The Edge
of Nowhere

Laura Bratcher Goins
Romans 15:4

Laura Bratcher Goins

ISBN 978-1-64569-976-7 (paperback)
ISBN 978-1-64569-977-4 (digital)

Christian Faith Publishing, Inc.
832 Park Avenue
Meadville, PA 16335
www.christianfaithpublishing.com

Cover design and illustrations by Cheryl A. Hart
Photo by Nate Weidner Productions
Author's logo by Cory Goins

Printed in the United States of America

Dedicated to

Bobby
my constant encourager

and

Debbie
my cheerleader

From the rising of the sun unto the going down of the same the LORD's name is to be praised.
Psalm 113:3

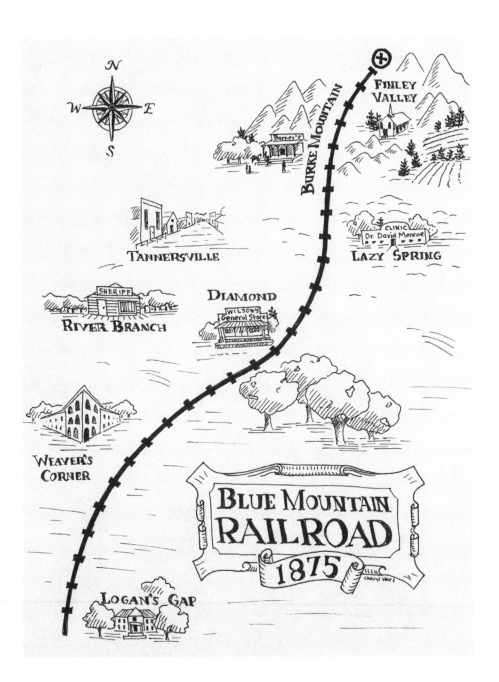

Chapter 1

The LORD is my strength and song
...he is my God.
Exodus 15:2

*A*nna was fifteen years old when she rode the train for the first time. And it was on this first train ride where she met Professor Higgins.

Mrs. McAfee was scheduled to accompany her to the train station, but instead, it ended up being Miss Avery because Mrs. McAfee had fallen seriously ill the night before. Miss Avery was by nature nervous and jumpy, and Anna would have rather walked to the train station than to be seen with her.

Yet she had no choice. Miss Avery *did* drive her to the train station, and Anna unconsciously ground her teeth as the funny little woman drove the horses painfully slow. Anna didn't say one word except to offer a whisper of a goodbye when she jumped from the carriage the moment they arrived. Miss Avery looked as if she was going to cry as she handed Anna's bags down to her. And for the first time ever, Anna felt sorry for her.

Anna knew it was doubtful she would ever see either of the women again or anyone else from the Children's Shelter for that matter. She would miss Mrs. McAfee the most, and the only reason she fought tears as she walked away from the carriage was because she wasn't allowed to even tell the older woman goodbye. "She is much too sick," they said.

Anna took her place in line at the ticket counter and watched as people standing and sitting around sprang to life as the inbound train hissed and groaned, creating a very noisy entrance. Many stood and began waving to those waving back from some very dusty windows. Others remained seated with bags resting at their feet. Mothers anxiously grabbed their children's hands while the fathers cautioned the young ones to stay back. Others raised their voices to continue their conversations over the noisy hustle and bustle all around them. Others stood in line like she did.

Everyone seemed to know exactly where they were going, everyone but her.

Anna had no idea where she was going or what was waiting for her at the other end of her train ride. It was only the positive promptings from Mrs. McAfee that kept her from running away in the dark of night, not giving any thought how she would survive on her own.

"Oh, Anna!" the older woman would cheerfully exclaim as she pushed and pulled at a lump of bread dough with her large overworked hands. Then she would turn toward Anna as she wiped her hands down her flour covered apron, not caring one bit that flour was dotting the clean floor as well as her sturdy shoes.

"There's an adventure waiting for you out there!" she would say as she pushed her fading Irish red hair away from her face with her arm. "I just know it! God has something special planned for you. I can feel it!"

Then suddenly, she would turn back around and pound on that lump of dough with no mercy, singing a song matching the beat with each thrust of her hand.

Anna loved this stout woman who sometimes laughed too loud and talked way too much. She was the closest thing to a mother Anna ever had, and even though she rarely hid her feelings and despite her cheerfulness up to the very end, Anna was quite sure Mrs. McAfee would ache inside when she left.

Oh, how she wished she could have hugged Mrs. McAfee goodbye and thanked her for believing in her! But now it was too late. This time, she couldn't hold her backed up tears, and they spilled down her cheeks blotting the starched white collar of her dress. She swallowed her sobs the best she could. She quickly wiped her face then inched in closer to the back of the man in front of her hoping no one noticed.

Slowly, the line crept forward, and it was finally her turn to stand before the window where she was supposed to pick up a one-way ticket waiting for her.

The uniformed man at the counter noticed the tag pinned to Anna's plain brown dress and nodded, politely ignoring her fragile state.

"Finley Valley, huh?"

Anna tried to smile.

He couldn't recall any other boys or girls from the Children's Shelter going as far as Finley Valley. He knew she had a long ride ahead of her, so he grabbed a metal pail from under the counter and set it right in front of her. Since it was covered, Anna had no idea what was inside.

"Here, my wife always fixes me way too much lunch," he said. "Think you could help me out by taking this off my hands?"

Puzzled, Anna first hesitated but then glanced back toward the people in line who appeared to be listening to their every word. She quickly turned back around and looked over the top of the pail into the slender man's patient face.

"Here, take it," he said. "There's blueberry muffins in there, made fresh this morning actually." The man pushed the pail a little closer toward her.

Anna timidly picked up the pail that was heavier than she thought, causing her to stumble a little before setting it on the ground by her feet. When she couldn't find any words that had courage enough to leave her mouth, she just simply smiled her thank you.

The man gave a slight nod with a wink then quickly stamped a ticket and handed it to her. His brown eyes were kind as they looked into her blue ones. He had witnessed this plenty of times before. It was never easy.

Everyone who lived in Logan's Gap knew once you turned fifteen years old, you had to leave the shelter. It was the rule. "You are too old now." It was obvious "no one wanted you," and besides, "we have to make room for others," they'd say.

Now you were expected to make your own way or go live with someone willing to take you in. In Anna's case, someone in Finley Valley agreed to temporarily take in an older girl who could "help a family in need."

The tag pinned to Anna's dress simply read, "Annaleigh Thompson; Destination: Finley Valley."

Chapter 2

But thou, O LORD, art a shield for me.
Psalm 3:3

*A*nna stood quietly off to the side as passengers of all shapes and sizes boarded the train in a uniformed single file. Her two small travel bags and the metal pail given to her by the man at the ticket counter sat carelessly about her feet. She wasn't ready to board just yet, so she lingered on the station platform where she could breathe in as much fresh air as she could. It was a perfect spring day, and she wanted to record every single thing around her.

The dogwood trees that lined the dirt road next to the train station were bursting with off-white blossoms marked with just a touch of pink that helped them look a little more interesting. The grand houses across the way stood at attention with wide white porches and fancy-looking rocking chairs that invited each guest to sit and stay awhile. The lazy river that flowed on the other side of the station was full to overflowing from all the spring rains, and little birds skimmed gracefully right above its surface as if they had no particular place to go.

Anna wished she was one of those birds—no cares, no worries, and no expectations.

She turned at the sound of two little boys chasing each other in a nearby field and smiled. She thought about how much she'd miss the younger children placed under her care at the Children's Shelter. She hoped the task wasn't given to the irresponsible Rebecca Dunlop who liked to yell and give orders instead of trying to understand that children needed some freedom to develop their talents and gifts. She pushed the thought from her mind and instead tried to focus on the daily instructions from Mrs. McAfee who always encouraged her to find the good in people and not to focus on their faults. But with Rebecca, she found that extremely hard to do. She kicked one of the bags at her feet, but it didn't make her feel any better.

Anna wondered just how sick Mrs. McAfee was and did all she could to quickly push that thought from her mind as well. She drew in a deep breath and held it a few moments before releasing it along with a long, gentle sigh. She never wanted to forget the only home she'd ever known because there was no promise she'd ever set foot on this station platform again. She reluctantly grabbed her bags along with the metal pail and headed toward the train just as the conductor stepped out on the platform and shouted.

"All aboard! Ten minutes, folks!"

Anna stiffened. Only ten more minutes and then she'd have no choice but to board the train or turn and run. But who was she kidding? She really only had one reasonable choice, and that was to board the train and do exactly what she was told. After all, that's what she'd been doing her entire life. She never had to think on her own, it was all done for her. "Anna, get up at this time." "Anna, eat at this time." "Anna, go do this and go do that." Now it all seemed strange and confusing to even have choices.

She realized if Mrs. McAfee had been able to bring her to the station, at least someone would be there to help her and see her on her way, to at least hug her and tell her goodbye. She headed toward an unoccupied bench and decided to sit her last ten minutes there instead of in a train car that was probably noisy and stuffy. No, she wasn't ready for that. Her heart settled down a bit, and she rested on a memory—on a memory she would never forget. Never.

She envisioned Mrs. McAfee working at the long wooden table in the kitchen, telling her the story she never tired of hearing…

> *Oh, Anna dear, it was a fine spring morning, it was. But it was right chilly, and I took care to wear a wrap that morning.*

I arrived as usual before the sun so I could begin making breakfast for all the sweet children that God had sent our way. I was stepping carefully up those uneven back steps when I looked up and saw a wooden box near the door.

I was saying to myself, Now what could that be, when I saw a tiny hand reaching out above the top of the box.

Oh my, oh my, I exclaimed! What soul would leave a sweet baby out in the morning cold?

My heart started pounding as I dropped my things so I could scoop you up out of that box and into my arms off that cold stone porch.

The kitchen was almost as cold as the outdoors, so I carefully placed you on the rug near the stove so I could start a fire. I knelt beside you, and what I saw when I pulled the blanket aside completely took my breath away!

Anna ignored all the noises around her as she recalled Mrs. McAfee's repeated excitement even though she had told her the same story so many times before. An unexpected smile warmed Anna's heart as she could almost hear the older woman's hushed voice...

You was an angel, Anna! Soft, curly blond hair and you smelled so nice, like you'd just had a lavender bath. You smiled and reached out for me with the chubbiest arms I think I'd ever seen. It was clear to see that someone had taken great care of you up to that point.

Then my heart grew heavy. I knew someone truly must have loved you, and no doubt someone had a broken heart out there having to leave their precious angel in someone else's care. I held your cold little hands and said a small prayer for them. I could only guess they had a good reason to leave you.

You had on the prettiest white dress with little blue flowers that matched your blue eyes. I had never seen a baby with such big blue eyes! Everyone here said they would darken, but I knew they wouldn't. God wouldn't bother making them so blue if He was gonna go and change them, now would He?

Anna squeezed the handle of her travel bag as she thought of the little white dress tucked away deep inside. She loved the older woman for thinking to keep it for her and presenting it to her the week before she left. Anna lingered on the rest of the story Mrs. McAfee told so well…

Well, of course, we had no idea your exact age, but I guessed you to be about six months old. And with all the babies I'd held in my life, I was a pretty good guesser.

I didn't notice the note that was left right away. I guess in my hurried excitement, it got wrapped up in your blanket.

"Dear Christian friends," it said and it was in an elegant hand, "please care for our little Annaleigh until we can come back for her."

That's all it said. Except it was signed "Thompson" and in a much hurried-looking manner.

No one knew if it was a first or last name, so it seemed fitting to just tag it on your first name so it could be a wonderful memory for you until they returned.

The older woman always paused at that point with tears forming in her eyes but would then quickly finish the story…

Annaleigh Thompson—I thought it was such a mouthful for a baby girl, so I called you Anna right off. You captured my heart that day and have every day since.

Well, that's how you came to us, our little Annaleigh. You was a gift straight from God to my heart.

Anna started at the sudden cry of the conductor.

"All aboard!"

He was standing on the top step of the passenger car, and he looked straight at Anna when he called out causing her face and neck to burn hot. So she clumsily gathered her things, took one last quick look around, then with her bags and pail that seemed heavier than they were before, headed straight for the big black train waiting for its last passenger.

Annaleigh Thompson slowly climbed the steps to the train car with the painful reminder that no one ever came back for her like they said they would. Because if they had, she wouldn't be on this train facing the unknown!

Chapter 3

I will call on the LORD,
who is worthy to be praised.
2 Samuel 22:4

*A*nna found a seat right away that suited her. It was all the way in the back, and she had the whole seat to herself. She stowed away her travel bags and the metal pail under the seat in front of her then untied her brown clunky shoes that were pinching her toes. All the other seats were filled, and most people were already settled and ready to go. Even the children were quiet.

She was just getting as comfortable as possible when an old gentleman boarded the train. He had a full white beard, though neatly trimmed, and he was obviously out of breath. He was dressed in a smart-looking dark suit with a gold chain hanging from his vest pocket, and he looked as if he could be someone important.

Anna hoped he was someone from the train company just checking on things before the train pulled away, but the blood drained from her face when she saw the conductor point her way. It appeared she wasn't to have a seat to herself after all. She looked down at her stocking feet as if she didn't know the man was heading straight for her. She didn't look up until she heard his voice.

"Do you mind if I sit here?" he asked kindly.

Anna thought it was a silly question since there was obviously nowhere else to sit. Nevertheless, she remembered what she was taught at the Children's Shelter and answered as politely as she could.

"No, sir."

She scooted over as far as she could, and he sat down, stuffing his oversized carpetbag and a small leather satchel under the seat next to her things. She thought he had a nice smile, and he smelled of a very sweet cologne that reminded her of peppermint candy. She couldn't tell how tall he was since he had already sat down, but his legs seemed to fit comfortably behind the seat in front of them, and after all, that's all that really mattered when riding on a train.

The very moment he sat down, the train lunged forward, and Anna felt a small panic rise in her throat causing her to gasp. Her journey had officially begun, and everything she had ever known would soon be beyond her reach. She just wanted to stop the train and run back to Mrs. McAfee where she felt safe and secure.

The kind gray-haired man noticed her anxiety, and not knowing any other way to help the pretty young woman, he silently prayed for her.

Against Anna's will, she eventually slipped into a sound sleep, and when she woke up, she could tell by the position of the sun that she had slept a nice part of the day away. It took her a moment or two to realize where she was, but the soft snore of the bearded man next to her and the cry of a baby toward the front of the train brought back the painful reality of her journey. Her foot bumped against the metal pail and she suddenly realized how hungry she was. She carefully reached to get it, her eyes never leaving the man next to her. But he began to stir, so she quickly drew back for fear of waking him. She decided, though disappointingly, the food could wait until later.

Anna also decided that looking out the window proved to be a waste of time. The sun was slowly descending toward the low rolling hills in the far distance, and there wasn't much to see anyway, she thought, just endless open ground as far as you could see. So instead, she laid her head back and quietly hummed a tune Mrs. McAfee taught her as a child.

"Sing this when you're afraid, Anna," she would say. "My mama taught it to me, and it brings me comfort to this day."

It did bring comfort to Anna, and as her body relaxed, she thought she might be able to sleep again, but the gnawing in her stomach reminded her she hadn't eaten since breakfast. And that was just cold oat cereal and a half glass of warm milk.

And *that* reminded her that Mrs. McAfee was sick in bed. Anna knew the kind woman would have fixed her a hearty breakfast before she left if she had been able and never would have sent her away with no food at all for the long trip ahead of her. She had determined not to cry on this trip, but this was the second time she was forced to wipe tears from her face. Then Anna turned her head toward the soft, raspy voice of the old man sitting next to her.

"That was a nice tune you were humming," he said.

"I'm sorry," she sobbed quietly. "I woke you up."

"That's all right. I was getting a crick in my neck anyway."

He stretched his legs out in front of him the best he could and combed his thick white beard with the tips of his fingers. He sat up to his full height then stretched out his arms until his fingers almost reached the seat in front of him. He closed his eyes and rocked his head from one side to the other.

Anna discreetly watched him straighten his sleeves and smooth the wrinkles in his suit. Then he pulled out a gold pocket watch and polished its glass front with a very clean handkerchief.

She hadn't expected him to glance her way, so when she quickly turned her face back toward the dirty window, she hoped with all her might he hadn't noticed her watching.

Anna liked him. She wasn't sure why, but she liked him. She turned back toward him when he cleared his throat.

"I'm Professor Higgins," he said, as he put out a hand toward her.

They shared a slow, gentle smile as Anna wiped her hands on her rough dress before accepting his warm handshake.

"I'm Anna."

"Nice to meet you, Anna."

"It's nice to meet you too," she said and really meant it.

The two sat in awkward silence for a few moments until Anna had the courage to ask, "You wouldn't happen to be hungry, would you?"

"Why, I'm absolutely starved," was his quick reply.

The professor watched as Anna eagerly grabbed the handle of the metal pail and clumsily pulled it up on the seat between them. He scooted over just a tad to make room.

"Why, what do you have there?" he asked.

"I'm not exactly sure. The man at the ticket counter gave it to me. But I do know it's food because he told me so."

The professor lifted a brushy eyebrow. Anna bit her lip.

"Oh, I love a good mystery," he said, rubbing his hands together. "And I bet you do too, Anna."

She nodded eagerly as she pushed the handle off to one side. The professor helped Anna pry the top off, then they both looked inside, almost bumping heads.

The old dented pail contained almost two of everything as if the person who packed it knew two people would be sharing its contents. Together, they began to pull out food little by little—two tart green apples, two hefty ham sandwiches, two very large and very moist blueberry muffins, and a container of sweet pickles to share. There was even a big glass jar of water to wash it all down along with a small tin cup. Lastly, Anna pulled out a soft cloth that she supposed was to be used to wipe your mouth and hands when you were finished.

They had no way of knowing that the man behind the ticket counter was working late into the night and his wife packed him enough for two meals. It never entered their minds, but of course, it did of the man who went home hungry. But no matter, it wasn't the first time he'd given his lunch away to one of the shelter children, and he, as well as his wife, knew it wouldn't be the last.

Anna felt energized after a good meal, and she tried not to choke on her blueberry muffin while laughing at the bearded man's silly stories of which he seemed to have an abundance.

The lowering of the sun and the harsh look of the woman in front of them caused them to lower their voices and snicker toward each other.

"Do you have a first name?" Anna whispered while trying her best to put the top back on the pail.

"Indeed, I do but you must promise not to laugh," he whispered back.

Anna stopped and studied his round face and red cheeks.

"Why would I do that?" she answered somberly. "That wouldn't be polite."

"Oh, you will understand when I tell you," he replied.

Anna inched toward him and waited eagerly.

"Applebee."

"Applebee?"

"Yes, Applebee. So what do you think?"

Anna leaned back and studied his face again.

"Well?" he prompted.

"I think it suits you."

"Really?"

"Professor Applebee Higgins—I like it. It's not plain and ordinary."

"No, it's definitely not that!" he chuckled.

"And how about *your* name? How did you come to be named Anna?"

"Annaleigh is my given name, I guess."

"You guess? Don't you know?"

"I never knew my parents. I've lived at the Logan's Gap Children's Shelter all my life until this very morning."

The professor cleared his throat and marveled at this young woman sitting next to him, and even though he normally wasn't at a loss for words, he didn't know how to properly respond. So he just nodded and listened.

Anna just kept on talking even though she wasn't sure why.

"My last name is Thompson, though no one knows for sure if it's really my last name. It's just a name that was given to me at the shelter when I was just a baby."

"I see."

"Someone left me outside the Children's Shelter in a wooden box with a note asking them to take care of me. The note also said someone would come back for me, but no one ever did."

Anna shrugged and looked down toward the floor.

The professor cleared his throat again.

"Well, Anna, sometimes, our misfortunes turn into our greatest opportunities," he finally said.

"You sound like Mrs. McAfee."

"And who is Mrs. McAfee?"

"Oh, she's the woman who found me. She cooks at the Children's Shelter, and she saved my life. It was very cold outside, and she said I could have died if I had been there too long. She found me outside on the kitchen's porch when she came to work early that morning."

"Someone was looking out for you."

Anna fingered the tip of her long blond braid.

"Who?"

"God watches over all of us."

"You sound like Mrs. McAfee again."

Anna flipped her braid across her shoulder.

"Mrs. McAfee sounds like a very wise woman. What else does Mrs. McAfee say?"

"She said God has something special planned for me and there's an adventure out there just waiting."

The professor shifted his weight so he could see her face a little better.

"Do you think she's right?"

"I don't know. It doesn't seem very special to have to leave everyone I know and care about to go live somewhere else."

"Sometimes, God does things that don't make sense to us."

"There you go again."

"What?"

Anna rolled her eyes, and the professor grinned causing his mustache to look wider than it really was.

"You sound like Mrs. McAfee again. 'Trust God,' she said, but I don't believe I can."

"Oh? Why not?"

Anna turned her face back toward the window. The orange sun was barely visible behind the rolling hills that had gradually gotten taller and more rugged since they left Logan's Gap behind. And the train car was growing darker, which made it hard to see anything around them.

"You know, I really don't think I want to talk about this anymore," Anna said in a voice so softly that the professor had a hard time understanding her.

So he left the conversation there and reached into his pocket and handed Anna a neatly folded handkerchief baring his initials.

"Night, Anna," he whispered.

Anna didn't answer but instead turned her head to hide those doggone tears again.

Chapter 4

For great is the LORD,
and greatly to be praised.
1 Chronicles 16:25

*E*leanor McAfee sat in bed sipping the warm chicken broth given to her by a kindly neighbor. She was following the doctor's orders the best she could, but it was hard to lie in bed when there was so much to do at the Children's Shelter.

Her head still hurt, but her heart hurt far more.

She thought of Anna all alone on the train, and her imagination was running wild with concern. Many children had come through the shelter and had faced the same fate as Anna, but Anna was different. Losing Anna was like losing her own child. All she could do was trust God for her protection.

"Please, God," she prayed, "bring someone into Anna's life to help her on her new journey. You knew all about this before we did, and only You know Anna's future."

As the cook turned her head toward her bedroom window where she could watch the rising of the sun, she had no idea God had already answered her prayer far in advance.

That same bright morning sun had made such a swift appearance within the train car where Anna and the professor were peacefully sound asleep, they missed its entrance as it rose above the range of now jagged hills that began taking various shapes and forms. Anna woke first and began tugging on the professor's suit sleeve.

"Wake up, Professor Higgins! The train is slowing down."

The professor opened his eyes and yawned.

"Yes, you're right."

They grabbed their shoes and started putting them on when the conductor announced their next stop.

"Diamond Station, five minutes!" he called out. "Diamond Station, five minutes!"

Anna was looking forward to stretching her legs. The professor offered to buy some food to refill their pail, and Anna had no choice but to graciously accept his offer. Mrs. McAfee had given her a little money but told her not to use it unless she just absolutely had to. It was safely tucked inside a sock in one of her bags.

Anna re-braided her unruly hair and straightened her dress. She hated the plain brown dress from the shelter, and the other clothes she had with her weren't any better—plain and ordinary. She hated plain and ordinary. She dreamed of cool light colors.

The professor was already standing in the aisle as were many others. Everyone seemed to long for a break as much as they did. Anna was surprised the babies and young children were as well behaved as they were, and she figured it must be because of the constant rocking of the train.

Only a few passengers had gotten off at the other stops. Anna wondered how many they would lose this time. Then a thought entered her mind. She wondered how far the professor was going before *he* got off. She knew for herself, Finley Valley was a far distance and she had no reason to be in a hurry to get there. There was a family waiting for her, but she had no idea what they were like or if they would be kind to her.

This was the first time she considered getting off at a different destination other than Finley Valley.

Who would know? she wondered.

She was suddenly jolted back to the present when she heard the professor calling her name.

"Anna? Are you coming?"

Anna saw the professor's outstretched hand and reached up and took it. She was so engrossed in her thoughts she didn't realize the train had come to a stop.

The conductor was giving instructions, and Anna strained to hear him over the rustling caused by everyone preparing to get off.

"Diamond Station!" he cried. "This is a four-hour stop, ladies and gentlemen. We will blow the whistle two times when we are close to leaving."

He paused until the chatter among the passengers died back down.

"Then you will have thirty more minutes to conclude your affairs and return to the train. Have a good and safe visit."

Then the conductor led the way down the steps and out into the sunshine.

Four hours! Anna relished the thought of such freedom, and the professor laughed at her opened mouth and arched eyebrows.

The mismatched pair followed the slow line of passengers to the front of the car and down the steps where the bright morning sun greeted them.

The professor turned as he helped Anna step to the ground and then suddenly bowed toward her.

"Would you grant me the pleasure of escorting you on a brand new adventure, ma'am?" His eyes twinkled, and his chubby cheeks were stretched tight from his broad smile.

Adventure! Anna thought. She could almost hear Mrs. McAfee saying, "See, Anna, I told you adventure awaits!"

Anna giggled and returned his bow.

"Yes, Professor Applebee Higgins, I would love to."

Chapter 5

Sing praises to God, sing praises:
sing praises unto our King, sing praises.
Psalm 47:6

The professor and Anna walked the wooden sidewalks of the town named Diamond and peeked in the windows of the various stores. Many of the other passengers were doing the same.

Anna was never given the privilege of going to town when she lived at the Children's Shelter. The children just weren't allowed, unless you counted the times she went to the dentist or like the time she fell and broke her arm and had to be rushed to the doctor. But to just window-shop? Never.

Professor Higgins watched Anna's eyes light up when they reached Wilson's General Store.

"Want to go inside?" he asked.

"Could we?"

"Of course, let's go see what's inside."

He held the screen door open, but it took a moment for her to walk through. She had never seen anyplace like it. It was already fairly crowded.

The professor gently nudged her, and she gingerly stepped inside.

Rows and rows of glass jars filled with an assortment of candy in all colors lined the busy shelves behind the long wooden counter. Overstuffed bags of flour and sugar were stacked near a barrelful of feed corn. Small wooden toys sat on lower shelves, just eye level for small children to admire and hopefully beg their parents to buy

28

them one or two. Rakes and hoes stood straight and tall against the wall in one corner. There were even watches and pretty jewelry resting beneath a glass countertop. There seemed to be something for everyone!

The professor tapped Anna's shoulder and directed her attention toward the back of the spacious store.

"Come," he said, "I want you to look back there with me."

Anna followed him to where dresses of various sizes hung on wood pegs. There were several pairs of shoes lined up on the floor beneath them in one perfectly straight line.

He asked her to sit in the chair next to a full length mirror and explained that he'd be right back.

Anna nodded.

Before she sat, she stood before the mirror and studied her reflection. Her long blond hair was flat from needing a good wash, and her rough brown dress was all wrinkled. She turned her head and noticed bits of hair sticking out here and there from her long braid that hung just past her small waist. Her shoes were new but clunky and old-fashioned. Her stockings were dirty. She glanced around and saw nicely dressed women with their nicely dressed children, and she was suddenly embarrassed by her looks.

She quickly sat in the chair and pulled her feet underneath. She was determined not to cry. It was silly to cry over such things, she thought. At the Children's Shelter, she was told to be thankful for what she had and never complain.

Anna *was* thankful, at least she tried to be. Mrs. McAfee used to tell her some of the biblical principles she learned when she was growing up.

"Be thankful," she would tell Anna. "And be content with what you have because there are always people that have far less than you."

Anna realized she hadn't thought about Mrs. McAfee as much as she had before and felt ashamed. Had she recovered from her illness, or was she still sick? Did the older woman even miss her?

Anna sat and wondered if she could ever be thankful for having to go live somewhere else. This was a nice town, but she wondered what Finley Valley was like.

Suddenly, she just wanted to go back to the train. She jumped up, and as she turned, she ran right into Professor Higgins' round belly.

"Whoa, girl!"

He caught her by her shoulders.

"Where are you heading in such a hurry?"

Anna's face turned crimson.

"I'm just, I'm just—"

He saw the horror on her face.

"What is it, Anna? What happened?"

He looked around for anyone or anything that might have frightened her and felt badly for leaving her alone.

Anna shook her head and pushed back the stray hairs on her forehead.

"Nothing. I'm just tired. I want to go back to the train."

"All right, we can do that, but I found someone who can help us find a new dress for you among these hanging here."

Anna politely smiled at the woman who was standing next to him. Her hair was as white as the professor's and the bun atop her head was neat but rested a little off center. She was a bit short and her figure betrayed years of plenty.

"This is the store owner's wife, and she made some of these dresses herself," the professor was saying.

He walked over and took a lovely pink dress off one of the pegs, but it was most definitely too large for Anna's slender frame.

"Well, what's your favorite color?" he asked, as he scanned the others.

"I guess I've never really thought about it before," she replied.

"Well, now's as good a time as any to choose one, don't you think?"

Anna hesitated but only a few seconds.

She pointed.

"Well, I like that green one with the pretty lace collar."

The professor turned toward the store owner's wife and smiled.

"Mrs. Wilson, I think we're ready to do some shopping."

Chapter 6

Because thy loving kindness is better than life,
my lips shall praise thee.
Psalm 63:3

A trip into town turned out to be far different than Anna expected.

And to her delight, Professor Higgins bought her two new dresses—the green one with the lace collar and a pale blue one with small white polka dots. These dresses were soft, not like the rough one she was wearing. And they were pretty and feminine. They weren't plain and ordinary. She couldn't stop admiring them while the professor talked with Mrs. Wilson.

"She will need five more dresses," he was saying. "A couple of them need to be of heavier weight for the winter months."

The woman nodded as she wrote down his specific instructions. She was having a hard time writing as fast as he was talking, so she had to ask him to "slow down, please!"

"Send them on the train to Finley Valley in care of Annaleigh Thompson," he explained. "I will make sure someone picks them up."

"Well, let's see," he continued. "We have two pairs of shoes, several hair ribbons, undergarments, and stockings. Can you recommend anything else?" he asked the store owner's wife.

Mrs. Wilson pulled him aside and spoke softly so Anna couldn't hear.

"You're absolutely right!" the professor suddenly exclaimed. "That's a grand idea!"

"Anna—"

She looked up at the sound of his voice to find him grinning from ear to ear, which helped her immediately relax. Up to that moment, Anna was speechless and a bit embarrassed from all the attention.

"Yes, Professor Higgins?"

She answered him but was looking at Mrs. Wilson because she kept nodding and nodding and Anna wasn't sure what was going on.

"Mrs. Wilson," the old man pointed, "has offered to take you upstairs to their home and let you refresh up."

Anna released a gentle sigh of relief.

"Would you like that?" he asked, studying her face.

"Oh yes, I would!" she exclaimed.

"It's settled then. You go with Mrs. Wilson, and I'll go find the barbershop."

The old man with the snow-white beard pulled out several bills from his pocket and handed them to the store owner's wife.

"Here, this should cover everything."

Mrs. Wilson's eyes lit up, and she didn't know how to exactly respond to his generosity.

But the professor held up his hand and refused to even discuss the matter.

Instead, he headed to the barbershop while Anna followed Mrs. Wilson up a narrow set of stairs to the upper floor. Soon, they stepped into a small living area that was warm and cozy, and Anna suddenly burst into tears.

Mrs. Wilson turned to Anna and immediately pulled her into her arms.

"What is it, Anna? What on earth is wrong?"

Anna couldn't answer, so the woman held her peace. Instead, she lovingly led Anna to a soft sofa, and there they sat in the comfort of each other's arms.

Meanwhile, the professor found the barbershop. But instead of going in, he headed back to the train station. He was relieved there was no line at the ticket counter.

The bald-headed man behind the counter looked up but didn't say anything.

"I'd like to exchange my ticket," the professor said.

Professor Higgins handed the man his ticket and waited as he seemed to move in slow motion.

"Where is it you want to go?" the man finally asked.

"Finley Valley."

He looked up with an odd look on his face.

"Finley Valley? Don't get many wanting to go there."

"And why is that?" the professor inquired with a hint of irritation in his voice.

"Never been there myself, but I hear tell it's on the edge of nowhere."

The professor arched back as the man spit a stream of tobacco into a rusty can.

"Well, then give me a ticket to the 'edge of nowhere.'"

"It's your money."

The man shrugged as he slid a ticket under the iron bars.

Professor Higgins paid the man and walked away with a slower step. "The 'edge of nowhere,' whatever did the man mean?"

He glanced at his pocket watch and picked up his pace. He didn't want Anna waiting for him. But what he didn't know was Anna was still safely cradled in Mrs. Wilson's warm embrace.

Mrs. Wilson was stroking Anna's hair when Anna gently pulled away, her face an absolute mess.

"Everything all right now, dear?"

She was patting Anna's knee.

"Yes, I'm sorry. It's just that you remind me of someone who is very special to me and your house is like the home I've always dreamed of. Where I come from, the furniture is hard, and nothing is pretty, just gray-like."

The older woman smiled and was nodding again.

She's much like Mrs. McAfee, only quieter, Anna thought.

"Well, dear, we need to hurry and get you cleaned up before your grandfather returns!"

Anna blew her nose on the hanky Mrs. Wilson gave her.

"Oh no, he's not my grandfather, just a friend, but a very good friend."

Chapter 7

For thou art my hope, O Lord God:
thou art my trust from my youth.
Psalm 71:5

*A*nna thought her long blond hair had never felt so soft or smelled so good. She was sure of it.

And Professor Higgins was pleased with his bath, haircut, and trimmed beard. He tipped the skilled barber well for "fine service." And the kindhearted Mrs. Wilson tucked away his generous payment to her in her money jar hidden behind the lard crock in the pantry.

It was a glorious day, and Anna and the professor walked arm in arm toward Diamond's only restaurant located in the Majesty Hotel.

"My, you look very pretty, Anna!"

She blushed. She *felt* pretty, but it was nice to hear someone say it out loud.

She had a very warm bath at the Wilson's, and Mrs. Wilson even let her use some of her special cologne her husband had given her on their last wedding anniversary. She was wearing her new blue dress with the tiny white dots.

"Your dress compliments your eyes—so blue," the professor said.

Anna blushed again.

"It's so soft and light. Thank you, Professor Higgins."

She released his arm and twirled in a circle, releasing a girlish giggle.

"You're quite welcome, Annaleigh."

Anna paused at the name rarely used by anyone. It actually brought back the memory of the note that was left when Mrs. McAfee found her as well as the added memory that no one came back for her like they said they would. For the first time in her life, a root of bitterness was beginning to form.

Anna reached over and took the professor's arm, and they continued down the wooden sidewalk listening to the sound of their shoes on the weathered boards. She was once again swept up in the moment, but this time, it was a wonderful moment of happiness and freedom.

Anna actually noticed very little around her. She felt like she was living a dream and never wanted to wake up.

The professor was wondering what would become of this budding young woman who was just starting to realize she had worth and purpose, even though he was sure she hadn't noticed it yet.

"May I ask what you did with the tag that was pinned on your other dress?"

"Oh, that. I have it here in my pocket."

The professor squeezed her arm and pointed up ahead.

"I see the hotel."

Anna quickened her step and tugged on the professor's sleeve.

"I'm starved! Let's go!"

The professor was surprised he had enough energy to keep up with Anna as much as he did. She reached the hotel first and waved for him to hurry, which, of course, he did.

Anna gasped as they entered the double doors. She stood in awe at the vaulted ceiling and the elegant furnishings. She felt like a queen entering a castle.

"Anna—"

She turned to look into Professor Higgins' kind eyes.

Then there was a moment of odd silence.

"What is it, Professor Higgins?" Anna asked. "Are you all right?"

There was another moment.

"Oh, never mind," he said. "I just needed to catch my breath is all."

Anna noticed the concentration on his face, and for a moment, she was confused.

But he had already changed the subject and was leading her into the dining room where they would feast on baked chicken, pan-fried potatoes, fresh baked bread, and apple pie.

Time just seemed to disappear.

Anna wiped her mouth with her cloth napkin then folded it neatly before laying it on the table.

"I can't eat another bite," she said.

"Nor can I," the professor announced.

"I don't ever want this to end, Professor Applebee Higgins!"

He laughed out loud at her girlish grin.

"Neither do I, sweet girl, neither do I."

So he ordered a cup of coffee and some hot tea so they could savor their adventure a little while longer.

The waiter had just set a tray of hot beverages before them when the train whistle blew.

Anna stiffened as the second whistle blast followed on the heels of the first, reminding the passengers they only had thirty more minutes to be back on the train.

The professor calmly picked up his cup of coffee and lifted it toward the pretty young woman seated across from him.

"Here's to thirty more minutes of sheer pleasure, Anna."

But Anna couldn't respond because those doggone tears had surfaced once more.

Chapter 8

The flowers appear on the earth;
the time of the singing of birds is come.
Song of Solomon 2:12

*I*t was no surprise they lost many more passengers on their stop at Diamond Station, and now the train car seemed strangely quiet and empty. Diamond had all the makings of a growing, vibrant place, and Anna was sad to leave it and Mrs. Wilson behind.

She knew both the town and the store owner's wife for only a brief time, but Anna strangely felt like she had known both all her life. Of course, that wasn't true. It just felt true.

The stop at Diamond had been bittersweet.

Anna and the professor found their usual seats in the back of the train car and settled in for the next leg of the trip.

"I bought you a little something, Anna."

The professor handed her a package wrapped in brown paper and tied with string.

Anna smiled but didn't reach for it.

"Go ahead, take it," he urged.

"I've never gotten a wrapped gift from anyone before," she said softly, almost a whisper.

The more time the old man spent with this brave young woman, he realized how much he had taken for granted. He couldn't help but feel a bit guilt-ridden.

"It's just a *little* something. Go ahead, open it."

Anna pulled the string and pushed the paper away to find a book and some pencils.

"It's a journal," he explained.

He turned to the first page and pointed to the inscription.

It read...

To Anna,

May you blossom and grow like the wildflowers we have enjoyed along our journey from our train window. Embrace the adventures God brings into your life and trust Him. You are never alone.

Your friend,
Professor Applebee Q. Higgins III

"I thought you could write down a few sentences every day so one day, when you're old and gray like me, you can go back and remember this part of your life."

Anna ran her hand across the journal's front. It was stained blue, and small flowers had been hand-drawn in one corner and filled in with bright colors. It was pretty and in no way plain or ordinary.

She loved it and held it to her chest.

"Do you like it?"

The professor bit his lip as he studied her profile.

She turned his way.

"Oh, I do! I really do!"

"The pencils are colored so you can be creative. I have a small knife you can have so you can keep them sharpened."

He pulled out a small, stainless steel knife engraved with his initials.

"It's something you can keep so you can remember me."

Anna accepted it and held it as if it was the most valuable thing she had ever held.

"What does the Q stand for and the three little lines?" she asked.

"Oh, that. The Q doesn't stand for anything."

"That's silly."

The professor smiled but held his laugh. She looked so innocent and serious when she said it. And after all, she was right.

"Well, the three little lines, as you call them, are Roman numerals."

"You're Roman?"

This time, he couldn't hold his laughter. He reached down and grabbed her warm hand.

"No, no, no. They stand for a number like the Roman's used in their day. It stands for the number 3."

"So your name is Professor Applebee Q. Higgins Three?"

"Not exactly. Instead of saying three, you say the third. I am Professor Applebee Q. Higgins the Third. That means my father and grandfather had the same name. I'm the third one to have it."

Anna shook her head and looked at him with her brilliant blue eyes.

"That's really silly for your parents not to take the time to come up with a name you could have for yourself."

To his surprise, she suddenly opened the journal and began writing.

This wasn't the same girl in a plain brown dress with messy hair that sat in the back of the train when they first met.

No, next to him sat a beautiful young woman in a brand new blue dress with ribbons in her soft, flowing blond hair, a budding wildflower beginning to bloom.

Chapter 9

Hear my prayer, O LORD,
and give ear unto my cry.
Psalm 39:12

There was an unexpected stop in a dusty little town called Lazy Spring.

And there was murmuring up near the front of the train car. Anna strained to hear what was going on.

"What is it?" she anxiously asked the professor.

"Not sure, let's just wait and see," was his reply.

Anna waited as he asked, and it soon became clear.

It was the young couple in the second set of seats. Something was most definitely wrong.

Anna fidgeted and stretched her neck as people began gathering around the couple. She looked up at the professor, but she didn't have a chance to say anything. He was already on his way to the front.

Anna waited in her seat, but it was a really hard thing to do. She started humming the tune Mrs. McAfee taught her.

Remember, Anna, sing or hum this little tune when you're afraid.

Anna wasn't afraid, but she was sure the young couple was.

Finally, the conductor came, and people parted for him to get through.

There was whispering, and then Anna saw it happen, the young woman fainted. Her husband caught her as she fell limp against him, and he looked completely scared to death.

Anna closed her eyes and began to softly sing.

> Moses saw the burning bush
> Don't be afraid, Moses, don't be afraid
> Noah and his family entered the ark
> Don't be afraid, Noah, don't be afraid
> David fled from angry Saul
> Don't be afraid, David, don't be afraid
> Jesus came to save us all
> Don't be afraid, Anna, don't be afraid

Anna thought back to Mrs. McAfee's rich, deep singing voice. At the end of the song, the older woman would insert a different child's name from the Children's Shelter each time she sang it.

Anna opened her eyes and whispered in the direction of the couple, "Don't be afraid."

She studied the professor's face as he pushed past some people and headed back toward her.

"Anna, I'm going to have to leave you here. I'm going to try and find a doctor. You stay here, and I'll return as quickly as I can. Don't go up front. Don't leave your seat. Promise me."

Then the old man was gone before Anna could say a word.

She hummed her tune and reached for her journal and pencils. She flipped to a clean page and began to write, blocking out everything going on around her.

The conductor asked everyone to "please return to your seats" and explained that help was on the way. The young husband nodded his head with clear relief written on his face.

But an hour later, there was no sign of the professor. The woman was conscious but softly weeping, and her husband looked beside himself with worry.

Anna decided to pray. She thought back to the times she listened to Mrs. McAfee pray for a sick child or the time the cook prayed for the gardener who had cut his leg while chopping vines. She sat very still and tried very hard to think of just the right words.

"Dear God"—she paused a moment—"the lady in the front of the train needs help. Will You please help her? And please bring Professor Higgins back soon! Oh, and please help her husband too."

Anna hesitated and couldn't think of anything else to say. She wondered if God really heard her. She had never prayed all by herself before. The staff at the Children's Shelter took turns praying before meals. And Mrs. Jamison, the shelter's director, read from a big black Bible before breakfast every morning while all the children sat arrow straight with their hands neatly folded in their laps. It was the same routine every single day. Anna never really listened, and now she wished she had paid more attention.

She was struggling to stay awake when she heard a familiar voice. It was the professor, and he had a man with him. Both of them were out of breath, especially the professor. The man rushed to the young couple's side.

Every eye was on the tall, rugged stranger whose beard was just a tad bit lighter than his thick brown hair. Then every eye grew wide when the man's face paled as he pulled his hand away from the woman's forehead.

"What is it? Are you a doctor?" someone asked anxiously. Then all was quiet. Everyone held their breath.

The man stood to his feet and addressed everyone.

"My name is Dr. David Monroe, and I believe this woman to be gravely ill."

Anna heard gasps all around. The professor looked right at her with concern written on his face.

"What does she have? Is she contagious?" people were asking, voices rose.

The doctor spoke in a clear, calm voice, "If it's what I think it is, no one is leaving this train."

Chapter 10

Give unto the LORD
the glory due unto his name.
1 Chronicles 16:29

*A*nna's thoughts flew straight to Mrs. McAfee. When Anna left the Logan's Gap Children's Shelter, all she knew was the woman was seriously ill. She had no way of knowing if she had recovered or not.

Now this.

"Is everything going to be all right, Professor?" Anna asked.

The kind, old man laid his hand on Anna's knee.

"I don't know, child, I just don't know."

He looked tired and worn out. The new clothes he wore that he bought in Diamond were dusty, and he smelled of sweat.

"You should rest, Professor Higgins."

He gently nodded his head, and Anna held his hand until he quietly dozed off.

But the whole train was abuzz.

The doctor left with strict orders for everyone to stay on the train. He would return with a solution soon, he said, and in the meantime, he had given the sick woman some sleeping powder and something to reduce her fever. Both she and her husband appeared to be asleep.

Anna wasn't sleepy, so she counted people instead.

Of course, there was herself and the professor and the woman who was sick and her husband. That made four. But Anna hadn't really noticed the others before now. She figured why did it matter because

44

once someone got off at their destination, they would probably never see each other again. But things were different now—very different.

Anna scanned the train car from her back seat.

There was an older couple who was sitting right in front of the young couple until they moved to one of the back rows near Anna and the professor. That made six.

Right across from them was a family of five taking up two rows of seats. They were the ones who had the baby Anna heard crying from time to time. They too had moved from the front to the back. She counted in her head. That made eleven.

There were two men traveling together who looked to be cattlemen, another family of three, and a woman traveling alone.

All in all, there were only seventeen passengers left on this part of the trip. Anna wondered if any of them were going to Finley Valley like she was.

Everyone seemed on edge except the two men traveling together. She couldn't tell if they were bothered or not. Anna wondered if everyone was on edge partly because it was so stuffy in the train car. Being restricted to the train made her want to get off more than ever.

Minutes seemed like hours, and Anna stood to stretch her legs just as the doctor boarded with news.

"Attention, attention, ladies and gentlemen!" the conductor shouted.

Certainly, no one could have slept through that, and the professor woke with a start.

"Dr. Monroe has an announcement."

Everyone was quiet and listened intently.

"We have set up a temporary hospital in a nearby boarding house. Everyone will be moved there for the time being," the doctor explained.

Quiet turned into chatter.

"Listen, listen."

The doctor held up both hands.

"We will take this woman and her husband first and get them settled. Then we will escort each of you as we are ready. Bring all your belongings with you—everything."

The questions began to fly, and the doctor just stood there until everyone realized he wasn't going to answer any questions. He pointed to a younger man standing next to him.

"Luke, here, will be the one coming for you. Just follow his directions exactly, and things will go smoothly."

Standing beside the thirty-year-old doctor stood a younger version of himself. The same thick brown hair, same blue gray eyes, and the same tall, lanky build. The only thing missing was the beard. Anna was sure he must be the doctor's brother. She thought he was very nice looking, and she was taken completely by surprise when her face warmed. She looked over to see if the professor had noticed and was relieved he hadn't.

Dr. Monroe and his assistant escorted the sick woman and her husband off the train, and eventually, everyone was taken to an old, worn-out house away from town. It looked as if no one had taken care of it for a very long time.

Someone eventually asked the question everyone else wanted to ask.

"How long will we be here?"

The doctor rubbed his eyes.

"I'm afraid I don't know the answer to that question right now. We have quarantined Mr. and Mrs. Landry, and we've done the best we could with the short notice we had to make everyone as comfortable as possible. Some of you will have a room, but some will have makeshift beds in open areas."

A murmur began to spread.

The doctor spoke above it.

"We will make any changes we have to. Please be understanding. This isn't the time or place to complain."

"You just can't disrupt our lives with no explanation!" someone called out.

The doctor sighed and pondered on the faces staring at him.

"I'll know more in the morning. Please just trust me. I'll have Luke bring breakfast around early. So please, please settle in the best you can. I'm sure all of us will be able to think more clearly when we've had some sleep."

One by one, everyone reluctantly nodded their heads and prepared to turn in for the night following Luke's orders as to where they would sleep.

The doctor wasn't ready to confess just yet that his suspicions had most likely been confirmed when he saw the rash forming on Mrs. Landry's arms and face. He had seen something like this before and not that long ago. His palms grew sweaty thinking about it, and he stuffed his hands into his pockets.

He finally headed to bed like the rest but not before checking on the sick woman and her husband. The man held his wife in his arms as she slept peacefully from the medicine Dr. Monroe had given her earlier. His eyes were red and swollen. The doctor's heart ached for the man who couldn't be more than twenty years old. She, on the other hand, appeared to be even younger. He feared for their future.

The doctor laid awake that night, rehearsing over and over in his mind how he would deal with the situation if it was to get out of hand. He wasn't sure he and Luke could handle it alone.

Dr. David Monroe finally drifted off to sleep and, for at least a few hours, would have nothing at all in the world to worry about.

Chapter 11

Rejoicing in hope; patient in tribulation;
continuing instant in prayer.
Romans 12:12

The doctor sent a telegram first thing the next morning. He knew he had to prepare for the worst and he didn't have enough medicine to treat everyone in case more came down with the illness. He only hoped help would arrive in time.

He handed the message to the clerk.

"Please mark it urgent and don't speak of this to anyone."

The clerk read the note and just stood there motionless.

"Quick, man, we can't delay!" David exclaimed.

The clerk jumped into action, and David headed toward the old boarding house. It wasn't an ideal place to set up a hospital, but it was far enough from town to keep any illness contained. He just hoped his suspicions were wrong. He spotted Luke across the street.

"Hey, Luke!"

Luke turned then headed toward him.

They shook hands in greeting.

"How's the food coming?" David asked.

"I was just heading that way to check."

"Well then, I'll give you a hand. I was just heading back to the boarding house. It was a quiet night, and Mrs. Landry was resting easy when I left this morning. I hope her husband escapes it, but I'm not sure how. He refuses to leave her side."

David started to cross the street, but Luke didn't follow. The doctor turned back toward him.

"What is it?"

"I saw the rash on Mrs. Landry's arm and face. What's going to happen to her?"

David rubbed the back of his neck.

"I've seen something like this before. Right before coming here, I witnessed an epidemic that nearly wiped out half the town. We worked night and day to save everyone we could. We lost many, too many. We just weren't prepared, and I'm concerned we may have the same problem here. I've wired for more medicine."

"You think this is the same thing?"

"I fear it is, Luke. But this time, we might be able to contain it to only the passengers on the train."

Luke ran his fingers through his thick brown hair.

"What are their chances?"

"I'm hoping the Landry's will be the only ones. We will keep them separated from the others, but I can't take a chance that no one else has been infected. We will have to wait. That's sometimes the hardest part."

"How long?"

"At least a week if no one else shows signs, maybe longer just to be sure."

Luke shook his head and sighed.

David laid a hand on the young man's shoulder who was only five years younger than he was.

"Luke, I know you're here to learn doctoring, but I won't ask you to go back over there if you don't want to. I would feel responsible if—"

Luke cut him off.

"No. What kind of doctor will I ever be if I run from treating people in need?"

"Are you sure?"

Luke hesitated, but only a moment.

"Yes, I'm sure."

The doctor slapped Luke on his back and smiled.

"Then let's go get that food. I don't want to be gone too long."

Dr. Monroe and his intern loaded a wagon with hot food along with a few supplies from the general store then headed to the boarding house that had been abandoned when the owner, Widow Marion, got married to one of her boarders and moved away.

They were almost to the house when they saw someone walking toward them.

David reined in the horses and pulled alongside Professor Higgins. The professor stopped to take a breath before speaking.

David could tell by the look on the old man's face something was terribly wrong. He handed the professor a canteen, but he waved it away.

"Someone else…is sick. One…of the women…she has small children…"

David threw the reins to Luke as he jumped from the wagon and ran the rest of the way to the house.

The professor looked up at Luke, worry covered his face.

"The passengers deserve to know the truth. We all do," the professor said as soon as he caught his breath.

"And they'll get it when the doctor is ready. But first, let's get this food inside so we can take care of the people who *aren't* sick."

Professor Higgins agreed and accepted the short ride back to the house. He wanted to take Anna far from the others and protect her, but he knew he couldn't. He felt helpless, but they would just have to ride out the situation along with everyone else.

Luke jumped down and started unloading. The professor gave him a hand.

"I've never been in a situation like this before," Luke confessed. "We are going to need something powerful to fight this!"

Professor Higgins nodded as sweat formed along his hairline.

"Prayer—there's nothing more powerful than prayer."

Chapter 12

Trust in the LORD
with all thine heart.
Proverbs 3:5

$\mathcal{M}$rs. Landry recovered, but Mr. Landry died only days after contracting the illness. He was buried under the shade of a large oak tree in an open field near the boarding house. He and his young bride had only been married three months and were heading west to start a new life together. She would soon find out she was pregnant.

The professor and Anna slowly walked back to the house with the others. David offered a few words of comfort at the grave site because they couldn't risk asking the preacher to come.

The older couple who sat in front of the Landry's on the train were both sick, as well as Mrs. Campbell and one of her children. The Campbell family sat directly across from the Landrys.

David was taking every precaution to keep the illness from spreading, but he felt like he was losing the battle.

"Where is that medicine!"

The doctor threw a wet towel to the floor.

"It should have been here by now! I only have enough fever reducer for one more day, two perhaps."

Anna pulled her hair back with a ribbon and walked over to the doctor.

He took a deep breath as she approached.

"Hello, Anna. I'm sorry."

David searched her flushed face.

"Are you feeling all right?" he asked.

"Just a little tired is all. It's hot."

"It is that." He reached out and felt Anna's forehead.

"Maybe you should rest. Are you sure you're feeling all right?"

"I came to offer some help. You and Dr. Luke need to get some rest."

David looked into Anna's bright blue eyes. She seemed older than her fifteen years. He knew Luke would have been pleased to hear her call him "Dr. Luke."

"I used to live at a Children's Shelter. I know how to take care of babies. I can help with the children."

Her eyes held his.

The doctor stood thinking but finally nodded his approval.

"Thank you, Anna. I appreciate it."

She walked over to Mr. Campbell and reached for the baby on his lap. He didn't refuse.

"Is Mrs. Campbell better?" she asked.

"Doc says she's resting easy. He won't let me go in to see her or little Timmy."

He stood and starting pacing.

Anna bounced the baby girl on her hip.

"What's her name?"

"Sarah—after her mother."

Anna had just sat down when the professor found her.

"Anna, what are you doing?"

She didn't know how to answer. He seemed cross.

"Leave the baby and come back with me."

Anna glanced toward Mr. Campbell.

"He's right, Anna. You shouldn't be around us."

She handed Sarah back to her father and followed the professor back to their cots.

Anna sat quietly.

"I'm sorry, Anna. I just don't want you to get sick like the others. I shouldn't have talked to you that way. I'm very sorry."

"When are we going to leave?" she asked, barely above a whisper.

"I don't know. I don't think anyone knows."

Anna turned away.

The professor took his hand and gently turned her face toward his as he sat down next to her.

"What is it, Anna?"

She paused and, looking down at her feet, spoke softly.

"At first, I was scared to leave the shelter, and then I was just sad. But when I met you, I started thinking less of the shelter, and well, you made me happy. You made me feel like I was a real person."

The professor smiled and reached over to hold her hand.

"You are very much a real person, Anna."

She raised her head.

"We had so much fun in Diamond, and Mrs. Wilson was wonderful. The dresses, the big hotel, my journal—I was starting to forget all my sadness and trouble."

"But now?"

"Oh, Professor!"

Anna flung herself into his arms.

"Why do bad things happen? Why did Mrs. Landry's husband have to die? Why is everyone getting sick!"

The professor stroked Anna's hair and kissed the top of her head.

"We don't always know why, little one. But we know God is with us. We just have to trust Him, Anna."

"I try, Professor, I try, but it's not working. I just want to go to Finley Valley and forget all this. Any place has got to be better than here!"

The professor held her tightly and thought she was probably right.

Chapter 13

God is our refuge and strength,
a very present help in trouble.
Psalm 46:1

*T*he professor hoped everything would get better, not only for Anna's sake but for everyone.

But his hopes were just hopes.

The medicine David was looking for came a couple of days too late to help the Campbell family.

Both Mrs. Campbell and her three-year-old son, Timmy, died on the same day.

And the professor gave in to Anna's pleas and allowed her to help with the children while he did his best to comfort the grieving husband.

He waited until David left the man's side then walked over and gently sat down next to him. Mr. Campbell barely acknowledged the professor's presence.

"What can we do to help?" the professor asked, as he laid a hand on his shoulder.

Mr. Campbell shook his head then buried his face in his hands. His body began to shake from his violent sobs.

The professor didn't try to comfort him at that moment but instead just gave him time to grieve openly. He waited patiently.

Anna glanced toward the professor, and she looked as if she was going to cry as well.

The professor's kind eyes spoke directly to her heart, and she quickly turned her attention back to the children. She began to hum.

Professor Higgins was proud of Anna. He wished he could have spared her from the pain and suffering everyone was feeling from one degree or another. But on the other hand, he knew firsthand that adversity made a person stronger to help endure greater hardship later if necessary and to help others going through something similar. He had no doubt if they were spared, she would indeed grow up a little more from the experience. In fact, he thought, she already had.

Mr. Campbell wiped his eyes with a handkerchief slipped to him from another passenger who was sitting nearby. Finally, the grieving husband answered the professor's original question through soft, halting sobs.

"How can you help me, you say? I would ask you to take away the hurt, but I know you can't do that."

The professor was shaking his head.

"I can't but I know Someone who can lessen the hurt and bring you comfort."

The husband looked at the professor with questioning eyes.

"God is able to comfort us even in our deepest sorrows," the professor tried to explain.

Mr. Campbell's face fell, expecting quite a different answer. He looked past his red swollen eyes deep into the professor's compassion-filled eyes. His voice was controlled and steady.

"Is He the same God that took my wife and son away from me?" His voice was hard with bitterness, and his eyes narrowed, portraying the same bitterness.

The professor tugged at his snow-white beard as he pondered on this broken man who dropped his head back into his wet hands. The aged man spoke in a soft, raspy voice.

"I had a child once who died."

Mr. Campbell sat up slowly. The professor continued without looking at anything in particular.

"A little girl. She died along with her mother."

Several seconds passed without a word spoken.

"How did you cope? How did you go on?" Mr. Campbell finally asked.

"Well, honestly, I got mad," the professor answered. "I got mad at the doctor. And I got mad at God."

Mr. Campbell drew a deep, shivering breath and wiped his eyes.

"What did you do?"

"Well, I stood at the funeral and watched them bury my wife and child, and then I rode away. Simply rode away from everybody and everything."

The professor glanced over at Anna first and then toward Mr. Campbell. Anna didn't appear to be paying attention.

"I've never been back," the professor said.

Mr. Campbell searched the old man's face.

"So that's why I'm traveling on the train. I was on my way to make things right, apologize to my wife and baby girl for walking away, for being a fool."

"I don't think anyone would call you a fool, Professor—nobody."

"Perhaps, perhaps not."

A different type of sadness fell upon the grieving husband. The tables had turned a new direction.

"Well, enough about me. How about we ask for the help we both need right now, including the older couple who is still struggling from the illness?"

The professor bowed his head and began to pray out loud. Several around them bowed their heads as well. But Mr. Campbell just watched. He wasn't ready to ask for help from something or Someone he didn't understand.

Chapter 14

Be not afraid…
for the LORD thy God is with thee
whithersoever thou goest.
Joshua 1:9

The older couple recovered, but the husband was so weak they decided to stay on in the little town called Lazy Spring. Everyone said it was a miracle they even survived.

The woman traveling alone was a great asset to David. Her father was a doctor, so she had the natural ability to assist him. It was no secret she probably wouldn't be getting back on the train when it came. She and the good doctor were spending a lot of personal time together.

Because of that, Luke decided it was a good time to take all he had learned from David and the schooling he had and put it to good use somewhere else. His dream was starting to take shape. He was excited and motivated.

The two "cattlemen" turned out to be bankers of all things, and they stayed as far away from everyone as possible. It was no wonder they stayed well.

The family of three was untouched as well and eagerly awaited for the train to take them to waiting family members. They quietly stayed to themselves, and no one blamed them.

No one was quite the same after the long weeks in the old boarding house, especially Mr. Campbell. It was an experience that would stay with everyone forever. Lasting friendships were made, even though it was unlikely most of them would cross paths ever again.

Mrs. Landry quietly grieved for her husband, and the professor found her and Anna sitting in the sun.

"Good morning, ladies."

Anna and Elisabeth Landry looked up toward the professor and smiled.

"Anna, the train should arrive in about an hour," he said. "Dr. Monroe says we will load the wagon soon and for everyone to be packed and ready."

Elisabeth hugged Anna.

"You have been a great comfort, Anna. I will miss you."

Anna pushed a stray hair from her face.

"Mrs. Landry, what are you going to do now?" Anna asked.

The professor listened eagerly for her reply as well.

"I just don't know. I guess the easiest thing to do is to stay here. Andrew always said I was the best cook ever."

The young widow paused and waited until she was able to control her urge to cry.

"And I can sew a pretty good stitch. Maybe someone would trade my services for a place to stay until I can make some clear decisions."

Anna looked up at the professor. They shared a genuine concern for the woman.

"Besides, I couldn't bear to leave Andrew," Elisabeth added.

The professor nodded. He knew right well how it felt to leave a fresh grave. He handed Elisabeth Landry some money.

"I can't—"

"Yes, you can, and I insist. God has been very good to me."

"Thank you, Professor. And thank you, Anna. I will never forget either of you."

"Nor shall we," the professor said.

David called from the door of the boarding house.

"We will load in fifteen minutes!" he cried. "Make ready everyone!"

Professor Higgins and Anna walked back to the boarding house but not before they walked across the open field with Elisabeth to visit Andrew's grave. Tears were shed, and tight, warm hugs were given.

Soon, the small remaining group pulled in front of Lazy Spring's train station.

It seemed ages since they last rode the train. Anna knew Mrs. McAfee would think she was in Finley Valley by now. She asked the professor if there was any way to let her know what was going on.

"I will inquire at the ticket counter," he said. "We should have time to send a telegram, I would think."

The professor helped Anna from the wagon then walked around to the other side to talk with David.

The two men shook hands.

"Anna and I can't thank you enough, Dr. Monroe."

"Don't thank me. You and Anna helped me more than you know. I was just doing my job."

"And you do that job very well."

"If you are ever back this way, please stop in," David said. "Thankfully, it should be under much better circumstances! Lazy Spring is a nice little town."

"We may just take you up on that, Doctor."

Others gathered around to thank the doctor, so the professor slipped away feeling beyond thankful that God spared Anna and himself for more days ahead. Now they could pick up on their journey where they left off.

Chapter 15

Casting all your care upon him;
for he careth for you.
1 Peter 5:7

"It's not much further now, Anna!"

Anna was waiting for the professor on a weathered bench near the ticket counter when she looked up, hearing his cheery voice. Her mind was busy with many different thoughts, various thoughts and memories she would have preferred not to have entertained right then. But she couldn't push them away for some reason.

The professor sat beside her with a huff.

"The man at the ticket counter says we are less than a day from Finley Valley. Our journey is near completion!"

Anna didn't try to hide her uneasiness and produced neither a smile nor a frown.

The professor paused, puzzled with her demeanor.

"Well, what if I showed you this? Does this help make things better?"

In the professor's hand was a yellow telegram receipt.

Anna immediately broke into a smile, and she gladly received the paper from his hand.

The professor hadn't seen that smile in a very long time. He breathed a sigh of relief after observing her from the line at the ticket counter.

"You were able to send Mrs. McAfee a message!" she cried. "Oh, thank you, Professor Higgins!"

"Yes, she will know you were delayed and are safe and sound. You will probably be in Finley Valley before she receives it."

He didn't miss the strained look on Anna's face.

"Did you tell her about the sickness and, well, everything that has happened?" Anna asked solemnly.

"No. I thought I'd let you do that, perhaps one day, when it's a distance memory."

Anna nodded.

"Thank you, Professor Higgins."

The professor stood and held out his hand toward her.

"We better board. All the good seats will be taken."

Anna didn't move.

"What is it, Anna?"

"I was thinking about Mrs. Landry. She'll be all alone."

"She's a strong woman, Anna. She will be just fine. I have no doubt."

"But how do you know?"

"For one thing, Dr. Monroe will look in on her. I specifically asked him to, and he has happily agreed."

Anna still sat.

The professor sat back down and searched her blue eyes.

"Listen, she and I had a good talk. It was right after I tried to comfort Mr. Campbell."

Anna clearly remembered the talk he had with Mr. Campbell when the man was grieving his wife and son. She wasn't ready to tell him she had overheard everything that was said, including the part about the professor's loss of his own wife and baby girl.

Professor Higgins noticed the look on her face and felt he needed to explain further even though he could tell the train was preparing to leave soon. He had no idea the look on her face wasn't concern so much for Elisabeth but for him.

"Mrs. Landry, Elisabeth, was saved when she was a little girl. Her husband was saved as well. Because she and Andrew had given their lives completely to Jesus Christ when they were young, they learned to rely on Jesus. She will find her strength and comfort in Him. So don't worry, Anna. She's strong."

Anna just sat there with a blank look on her face.

The professor cringed inside. This conversation was much too soon, and Anna clearly didn't understand what he was trying to say. With the train's departure pressing down on them, this conversation would have to wait until a later date when Anna was ready.

"Anna, we need to board very soon."

The professor watched the conductor walking from the front of the train toward the passenger car.

The professor began to stand.

"I don't want to go to Finley Valley," Anna said suddenly.

The professor was taken back and sat back down.

"But, but you have to—I'm right here with you if that is what you're concerned about."

"I don't *have* to go. Who says I have to go?"

"Well, no one, I suppose. But I believe you should give it a try. You can't—"

Anna abruptly cut him off.

"What? I can't make it on my own?"

The professor was shocked at Anna's change in behavior and was growing somewhat annoyed. He took a deep breath and continued the conversation.

"No, Anna, that's not what I was going to say, but that is a true statement."

He waited to see what else she had to say. Obviously, she had other things on her mind.

"Is that your destination too?" she asked.

Anna watched his expression carefully.

"Yes, yes, it is. I want to see you safely there, of course. I exchanged my ticket when we were in Diamond."

"So we passed the stop where you were really going?"

The professor sat up straight and thought about his words carefully.

"Anna, I have no set schedule. And yes, we passed my original stop. Like I said, I traded my ticket at Diamond so I could accompany you to Finley Valley. I care about you."

"Why? Why do you care about me? No one ever cared for me. I was abandoned when I was left at the shelter. If anyone really cared, they would have come back for me like they said they would. I waited and waited. No one ever came! I wish Mrs. McAfee had never told me about the note that was left with me when she found me."

"You have told me so much about Mrs. McAfee, Anna. You know *she* cares for you."

The professor reached out to hold her hand, but she pulled away and turned from him.

"If anyone cared, they wouldn't have sent me away. Don't you think I know what the others are saying about me? Poor Anna this, and poor Anna that. If Mrs. McAfee had really cared, she wouldn't have let me go. I'm sorry you sent that telegram!"

"I'm sure she didn't have control over your situation, Anna. You have to understand."

"I *do* understand. I'm beginning to understand more than you know!"

The professor was taken back. He had no idea she had so much hidden inside or the struggle she apparently was fighting and had been fighting for a while it seemed.

"Anna, from the moment I met you on the back seat of that train, I knew you were someone very special. And each passing moment confirmed it. You are bright and sensitive. You are also smart and witty. You are an amazing young lady. You just need to believe in yourself."

He paused for a reaction, and since there was none, he continued.

"Anna, I agree with something you told me early on about what Mrs. McAfee once told you."

Anna didn't move.

"She said she believed God had something special planned for your life. I agree with her! Don't quit now. Just as God is about to show you wondrous things! He has a plan for you, Anna. He has a plan for me. I'm just a little late letting God show me some things. I'm on a journey too. And I have enjoyed sharing our journeys together."

The professor gently took her shoulder and turned her so she had to face him.

"Now look at me. Look at me, Anna."

"It's time to realize that you aren't a child anymore. You are a young woman with strength and character. You are a beautiful person, inside and out. Don't let anybody or any circumstance convince you differently. You must stand strong. If you quit now, I truly believe you will regret it."

Anna didn't cry. She didn't want to this time. She honestly didn't know how she felt right then. So much had happened since she left the shelter, and she was having a hard time figuring out what she wanted to do.

"Anna, only *you* can make the decision you think is best for you. And I will stand by any decision you make."

The conductor chose that very moment to announce the ten-minute warning.

"All aboard!" he yelled.

The professor stood to his feet and squared his shoulders.

"You have ten minutes, Anna."

The professor then left her on the weathered bench all alone.

It was the second hardest thing in his life he had forced himself to walk away from.

Chapter 16

Call unto me, and I will answer thee,
and shew thee great and mighty things,
which thou knowest not.
Jeremiah 33:3

*L*uke thanked the man for the ride, grabbed his bags from the back of the wagon, then ran as hard as he could. His long legs ate up the distance quickly.

He heard the conductor give the ten-minute warning, so he slowed a bit. He could surely get his ticket and get on the train within ten minutes, he thought.

He rounded the corner of the station and just about ran over the professor.

"Professor! Forgive me. Are you all right?"

The professor held his hand to his heart.

"Just startled a bit, son. No harm done."

"I'm sorry, but if you'll excuse me, I need to purchase a ticket for the train, and it seems I don't have much time. Are you about to board?"

"I'm not sure."

Luke hesitated for just a moment then continued on. He didn't want to miss the train. He was just about to reach the ticket counter when he saw Anna sitting on a nearby bench. She was wiping her eyes, and he wanted to stop but knew he couldn't. But as soon as he purchased his ticket, he ran straight to her.

"Anna, what's wrong?"

Luke was the last person she expected to see. And when he reached her, she turned away, struggling not to cry.

"What is it, Anna?"

Luke searched around for the professor but didn't see him anywhere.

"Does the professor know you're here? Let me help you to the train. I fear we both may be left behind if we linger."

Just then, the conductor yelled his last cry.

"Last call! Last call! All aboard!"

"Come on, Anna. Let's go!"

He grabbed her bags and struggled to carry both his and hers. He motioned with his head.

"Come on!"

Anna stood and followed the young doctor-to-be, but she could barely keep up with him. She needed to find the professor. She couldn't leave without him knowing! What had she done?

"Dr. Luke!" she cried.

Luke turned but continued his pace.

"I can't leave without the professor. I can't get on that train!"

"I'm sure he's close by!" he yelled back toward her.

Just as they reached the steps leading to the train car, the conductor gave the signal for the train to pull away.

Panic rose within Anna.

"No! I can't!"

Luke literally pulled her up the steps, and when they reached the top, they both fell into a heap on top of their bags, safely in the train car. And there standing right above them was the good professor.

"Glad you both could make it," he said calmly.

He reached out with both hands and helped Anna and Luke to their feet.

The train began to build up momentum as Professor Higgins led them to seats he had secured earlier. Near the back of the car, Luke was able to sit directly across the aisle from them.

Anna hugged the old man, and he hugged her. She didn't want to let go.

She started to say something, but the professor put his finger to her lips.

"Shhh. We'll talk about it later. Right now, let's just get settled."

Anna nodded and laid her head on his shoulder, slipping her arm through his and squeezing tightly.

The professor was able to finally relax. He was tired. The last few weeks had been stressful, and he longed for some order in his life. He had a slight headache after his earlier conversation with Anna, but he was relieved they were finally on their way to their original destination.

He wondered how Elisabeth Landry was doing. Mr. Campbell was on the train with his four children and appeared to be handling things just fine. The train was almost full, and the sun was hiding behind some very dark storm clouds. The slow rocking tempted many to sleep, including Anna. The professor was sure he would fall victim anytime. He made sure Anna was comfortable then turned to check in with Luke.

"Glad you could join us, Luke. Thank you for getting Anna on the train."

"I'm just happy we made it! I figured you and Anna got separated somehow. I'm lucky to have run across her when I did. I don't know if she would have made the train in time otherwise."

"I actually knew where she was."

The professor looked smug.

Luke politely nodded.

"And did you know she was near tears?" Luke asked, his furrowed brow giving away his concern.

"I suspected so. I was watching. I wouldn't have left her if that's what you're thinking. But thank you for persuading her. I was just about to go get her myself when I saw you. I thought I'd watch and see what happened before I made a move."

Luke's expression hadn't changed.

"I had already talked to the conductor," the professor said as he continued. "They wouldn't have left without us."

"Well, actually," Luke said, "she had no choice but to follow me. I just grabbed her bags and took off!"

"I'm very grateful, Luke. She will be too, if not now, then in the days to come."

The professor looked down at Anna's peaceful expression. She was sound asleep and heavy against his arm. He fought to keep his own eyes open as he thanked God for answering his prayer and always in a way he never expected.

Chapter 17

Make a joyful noise unto the LORD, all the earth:
make a loud noise, and rejoice, and sing praise.
Psalm 98:4

The professor and Anna never expected to see Luke on the train heading away from Lazy Spring, so the professor decided the only way to find out why was to ask.

"So where are you heading, Luke?" asked the professor.

He, Luke, and Anna snacked on flakey biscuits and raspberry jam that the professor purchased before he boarded the train, just before Luke almost ran him over at the train station.

They all napped better on the train than any night at the boarding house. There, no one fully relaxed knowing someone was fighting for their life. None of them realized how tired they were and they'd all slept much longer than expected.

"I'm heading to a remote area just north of here," Luke said.

It was just the beginning of Professor Higgins' many questions.

"I grew up there, and it's always been my dream to go back one day after training to be a doctor. It's been longer and harder than I thought, but I think I might be ready."

"I'm sure you are. I can tell you're excited. Do you have family there?"

"My parents are there, and I have an older brother. He's married and has three young children."

"That will be quite a family reunion. Family is important."

Anna had been listening but then turned her head toward the window and pondered on the tall, jagged mountains in the distance. She wondered what it would be like to have family—any family.

Luke stood and stretched his long frame, running his fingers through his thick brown hair.

"They're all I've got, all except Uncle David. Dr. Monroe, he's my father's baby brother."

Anna had only been halfway listening until that moment.

"So that's why you look alike!" she exclaimed, suddenly sitting up straight in her seat.

The professor jumped then chuckled.

"I'm afraid you startled me, girl!"

They all enjoyed a good laugh. It was the makings of a great day.

Anna had been very quiet on this part of the trip, so the professor was happy to see her finally perk up a little.

Professor Higgins was still peppering Luke with questions, and discovered he was happy to talk about his family.

"I look more like my Uncle David than either my father or my brother. We are actually very close. I'll miss him for sure, but I knew it was time to move on. So I quickly packed all my things, and well, here I am. I admit to being a little impulsive at times. Hard to sit still. My father often threatened to tie me to a chair when I was younger! My brother is the quiet one."

He had earned the professor and Anna's full attention. It was nice to have him along for this part of their journey.

Luke yawned and then casually added, "And it's barely a day's ride from Lazy Spring to Finley Valley. Not too much longer now."

That really got both the professor and Anna's attention.

"You are going to Finley Valley?" they both asked at the same time.

"Yes, you know Finley Valley?"

Luke turned and faced them, his long legs in the aisle.

"Well, no," the professor began to explain, "but that's where we're heading."

"I just assumed you were going to Burke Mountain. It's a large trading station and very popular."

Luke looked around at all the other passengers.

"Most of these people will get off there. Finley Valley is as far as the train goes. It turns around there.

"What takes you there?" Luke asked. "Do you have family there? Because if you do, I'm sure I'd know them. Everyone knows everyone there. Absolutely no secrets!"

He laughed out loud, and the people in front of him turned and looked his way.

Luke politely nodded toward the family and the toddler with them shyly smiled and waved.

"He's adorable," Anna said, realizing how much she missed the children at the shelter.

"He looks to be about the same age as my youngest nephew," Luke said. "Maybe two years old?"

Anna agreed his estimate was probably correct.

"Say, if you're around long enough, maybe you'll get to meet my nephews. They have an older sister as well."

"I'd like that," Anna shyly replied.

Then they all sat quietly for a few minutes. The mountains seemed to rise higher and higher as they came into closer view.

The professor and Anna turned their faces from the window just as Luke let go of a loud sigh.

"I'm ready for a break," Luke said and stood again. "We will be coming up on Burke Mountain Station anytime. I know a place there that serves a spread of food fit for a king and at a good price!"

"That sounds wonderful," Anna said, rubbing her stomach.

She glanced up at the professor.

The professor assured her he agreed.

"A nice, relaxing meal right now does sound wonderful," he said.

"My treat then," Luke said. "And then I'll show you around. It's a longer stop because even the train crew takes advantage of the good food and the large trading post. People travel a long way to trade and sell there."

Luke pointed out that many passengers had large packs with them, full of wares and many interesting things to sell.

Anna tingled with excitement. It was an unexpected surprise so close to her destination. Another adventure!

She reached for the professor's hand. He had been right.

She couldn't quit now.

Chapter 18

For the LORD thy God,
he it is that doth go with thee;
he will not fail thee, nor forsake thee.
Deuteronomy 31:6

They could hardly keep up with Luke's long strides.

The professor mentioned he needed some comfortable shoes, so that's where they were heading.

"I know exactly what you need!" Luke exclaimed. "And I know just the place."

Burke Mountain Station was nestled among a small group of Blue Mountains climbing high in all directions. They reached up among the white fluffy clouds, and the only word Anna could think of was *majestic*. It was a sight that would take anyone's breath away, she imagined.

Anna had never seen anything like it. It was beyond description, and she wasn't sure how she'd explain it in her journal. There just weren't the right words, so she decided she would take her colored pencils and try to draw them instead.

Professor Higgins held Anna's hand tightly as they weaved around people, trying to keep pace with Luke. She could tell he was struggling, so she slowed down. Luke would just have to slow down too.

Anna hadn't seen this side of Luke before. But she decided none of them were themselves in Lazy Spring.

She hoped to return there to see Elisabeth Landry sometime soon. Elisabeth was like a sister to her in some ways. They weren't that far apart in age really, and they were just getting to know each other when Anna had to leave.

Now that she knew Lazy Spring wasn't too far away, maybe she could visit, she thought. Surely, Luke would be visiting his Uncle David from time to time. Then she overheard him telling the professor that he often did go visit, he, along with his family sometimes. And it always included a fun stop at Burke Mountain!

She was having so much fun, she forgot all about her reason for going to Finley Valley for the moment. She forgot there was someone waiting for her, someone she knew nothing about…"a family in need."

Many people throughout the trading post, which seemed to stretch forever, knew Luke and threw their hands up in greeting. He was certainly no stranger to Burke Mountain.

In no time, they had found shoes for both the professor and Anna. They were soft leather, and Anna wondered how she had ever lived without them! The professor let her buy two pairs. One was decorated with blue beads, and the other stained with colorful flowers and designs. Neither was plain or ordinary in her mind. She chose to wear the pair with the blue beads.

But it was time to find something to eat. So Luke led them to a large cabin-like dwelling. Smoke rose from twin chimneys, and the smell of barbequed meat assaulted them long before they reached the door. The place was crowded, but they found a table in a far corner. The tables and chairs were made of rough wood and jars filled with lit candles sat in the middle of all the tables. The sound of laughter was everywhere. The walls were made from huge split logs.

Anna couldn't stop staring. Animal skins littered the walls as well as antlers of all shapes and sizes. She saw a large stuffed cat, and Luke had to explain it was a mountain lion and not just an ordinary cat that had grown that large. There was sawdust on the floor, and strings of small lanterns above their heads gave out as much light as they could. It was a bit smoky but not too bad. The food smelled heavenly.

Diamond was nice, but Anna had found her new favorite place. This was so interesting, so exciting. What else was out there she had never seen? she wondered. She decided right then and there she wanted to travel one day and see other places. She hoped her dream of doing so would come true, and she closed her eyes and wished away! This was beyond anything she could have ever conjured up in her mind.

Luke smiled at the innocence that flooded over Anna as he observed her wide eyes and open mouth as she sat across from him. It was refreshing to see someone so excited over, well, over almost everything. He had no idea what her story was, so he had no idea what she was experiencing inside. He had no idea that this extremely fascinating girl had never been away from the place she called home—a place called home that was never her idea, never anything she would have chosen, a place that never allowed her to experience real life.

Along her journey, Anna had already experienced much about life, and the professor was glad he was there to share it with her.

Anna was growing up and growing up quickly.

Chapter 19

Take therefore no thought for the morrow.
Matthew 6:34

*L*uke was right.

Most of the passengers *did* get off at Burke Mountain Station. Only four remained on the train heading toward Finley Valley. It was the last stop before the train turned around and went the other way, so unless you were specifically going to Finley Valley, you had no reason to take the train that far.

Anna was curious now. She wasn't afraid, but she was extremely nervous. She fingered the tag given to her at the Children's Shelter that would identify her when she got to Finley Valley.

"Annaleigh Thompson; Destination: Finley Valley."

Instead of pinning it to her dress, she decided to just carry it.

Well, Finley Valley will soon be a reality, she thought.

Anna took a deep breath and steadied her hands.

The professor had taken her to the hotel at Burke Mountain where she washed and changed into fresh clothes. Her hair was clean and shiny and pulled back into a loose ponytail. Small wisps of blond hair encircled her face. She smelled nice, and she wore her green dress with the lace collar. She put away her soft leather shoes and wore one of the pairs she had gotten at the general store in Diamond.

She was as ready as she was ever going to be!

Anna looked nice, and the professor and Luke told her so. She blushed at their compliments.

"You know, Anna, the people you are going to stay with were probably looking for you on the train weeks ago," the professor said.

Anna never thought about that.

"So what should I do? What if no one comes for me?"

He reached for her hand.

"Well, you know you aren't alone. I'm not going to leave you. I will make sure you get settled."

"Do you know their name?" he asked.

"No, I don't."

"That's all right. We will ask around. Luke knows everyone, he says."

The professor was so glad Luke was with them, and he felt it was no mistake that Luke chose to go home to Finley Valley the very same time they were traveling there.

Luke was up at the front of the train talking with the only other passenger. It was obvious they knew each other well.

Professor Higgins had no doubt Luke would be welcomed as a doctor in a community where he was so well known. It was obvious people liked him everywhere he went.

The conductor announced that their arrival would be only about fifteen more minutes.

Anna had come too far to think about turning back now, but it was nice to know she could. These people weren't adopting her, they were just giving her a place to stay in exchange for helping them with a specific need. But if she decided not to stay, she couldn't return to the Children's Shelter. Maybe she could go live with Elisabeth Landry or maybe even Mrs. Wilson from Diamond, she thought.

She didn't have any money other than what Mrs. McAfee had given her. And then she had a dreadful thought!

"Professor, where are you going from here?" she asked.

"What?"

He wasn't prepared for the question.

"When we get to Finley Valley, *my* journey is done. But you will need to finish yours."

"I guess you're right, Anna. But I won't leave until I know you are settled. You have Luke, you know. I'm sure you can count on him to help you anytime."

Anna nodded. It was true she had someone she knew in Finley Valley, but the thought of losing the professor was almost unbearable.

"Will I ever see you again?" she asked.

The professor had rehearsed over and over what he would say when this time came. But now he was at a loss for words.

"Of course, you will. I can come visit."

Anna watched his expression. He looked sad. She hadn't seen him that way before, and it concerned her. This was a different type of sad she didn't understand.

"Professor—"

"Anna, we can have a long talk after you are settled. Right now, let's just focus on what's ahead."

Anna knew that meant their conversation was over. She just sat quietly until they pulled into the Finley Valley Station. She wasn't feeling that well anyway.

Chapter 20

I will strengthen thee;
yea, I will help thee.
Isaiah 41:10

$\mathcal{F}$inley Valley wasn't anything like Anna expected.

She stepped onto the wooden platform and stopped. The professor had to urge her to move forward so the rest of them could step from the train.

After Burke Mountain Station, Finley Valley Station looked miniature and deserted. It wasn't dirty or falling down or anything, it just wasn't what she expected. She was at a loss for words.

She wanted to run. Sheer panic coursed through her. She couldn't do this. This was so final!

The professor and Luke were busy with the bags and had no idea what she was feeling.

Anna walked over and sat on a bench that looked to be freshly painted. Large flower pots sat on either side, and Anna ran her hand across the top of the flowers closest to her. They were a mix of vibrant colors and far from plain and ordinary, she thought. They did indeed brighten things up.

She wiped a bead of sweat from her hairline.

"Anna—"

The professor sat her bags down by her feet and took a seat beside her.

"You look pale. Are you feeling all right?"

Anna didn't have time to answer. She suddenly fainted away, and the professor caught her as she fell heavily against him.

"Luke! Luke!" the professor cried.

Luke rushed over and knelt beside Anna. Professor Higgins laid her the rest of the way down on the bench and stood over them. His heart was racing.

"She's burning up! Put her legs up on the bench," Luke instructed.

The professor quickly jumped into action.

Luke opened one of Anna's bags and pulled out the first item of clothing and crumpled it up to put under her head.

The professor and Luke locked eyes.

"You don't suppose—"

"No, it's been too long. If she was going to catch the illness like the others at Lazy Spring, she would have shown symptoms before now."

"Are you sure, Luke? Dead sure?"

"Yes, well, not one hundred percent sure, but it wouldn't make sense."

The professor just stood there thinking.

"Stay with her. I will get some water," he finally said.

The other man that was on the train with them was standing nearby and offered his assistance.

"I will get it! You stay with her."

Soon, he returned with a bucket of cool water and some small towels.

The professor was pacing back and forth and watched as Luke ran a cool, wet towel across Anna's forehead and face.

Anna opened her eyes and tried to sit up.

"No, no, little girl, just lie still a few minutes." Luke's voice was kind and gentle.

Anna was confused.

"You fainted is all, just lie still."

Anna's head was hurting, so she did as Luke instructed. Her stomach was upset.

Luke turned his head to the sound of a galloping horse heading up the trail beside the station.

"The man from the train is going for help," the professor explained.

"Good. We need to get her somewhere comfortable and out of this heat."

Anna lay there with her eyes closed, clutching the tag with her name and destination.

Luke carefully took the tag from her, and Anna didn't even open her eyes.

"What's this?" he asked the professor.

"Anna has traveled all the way from the Children's Shelter in Logan's Gap to help a family here. It's the tag they gave her to identify herself."

"Shelter? What family?"

"I don't know, and with our late arrival, I'm certain they wonder if she's even coming."

"I'll ask around, but right now, we just need to get her someplace where we can keep an eye on her." He slipped the tag into his pocket.

The professor nodded in agreement.

The man returned. And following close behind was another man with a small wagon.

The man with the wagon pulled the horses to a hard stop, jumped down, and ran toward the situation.

"Luke!" he cried.

"Brandon!"

Luke was never happier to see his brother.

Chapter 21

And be ye kind one to another, tenderhearted.
Ephesians 4:32

$\mathcal{T}$here was no time for handshakes or hugs.

Luke's brother, Brandon, did just as Luke asked him to as they carefully helped Anna into the back of the wagon where Brandon had thrown a couple of blankets.

Professor Higgins insisted on riding in the back with her and gently laid her head in his lap. He was clearly worried and upset, and Luke was concerned for him as well.

Anna was awake, but her head hurt so badly she didn't try to talk other than to ask for more water.

The wagon climbed the trail beside the station, and the professor held on the best he could so he and Anna wouldn't slide toward the back. It seemed as if they were going straight up.

Brandon pushed the horses, and they strained to make the hill while Luke kept watch on the passengers behind them.

"What's going on?" Brandon asked, shouting to be heard. "What's wrong with the girl?"

"I'm not sure," Luke shouted back. "We just need to get her to your house where she can rest."

"I sent Dan for Doc Stevens," Brandon said. "Dan said he rode in with you on the train."

Luke just nodded.

"And I asked Melissa to get a bed ready."

Luke nodded again, turning to see how the professor and Anna were doing.

The professor looked as badly as Anna, he thought.

It was unusually warm, but a breeze began to stir as they crested the small rocky mountain.

The wagon finally leveled out then started a descent into a fertile valley below. The professor wished Anna was well enough to see what he was seeing. He couldn't believe his eyes—Finley Valley.

From this vantage point, he could see the entire valley from a bird's-eye view. Well-manicured farms dotted the land in all directions, and a narrow yet vibrant river flowed through the area almost dividing the land into two equal parts. Strong, hardy trees stood tall and lush on either side of the water. And he saw a wide, wooden bridge that led into the heart of town where colorfully painted buildings stood in two perfectly straight lines.

As they descended the bumpy mountain, he could make out the movement of people as well as horses and wagons on the main street. New construction on a building near the church kept a number of men busy.

The ride was rough, and the professor hung on to the side of the wagon and Anna. He was sure he felt every bump in the road.

Brandon didn't have to steer the horses from there. They knew where to go. They slowed at the bottom of the mountain and headed left.

Soon, they pulled up in front of a modest frame house where a woman stood on the porch with two little boys by her side. She was tall and slender and her light brown hair that didn't quite reach her shoulders danced in the brisk breeze.

She held the screen door open as Luke carried Anna to the nearest bedroom and laid her on clean white sheets. The professor and Brandon weren't far behind.

Brandon led the professor to the parlor where he could sit comfortably then headed to the bedroom. His wife, Melissa, was already doing whatever she could to make Anna comfortable.

"What's wrong with her?" she asked Luke in a whisper.

"I'm not sure, but she fainted at the station, and she's burning up with fever."

Anna slowly opened her eyes and looked up into Melissa's big brown ones.

Melissa smiled and pushed all the little stray hairs away from Anna's face.

"Hello there," Melissa said softly. "Don't worry, you're in good hands."

Then everyone heard swift feet in the hall. Doc Stevens was there.

The older man with thinning hair and wire-rimmed glasses rushed to Anna's side and was quick to sit on the bed beside her.

"What can you tell me, Luke?"

He laid a calm hand on Anna's hot forehead.

"Well, she fainted, and when I felt her head, she was burning up. We had just gotten off the train, and then we came here as quickly as we could. She's complaining of a headache and—"

Luke hesitated so the doctor stopped and looked up at the young, upcoming doctor.

"And what?"

She's been exposed to an illness—to an illness that recently took some lives in Lazy Spring.

The doctor immediately stood to his feet.

"Melissa and I can handle it from here. Everybody else, out!"

Luke was slow to respond.

"But I don't really think—"

"I said, out!"

One look from the experienced doctor, and Luke knew he was defeated. He looked down at Anna then left. With a concerned look from Melissa, Brandon had already gone to round up their boys.

Luke stood outside the door listening for anything he could hear. As a doctor, he knew it was vital to use sound judgment and never put others in danger. He had broken a fundamental rule. It all just happened so fast, he reasoned.

Even his Uncle David had isolated the passengers from the train from the town as a precaution. And he probably spared lives because of it. Here, Luke knew he might have put his own family at risk.

Maybe he wasn't fit to be a good doctor after all, he further reasoned.

Chapter 22

*Bear ye one another's burdens,
and so fulfil the law of Christ.
Galatians 6:2*

Anna was asleep, and everyone else met in the parlor, except Melissa and Brandon's two young sons.

"We can't take any chances," Doc Stevens was explaining. "We need to move her somewhere else or move everyone *here* somewhere else. Which is it?"

No one missed the fact that the doctor looked frustrated and sounded even more so.

"We must treat this with utmost care and very quickly," he added with more emphasis than he had before.

Luke suddenly stood, shaking his head.

"I'm sorry. I should have thought—"

"There's no time for that now, Luke," the doctor said with a wave of his hand. "Sit back down."

Melissa stood slowly then took a deep breath.

"I'll stay with her."

She looked down at her husband for his reaction.

"I've been exposed as much as anyone."

Brandon reached up and held her hand.

"She will need a woman to see to her needs properly, so I guess that makes me the best and only choice to stay and care for her."

"Brandon, you can't let her," Luke began to blurt out.

"Melissa's right," Brandon said, cutting Luke off. "She's the best one to stay, and we all know when Melissa makes up her mind—well, let's just say she's bound and determined."

Melissa smiled at her husband, he squeezed her hand.

"Besides, from what you say, Luke, she probably isn't contagious with the same illness you dealt with in Lazy Spring, right?" Brandon added.

"No, she shouldn't have the same illness, but I don't know—I just don't know. It was an illness I wasn't familiar with. If only Uncle David was here, he would know exactly what to do."

The professor took his turn and stood. He looked tired and worn out. His wrinkled clothing seemed to mirror how he felt.

The room was quiet, everyone waiting to hear what he could add to the situation.

"I'll go get Dr. Monroe from Lazy Spring. I'm not doing any good here, and I'll never forgive myself if I don't at least try every option available to see Anna gets well."

Luke began to protest.

Doc Stevens stood this time and motioned for the professor to sit and for Luke to be quiet.

"Sounds to me like you have it all planned out. There's nothing more I can do here right now, so I'm going to make some other calls. I'll check back in when I can."

He shook hands with Brandon and the professor. He nodded toward Melissa. He then walked over and put a hand on Luke's shoulder.

"Take good care of the girl. I believe in you, Luke."

The doctor waited until Luke looked up at him. His voice was gentle.

"You will make a fine doctor, Luke. I'm counting on you. I won't live forever, you know," he said with a smile. "Someone needs to take my place."

Luke couldn't speak, so he just nodded his head.

Brandon and Melissa made quick arrangements to take the boys to their grandparents. Brandon would stay there with the boys until further notice.

Luke insisted he stay in the bedroom next to Anna's and Professor Higgins would immediately go to Lazy Spring to get Dr. Monroe.

Doc Stevens had already left.

Finley Valley had welcomed Anna at last but not in the way anyone expected.

Chapter 23

Be still, and know that I am God.
Psalm 46:10

$\mathcal{P}$rofessor Higgins stepped off the train in Lazy Spring. So much had happened since he, Anna, and Luke had left.

He soon found a ride into town and located the small, but impressive, medical clinic run by Dr. David Monroe. The doctor had just finished with a patient when he saw the professor coming through the door.

"What are you doing here, Professor?" he asked, as he scribbled something on a medical chart.

"Did you and Anna decide not to leave after all?"

The professor shook his head.

"I'm here because Anna is very sick. And no, we *did* leave, along with Luke in fact."

"Anna is sick?" He gave the professor his full attention.

"Yes! When we got off the train at Finley Valley, she fainted. Thank goodness Luke was there to help."

"Go on, Professor," David said with a frown.

"Is she hurting? Is she with you?"

He was already packing his medical bag.

"She has a high fever and was complaining of a bad headache."

David stopped.

"Does she have a rash of any kind?"

"I don't think so. I didn't hear about any rash, but a Dr. Stevens was there to check on her."

"Good, good. What did Doc Stevens say?"

"I don't know. I wasn't in the room where Anna was, but Luke mentioned to him that Anna had been exposed to an illness here, so Dr. Stevens took precautions and sent Luke's brother, Brandon, away with his two sons."

"Brandon? So Anna is at Brandon and Melissa's?"

"Yes, and Melissa stayed back to help with Anna's care."

David slammed his bag shut.

"Foolishness! Melissa shouldn't be there! She has Megan and the boys to consider."

"Do you think Anna could have the illness?" the professor was asking. "I was thinking—"

"What you and I think, Professor Higgins, doesn't matter. Since she's been exposed to the illness, and you know firsthand what that illness can do, all precautions should be taken. Luke should have known better than to take her to Brandon's."

"He knows that now, Doctor."

"Well, we can't change what's already happened."

The professor nodded. He thought back to how sorry Luke was for not being more careful.

"You will have to stay here, Professor."

"Why?"

"The train won't be heading back that way anytime soon. I'll have to go on horseback."

"Is that possible in this mountainous region?"

"It *is* possible. I've done it before, just not in a long time. You go find a room at the hotel and rest up. You need the rest, and I will send word as soon as I can."

The professor didn't argue. He couldn't remember when he had been so exhausted.

"Hopefully, Anna is just fatigued or has a nervous stomach," the doctor continued to say. "She shared with me how she came to be traveling to Finley Valley. She may just be exhausted and, well, scared. We've had some unusually warm temperatures too."

The professor began to pace back and forth.

"I hope you're right, and it's nothing serious."

"In any case, she's in good hands. Melissa and Luke will see to her needs. Melissa used to assist Doc Stevens in the past, and she's a great nurse. Now you go and I'll head out."

The two men parted ways.

But in the meantime, in Finley Valley, Melissa sat on the side of Anna's bed trying to calm her but with little success.

Anna tossed her head back and forth. She was calling out for someone.

"Who is she calling for? I can't understand what she's saying, can you?"

"No, I can't," Luke answered.

He listened carefully.

"Mrs. McAfee, please don't make me go," Anna was saying.

"Must be someone she knows from the Children's Shelter—a Mrs. McAfee."

"She's from a shelter?" Melissa asked.

She was so surprised.

"I just found out. The professor said she's here to help out a family. I have no idea who."

"I was wondering why she and the old man were here."

"Yes, Professor Higgins. He's accompanying her, and they are very close. I don't think they're related, but he is very protective of her."

Anna was still tossing about making a mess of the bed sheets.

"Melissa, bring some cool water from the well. She's starting to feel feverish again."

"Doc left some powder but said not to give it to her again too soon so you won't run out," Melissa explained.

"Well, let's cool her down, and we'll go from there."

"All right, I'll hurry."

Melissa headed toward the door but then turned.

"And, Luke—"

Luke turned his worried face toward hers.

"You might want to check along her hairline. She has some small red bumps there."

"Bumps?"

Luke closed his eyes and groaned.

"Oh, please no."

Chapter 24

But let all those that put their trust in thee rejoice:
let them ever shout for joy, because thou defendeth them.
Psalm 5:11

$\mathcal{M}$rs. McAfee came to work very early as she did every morning. She was starting a fire in the cookstove when she saw a yellow piece of paper on the table nearby.

What is this? she wondered.

To her delight, it was Anna's telegram! The older woman held it to her chest before she even read the message. Warm tears showed up without warning.

"Thank you, Lord, for such a gift today."

She sat in a nearby chair with trembling hands. She read…

"Will arrive F V soon. Delayed. I am well. Anna."

"She is well!"

Eleanor McAfee burst out in song through a flood of happy tears.

"Oh, our many blessings, how bountiful is Your grace. We will sing Your praises until we see You face-to-face."

Anna was safe! It was news she longed to hear. The days had been so lonely without Anna. Eleanor McAfee went about her daily routine enduring the emptiness that comes from losing someone. But she knew it was the way things were and there was no use stewing over it. She was just pleased to know Anna was all right.

What the older woman didn't know was Anna was very sick and was calling her name.

Melissa and Luke stood over Anna as she thrashed about, call-ing the cook's name.

"What is it, Luke?" Melissa asked, handing the very cold well water to him.

Luke's face had gone pale. He took Melissa's hand.

"I want you to leave, Melissa."

"Luke, I'm not going to do that. Tell me, what's wrong."

"The people in Lazy Spring who died, they started with a fever just like Anna's. And everyone who had the illness developed a rash somewhere."

Melissa just stared for a moment, trying to understand what he was trying to say. But then she realized.

"The red bumps on her forehead."

Luke nodded.

"So you think she has the same illness?"

"I think she does. So I want you to leave. Go to Mother and Father's house with Brandon and the boys."

Melissa stood tall.

"Does a doctor walk away from his patient? Well, neither does a nurse. I have helped Doc Stevens many times, and I never once left his side when times got rough."

"This isn't the same, Melissa. Please don't argue with me."

"With all due respect, Luke, I don't think it's proper for you to care for Anna alone. She'll need care that you, well, you know what I mean."

Luke thought for a moment then dropped his head.

"All right. We'll take turns watching her. You go get some rest, and I'll keep cooling her down."

Melissa nodded.

"I'll get more water first," she offered.

Anna moaned and Luke just couldn't believe what was happen-ing. He hoped the professor had reached David and he was on his way. He needed some advice, some help with this!

Melissa brought the water, and Luke bathed Anna's face. Anna continued to mumble.

"I will do anything," Anna was saying. "Please tell them I'll do anything to stay!"

Luke continued to bath her face.

"Please don't make me go. Please don't make me go."

Anna was reaching out as if someone was in front of her.

Luke felt as if he was intruding on someone's private conversation, and although he felt uneasy, he listened carefully.

"I'm scared, Mrs. McAfee. I'm so scared."

Luke wondered what Anna went through at the Children's Shelter.

"Hold me, Mrs. McAfee. I'm so hot. I'm so hot."

Luke prepared the powder that Doc Stevens left and made Anna slowly sip it until it was gone.

She continued to toss and turn, and her blond hair was tangled, her face flushed.

"I'm so scared. Please hold me. Please."

Luke sat down on the bed beside Anna then tenderly enveloped her into a warm embrace. She gradually relaxed against him and soon fell into a peaceful sleep.

Chapter 25

Let thy mercy, O LORD, be upon us,
according as we hope in thee.
Psalm 33:22

*P*rofessor Higgins was ashamed he slept so long. He pulled out his pocket watch and was surprised how late it was. He had missed the evening meal, and the sun was getting ready to go to bed.

He decided to search for Elisabeth Landry, and he didn't have to search very far.

She had already found a job in Lazy Spring's hotel restaurant, and when Professor Higgins walked in to order a cup of coffee, she was the one who waited on him.

"Professor Higgins! Whatever are you doing here? Where's Anna?" she asked, as she reached out to hug him.

"She's not with me."

"What happened? Did you miss your train?"

"No, we made it to Finley Valley, but I had to come back to see Dr. Monroe."

Elisabeth poured coffee into his cup. She wanted to ask him why but decided it might be too personal, so she didn't.

"Elisabeth, what time do you finish here? I'd like to talk to you about something."

"Why, of course. I'm done in about an hour."

"All right, we can talk then. I'll wait for you in the hotel lobby."

She noticed his strained look.

"Is everything all right, Professor?"

"Nothing that can't be fixed, I'm sure."

He produced his best smile.

Elisabeth continued to help other customers while the professor sipped his hot coffee. He admired Elisabeth's strength to go forward without her husband. She would be fine, he thought. Yes, *she* would be fine, but he wasn't so sure about Anna. But he had faith that David would know what to do to help her. He wondered how long it would take to reach Finley Valley on horseback.

The professor decided a walk would do him some good, so he headed out to walk Lazy Spring's main street. He had to make some decisions, and with Anna so sick, everything he had previously planned to do after getting Anna settled would have to wait. But he also knew he couldn't wait too long.

The street was quiet. Most people were settling in for the night, and the night air was pleasant.

Lazy Spring wasn't a large town by any means, but it had all the signs of a growing one, the professor thought.

It was indeed a bit rough around the edges, but there were clear signs that improvements and additions were taking place. A faint hint of fresh paint lingered in the night air. Most of the wooden sidewalks appeared to be new. The impressive town clock that was in the process of being erected proudly displayed the town's simple name in bold, distinct letters across the clock's handsome face. The professor's faithful pocket watch revealed the clock's time was a perfect match to his.

He smiled and took a deep breath.

Lazy Spring was comfortable, he decided. He was beginning to understand David's deep love for the place. And he had no doubt the lazy little town returned that love.

The professor reached David's clinic and paused. The hand-painted sign above the clinic appeared to reflect the town's gratitude. It was grand for a humble medical clinic and obviously painted with great care by someone skilled in their craft. There was a note on the door saying the doctor was away on an emergency and to refer all matters to Sam at the barbershop.

He didn't remember the doctor putting a note there. He was tired and wasn't thinking clearly when he was talking with David, he reasoned. The opportunity to sleep was what he needed to get through the next several days until the train came back that way.

The moon had replaced the sun, and the professor sat on the hard bench outside the medical clinic. He gazed into the night sky and recalled all that had happened in the past weeks.

He remembered when he first met Anna. She was so shy and scared. What she didn't know was he was sometimes shy and scared as well. He drew a good amount of strength from her, knowing he had to be the strong one to see her through her difficulties. It helped him forget his.

He wondered what it would have been like to have raised his own daughter and to share an entire life with his wife instead of the many years without her. The hurt was still there after all the years that had passed. But Anna filled a void. She was just what he needed as he sought to mend some past hurts.

He bowed his head.

"Father, please don't take Anna away from me too, just now, when I need her most."

His prayer was simple but to the point. The professor continued walking and let his thoughts carry him wherever they wanted to go. He was too tired to fight anything right then.

But his thoughts were interrupted when he heard commotion near the train station. Lanterns were blazing. He walked that way.

He was surprised to see the train. It was supposed to only make a quick stop at Lazy Spring and move on. He asked a workman nearby, "What's going on?"

"We've had to make some repairs, but I think we almost have it now."

The professor nodded while his thoughts raced in a new direction.

"When do you think she'll be up and running?" the professor asked with keen interest.

"I think she should be able to head out first thing in the morning, sir."

"Thank you, thank you!" the professor exclaimed. "You've been a great help."

He shook the man's hand with purpose, pumping it up and down.

The workman chuckled as Professor Higgins suddenly turned and hurriedly headed back the direction he came.

"You're welcome!" the workman cried out. But he doubted the old man heard him.

The gray-haired man with the beard to match clearly had his mind somewhere else.

Chapter 26

For in thee, O LORD, do I hope:
thou wilt hear, O Lord my God.
Psalm 38:15

*E*lisabeth sat patiently in the hotel lobby, wondering what had become of the professor when he pushed through the door. He had a huge smile on his face.

She stood so he could see her, and he came her way.

"Sorry, I'm a little late. I took a walk," he explained, trying to catch his breath.

Elisabeth nodded.

"Oh, that's all right. I don't have any plans this evening, just to bed early probably."

The professor noticed a hint of sadness.

He sat then took her hand.

"How are you, Elisabeth? How are you, really?"

"I'm fine. Every day without Andrew has had its challenges. Sometimes, I forget he's gone. It doesn't seem real, like it's just a bad dream where I'll wake up and everything will be just like it was before he died."

The professor wisely let her talk.

"I lie in bed wondering what will become of me, how I will support myself. But then I remember God is with me. So then I do my best to trust Him and take it one day at a time."

The professor nodded.

"I like it here, though. Everyone has been so kind. A small town like Lazy Spring is very welcoming."

But the professor detected a slight pause.

"But it's not what you really want?"

She sighed.

"I'm not sure. I guess I just wonder what it could have been like if Andrew hadn't died and we were on our own land right now, preparing to build. Then I tell myself to not dwell on such things, to just move forward."

"Have you seen Dr. Monroe?"

"Yes, he was kind to check in on me."

"Good, good. I had asked him—"

"I'm going to have a baby," she said abruptly.

The professor stopped midsentence but recovered quickly.

"Such good news, Elisabeth!"

"I just kept wanting to cry, and I have been so sick to my stomach. I just thought it was from losing Andrew. But then it was clear."

"Elisabeth—"

She paused and looked at the professor.

"I'm sorry to interrupt, but I came to tell you that Anna is very ill."

"Oh, Professor!"

"She came down with a fever, and she's with Luke and his family right now. I came to get Dr. Monroe to see if he could be of any help. I could tell Luke was needing not only his medical advice but some emotional support as well."

"I heard Luke left for Finley Valley. I knew that was where you and Anna were headed, so I assumed you'd be riding on the train together."

"Yes, I don't know how I would have handled it alone. Luke jumped right in and took over, and now Anna's resting at his brother's home. Luke's sister-in-law has been a great help to Anna and a comfort to me."

"You must be frightened."

"Yes, I am. But like you, I'm trying to trust God. But it's not always easy."

Elisabeth just nodded and squeezed the old man's hand.

They sat in silence for several minutes. Elisabeth was fighting tears, and the professor was tossing around some ideas that were just forming. The hotel lobby had cleared out, and Elisabeth was getting ready to turn in for the evening.

"I believe I'll head upstairs now, Professor. I'm so sorry about Anna. Will I see you tomorrow?"

"Wait, I have an idea, Elisabeth. Please, sit back down a minute."

He sat on the edge of his chair and explained.

"I want you to go with me."

"With you? Where?" she asked as she sat.

"The train hasn't left the station yet due to needed repairs. Elisabeth, I'm going to be on that train tomorrow heading east, and I want you to go with me."

"But why?"

"I have an idea, but first, I could use your help."

Elisabeth sat there, pondering on his words.

"I don't know, Professor. I have my job here, and I need the income."

"Don't worry about the money. I will talk with the hotel manager and settle everything."

Elisabeth just sat there not knowing what to say.

"God has blessed me, Elisabeth. I can afford to pay for anything you need. You see, I asked God to allow me to use what He has so abundantly given me to help others in need."

A smile graced her face. She was thinking.

"And, Elisabeth, God seems to keep answering that prayer! Will you trust me and go?"

He searched her face and held his breath.

"Well, all right then. I'll go. I really have nothing to lose."

Chapter 27

Trust in him at all times...
pour out your heart before him:
God is a refuge for us.
Psalm 62:8

*A*nna was propped up against an overstuffed feather pillow, trying her best to drink the broth that Melissa was patiently feeding her.

"You can do it, Anna, at least one more spoonful."

Anna closed her eyes and gently shook her head. Her hair was neatly combed and braided off to one side, and she looked fresh and clean in one of Melissa's nightgowns.

Luke popped his head through the doorway.

"How is she?"

"Weak. But her fever is down. I wish she'd try to eat something, though."

"Don't rush it. I gave her some more powder this morning. She's probably just sleepy."

"So why aren't *you* sleeping?"

"Couldn't. I'm too wound up. So I can take over from here, Melissa."

"I just got here! You aren't going to do anybody any good if you don't rest. You don't want to get run down and sick. Then I'd have two of you to care for!"

Luke walked over and took the bowl and spoon from Melissa.

"Melissa, why don't you go check on Brandon and the kids? I can do this."

"You know I can't do that, Luke. I don't want to take a chance if for some reason I'm infected."

Luke walked around the bed and looked down at Anna. She was resting peacefully.

"I guess you're right, Melissa. We're both here for the long haul. And your woman's touch is obvious. She looks so much better."

Melissa reached for Anna's hand. Anna stirred a little.

"What do you know of her?" Melissa asked.

"Well, when we were in Lazy Spring, I was busy with Uncle David treating the ones who were ill. I didn't notice her much. But when things settled down, I got to know some of the passengers a little better."

"Passengers?"

"Oh, I guess I didn't mention that. When the train made an unexpected stop at Lazy Spring, they had a sick passenger, and she needed immediate medical attention. Ended up, she had a grave illness, which unfortunately spread to a few others. The professor was the one who came for Uncle David and myself, seeking medical help. He and Anna were among the passengers."

Anna groaned a bit. Melissa's heart softened toward the pretty blond haired girl who had traveled so far.

Luke continued.

"We housed all the passengers in an old boarding house to keep everyone isolated, like I should have with Anna."

"You didn't know, Luke."

"I didn't know, but I suspected there could be a chance. I guess I just didn't want to consider the possibility. Even the professor questioned the possibility. Anyway, we sadly lost a few, but the majority survived even after being in close quarters on the train."

"That's good."

"Yes, it is. The hardest thing is waiting. None of us would have been surprised if the original woman with the illness had died, but she ended up surviving, and her husband died. But we made the mistake letting him stay with her. We should have separated them. After that, we separated anyone that came down with it."

"She looks like a fighter."

Melissa straightened the collar on Anna's gown.

Luke smiled.

"I'm sure she is. She grew up in a Children's Shelter, remember?"

"Wonder what that was like."

"I don't know, but I have heard stories about some of those places. And I must say, Anna was a great help with the children at the boarding house. She seems older than her age. I guess you have to grow up quickly in a place like that."

"How old *is* she?"

"Fifteen."

"I guessed she was only fifteen or sixteen. She's too young to be sent out on her own, don't you think?"

Luke nodded.

"But she has the professor."

"What do you know about him?"

"Nothing really. I *do* know he was a big help at the boarding house. He had a way of comforting people and quietly taking charge. He's a religious man."

"He seems frail somehow. Do you think he's sick too and just didn't say?"

"I don't think he'd do that. He knows the danger. I just think he's exhausted from the ordeal at Lazy Spring and all the traveling."

"So why is he called 'professor?'"

Luke scratched his head.

"You know, I don't know."

Chapter 28

And the peace of God, which passeth all understanding,
shall keep your hearts and minds through Christ Jesus.
Philippians 4:7

Dr. David Monroe slid from his saddle and lifted his horse's front leg. A stone had wedged into the horse's hoof causing him to limp. It didn't take too much effort to pull it out, but David knew it was sure to have left a bruise.

"Of all things! This isn't the time for this!"

David led his horse under the shelter of a group of trees and built a fire. He would have to sleep there for the night and see how his horse was doing in the morning. He felt he was paying the price for driving his horse too hard on the rocky path.

He settled in under a cloudy sky wondering if Anna was better or was suffering from the illness that had taken the lives in Lazy Spring.

No matter. Luke and Doc Stevens would just have to make the best decisions they could concerning her care. His thoughts were on Melissa as well. Luke never should have gotten her and Brandon involved.

And with that thought, he fell asleep.

The next morning brought rain and lots of it.

David led his horse carefully down a wet, narrow trail while the professor and Elisabeth boarded the eastbound train, heading the opposite direction.

They were all concerned about the same thing—Anna's condition. And none of them knew what was going on.

Rain was also falling heavily in Finley Valley, which woke Melissa from a sound sleep. She dressed and headed downstairs to check on Anna and Luke.

Both were sleeping soundly, so she tiptoed into the kitchen to make a fresh pot of coffee.

She wondered how Brandon and the children were doing. Was she selfish to stay behind? No, she didn't think so. If she was sick, she would want someone to care as much. There were always risks in being a provider. She loved Brandon for standing behind her decision.

She sat at a small table and waited for the coffee to heat. She pulled the curtain away from the window and watched the relentless rain pelt the ground. They needed a good rain.

Just as she was pouring her coffee, a loud knock came at the door. As she approached, she could see the blurry outline of a man.

Thank goodness! she thought. *It must be David!*

But it wasn't David; it was Doc Stevens.

"Doc! Come in out of the rain. I didn't expect to see you back this way so soon."

Doc handed his wet coat to Melissa's outstretched hand.

"I had to come back this way to check on Mrs. Jennings. She's due to have that baby any time. So I thought I'd check in on the girl. How is she doing?"

"I haven't checked on her this morning yet. She and Luke were sleeping so soundly I thought I'd let them sleep. How about a hot cup of coffee?"

"That sounds good. Any food to go with that coffee?"

He gave her a mischievous grin.

"I think we can round up something. Come on in the kitchen."

Doc had just sat down when Luke appeared at the kitchen door. His dark brown hair was a mess.

"Doc, glad you're here."

"Morning, Luke. It's nice to find you and the girl sleeping. That sounds like improvement to me."

"Thank Melissa for any improvement. She has a certain touch I don't seem to have."

"Most women do, Luke."

While the men enjoyed Melissa's scrambled eggs, bread and honey, and fresh milk, she grabbed that opportunity to check on Anna.

Anna's room was dark without the benefit of the sun, so Melissa let her eyes adjust to the darkness before venturing too far. She felt for the chair and sat down.

"Professor, is that you?" Anna asked anxiously.

Melissa felt her way to Anna's bed.

"No, Anna, it's Melissa. The professor isn't here right now."

"May I have a drink of water?"

Anna's voice was weak, but it was good to hear her voice.

"Why, of course, you can, Anna."

Melissa practically ran back toward the kitchen.

"Luke! Doc! Anna is awake asking for water."

"Thank goodness!" Luke exclaimed and headed to Anna's room. Doc was right behind him.

Luke lit the lantern next to her bed just as Melissa came in with the water.

And as Anna turned her face toward them, none of them were prepared for what they saw.

Chapter 29

And it shall come to pass, that whosoever shall
call on the name of the Lord shall be saved.
Acts 2:21

"Are you comfortable, Elisabeth?"

"Yes, very. If only my stomach would settle down."

The professor's face was sympathetic.

"I remember my wife feeling sick just like that with our child. But I also remember it passing after the first two or three months."

"That's good to know. I didn't know you were married, Professor."

"I'm not actually. My wife died a long time ago."

"Oh, I'm sorry."

"Our baby girl died with her. They both died during childbirth."

"Oh, Professor, I'm so sorry."

"Like I said, it was a long time ago. Time has a way of healing the hurt. I'm not saying it doesn't still hurt, but I have healed for the most part."

Elisabeth didn't know what to say, and Professor Higgins sensed that.

"We have had many new medical advances since then, Elisabeth. When it's time for your baby to come, I'm sure you won't have any problems."

"Oh, I wasn't concerned about that. I'm not worried. I have actually seen babies born since I'm the oldest in my family. I just wish Andrew was here."

The professor nodded.

"Andrew didn't even know we were going to have a baby."

"Well, it's nice that you'll have a little one to remember him by, don't you think?"

"Yes, it will be. I'm just a little unsettled thinking of having to go through all this alone. I've considered heading back east, back to family."

"Elisabeth, I have some thoughts about that. Would you allow me to tell you what's on my mind and then I'll leave you with your decisions? Like I said earlier, I am able to help you with your needs. I think you just need some time to prayerfully consider your options. Not rush into anything. You've been through a lot."

"Thank you for the opportunity, Professor. I admit I was feeling anxious. Everything happened so fast. Everything I had hoped and dreamed for has changed. If only I hadn't gotten sick. It was my fault Andrew and the others died. My illness affected so many people."

Elisabeth turned and looked right at the professor.

"I have to live with that for the rest of my life."

"Now wait right there, Elisabeth. None of this was your fault. I had no idea you were carrying that burden."

"It's probably time to move back home and start over. No one there knows any of the details. I would be able to live there knowing no one was judging me."

"Judging you?"

Professor Higgins couldn't continue because Elisabeth suddenly burst into tears. Others around them on the train tried to politely not look their way. He pulled Elisabeth into his arms, and she shook with sobs.

"It's all right, Elisabeth. You cry. You cry all you want."

The professor realized he had never seen Elisabeth cry until then. She most likely hadn't allowed herself to grieve.

It was time for Elisabeth to begin the healing process, and it was time for him to complete his.

The professor held Elisabeth until she fell into a fitful sleep, then he gently moved her to a more comfortable position.

Hopes and dreams do change, he thought. The abrupt changes in his young adult life had made him bitter toward everyone and everything. If he had anything to do with it, he wasn't going to allow Elisabeth to make the same mistakes he had.

He blamed himself for his wife and baby girl's deaths when it happened. He had thought over and over through the years about what he could have done differently to have changed the outcome.

But then everything changed one day when he happened upon a man hurt, lying by the side of the road. He was in bad shape and needed medical attention. The man had been robbed, beaten, and left for dead.

The professor carefully placed the man on his horse's back and walked to the nearest town. He left instructions with the local doctor to care for him and explained he would pay for everything. He left enough money to do just that. He promised to return and settle up any other debts that might occur. And he kept his word.

When the professor returned, he found the man recovering and doing well. The man thanked him and in return offered him a gift that would change the professor's life forever.

In exchange for the professor's kindness, the man told him of a similar story in the Bible where a compassionate passerby helped a stranger who was hurt on the side of the road and did something much like what the professor had done for him.

Professor Higgins listened carefully, and as his heart softened, the stranger explained the love of Jesus Christ and how Jesus came to rescue all of us. We just had to receive that love.

The professor gave his life over to Jesus Christ that day, and nothing had been the same since.

Chapter 30

Let not your heart be troubled:
ye believe in God, believe also in me.
John 14:1

"Luke, I'm going to leave this with you and Melissa. I have too many people that depend on me. I just hope this doesn't get out of hand."

Doc Stevens didn't mince words.

"I won't be back anytime soon."

Luke sighed. He looked over at Melissa as the doctor left the room and the house.

She was holding back from saying anything and chose to not comment.

Just a few moments later, Anna was awake asking questions.

Melissa made the first move.

"Anna, it's Melissa."

Melissa wasn't afraid to sit on the bed next to her.

"We haven't officially met, but I'm Luke's sister-in-law. I'm married to his brother, Brandon."

"Where am I?"

"You're in my home. You needed to rest so you could get well. You are very ill, Anna."

Anna looked over at Luke who was pacing the floor.

"Where's the professor?" she asked. "What's wrong with me?"

Luke stood at the end of her bed, his knuckles white from holding on so tightly.

"He left to go get Dr. Monroe from Lazy Spring," Luke was explaining.

Luke hesitated but he felt Anna had to know.

"I think you might have the same illness Mr. and Mrs. Landry and the others had. You've been very ill, Anna."

Anna's face and arms had random, small and large bright red bumps, but she seemed to be doing better.

"How are you feeling right now?"

"I'm just very tired and very thirsty."

"And your head?"

"My head is fine right now."

"Can you eat something?"

"I think so."

Luke didn't have to ask; Melissa had already headed for the kitchen.

He took Melissa's place on the bed.

"If I'm so sick, doesn't that mean you and Melissa can get it too? And the professor?"

"Well, yes, that's true. But someone has to care for you."

"I feel bad."

Luke was concerned.

"Where do you feel bad?"

"I mean, I feel badly that I'm sick and someone else might get it."

"Don't worry about any of that. I'm sure you didn't plan on getting sick, now did you?"

Luke made a funny face.

Anna smiled a weak smile.

"No, I guess I didn't."

"You seem better. And that's good news."

Anna nodded.

"When will the professor get back?"

"I'm not sure, but he will have to wait for the train to come back this way."

Anna sighed.

"This trip hasn't been anything like I imagined. It's been so good but not so good too."

"That's how life is, Anna. We never know what a day might bring. We seem to be sailing right along doing fine when suddenly something happens to upset the apple cart. We just have to take one day at a time, all of us."

"You sound a lot like the professor."

"I'm assuming that's a good thing?"

Anna was quiet but smiled.

Luke took that as a yes and returned her smile.

"How do you know the professor?"

"I met him on the train. The only seat available when he boarded was next to me, so he had to sit there. But before long, we became good friends."

Luke laughed at her expressions.

"I'm sure he's helped you a lot."

Anna paused, her head beginning to hurt again.

"I was scared at first, but he helped me not be so scared. Then he bought me things I needed. He's coming back, right?"

"Of course, he is. You just have to hurry and get well so when he gets back, he'll see you are as good as new."

Anna's eyelids grew heavy.

"What about that family? Do they know I'm here?"

"Don't go worrying about that right now. They've had to wait this long, I think they can wait a little bit longer."

Melissa brought in a tray of hot food but stopped as soon as she stepped into the room.

"I don't think she's going to be eating that right now," Luke said.

Anna had fallen off to sleep.

"She seems better," Melissa whispered.

"I know. I can't make any sense of this, but sometimes, illness can be a mystery. We're going to have to give this some more time."

Melissa stood there, still holding the tray, looking down at Anna.

"I feel sorry for her."

"I don't," Luke quickly replied.

"You don't?"

"No. She's in a good place. Finley Valley is so mountainous and removed from everything, not many care to live here. And it's for that reason I love this place."

"I've grown to love it too, Luke."

Melissa sat in the chair and began eating what she fixed for Anna.

"I don't think things happen by mistake, Melissa. It's no mistake Anna is here. Whoever she is here to help might really need her. Do you know of anyone here that wouldn't love this girl?"

"Absolutely not! She's so sweet and brave!" Melissa wiped the corner of her mouth. She held back a few tears.

Luke pretended not to notice.

"It's our job to see she recovers," Melissa said. "David should be here soon, so we will see what he says. It would be terrible if anything happened to her."

"If she has the same illness, well, let's just say I watched it spare some lives but take others."

"I'm so thirsty."

Anna moaned a little, but her words were understandable.

She reached out toward Luke, and he grabbed her hand. She hadn't opened her eyes.

"I'll get you some water, Anna. Just relax," he said.

But she held tightly to his hand and wouldn't let go.

"Am I going to die, Dr. Luke?"

Chapter 31

*And God is able to make
all grace abound toward you.
2 Corinthians 9:8*

*D*avid rode into the Finley Valley train station. No one was around.

The rain had stopped, and the sun was peeking from behind some white fluffy clouds. Humidity had set in, and the doctor longed for a good bath. He sat on a bench and plotted his next move. He observed the colorful flowers in the pot next to him as he fought sleep.

Professor Higgins and Elisabeth, on the other hand, sat at a table in the Majesty Hotel in Diamond. The professor ordered a light meal for both of them with hot tea for Elisabeth and hot coffee for himself.

He thought about the last time he ate there with Anna. He and Anna had sipped their hot beverages until they had to board the train that would eventually take them to Finley Valley. It was a great time, he thought. It wasn't until the stop at Lazy Spring that things changed. And they changed dramatically. It had changed everything! The professor thought he'd be used to changes, but they always seemed to take him by surprise.

Elisabeth cleared her throat.

"What are you thinking about, Professor?" she asked. "You seem so far away."

The professor shook his head a bit.

"I was just reminiscing. Anna and I ate here not that long ago."

"Well, see that table over there?" Elisabeth asked, pointing toward a far corner.

The professor nodded.

"Andrew and I sat there. We held hands and talked about all our plans. We were going to build a house and plant the fields together. We agreed to wait at least a year before we started a family."

The professor sipped his coffee and pulled at his white beard that needed a good trim.

"Andrew would be so surprised we have a baby on the way."

"He would be happy."

She nodded.

"He would!"

"Would you like to walk around and stretch your legs before boarding?" he asked.

"That sounds like a wonderful idea!"

They finished their beverages and headed out down the wooden sidewalks toward the shops and establishments.

"Since we have a little time, I have an idea, Elisabeth."

"You are full of ideas, Professor Higgins. What is it this time?"

He laughed out loud then realized he hadn't laughed like that in a very long time.

"I need a bath and a good haircut and trim."

He pulled at his beard.

"How would you like to freshen up as well?"

Elisabeth seemed uneasy with the question.

"I know a woman at the general store who can help us," he went on to explain. "Her name is Mrs. Wilson. What do you say?"

He waited for Elisabeth's reply.

"All right, I think I'd like that very much."

"Good! Then let's go!"

Mrs. Wilson was thrilled to see the professor. She cried a little when she heard about Anna and asked the professor to please send word when he knew of her condition. The kindhearted store owner's wife led Elisabeth upstairs, and they sat on the same sofa where she had held Anna in her arms. It seemed like a long time ago.

"How far along are you?" Mrs. Wilson asked.

Elisabeth gasped.

"I, I didn't realize I showed yet."

"Oh, I could just tell by the way you hold yourself, dear."

"Not far along at all actually. I haven't even thought about when he or she will arrive."

"You know, I have some cloth just sitting around downstairs and a blanket or two I knitted for special occasions. You go on and get in that bathwater, and I'll head down there and rummage around."

Elisabeth couldn't find the right words.

"I don't know how to thank you."

"Oh, don't thank *me*. The professor told me to let you have anything you wanted or needed. I just want to help a little bit too. We will fix you right up!"

Elisabeth couldn't hold the tears.

"I'm overwhelmed. God has been so good to me."

The older woman handed Elisabeth a handkerchief and slipped away.

The professor soon showed up looking all trim and light on his feet.

He found Elisabeth wearing a new pink dress with a white lace collar. Her soft brown hair was pulled up loosely away from her face, and her smile was radiant. Her large brown eyes revealed a bit of a twinkle and her new dress fit her petite frame perfectly. She held several brown packages.

And Mrs. Wilson stood in the distance beaming from ear to ear.

Soon, the professor and Elisabeth slowly walked back to the train, the professor carrying her packages.

"Elisabeth—" The professor stopped right before they reached the steps leading up to the train car.

"What is it? Are you not well?" she asked.

"Oh no, I'm fine. I'm fine."

"Are you sure?"

"Yes, quite sure."

He took a deep breath.

"I'm not getting on the train with you."

She grew nervous and almost fearful.

"What do you mean?"

"There's something I need to do, something I've been putting off."

"I don't understand, Professor. You can't just leave me."

"I know that. I've been thinking since we've been here. I know a family not far down the tracks. I have known them for many years. You can go there and wait for me."

The train whistle blew which made them both jump.

"Professor, I know you think I'm very young."

His look confirmed what she was saying. So Elisabeth stood straight and as tall as her small frame allowed.

"I *am* young. But I'm young and strong. Losing Andrew has given me strength to persevere, and I'm determined not to crumble but to conquer. Being pregnant is not a weakness, Professor Higgins. It just means I have to look out for two now."

The professor pulled at his beard, enjoying what he was witnessing.

"Whether you like it or not, I'm going with you!"

Elisabeth Landry then stepped on the train to retrieve her belongings. She looked back at the professor.

"Well, you coming or not? Or do you expect me to get both *your* things as well as mine?"

The professor raised an eyebrow then followed her aboard. Things were going exactly as he had hoped.

Chapter 32

Cast thy burden upon the LORD,
and he shall sustain thee.
Psalm 55:22

$\mathcal{D}$avid rode up the small mountain and down into Finley Valley. It had been a while since he'd been there. It was a beautiful, peaceful place.

He started to head straight to Brandon and Melissa's house but decided to make a quick stop first since it was on the way.

He rode up in front of a well-kept, established home and tied his horse to a post on the front porch.

Two little boys ran out to greet him.

"Uncle David! Uncle David!" they cried.

Brandon was close behind.

The two men shook hands while the two boys jumped up and down.

"How's Anna?" Brandon asked.

"I actually just got into town, so I haven't seen her yet. I was going to ask you the same thing."

"I promised Melissa I'd stay here. I have no idea what's going on."

"You look worried."

"I am. Does it show that much?"

"Yes, it does."

David put his arm around Brandon's shoulder.

"Your parents at home?"

"Yes, in fact, they're out back with Megan."

"How *is* Megan?"

"Great. She gets around better than we do."

The men and boys walked around the nice home and found Brandon's parents sitting on a porch swing. Parked in front of them was a little girl sitting in a wheelchair.

David was welcomed by everyone.

He waved at his brother and sister-in-law but went straight to Megan.

"I see you're as pretty as the last time I saw you. No wait, I think you're prettier!"

Megan grinned and sat up as straight as she could.

"I'm six now."

She held up six fingers.

"That's right! You had a birthday."

Megan was nodding.

"Yesterday," she announced proudly.

"I seem to have forgotten all about that."

Megan's face fell but then lit up just as quickly.

David had pulled a small package from his shirt pocket.

"Happy Birthday, Megan."

Everyone was watching, including her younger brothers.

"What is it?" one of boys asked.

Megan's youngest brother, Ramon, couldn't stand not knowing.

"It's *her* birthday, pig brain," replied her other brother, Brady. "Wait till she opens it!"

"Now, boys," corrected their grandfather, "none of that."

The boys sat on the back porch steps as they were told then threw each other a look.

Megan tore open the paper.

She gasped.

"It's a 'monica, Daddy!"

"A *har*monica, dear."

"Thank you, Uncle David!"

She didn't wait to try it out, and squeaks and squawks soon filled the air.

"I guess we'll be enjoying that for a very long time, David."

The doctor laughed.

"I'm sure you will think of me often now."

"Yes, yes, we will," Brandon replied, rolling his eyes.

David bent and kissed little Megan on the cheek then walked over and greeted Brandon's parents. Brandon's father was David's brother who was much older.

"You look tired, David," his brother said.

"I am. It's been a long trip, but I can't delay any longer. I need to check on our patient over at Brandon and Melissa's."

They understood, especially Brandon. He was eager to know how Melissa was doing as well as Anna. He hadn't told his parents the severity of the situation because all had agreed to stay quiet until they knew something for sure.

"I have a favor to ask, though," David said.

His brother, Frank, stood from the swing.

"I'd like to leave my horse here. He needs some water and food and a good rub down."

"We'll take care of it. You can take one of the horses in the barn."

"Have you eaten, David?" Brandon's mother asked.

"No, no, sit down. I'm fine. I need to get on over there. Brandon, if you could help me with a horse, I'd appreciate it."

"Sure thing."

"I'll send some food with you," Brandon's mother insisted.

She wheeled Megan into the house while her brothers jumped from their spots after their grandfather gave them the signal.

The men had reached the barn, and Brandon looked back to make sure no one could hear.

"What will you do if the girl has the illness?"

"All I can do is make her as comfortable as possible. Then we'll wait."

"Wait? How long?"

"I can't answer that, Brandon. Every patient is different."

Brandon pushed his fingers through his dark blond hair.

"I'm worried sick, David."

"Worry doesn't help."

Brandon looked annoyed.

"What would *you* do if you were in my shoes?"

"I know I wouldn't just sit around doing nothing."

Brandon took a deep breath.

"And your suggestion?"

"Take the boys out somewhere. Play a game with Megan."

"Megan—she needs her mother."

"Looks like your parents are a big help."

"They are. It's just not easy to pretend the girl has a stomach ache or something. They are going to realize soon there's a reason Melissa is there and not here."

"Help me with a horse, Brandon, and I'll see what I can find out. Let's just pray no one else gets it."

"Pray?"

"Yes, that's what the professor would do. Says it's powerful."

"I sure hope so, for everyone's sake."

Chapter 33

He healeth the broken in heart.
Psalm 147:3

$\mathcal{M}$rs. Wilson stored their things for them.

And what the professor didn't know until that day was Elisabeth was an excellent horsewoman.

"I'm not the only one full of surprises, Mrs. Landry. Who taught you to ride like that!"

Elisabeth released her hair and shook it until it fell past her shoulders. She dismounted and tied her horse to the fence railing.

"Oh, that felt good! My father taught me. He taught all of us to ride. We lived on a ranch."

"Back east? A ranch?"

"It was a horse ranch. It was my father's dream, and over time, he fulfilled that dream."

The professor removed his hat and wiped his brow. He tied his horse as well.

"It's a hot day. Let's sit a minute before we go on."

"How much further?"

"Just over that rise, but I'd like to walk from here. You up to it?"

Elisabeth nodded.

The professor handed her a canteen.

"Maybe I should go alone. Would you mind?"

"No. I can wait right here."

The professor sat quietly.

Elisabeth reached over and squeezed his hand.

"You're doing the right thing, you know."

He sighed. "I sure hope so. It wasn't an easy decision, but I felt it was the right one."

"It's time for closure, a time to release all feelings and, well, leave them here."

He agreed but he didn't move.

"I can go with you if you want."

"Give me a minute to think about it."

The professor was stiff from the ride, but he walked over to a small brook and rinsed his hands. He ran his wet hands over his red face and breathed in the smell of nearby pines.

Memories rushed through him as if he had never left, even though it had been many years.

This was his journey. He never expected to share the journeys of others along the way. His journey had taken a back seat up until now. He thought he would do what he set out to do and go home, just like that. God seemed to have other plans as usual, he thought.

This was harder than he ever expected.

"Professor, are you all right?"

"No, actually, I'm not."

"Is there anything I can do?"

"Well, I dragged you into this by taking you from Lazy Spring. I suppose it was never meant for me to go this alone."

"I believe you're right. I would be the one who could truly understand your grief."

"Yes, you're right. You are the one I needed all along, and God allowed our paths to cross. I could never have brought Anna. She wouldn't be ready for this."

"She may be more ready than you think. She experienced a lot in Lazy Spring. Death in any form isn't easy. It does something to you."

"I wonder how she's doing. I just don't think I could handle losing someone else I have come to love so much. Not knowing is almost too much to bear right now."

Elisabeth had to be the strong one right then. The professor had been the strong presence for so many along his journey.

"I'm going with you, Professor. But first, let's draw strength from the Strength Giver."

They knelt on the ground, and Elisabeth prayed first. Her prayer was simple, and as she prayed, she felt her burden begin to lift. She asked God to help the professor as he faced his own burdens that he had carried many years.

The old man and the young widow cried from way down deep within. They were grieving. They were releasing all worry, fear, bitterness, and sorrow. It hurt but it also felt good.

God was there with them.

The professor stood and helped Elisabeth to her feet.

"I'm ready," he said.

"Me too."

Chapter 34

I will strengthen thee, yea, I will help thee.
Isaiah 41:10

"She doesn't look well at all," Luke said.

Melissa agreed.

"Where in the world is Uncle David!" Luke exclaimed, as he turned toward the bedroom window.

"I'm right here, Luke."

Luke whirled around and saw David standing in the doorway. He was dirty and tired, but he was there. Melissa thought his thick, full beard looked good on him.

"Oh, thank goodness!" Luke exclaimed, as he headed David's way.

The men embraced. David smiled toward Melissa, and she gave a quick wave.

"How's our patient?"

"Earlier, she was doing pretty well, but now she's, well, you can see."

David sat on the edge of Anna's bed and listened to her heart and lungs the best he could.

"She seems to be breathing fine. And she doesn't seem to have any fever."

"I gave her the last of the powder Doc Stevens left."

"Let me see the bottle."

David took a whiff.

"Yes, that's what I thought he'd give. It's been working, right?"

"Yes, but that's the last."

"Don't worry, I have more, so we're in good shape."

David lifted Anna's arm and carefully looked her over.

"This isn't like the rash the others had."

"It's not?" Melissa asked.

"No. This is different."

"So you don't think she has the same illness?" Luke was asking, holding his breath.

"I'm not ruling it out, but I don't think so. But whatever she has is making her very sick, it seems."

Melissa went for some coffee, but David caught her before she went out the door.

"Brandon is worried."

"I know. I just couldn't leave her for some reason. She needed a woman here."

The Lazy Spring doctor nodded.

"I think we should get her outside in the sunshine."

"Now?" Luke asked, surprised.

"Yes, now. I think she needs some fresh air. It's not going to hurt her to get up, Luke."

Luke called Anna's name then gently shook her shoulder.

Anna struggled to wake. The powder had done its job.

"Has she eaten anything?" David asked.

"Very little."

"And to drink?"

"A sip here and there."

"Luke, move over. I'll do this."

Luke hesitated.

"What's wrong?" David asked.

The doctor was beginning to get annoyed.

"I'm not sure I agree she should be forced to do this."

"Luke, man, she has been lying in bed too long. She'll be so weak it will be hard for her to recover. She's not eating or drinking. She needs to move. I know what she needs. You wanted my help."

Luke hesitated again.

"Trust me, Luke. Don't you want to see her well?"

Luke slowly stepped aside.

"Grab her other arm, and we will walk her outside," David instructed.

Anna resisted.

"Anna—"

She finally opened her eyes.

"Good girl. We're taking you outside to get some fresh air and some healthy sunshine."

Anna nodded that she understood, but suddenly, out of nowhere, Luke bent down and swept the fifteen-year-old into his arms.

David stood back, astonished.

"Well, Dr. Monroe," Luke was saying, "what are you waiting for? Lead the way."

David left the room with Luke following close behind. He whispered to Melissa as they passed in the hall, "She's going to be fine. I'd bet my life on it."

Chapter 35

I will lift up mine eyes unto the hills,
from whence cometh my help.
Psalm 121:1

"I've asked around town, and I haven't run into anyone who was expecting a girl from the Children's Shelter in Logan's Gap."

"I wouldn't worry about it," Melissa said. "She can just stay with us."

Luke sat down at the table across from her.

"She can't live here the rest of her life."

"So where do you think she should go? Back to the shelter?"

Luke stood quickly, almost knocking over his chair.

"No! That's no place for her. I don't know. I just don't know."

"Then let her stay here until you *do* know. The professor could take her back with him maybe?"

"What's an old man going to do with a girl like Anna? She needs someone to help her, protect her. She's never been on her own before."

"She's not a child, Luke. Have you noticed that, or have you been too busy to notice?"

Luke's face grew warm.

"Of course, I've noticed."

Melissa sat smiling at her brother-in-law.

"What?"

"Oh, nothing, just observing."

"Now wait a minute, it's not like that. She's young, Melissa. A good ten years younger than me."

Melissa just sipped her coffee, continuing to smile at her red-faced brother-in-law.

"Oh, never mind. You women are always trying to make something out of nothing."

Melissa just raised her eyebrows and leaned back in her chair.

Luke sighed. "I'm going to see what's going on in the other room."

Luke had barely stepped into the hallway when Brandon rushed through the front door and met him head on. The screen door slammed, echoing through the entire house.

"I came as soon as I heard everything was all right. Where's Melissa?"

Luke pointed, rolling his eyes, then headed into Anna's room.

Anna was dressed and sitting in the chair. David was sitting on the edge of the freshly made bed.

The doctor from Lazy Spring was explaining some things to Anna.

"I've seen this condition before, only in children so far and maybe one other near your age. It's not fatal, just annoying. And it can make you very sick, especially when you're run down and not eating properly."

Anna scratched her arm.

David shook his finger at her.

"None of that. Maybe you can get a warm bath later on, it will soothe the itching some. I'll let Melissa know."

"Your red bumps are already fading. They will all go away, but if you keep scratching, they may leave some scars."

Anna nodded.

"And you're too pretty to have that happen."

She blushed and glanced up at Luke.

David followed her look.

"So, Luke, I guess you can go home now. Anna's on the mend, and I hear Brandon's back already. I'm sure your parents will be glad to see you."

"That's why I came in. To say goodbye and to say thanks."

David stood, and the men embraced.

Luke's uncle pushed him away but held tightly to his shoulders.

"You are going to make a good doctor, Luke. You just have to believe in yourself."

"I'm starting to doubt my abilities."

"There you go."

"I'm seriously considering stepping back from doctoring. Maybe I'm forcing something that's not really there. You are so good at it."

"I didn't get good all at once, Luke. You tend to rush things. Just slow down."

"That's exactly what I intend to do."

The men embraced a second time.

"Well, I'm heading out." Luke nodded toward Anna.

"I'm glad to see you doing so well, Anna. You scared us, after Lazy Spring and all."

He shuffled his feet back and forth.

"Well, I need to go. I haven't seen my folks yet, and I know Mother is probably pacing the front window."

"No doubt, Luke. Go get some rest and take some time off."

Luke nodded.

"Will we see you before you head back to Lazy Spring?"

"I'll be around a couple of more days. I promised Megan I'd stop back in."

"Good. She'll love that. I'll see you around then."

With that, Luke left the house, Brandon and Melissa laughed in the kitchen, and the doctor went upstairs to get some needed sleep.

And Anna, she took a walk in the sunshine. The most she had seen of Finley Valley was from her bedroom window. It was time to get acquainted.

Chapter 36

Nevertheless we, according to his promise,
look for new heavens and a new earth,
wherein dwelleth righteousness.
2 Peter 3:13

"I want you to come to Finley Valley with me. I want you to move there."

Elisabeth and the professor walked up the gradual slope toward the top of a grassy hill.

"You certainly don't mind getting to the point, Professor."

"I'm not sure there's a future for you in Lazy Spring."

"But Andrew—"

"I know. It would definitely have to be your choice. I'd never force you into anything, but you need to think of what's best for *you* right now."

Elisabeth was quiet as they climbed.

"Andrew is gone, but he would want the best for you too."

Elisabeth nodded.

"I'll think about it."

They reached the top of the hill, and below them, a short distance away, was a log cabin that was almost completely destroyed from lack of care. It was covered with vines and overgrowth.

The professor drew a deep breath.

"I haven't seen that cabin for more years than I care to admit. Well, Elisabeth, that's what I walked away from."

"Ellen and I worked together to build her. We did it all by ourselves. We were so much in love we didn't notice how much work it was. It really was built with love."

"It's in such a beautiful location, Professor."

"It *is* beautiful. We searched for just the right spot. Our porch faced the rising of the sun each morning. And the view of the mountains could be seen from our large bedroom window. Every detail was planned out. We added the two small bedrooms for the children we hoped to have. And the kitchen! I made the kitchen long and roomy just like she asked. I was going to build a long table, but I never had the chance."

"Be careful going down this way, Elisabeth."

Elisabeth stepped carefully, but she was more concerned for the professor. He was red in the face from the heat, and his breathing was labored.

"We can rest a few minutes if you want," she offered.

"No, since we're here, I'd like to just go on down and look around. And don't give me those looks. I'm just not as young as I used to be."

He was right. He was getting up in years.

The cabin was in such disrepair that to live in it again would be impossible without tearing it down and starting over.

The professor just stood in front of it and stared.

"It's worse than I ever imagined."

"What are you going to do with it?"

"Burn it."

It wasn't the answer Elisabeth expected, but it was something she would probably do as well.

"Now?"

The professor shook his head.

"No, not now."

"Come, I'll show you what I really came here for, and then I'll need a few moments alone."

The professor and Elisabeth walked through tall grass and weeds until they came to an area that had been fenced off. Everything was overgrown, but if you looked carefully, you could see the gravestone.

"I'll let you go on alone, Professor. I'll sit here on this log in the shade."

He looked at her.

"I'll wait. You take all the time you need."

Professor Higgins walked over and began pulling grass and weeds until he could read the full inscription on the grave stone.

Ellen Mae Higgins and daughter.

He had them buried together, the baby in her arms.

He wept. He thought he would have more control, but he didn't. He wept unashamedly.

"I'm sorry Ellen. I'm so sorry. I shouldn't have left the way I did. But I was angry and hurt."

He wiped his face and found some control.

"I was bitter. I was young and reckless, not caring about anyone but myself. You were all I cared about. And to lose our baby girl, it was just too much. I've come to say goodbye the right way and to end this chapter of my life. I have carried so much guilt, but no more."

He stood from his kneeling position.

"Ellen, I found the faith you always prayed I'd accept. I'm free from the burdens I rode away with that day.

"So I'll see you and our baby girl again. Until then, Ellen. Until then."

Chapter 37

Therefore my heart is glad.
Psalm 16:9

"Luke! Oh, Luke!"

Luke's mother turned from clearing the breakfast dishes off the table when she heard his voice.

"Oh, Luke!"

Luke stood with his arms wide open.

"Hello, Mother."

She fell into his arms.

"We have been so worried! How are you?"

"I'm fine, Mother. Just ready to do some relaxing. Where's Father?"

"He's in the barn with Megan."

"How is it going with Megan? I'm sure she keeps you busy."

"That she does. She can't walk, but she runs me around plenty."

"Are you up for it, Mother?"

"Megan? You mean with Megan?"

He nodded as he scooped up the last biscuit from a bowl on the table.

"I admit it's a lot of work sometimes, but Melissa has her hands full. I'm happy to help when I can."

"Well, I can take her and the boys home in a few days. Uncle David says it's best to wait before bringing them over."

"How is the girl?"

"Doing well! She's making a full recovery thanks to Melissa and Uncle David."

"And you too, Luke."

She poured him a glass of milk and pushed the butter closer to him as he sat.

"I lost my head. I missed some of the basic things she needed."

"Like what, dear?"

"I don't know. She just wasn't getting better."

"She just needed rest, Luke. David probably came at just the right time. You and Melissa did your part, and now he's done his. That's teamwork."

"I suppose."

She sat down across from her son.

"What's wrong, son?"

"I don't know, Mother. I thought I knew what I was going to do for the rest of my life. Now I'm not sure."

"And that's all right. Sometimes, life changes our direction. We just have to be willing to let those changes shape us into what we should be."

"I suppose."

She stood and began clearing the rest of the table.

"I'll finish here and you go change out of those clothes. I bet you have other clothes that need washing. Am I right?"

Luke chuckled.

"I'll go fetch them."

"Good. Put them out on the back porch. I'll soak them out there. Then you can go check on Megan and your father out in the barn. Megan will squeal with delight when she sees you."

She gave her son another hug.

"We are so glad you're home, Luke."

He just nodded.

Luke grabbed his bags from Brandon's wagon and brought them to the back porch where his mother was already setting out a couple of metal wash tubs.

"I'll put some water on the stove to heat," Luke said.

"Thank you, son. By the look of these pants, they will need to soak for days!"

"Oh, I was wearing those when we stopped in at Burke Mountain. We covered a lot of ground, including a quick hike up one of the mountain trails."

"That's always a fun stop! Did you stop in Barney's Place for their smoked meat?"

"Sure did. Mother, there's so much to tell since we last talked. You haven't met the professor or Anna."

"Anna? She's the girl who was so sick?"

"Yes. And the professor, he came to Finley Valley with her. I'll go put that water on the stove, and then we can talk after I go out and see what Father and Megan are up to."

"Fair enough. And I'll fry up some chicken for later, your favorite."

"It's a deal."

Luke set the kettles on the stove and stepped back out on the porch.

"Luke—"

"What is it, Mother?"

"Where did you get this? This tag in your pocket from the Logan's Gap Children's Shelter."

Chapter 38

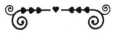

The LORD is great.
Psalm 99:2

$\mathcal{E}$leanor McAfee couldn't sleep. She had received a second telegram explaining how sick Anna was. She was so worried she knew sleep wouldn't come any time soon.

She headed back into her parlor and sat in her green overstuffed chair by the fireplace. She prayed for Anna. She was glad she had reached Finley Valley. Surely, someone there would see she received proper care.

She picked up the folded telegram and looked for the name.

Oh yes, Professor AQ Higgins. He had sent the telegram. She prayed for him too and silently thanked him for thinking of her. She wondered who he was and how he knew Anna. She was thankful because she knew God was certainly looking out for Anna and her needs.

Many miles down the train track from her, the professor and Elisabeth waited in Diamond for the train to return so they could head back to Lazy Spring and then on to Finley Valley.

They heard Mrs. Wilson coming up her back steps.

"Here I am!" she cried. "Hot food from the hotel. I've never been much of a cook, but I can sew a fair bit."

"I enjoy sewing as well," Elisabeth explained.

"And I'm guessing you can cook since you didn't mention cooking?"

"Well, yes, I do enjoy it. I come from a large family with all girls, and we all learned to cook and sew."

"I only had one sister myself. I married very young, and she did most of the cooking."

"How about you, Professor?" Mrs. Wilson asked.

She set the table quickly and proceeded to dish out from tins of steaming hot food.

Both women were looking toward the old man.

"Oh, huh, well, I grew up back east actually."

"I knew it," Mrs. Wilson whispered toward Elisabeth. "Here, sit both of you. Let's eat some of this good food before it cools off. My husband is busy in the store, so he said to eat without him."

"It's so nice of you to let us stay with you, Mrs. Wilson," Elisabeth said.

"Well, there's no sense in paying for a hotel room. And to tell you the truth, I'm hungry for company."

The professor offered to pray so they could get started. He thanked God for the food and His watch care over them. He prayed for Anna's speedy recovery.

"So…Professor, you grew up back east you were saying?" Mrs. Wilson began.

He nodded.

"I did. I was an only child. My mother was never able to have anymore children. My father was a schoolteacher, as was his father before him, and since I was the only child, my mother was able to assist him with his students. They eventually purchased a building, and over time, they established a well-respected school for both men and women. I grew up, well, learning."

"What brought you west?"

"I fell head over heels in love."

Both of the women stopped eating.

Elisabeth wiped her mouth and looked across the table at the professor who seemed a little embarrassed over all the attention.

"You are still full of surprises, Professor Higgins."

Mrs. Wilson was all ears.

"It's true." He shrugged. "A family, who lived not far from here actually, sent their daughter east for education and grooming. The moment she walked into my classroom, I couldn't speak, I couldn't think, she was so beautiful."

The women shared a smile. The food was forgotten for the moment.

"I was lecturing in a small university, and I was right in the middle of a sentence when I lost all thought of what I was saying. She had arrived late for class and two weeks into the school year. It was like she appeared out of nowhere. I was watching her and the whole class turned to see what I was staring at."

The women laughed.

"She had walked into a classroom of all men. The men and women were taught separately in the universities then."

"Every eye was on her. She didn't flinch. She just sat there, tall in her chair with her hands in her lap. I even remember the white dress she was wearing and how her hair was pinned back."

"What did you do?" Mrs. Wilson asked.

"I finally found my voice. The classroom was as silent as a winter's night. All eyes were now on me."

"I walked over and introduced myself and politely explained that she had made a mistake."

"Was she embarrassed?" Mrs. Wilson asked. "Surely, she could see it was all men."

"Embarrassed? No. She proceeded to tell me and the class that she came to learn from Professor Higgins. She had heard so much about him and wanted to know where he was. The class laughed."

"'*I'm* Professor Higgins,' I admitted. 'And this is a class for men only. I can direct you to a women's class.'"

"'You, you are the professor? she stammered. You're younger than I expected.'"

"She looked me up and down."

"'Not all professors are old men with white beards, Miss—'"

"'Fisher—Ellen Fisher, she said.'"

"'Well, Miss Fisher, like I said, I can direct you to a women's class.'"

Mrs. Wilson interrupted.

"Wait right there, Professor! I'll make a pot of tea, and we can sit on the sofa where we can be more comfortable."

"No, no, actually, I've said enough."

The two women tried to speak at once.

"You can't leave us hanging now!" Elisabeth exclaimed.

"No, you can't," Mrs. Wilson was saying. "Did she go to the women's class?"

"Yes, she did, but only after I agreed to teach her privately about some of the fundamentals I was teaching the men. She had a strong will and an even stronger spirit."

"Was she upset she had to leave the class?" Mrs. Wilson asked.

"No. She did exactly what she had set out to accomplish by interrupting that class."

"And what was that?"

Elisabeth asked this question.

"That she wasn't going to let anyone keep her from doing what she had set out to accomplish. Not even a class closed to women. No eastern culture was going to define who she was. She was a determined young woman. She may have been in the east, but she was west through and through. And she wanted everyone to know that."

"Were you upset?" It was Mrs. Wilson asking again.

"Upset? No, I fell in love with her right then and there. I asked her to marry me three months later, and when the semester was over, I found myself following her out here."

"Any regrets?" Elisabeth asked, her mouth wide open.

The professor, who had become that "old man with the white beard," took a deep breath and sighed.

"No regrets. She was the best thing that ever happened to me. She made me the man I am today. Beneath that tough exterior, she was soft. She was kind and caring and treated me like a king. She was everything for which I had ever dreamed. She never gave up on me. Never."

He slowly stood to his full height and smoothed his pants and brushed his fingers through his white beard.

"Professor—"

Elisabeth was getting ready to speak.

He held up a hand.

"I'm fine, Elisabeth. I'm better than I have been in many long years."

Mrs. Wilson sat quietly, first looking at Elisabeth and then up at the professor.

"And now, Mrs. Wilson, how about that cup of tea?"

Chapter 39

Bless the LORD, O my soul:
and all that is within me,
bless his holy name.
Psalm 103:1

*M*elissa was picking wildflowers on the side of the hill behind their home when Anna walked up to greet her.

"Anna, you're looking well."

"I feel much better. May I help?"

"Sure. I love wildflowers. I wanted to pick a large bouquet for the supper table. We're having a special supper tonight."

"I can help. I'm feeling somewhat useless."

"You've been sick, Anna. No one has expected you to do anything but get well."

"I used to live at a Children's Shelter, and we were busy all the time, even when we didn't feel well sometimes. But we weren't allowed to help with the food. We had a cook, and she had helpers." She thought back to Mrs. McAfee but was trying very hard to pay close attention to what Melissa was saying.

"Well, you're here now, and while you're here, I'd love a couple of extra hands, including some help with the cooking. My children arrive home tonight. Maybe you could help with them."

Anna's eyes lit up.

"I would love to. At the shelter, I helped with lots of children! All the older girls did. I never minded it like some of the others."

Melissa's basket was full, and she laughed out loud as she led the way to the house.

"Well, I have two little boys that don't know the meaning of 'slow down' and a feisty, little girl who can hold her own! Still ready for the challenge?"

"Of course! I hate plain and ordinary. They sound like neither."

"Then you should get along with them just fine. Come on, you can help me with supper. The whole family is coming over tonight."

"The whole family?"

"Yes, and they like to eat!"

Anna practically ran to keep up with Melissa's long strides. She liked it there.

Melissa found a large vase, and she let Anna arrange the flowers any way she liked. Together, they laid the lace tablecloths on the long tables out on the sunporch.

"This room is nice. I didn't realize it was here."

"Brandon built this right after our daughter was born."

"What's your daughter's name?"

"Megan. She was born weak. She never could hold her head up well. Doc Stevens said she needed lots of care and sunshine. So Brandon, being the type of father he is, built this."

Melissa straightened one of the tablecloths.

"You'll meet her tonight. In fact, she just had a birthday. She's six now, which is hard to believe."

"I'd like that. We need another girl around here."

"Indeed, we do! Come on, I can show you how to peel potatoes."

Not too far down the road, Luke and his mother were still on the back porch as she prepared to soak some of Luke's clothes.

She held Anna's tag.

"I forgot all about that," Luke said. "I meant to return it."

"Where did you get it?"

"It's Anna's. I took it from her hand when she fainted. It's supposed to identify her. She's here to help a family in the community, and she was supposed to pin this to her dress. But I haven't been able to find—"

"Anna—Annaleigh."

"What is it, Mother?"

"How silly of me."

"Mother?"

"I never saw the connection."

"What connection? You aren't making sense."

She turned and ran toward the barn.

"Frank! Frank!"

Her husband came running toward her.

"What is it, Martha? What's wrong?"

"Nothing is wrong. Oh, Frank."

She hugged him and then looked toward Megan who was trying to push her wheelchair toward them.

"She's here, Frank! She's been here all along."

"Who? What?"

"The girl we sent for from Logan's Gap. She's the sick girl over at Brandon and Melissa's!"

"Annaleigh is here."

Chapter 40

*Giving thanks always for all things
unto God and the Father in the name
of our Lord Jesus Christ.
Ephesians 5:20*

*E*lisabeth had made her decision. She would go to Finley Valley with the professor and try it for a month, maybe two if all went well. Then she would make her final decisions.

"Sounds fair," the professor said.

Quick arrangements had been made at Lazy Spring, and the train was just about ready to pull into Burke Mountain Station.

"You're worried, aren't you?" Elisabeth asked.

Elisabeth caught the professor's attention.

"Some, well, yes, quite a bit. I never heard from the doctor. I checked the telegraph office at Lazy Spring. I'm sure he said he'd let me know something."

"He's probably just busy. You know how doctors are. I'm sure she's fine."

She patted his knee.

"That's been my prayer. I'm not sure what I'd do if she didn't recover."

"You'll see her soon, only a few more hours."

"Yes, finally."

The train came to a stop, and the two waited until the train car emptied. Elisabeth was the first to stand.

"I can go get us something to eat and bring it back here if you prefer. You look tired."

The professor stood.

"Maybe a bit tired, but not too tired to take you to the finest eating establishment at Burke Mountain! It's called Barney's Place."

Elisabeth raised her eyebrows.

"Well, lead the way then Professor."

They walked the streets along with the other passengers, some of them setting up tables to sell their wares. Elisabeth had never seen any place like it. The outdoor shops and all the trading back and forth—this place was full of life and excitement!

"So what do you think, Elisabeth?"

"I love it, but I don't think I could live here. I like things a little calmer than this."

"Me too. Let's walk, I'll show you around."

Both the professor and Elisabeth were able to set aside all their yesterdays and focus on the moment. They were just about ready to turn around and head back the way they came when they passed a man sketching portraits.

"Let's stop and get our portraits done, Professor!"

The professor was shaking his head.

"No, you go ahead. I'll watch."

"Oh no, you don't. We're both doing this. It will be something we can look back on and remember about this time in our lives!"

The professor watched as the man sketched a mother and daughter. He pushed away his thoughts before they had a chance to form.

"What do you say? Please...Professor?"

"Well, all right. But only because I can't say no to a woman's pleas."

Elisabeth laughed. She was so pleased the professor had come into her life at this time. He had become a rock when she needed one so badly. She knew Anna felt the same way, even though she probably didn't realize it yet. She knew one day Anna would see it and be forever grateful.

Elisabeth sat down in front of the artist first.

The man tilted her head up a little and asked her to push her hair away from her face.

"We want to capture your full beauty," the man explained.

Elisabeth turned a shade of pink.

"Fine, fine. Exactly what I wanted! So beautiful!"

The professor watched as the man first traced her face and shoulders then started filling it in with thicker strokes. He was capturing the young woman's spirit whether he realized it or not.

Elisabeth glanced up at the professor, and her eyes sparkled as she tried to sit very still.

He smiled his approval with a nod and a wink.

Elisabeth was beautiful with a whole lot of spunk. His Ellen was like her. He prayed right then that God would bring the right man into her life at just the right time, someone who would appreciate her for who she was and who would love her baby without restricting her from clinging to a piece of Andrew through that child.

Elisabeth noticed the look on the professor's face. She gave him a questioning look.

He just nodded again, ignoring her silent plea to know what was on his mind.

"You're doing great!" he called out.

The artist turned toward the professor and agreed with a hearty nodding of his head.

"Excellent!" the man exclaimed.

Elisabeth will do well in Finley Valley, the professor thought. What little time he was around Luke's family, he knew she would be in good hands.

Finley Valley—it had turned out to be vastly different from what he had ever imagined. It was a place where someone could live peaceably without the noise and bustle of a place like Burke Mountain. It was remote and untamed in a way, right on the edge of nowhere. It was a place where he could comfortably leave Anna and Elisabeth and not worry.

Professor Applebee Q. Higgins III's job was coming to an end. Now he just needed to decide the best plan for himself.

Chapter 41

Give thanks unto the LORD,
call upon his name.
1 Chronicles 16:8

Anna sat with her journal in her lap. She hadn't written in it for a long time. She traced her finger over the picture of the mountains she had drawn after they left Burke Mountain. She loved that place and hoped to go again soon. She thought back on the fun she had with Luke and the professor. It wasn't that long ago, she thought. It just seemed that way.

She wondered where the professor was. Luke said he would be back soon.

Melissa called for her.

"There you are. Would you like to help me snap some beans?"

"I've never done that before. You'll have to show me."

"Of course, I will! Come on, we'll sit out on the back porch. There's a nice breeze right now. It's cooling down some."

Melissa couldn't help but think about how her daughter, Megan, would never be able to walk and run like other children. Her arms weren't strong, and she tired easily in her chair. She often needed someone to help her by lifting her from her chair and letting her lay down for periods of time.

She would never be like Anna.

Melissa watched Anna snap the beans just as she showed her. She was pretty with her long, flowing blond hair. Her eyes were so blue. For a girl to have grown up in a Children's Shelter, Melissa thought she was capable and motivated. She wondered about the details of her life and decided to just ask.

"Anna?"

"Yes, Melissa?"

"Do you mind my asking about your life at the Children's Shelter?"

"No, but there's not much to tell really."

"So how old were you when you came there?"

"I was just a baby. The cook found me lying on the back porch one cold morning."

Anna thought about the story Mrs. McAfee would tell her so often.

"'You was an angel,' she'd say. Her name was Mrs. McAfee. She was sort of like a…mother."

Melissa recognized the name. It was the name Anna called out when she was so sick.

"So you lived there all your life then?"

Anna nodded. "Someone left me there, and there was even a note."

"So do you know your parents' names or at least something about your past? Anything?"

"All I know is what Mrs. McAfee told me. I don't think the shelter would have been happy to know she told me so much, but she did. I spent as much time with her as I could. I would sneak into the kitchen and watch her cook. She loved to sing and tell stories."

She and Melissa laughed as they rocked in the chairs on the porch. Both of them had a bowl on their lap.

"Do you like to sing, Anna?"

"I do. It comforts me and helps me forget about things if I'm worried."

"It comforts me too, Anna. I like to sing, and I sing with Megan all the time. She loves music."

"I'm sure we'll get along just fine then," Anna said. "I can't wait to meet her."

Anna was snapping and rocking away.

Where did this precious girl come from? thought Melissa. *I'm getting so attached to her already. But I can't, she will go live with someone else.* She wondered about this girl's future.

"Do you know what the note said, Anna?"

"Yes. It asked them to take care of me until someone came back for me. But they didn't. No one ever came back."

Anna slowed her rocking and became quiet.

"I'm so sorry, Anna. Is that all it said?"

"Uh, there was a name on the bottom. Thompson. No other name. The note said my name was Annaleigh."

"Annaleigh? I like that."

"They gave me the last name of Thompson since it was on the note."

"Do you have that note with you? Did you get to have it since they sent you away?"

"Mrs. McAfee saved it for me along with the little dress she found me in. It was white with little blue flowers. Oh, and the blanket she found me wrapped in the day she found me. I have that too."

"Mrs. McAfee sounds very special."

"She is. She was."

"Maybe you'll see her again one day," Melissa encouraged.

"I hope so. I miss her so much."

Chapter 42

*By him therefore let us offer the sacrifice
of praise to God continually, that is, the
fruit of our lips giving thanks to his name.*
Hebrews 13:15

*S*upper was on the table. Melissa and Anna stood back and admired
the spread of food.

"I couldn't have done it without you, Anna. Thank you."

"It was fun. I didn't realize how much fun cooking could be."

Melissa gave her a side hug.

"The flowers add just the right touch. You did a great job,
Anna."

Anna beamed. While they straightened the plates and cups just
right, they heard horses approaching.

"They're here!" Melissa exclaimed.

She ran past Anna. Anna just stayed back, not feeling comfortable enough to go meet them.

The boys were on the porch before Melissa reached the door.
As she opened the door, two-year-old Ramon ran and grabbed her
around one leg. Brady, being the older at four years old, just stood by
with a smile on his face. But Melissa pulled him close to her side as
she smothered both boys with kisses.

"I believe you have grown since I last saw you!"

She playfully messed their perfectly combed hair.

"You boys run on and wash those hands. Supper is waiting and
on the table!"

They took off down the hall and into the kitchen, playfully fighting all the way.

Brandon carried Megan up the porch steps and into Melissa's arms. The six-year-old's weight didn't quite match up to most six-year-olds.

"My big girl, you look so pretty in that dress. Grandma make that for you?"

Megan nodded and then snuggled against her mother.

"I missed you, Mommy."

Brandon reached for Megan, but Melissa shook her head.

"I'll take her. I have someone I want her to meet."

Luke helped his parents from the wagon, and David led his horse and the team from the wagon to the barn.

Brandon brought Megan's wheelchair to the sunporch. He watched as Melissa introduced Megan to Anna. Anna was shaking Megan's hand when he sat the wheelchair beside them.

"Can I sit next to Anna, Mommy?"

"Why don't you ask her?"

"May I please sit next to you, Anna?"

Megan was all politeness.

Brandon raised his eyebrows toward his wife and whispered, "I think she's found a friend."

He took Megan from Melissa then carefully sat her in her chair, straightening her dress around her legs.

"I can roll her to the end of the table if you like," Anna suggested. "There's a perfect spot for both of us right on the end."

"That would be nice, Anna. Thank you," Melissa said.

Frank and Martha Monroe walked up next to Brandon and Melissa. The four of them watched as Anna wheeled Megan toward the end of the long table.

"So that's Anna."

Melissa nodded. "Yes, that's Anna."

"And I'm Luke," Luke teased, as he came up behind them. "Let's get this supper started."

Everyone was grabbing a chair as David came through the door. He chose the seat on the other side of Megan.

The family was finally together again.

Anna scanned the faces of the Monroe family as they laughed and joked with each other while pushing their napkins into their laps. The boys chose to sit on either side of their grandfather.

Martha sat just down from them next to Melissa. Anna could tell the two women got along well. Brandon sat next to Melissa quietly holding her hand as he listened. Luke sat down across from his Uncle David and next to Anna.

As Frank stood to his feet, everyone quieted and gave him their full attention.

"We want to welcome Anna to our table tonight."

Everyone looked her way and smiled or nodded, even the two small boys. Megan squeezed Anna's hand and grinned from ear to ear.

Frank continued, "We are thankful we can all be together tonight and, most of all, for Anna's full recovery. We have much to be thankful for this evening. Let's bow our heads and give thanks."

The sunporch was quiet as Frank said a quick prayer.

Brandon had just passed the potatoes when they heard a horse coming into the yard.

"Who in the world?" Martha asked. "And right at suppertime."

Brandon went to see.

Chapter 43

I will sing unto the LORD as long as I live.
Psalm 104:33a

"It's Dan."

Brandon and Luke had quickly slipped away from the supper table to see who had arrived.

"Hello, Brandon, Luke."

"What's up, Dan?" asked Brandon.

Brandon held to the horse's bridle and stroked the horse's damp neck.

The man didn't bother to dismount.

"I just came from the train station and ran across that old gentleman who was with Luke and the girl that got sick a few weeks back."

"The professor?"

"Don't recall his name, but he's white headed with a white beard."

"That's the professor. We've been expecting his return."

"He has a woman with him, and he said he needed a ride here. I only have my horse, so I couldn't help them out. Told him I'd ride here and let you know."

"Thanks, Dan. We'll head out and pick them up. We just sat down for supper, care to join us?"

"No, I'm needed home. It's tempting, though, maybe next time."

Dan then nodded and took off down the dirt road at full gallop.

"I guess supper will have to wait," Luke said. "I'll hitch up the wagon and go."

"I'll help you hitch up the wagon, but I promised Melissa I'd help tonight. Otherwise, I'd go with you."

"I don't mind going. You're the host tonight, so go do some hosting."

"I can still help you."

The brothers walked toward the barn. Luke was tall and lanky like his father and David, but Brandon favored his mother. He was shorter than Luke and carried his weight differently.

Brandon always had to push himself to keep up with Luke's long strides, and this night was no different.

"Who do you think the woman is?" Brandon asked.

"I don't know, but I guess we'll find out soon."

Melissa showed up at the barn at that moment.

"What's going on? Anything wrong?"

"No, Dan Worley stopped in to let us know the professor is here at the train station. Luke's going to go pick him up."

"Can't you eat first, Luke?"

"I can wait. They're probably tired and hungry, and it will be dark soon. I can eat with them when I get back."

"I'll set another place. We have plenty."

"Set two places. Dan said the professor has a woman with him."

"Oh, I'll set two then."

She looked at Brandon. He shrugged.

"I better get going," Luke said. "Brandon, give me a hand real quick, and I'll be on my way."

Brandon and Luke hitched up the horses to the wagon, and Luke headed out.

Melissa didn't have a chance to head back to the house because Brandon reached out and pulled her toward him.

He searched her eyes.

"I love you, Melissa."

She allowed herself to be pulled into his arms.

Brandon held her tightly.

"I was so worried about you."

Melissa pulled away just far enough to look into Brandon's eyes. "I was fine."

"Maybe, but I wasn't."

Brandon held Melissa's face, then he tenderly kissed her.

"Don't ever do that to me again, Mrs. Monroe."

Melissa let her husband kiss her again, this time slowly and sweetly.

"Mommy—"

Melissa and Brandon suddenly pulled apart at the sound of Brady's voice.

Brady just stood there staring.

Melissa pushed her hair behind her ears as she smiled a crooked smile. Brandon slipped his hand into hers.

"What are you doing?" the little boy asked.

"Well, we were helping Uncle Luke with the horses."

Melissa released her husband's hand.

"I'll head back to the house," she said. "Everyone will be finishing up."

As Melissa gave a backward glance, Brandon kneeled before his four-year-old son.

"We were wondering where you were, Daddy."

"I'm right here, son. What do you say we head back with Mommy and finish our supper?"

Brady jumped up and grabbed his father by his neck and hung on tightly.

"I love you, Daddy."

"I love you too, Brady."

Brandon then picked up his son and gave him a piggyback ride back to the house where everyone was enjoying their time together.

Chapter 44

I will sing praise to my God while I have my being.
Psalm 104:33b

*D*avid was helping Megan with her last bite of potatoes.

"Did you leave room for dessert, Megan?" he asked.

She nodded her head the best she could.

"Do you like dessert, Anna?" the little girl asked.

"I love dessert. I helped your mommy make a cake," Anna whispered.

Megan's eyes lit up.

Anna held her finger to her lips. Megan did the same.

David winked at Megan then turned his attention toward Anna.

"So, what are your plans now?"

"I'm not sure. I guess we will have to find the family who sent for me."

Anna sat quietly, her demeanor obviously changed.

"That saddens you?"

"It does. I really like it here at Melissa and Brandon's."

"I know most of the families in Finley Valley. I can't think of anyone who wouldn't be nice to live with or who wouldn't be thrilled to have you."

Anna just smiled a gentle smile and shrugged a bit.

David looked across the room and watched Melissa and Brandon heading back in with Brady.

"Melissa will miss you. I heard her say so."

"You are really lucky to be part of this family, Dr. Monroe. I've never had a real family."

The doctor wasn't sure what to say. He paused a moment.

Anna flipped her long hair across her shoulders and pushed around the food on her plate.

David observed how much Anna had matured since the incident at Lazy Spring.

He wasn't afraid to speak up.

"You're growing up, Anna. Wherever you go, they will love you. I have no doubts."

"I sure hope so. At least I hope I can come back here to visit."

"I'm sure they hope so too. I don't know why you couldn't."

Megan's head was bobbing as she struggled to stay awake.

Anna gently laid Megan's head to one side, and the little girl quickly lost the battle and fell asleep. Anna then placed Megan's hands in a comfortable position. She held on to one of her hands while she continued talking with the doctor.

Melissa sat down next to her mother-in-law.

"Anna sure is gentle with Megan," Martha pointed out. "Did you see that?"

Melissa nodded.

"Anna's been good company and a big help. Megan took right to her."

Martha studied Melissa's face.

"What is it? Clearly, something is bothering you."

Melissa looked to make sure Brandon couldn't hear.

"You're going to think I'm terrible."

"No, I'm sure I won't."

"Having Anna here makes me realize that Megan will never help me with supper or walk up the back hill to help me pick wildflowers or run and play with her brothers."

Martha wisely chose her words.

"Megan isn't Anna, Melissa. They are different girls with different futures."

"I know, it's not fair to compare. I was just being honest with my feelings. I would never be able to tell Brandon what I was thinking. I'm glad I can be open with you."

Martha hugged Melissa warmly.

"You know, Megan has so much to offer. Even though she's in a wheelchair, she is bright and intelligent. She is almost always happy. And she can talk your leg off! She can sing too!"

Melissa laughed. "I know, she is a joy. She has far surpassed Doc Stevens' expectations and ours."

"That's because she has an amazing mother who has worked with her and has given her love and undivided attention. I know it's hard work, Melissa. We all know that, and we are very proud of you and Brandon."

Melissa looked over at her sleeping little girl and held back a tear. She turned her head when she heard Brandon's voice.

"Everything all right here?" he asked.

He placed his hands on Melissa's shoulders.

"Yes, everything is fine."

Melissa squeezed Martha's hand.

"I can help you with that dessert now," he said.

"Thanks, sweetheart. I'd like that."

Brandon and Melissa headed for the kitchen.

Martha sighed. She decided to keep her plans for Anna a secret a little longer. She would know the right time to bring it up and now wasn't that time.

Chapter 45

My tongue shall sing aloud of thy righteousness.
Psalm 51:14

𝒫rofessor Higgins told Elisabeth story after story until she couldn't laugh anymore.

"Stop, Professor! I can't take anymore. My baby will get sick from my body shaking with laughter! You will never convince me all your stories are true."

"So you doubt my integrity?"

"Yes, I do!"

They both had a good laugh.

"I thought someone would be here by now. It's going to be dark soon."

"This isn't a very big place, is it?" Elisabeth asked, as she looked around the Finley Valley train station, which was nothing more than a bench on a small platform with a ticket booth that looked no bigger than a large crate standing on end with a hole cut out.

"I think you'll like what you see beyond here, Elisabeth. You won't be able to see much in the dark, though."

The professor sighed.

"If I don't hear something about Anna soon, I'm going to go out of my mind."

About that time, they heard a wagon coming down the hill.

It was Luke. He pulled the horses to a stop right next to the platform.

"Professor, good to see you," he said, as he jumped from the wagon.

They shook hands.

"Please, Luke, how is Anna? I haven't heard a thing since I left here!"

"She's well, Professor. She gave us a scare, but she's well."

"Oh, thank goodness!"

The professor moved toward Elisabeth with great relief on his face. "She's well. Isn't that wonderful news?" The professor barely held his composure.

"It's great news, Professor," Elisabeth said.

That's when Luke noticed who Elisabeth was. He had never seen her with her hair down. She looked happier, healthier.

"Mrs. Landry?"

She nodded.

"You can call me Elisabeth, Luke."

"I heard the professor had a woman with him, but I never expected to see you again so soon."

He shook her hand as well.

"It's sort of a long story," she said.

She glanced over at the professor.

"Well, let me help you into the wagon, and you can share your story later if you want."

"My sister-in-law fixed a really nice supper tonight for the whole family, and you've been invited. Sort of a celebration. Now we have even more to celebrate with you two here."

They piled into the wagon, the professor up front with Luke and Elisabeth sitting in the back with all the blankets.

"Hold on, Elisabeth," the professor warned. "It's quite a climb up this mountain." He could hardly contain his joy and relief over the news about Anna.

The sun was setting as they made the journey to Brandon's, and Elisabeth witnessed the beauty of Finley Valley as they crested the small mountain. The sunset's rich orange and yellows mixed with a shade of purple made it even more spectacular.

Professor Higgins looked back toward her.

"So what do you think of Finley Valley now, Elisabeth?"

"It's beautiful. I thought it would be a dusty, run-down old town no one cared to come to. Didn't you say yourself that it was called the edge of nowhere?"

Luke explained, "Finley Valley is sandwiched between two very rugged mountain ranges. There are no more towns beyond here where the train could reach even if it wanted to. And because of the mountains and small valley, there just isn't much room for expansion. What you see is all of Finley Valley.

"Most people reach Burke Mountain with all it has to offer, and there's no interest in a small community like ours. No one bothers to come up the mountain to see what's here, which suits me just fine."

"Well, they are missing out is all I can say," Elisabeth said.

They rumbled down the mountain and turned left toward Brandon and Melissa's.

"It's not much further," Luke explained.

Brandon and Melissa's boys heard the wagon coming into the yard and stopped chasing each other just long enough to see who it was.

Most everyone else was on the porch waiting. David and Anna had stayed on the sunporch with Megan.

"Professor! Good to see you. Glad you made it finally. You look well," they were saying.

Melissa was trying to get a good look at Elisabeth. Their eyes met as the wagon came to a stop.

Melissa nodded with a smile, and Elisabeth returned that smile.

Luke's parents stood on the porch, and Brandon held on to the horses so he could get them to the barn before it got too late.

"Come inside! We have food waiting for you!" Melissa cried.

"We had a large meal at Burke Mountain," the professor confessed. "I think I speak for both of us when I say we aren't that hungry."

The professor glanced toward Elisabeth, and she was confirming what he said with a firm nod.

"Well then, come join us for cake. We have several things to celebrate, including a birthday my daughter had recently."

Luke helped Elisabeth from the wagon, and Brandon and the boys headed to the barn to put the horses to bed.

There were greetings all around, but the professor was distracted.

"Where's Anna?" he asked anxiously.

"She's inside. We didn't tell her you were coming. We wanted it to be a surprise."

Brandon and the boys returned, and everyone headed to the sunporch. They stepped back so the professor could go in first.

Anna was playing with Megan when she stopped and followed David's gaze.

There was the professor standing just inside the doorway.

No one said a word. They slowly filed in behind the professor as he walked slowly toward Anna.

She just sat there. She couldn't believe her eyes. Then she burst into tears of joy. Megan became frightened and reached for David. He picked her up out of her chair and placed her in his lap as he held her tightly.

"It's all right, Megan," he said. "Anna's just very happy right now."

The professor walked to the end of the table, squeezing the doctor's shoulder as he walked behind him. His eyes never left Anna's.

He knelt beside her.

"How's my girl?"

She looked at him with her brilliant blue eyes, which were flooded with tears. She fell against him.

"There, there, child. Everything is all right now."

"I thought I'd never see you again, Professor. I was afraid you weren't coming back."

"I told you I'd be here to get you settled. Well, here I am."

Anna hugged the man with the white hair and white beard.

"Wipe your tears, Anna," he told her. "I brought you a surprise."

Chapter 46

His greatness is unsearchable.
Psalm 145:3

*E*leanor McAfee sang at the top of her lungs. She didn't care who heard her or how early in the morning it was. She was happy!

"Anna is well," the professor had written in the telegram.

"Praise the Lord," she sang. "My God is gracious and good. His love is everlasting."

She maneuvered the uneven stone steps that led up to the kitchen's back porch. As she reached the top, she stood by the back door catching her breath before she entered. She looked down at the exact spot where she found Anna, in that box, just lying there with no more than a blanket on a very cold morning. It didn't really seem that long ago.

Since Anna was so warm when she unwrapped her, she couldn't have been there very long, she thought. She had never really thought about that before. As she lingered at the back door with the keys in her hand ready to unlock the door, she had another thought.

Suppose someone was watching to make sure Anna was taken safely inside? She had the same routine every morning. Anyone would know that if they had been watching her.

She shivered despite the warm morning. She looked all around her. The tall, overgrown bushes right there. Would they have been large enough to offer a place to hide that many years ago? Possibly.

She hurried into the kitchen and locked the door behind her.

It was so many years ago, why did it matter now? Why had it come to mind? Anna had moved on, and it sounded like she was in good hands with this professor. Her life was on a different course, and there was nothing left but to grow up and start real life. It was best she forget her past and just move forward, she thought.

Instead of starting a fire in the cookstove, she sat at the kitchen table instead. She fixed herself a nice cup of hot tea before starting breakfast, which she had never done in all her years working at the shelter. She needed to think.

Anna, on the other hand, was beginning to stir despite the early morning hour. The sun wasn't quite ready to peek over the horizon yet. She doubted anyone else was awake after a long evening at Melissa and Brandon's. She cradled her head in her clasped hands and stared up at the ceiling. The softness of her gown reminded her that she had moved far beyond living at the shelter. She sighed with contentment.

She had accepted Martha and Frank's invitation to stay with them for a few days. After all, she didn't have a real place to stay yet anyway. And she wasn't in any hurry to leave the Monroe family. But she knew it was only a matter of time.

Melissa and Brandon needed their home and routine back after all the events of the past weeks. Even she was wise enough to pick up on that. And certainly, Martha Monroe did too as she went around arranging places for everyone to stay soon after the cake was served, and they had sung happy birthday, though belated, to Megan.

Megan was there as well after begging and begging her parents to go to Grandma's where Anna was going to be. It was too late in the evening to argue with a determined six-year-old. She was sleeping in her grandparents' room, despite wanting to sleep with Anna. Grandma put her foot down on that subject, and even Megan knew arguing with Martha Monroe was to no avail, and it wasn't worth the time to try to change her mind.

The professor was there too, as well as Luke, along with David who announced he could only stay a couple of more days. They were bunking together in the small house near the barn. It was the original house Frank built before he and Martha married. It was still furnished and offered a place to stay when anyone needed it. And they certainly needed it now.

They had a full house indeed. And Martha was full of joy because of it, even though she tossed much of the night thinking of what she would fix for breakfast that would satisfy so many hungry men. Frank slept soundly and barely moved a muscle all night. Megan too slept soundly after such a tiring evening.

Anna was in the largest bedroom on the second floor, which had a private balcony. It was the nicest guest room in the house, and Anna felt like a princess lying in the soft bed that set high above the floor.

She rolled on her side and watched Elisabeth sleeping peacefully on a sofa that sat against a long wall. She too had been persuaded by Martha to stay with them. The young widow's brown hair spread across the pillow evenly as if someone had just combed it that way.

Anna couldn't wait for her to wake up so they could talk. The evening before was busy, and by the time they were settled for the night, neither of them wanted to do anything but sleep. In her hurried excitement, she had forgotten to thank the professor for bringing her. The professor couldn't have given her a better gift—someone closer to her age, like a sister, like, well, family! Anna sighed again. She felt safe. She felt like she had never felt before. There was nothing plain or ordinary about this life. She sighed one more time and bit her lip in thought.

Anna was sure she overheard Elisabeth telling David that she was probably staying a couple of months. She just wanted to hear it for herself. She prayed it was true.

The distinct aroma of strong coffee floated upstairs from the kitchen. Someone else was up after all. The sun was just beginning to pierce the darkness and show itself through one of the large windows in the room. Elisabeth was still sleeping soundly.

Anna hurriedly dressed and tiptoed from the room. She could hear voices when she reached the top of the stairs. She recognized Frank and Martha's voices and carefully began the descent down the stairs through the darkness.

Anna was just about to step on the bottom stair step when she heard her name. She pulled back and listened. They were talking about *her*.

Chapter 47

The LORD is nigh unto all them that call upon him, to all that call upon him in truth.
Psalm 145:18

"I'm just not sure we've done the right thing. This isn't the way I imagined it would be."

Martha Monroe's salt and pepper hair was neatly arranged in a loose, fashionable bun near the nape of her neck. If her hair had been allowed to hang free, it would have nearly reached her full-figured waist. She wasn't tall, but she wasn't short either. She paced the kitchen floor, opening one cabinet door after another.

Frank, whose tall, lanky frame mirrored David and Luke's, sat calmly at their kitchen table. Several gray hairs graced his dark brown hair here and there. He finally convinced his wife to sit down and share a cup of coffee with him.

"I agree it's not how we expected it," he said, "but give it time, things will work out."

He poured Martha's coffee then pushed the bowl of sugar toward her.

"Maybe we were hasty bringing Anna here. I just wanted to make a difference in a young woman's life. Was I wrong to try? Maybe it wasn't a good idea after all. We're older, she's so young, and the timing doesn't seem to be working well at all."

Frank was shaking his head.

"No, Martha, we both agreed to bring her here. It's no one's fault."

Martha held onto her hot cup of coffee with both hands, slowly nodding her head. Her thoughts were everywhere.

Anna stood on the stair step listening, her heart pounding. She sat down not knowing what to think.

So it was Luke and Brandon's parents that sent for her. Why hadn't they told her?

She tried to process what she had overheard, and before she could hear anything else, she headed back upstairs as quickly and as quietly as she could.

Martha got up from the kitchen table and started pacing again.

"Martha—"

"No, Frank, I'm all right. I think better this way."

He knew that.

"I know the timing isn't exactly as we planned, and there hasn't been a good time to tell the others, but I think it's *her* that's making a difference, not any of us, Frank."

He was nodding.

"Have you seen the way Anna works with Megan?" Martha asked. "And Megan has taken to her so quickly—Melissa too."

"It's true," Frank said. "Everyone is taken with her. She seems to fit in perfectly."

"It's time to get things straightened out, don't you think? Let her know?"

"Like I said, just give it time, Martha. Everything will work out in due time after things settle down."

"I sure hope so. The poor girl must be wondering what is to become of her."

Anna *was* wondering what was to become of her. At least now she knew who had sent for her. And she knew she should be happy it was in the Monroe family. Isn't that what she wanted?

But it was clear they weren't sure they wanted her now.

Anna sat on the top step.

She wondered if that was the reason her parents gave her away and never returned. Maybe once they had her, they weren't sure they wanted her either.

"Well, no one has to worry," she decided. She would make the decision for them.

Anna tiptoed back to her bedroom and was glad Elisabeth was still sleeping. She gathered some things and made the bed before heading down the same stairs and out the front door.

Martha heard the door.

"Oh my, I better start breakfast! I heard someone."

"It's early still, Martha. You have plenty of time. I'll go check on the animals, and whoever it is, you can just enjoy their company. Just put on more coffee. Pull out some of those biscuits you made the other morning with some of your prizewinning raspberry jam. Enjoy the company and the fact that Luke is home for a while."

Martha accepted her husband's peck on her cheek.

"Relax."

She waved as Frank grabbed his hat off the peg by the kitchen door and winked at her on his way out.

He was right. He always was. She loved him for his calm manner that always settled hers.

Martha closed her eyes and drew in a long, deep breath.

Yes, she would enjoy all the unexpected company and especially Luke's decision to come home for a while. He could be a big help to his father.

She grabbed her apron and looked out the window. The sun had risen quickly, and Frank was standing in the yard talking with his brother, David.

He must have been the one coming in the door, she thought. She was glad David was there so he and Frank could spend a couple of more days together.

She pulled out the biscuits and set them and the jam on the table in case some early birds came looking for something to eat. Her warm coffee sat at her place, untouched.

As she sat a stack of plates on the table, she pulled out her chair and sat. She added another spoonful of sugar to her coffee, and as she stirred, she began rehearsing in her mind all she needed to do that day.

But her thoughts kept drifting back to Anna.

She wanted to go upstairs and sit on the side of Anna's bed and tell her they were the ones who sent for her. But she'd wait like her husband said. It would all work out in due time, after everything settled down.

Now she felt at peace. She was happy Anna was there. Anna had indeed made a difference in their lives, and she was looking forward to spending more time with her, just taking some time, getting to know her.

Chapter 48

But let him ask in faith, nothing wavering.
James 1:6

*M*ost everyone was up and starting to gather in the large dining room. There was laughter and many cups of coffee poured. All the men were swapping some very interesting stories. Professor Higgins, of course, topped them all.

Martha was busy putting food on the table, and Frank had just brought Megan down, getting her settled into her wheelchair.

David teased the little girl, "Someone sure looks sleepy."

Megan smiled then hid her face against her grandfather.

David tousled her curly golden hair but was then distracted by a movement in the doorway.

Elisabeth was just entering the room, and all eyes were suddenly on her. Her lavender dress was simple, but stylish. The room quieted, and she felt a bit uncomfortable from all the sudden attention.

The professor immediately started her way, but David beat him there.

"Mrs. Landry, you look very nice this morning."

He led her to the table and pulled out a chair for her. That prompted everyone else to find a seat.

"I'm embarrassed to be the last one here. I'm sorry," Elisabeth said.

She tucked her napkin into her lap.

"Oh, you aren't the last. Anna hasn't come down yet," the professor said.

"She hasn't?"

Elisabeth scanned the dining room.

"I thought she was here with you. She's not in her room, and the bed's made."

"She's probably just outside or something," Martha remarked. "Did any of you see her outside?"

There was headshaking and a couple of no's.

"I'll go look for her," Luke offered, rising from the table. "The rest of you get started. Looks like Mother has everything about ready."

"I'll go with you," offered the professor, starting to rise.

Luke held up a hand.

"No, I'll go. She probably just took a walk. No doubt she has plenty on her mind right now."

They all agreed.

Luke looked in the barn first then walked around the immediate area. He headed back into the house and caught his mother as she came from the kitchen.

"Mother, go upstairs and see if Anna is up there and Elisabeth just missed her."

"Oh, all right."

But Martha couldn't find her. Luke discreetly looked in all the downstairs rooms, avoiding the dining room.

Frank showed up in the kitchen looking for his wife. She and Luke were talking softly.

"What's going on?"

"Luke didn't find Anna outside, and we've checked all through the house. She isn't here."

"Did you check the little house?"

Luke confirmed he did.

Martha looked at her husband.

"I'm worried, Frank."

"I'm sure she's close by. Probably just went for a walk and lost track of time. I'm sure she's fine."

"What should we do?" Martha asked.

"Luke and I can grab a horse. We can cover more ground that way and faster. Just go back in and make Elisabeth feel welcomed. Megan will need you."

"Oh, that's right—Megan. Let me get in there."

Father and son headed into the barn, and Frank noticed it right away.

The small brown mare was gone.

"I'm surprised she would take a horse without asking," Luke said.

Frank shrugged.

"She's young. Young people don't always think responsibly." He threw a knowing glance his son's way.

Luke's face reddened.

"All right, I get it. I haven't always been that responsible myself over the years. But I'd like to think I've improved with age."

Frank slapped his son on his back.

"I'm sorry, Luke. That was unkind of me. You're a high-spirited young man. And honestly, I wouldn't want you any other way."

Luke just nodded.

"Well at least she took the mare," Luke said. "She's smaller than the others."

"Well, that mare is high-spirited too, Luke. Hopefully, Anna has ridden before. Obviously, she can saddle a horse, so that's reassuring."

The men saddled their horses and headed down the beaten trail through the woods, hoping it was the most logical direction she would have gone.

Finley Valley didn't cover an enormous amount of ground, but it was dense in spots and large enough to get lost if you weren't familiar with the area.

The weather was clear, and the horses were eager for some exercise. The men picked through the trail, watching for signs that she might have passed through there.

So far, nothing was giving them any clues where she might have gone.

Chapter 49

In all thy ways acknowledge him,
and he shall direct thy paths.
Proverbs 3:6

*A*nna was hungry, but she didn't really notice. She had a lot on her mind.

She guided the small but muscular brown horse along the river, carefully watching the underbrush. The water was amazingly clear, and the air was cool under all the bountiful trees that nearly blocked the sun. She stopped in a clearing, which looked to be used regularly. All the grass had been worn away, and a rope hung from a sturdy tree branch. The rope was frayed at the end, obviously from plenty of use.

Anna envisioned the children who surely swung out over the water, jumping in, trying to outdo each other. She wondered if this was the spot where Luke and Brandon swam as boys. She also wondered if she would be brave enough to swing out over the water. She never had the opportunity to do anything like that. In fact, she had never swam before. She had never even been in water, she thought.

She cautiously dismounted and tied the mare to a slender tree. She rubbed the horse's nose and looked into its dark brown eyes.

"Life is easy for you, you know."

The horse stamped her foot as if she understood.

"I envy you."

She patted the horse's side. Frank Monroe took care of his horses. That was evident from the luster of her coat and carefully brushed mane.

"What's your name?" Anna asked. "I bet it's a really nice name."

The horse shook her head and softly snorted.

"I'll just call you Ruby," Anna whispered. "Your coat is almost red in the sunshine. Yes, I'll call you Ruby."

Anna walked to the river's edge and studied her reflection. Her hair was pulled back into a pony tail, and the dress she chose was one Melissa had given her. It was pale yellow and very light weight. It was soft and a bit too big.

She stooped far enough to run her hand through the cold water. She never expected it to be so cold and quickly pulled away.

Anna glanced around and noticed a fallen tree nearby. She made her way there and sat down.

She hadn't been away from the shelter that long, she thought, but in many ways, it seemed so long ago. She picked up a stick and wrote her name in the dirt—Anna—at least she knew Anna was her real name. Well, Annaleigh was. There was a certain comfort in knowing that was an absolute in her life. She surely had a middle name, she thought. She had never really thought about it before. Did she have a middle name? There was no comfort knowing she wouldn't be able to answer that question. And Thompson—was that her real last name? Probably not.

There were so many unanswered questions. Why did she have to be born to a family that gave her away? She thought she'd rather be like Megan. She couldn't walk but at least she knew her family and they all loved her.

Anna looked back toward the horse. She knew they would certainly be missing her by now. Maybe she should just go back. She could confess she had overheard them talking and agree to leave. That way, they wouldn't feel obligated, and she could just go live in Diamond or even Burke Mountain. Mrs. Wilson would surely take her in. That would probably be the best place to go, she thought.

Maybe Elisabeth would go with her. She didn't have anyone to hold her back. The two of them could find their way. But she definitely didn't want to live in Lazy Spring after all that happened.

She thought about the professor. He would probably be worried. He had been so nice and had given up so much for her. She probably wasn't being fair to him. He seemed tired and also sad. She could see it in his eyes even when he was trying to pretend otherwise. She hadn't had time to ask him about when he was leaving or where he was going.

She would miss Megan when she left and Melissa and Brandon.

She stopped. Thinking of everything and everyone was becoming very uncomfortable.

She remembered Mrs. McAfee and her solutions to every situation. "Pray, Anna. Sing, Anna. Trust God, Anna."

So where *was* God? Why didn't He just fix all this! She clenched her teeth and threw the stick to the ground.

She stood and straightened her dress, and a sudden breeze teased her hair. She knew what she should do, but she was tired of doing what she should do. She had been told what to do all her life. She lived by everyone else's rules, everyone else's ideals.

"God," she prayed, "if You really are out there, then You are going to have to show me because right now, I'm having a hard time believing what Mrs. McAfee has told me all my life!"

Anna ran toward the horse but tripped over a hidden tree root, cutting her hand and scratching her face as she hit the ground.

She slowly rose to her hands and knees, numb from what had just happened. The cut on her hand was filled with sand and dirt. It appeared to be deep, and even though the pain came slowly, it did indeed come.

She made it to her feet and wiped the dirt from her dress the best she could. Blood from her hand stained her dress, and that upset her even more.

She mounted the horse, and in her frustration, she spoke harshly and raised her voice to a level she didn't know existed.

"Get me away from here!" she called out to the horse she called Ruby.

"I don't care where, just get me as far away as possible!"

Chapter 50

Fear thou not; for I am with thee.
Isaiah 41:10

"It's so quiet."

Brandon rolled over and found Melissa staring at the ceiling. He pulled her close.

"Wasn't that the purpose of letting the boys sleep in? So it would be quiet?" he whispered.

"I suppose so, but it's *too* quiet."

Melissa sat up in bed and looked down at Brandon. He could feel her eyes on him.

"So what do you suggest we do?" he asked.

"We could head over to your parents and join them for breakfast. It's early. Surely, they haven't eaten yet."

Now Brandon was staring at the ceiling.

"I could help your mother," she added. "And you know Megan can be a handful."

"I'm sure she has plenty of help, Melissa. Anna and Elisabeth are there."

Brandon turned on his side away from her and pulled the down comforter up around his neck.

Melissa leaned over and whispered in her husband's ear, "Please?"

Brandon sighed.

"Mother went to all the trouble to arrange places to sleep at their place for everyone so you could have a break. So *we* could have a break—a quiet break."

"I know but I can't stand it. I want to be where everyone else is. I want to hear what's going on. We don't have to stay all day."

Brandon wasn't saying anything.

"I can get the boys up and dressed so you can get the wagon."

Brandon finally turned toward Melissa with defeat written all over his face. She smiled then quickly kissed him and headed down the hall to wake the boys.

But Brandon lay there, wanting just a few more minutes before getting up. Anything going on over at his parents' house could surely wait a few more minutes.

And that's where Melissa found him thirty minutes later.

"Okay, boys, time to wake your father!" she called out.

Brandon pulled the comforter over his head and braced himself.

With a little help from their mother, Brady and Ramon jumped on their father and started tickling him with no mercy.

The four of them created a noisy ruckus with pillows flying. The comforter had long hit the floor.

But Brandon suddenly sat up.

"Quiet!"

He strained to listen.

"Boys, quiet!"

Brandon headed to the window and looked out.

"What is it?" Melissa asked, her hair a tangled mess.

"It's Luke and Father."

"What do you suppose they want?"

"They're probably just out for an early morning ride. They're probably here to see if I want to join them."

Melissa didn't try to hide her disappointment.

Brandon walked over and sat beside her and pulled her close. The boys grabbed him around his neck.

"Tell you what. I'll dress real quick and go riding with them. But before I go, I'll hitch up the buggy so you and the boys can go on over to my parents' house. I'll just meet you back there."

Melissa nodded even though it wasn't working out the way she had hoped.

"Grandpa and Uncle Luke are here, boys!" Brandon suddenly exclaimed.

The little boys headed out of the bedroom at lightning speed. Their bare feet hit hard on the steps as they raced toward the front door. Melissa trailed behind them.

"Well, there went our quiet morning," Brandon said to himself.

Melissa met the men at the door. The boys were hanging on their legs.

"Brandon's getting dressed, he'll be right down," she said. "Come on in. And, boys, go find something else to do."

The boys reluctantly let go and headed into the yard after a gentle nudge from their grandfather.

Melissa held the door.

"Come on in."

"We stopped in to see if Anna might be here," Luke said, as he stepped past Melissa.

"Anna? No, Anna's not here."

Brandon joined them in the foyer.

"What's going on?"

"They're looking for Anna."

"No one has seen Anna since last night. We can't find her anywhere," Frank explained. We're out looking for her."

Melissa gasped.

"Oh no. Where could she be?"

"No idea," Frank said. "We just have to keep looking."

Brandon kissed Melissa real quick then grabbed his hat hanging by the door.

"I'll saddle up and help you. Let's go!"

Chapter 51

We love him, because he first loved us.
1 John 4:19

Elisabeth helped Megan cut her pancake into small, manageable pieces. And David kept making the little girl laugh when she should have been eating her breakfast.

Elisabeth was trying her best not to encourage Megan by laughing at the doctor, but she found it to be a nearly impossible task.

Professor Higgins stood, looking out the dining room window, his plate sitting empty.

"This isn't like Anna," he said. "She would want to be here with everyone else. She told me herself that she couldn't wait to talk to Elisabeth this morning. It just doesn't make sense."

Martha came and stood by the professor.

"Don't worry. If she went for a walk and got lost, Frank and Luke will find her. They know every inch of the woods."

She did her best not to show that she too was very worried.

"I should be out there helping," he said.

David stood.

"I'll go out and look around again. Maybe we're just missing something. Professor, I think it's best that you stay here with the women."

"Please, Professor, sit and eat something," Martha coaxed. "Not eating doesn't help Anna one bit."

Every eye was on him. They were all concerned about Anna, but they were concerned for him as well. He looked strained from worry.

"Mrs. Monroe, would you mind helping Megan?" Elisabeth asked. "I'm afraid I'm feeling a little queasy this morning."

"Of course not. Are you ill?"

Elisabeth looked first at the professor then David.

The exchange of eyes didn't escape Martha.

"What is it? Did I miss something?"

"No, I'm not ill. I'm expecting."

Elisabeth blushed as she said it and looked away.

"Why that's wonderful, dear. Why don't you go lie down a little while? All this worry about Anna can't be good for you. I can make a nice cup of tea if that would help."

"Actually, if Dr. Monroe doesn't mind, I could use some fresh air."

"Oh, of course," he replied, "I'd enjoy some company."

Elisabeth and David headed outside, which left only the professor, Megan, and Martha sitting at the table. Megan was unusually quiet. She hadn't said a word about Anna.

Martha helped Megan while trying to keep the professor's mind on other things. She poured the professor a hot cup of coffee.

"Thank you, Martha, another cup of coffee sounds real good right now." He waved away the bowl of sugar she offered.

"It was good of you to bring Elisabeth for a visit," Martha was saying. "She seems like a very nice girl and so young to be a mother soon."

"Elisabeth *is* young but strong and very brave. She proved that to me in the little time I've spent with her. She's very mature for her age. She's been through a lot."

"I can see the maturity. She sounds well educated as well."

"She is. She traveled from the east with her husband. She's the oldest of all girls, and her parents did quite well for themselves, it seems. Her father owns a horse ranch, and she's an excellent horsewoman."

"So where *is* her husband, if you don't mind my asking?"

The professor sipped his coffee.

"Her husband passed away just a short time ago."

"Oh, the poor girl!" Martha slumped back into her chair. "And to be expecting all alone."

"He was the first victim of the illness at Lazy Spring. Dr. Monroe did everything he could to save him."

"I've had little opportunity to talk with Luke or David about what happened there. I've almost forgotten it even happened after all our concern over Anna's illness."

"Elisabeth was the first to have the illness that killed her husband. She blames herself for his death and the others that died. She feels guilty that she survived and he didn't."

"That's a heavy burden to bear."

"Yes, it is."

"I'm glad she's here. And we will help her all we can."

Martha rose.

"Well, I need to take Megan back upstairs so she can lie down. If you need anything, please help yourself. I'll be back down soon."

The professor walked back to the window and watched Elisabeth and David as they walked toward the barn. It was hard to imagine the direction life had taken him to this point. He prayed Anna was safe and would be found soon.

Elisabeth glanced back toward the house.

"Dr. Monroe?"

"David."

"All right...David. I have some questions concerning my pregnancy, and I'm also concerned about the professor. I'm so worried about Anna too. I'm afraid I just want to cry all the time. I'm not normally like that, and frankly, I hate not being in control of my feelings."

The doctor chuckled.

"Many women are emotional during their pregnancies, and stressful situations can heighten that feeling."

Elisabeth nodded and, suddenly feeling somewhat awkward, decided to change the subject.

"I feel helpless about Anna. I do know how to ride, and I'd be happy to help look for her."

David stopped in his tracks and turned to face her.

"No! Elisabeth, that's not a wise idea. If you were thrown from a horse, you might lose your baby since you're in your early stage of pregnancy."

He was relieved she didn't argue and just nodded instead.

"It's so difficult right now," she said. "I'm just not sure what to do with my life. I would never want Martha to think I don't appreciate her offer to stay with them, but I'm not sure I'm ready to live with someone right now. I know the professor means well by bringing me here. I'm not sure what my choices are actually."

Elisabeth seemed frustrated, and David thought about what he could or should say.

"Well, I've actually been thinking of a way I might be able to help you. It's been on my mind a while now."

"Thank you."

Together, they checked the barn and the small house and called Anna's name along the tree line. Neither of them expected to find her, but doing nothing was difficult. This way, they felt like they were at least doing something.

"Why haven't you married, David?"

He hadn't expected that question but didn't hesitate to answer.

"I've been waiting for the right woman."

"What about the woman from the train that stayed back to help you?"

"Oh, Peggy?"

"Yes, I had forgotten her name."

"She was very nice and was very helpful, but I had to explain to her that she just wasn't the one."

"So you broke her heart?"

The doctor laughed at Elisabeth's mischievous grin.

"Maybe I did at that. Let's just say she wasn't very happy when she boarded the train to go back home."

There was a time of silence, but it wasn't awkward.

"Elisabeth?"

"Yes?"

"I know you miss Andrew, but are you ready to accept what has happened and move on?"

"You mean just forget him like it never happened? Sure, that's easy."

David sighed and stopped.

"I guess I may have deserved that. I wasn't trying to pry, Elisabeth."

"I'm sorry. I'm just so tired of people giving me advice about how to 'move on.' I'm just trying to take one day at a time right now. I wish I could just go someplace and be alone for a little while, where I don't have to talk to anyone, to accept the fact I'm really going to have a baby! That I'm going to have a baby without its father."

David was thinking.

"Well, while you're here, you should check in with the local doctor. Doc Stevens is getting up in years, but he is a fine doctor because of his many years of experience. I learned much of what I know from him."

Elisabeth nodded. "I will. Thank you."

"And you need to take care of yourself. Worrying isn't healthy. And you need to stay healthy."

"You sound like a doctor."

"Because I am one. And because I'm a *good* one," he teased.

Elisabeth walked a little bit ahead of him, making no comment.

David suddenly reached out and took her arm and turned her toward him. He held on to her with both hands tightly clasped on each of her arms.

She felt his fingers tighten.

"Elisabeth, I'm sorry I couldn't save Andrew. You don't know how sorry."

He looked deeply into her eyes.

"I am so sorry."

"Do you think I blame you?" Her eyes began to fill with tears.

"Do you, Elisabeth?"

"No...I don't know."

She struggled free from his grasp.

"If anyone is to blame, it's me!" she exclaimed with hot tears streaming down her face. "I'm the one who got sick and should have died, David! It should have been me!"

"I don't have all the answers, Elisabeth, but I do know you can't blame yourself."

She turned so he had to say whatever he thought he needed to say to her back.

Her body trembled.

"Elisabeth," his voice was soft and tender, "please look at me."

He gently turned her around and stooped down so he could look directly into her eyes.

She was quietly sobbing.

"What I'm going to tell you might cause you to turn and run, but I have to say it or burst."

She waited.

"I'm in love with you. It may be wrong, but I fell in love with you at Andrew's burial. I've tried to shake it, but I can't. I don't know how you feel about me, but I love you, and I would love that baby."

Chapter 52

For I the LORD thy God will hold thy right hand,
saying unto thee, Fear not; I will help thee.
Isaiah 41:13

The small brown mare carried her rider down the trail that followed the river harder and faster than Anna ever wanted to go.

"Ruby, please!" Anna cried.

She pulled back on the reins, but it didn't make a difference. The horse was given permission to have her own way, and no amount of coaxing was going to change anything.

But Anna didn't know that. She was pleading with the horse to stop.

The ground below her feet was a blur, and the low-hanging branches above grabbed her hair and stung her face.

"Stop, oh, please stop!"

Anna let go of the reins and grabbed the horse around its neck, holding on for dear life.

She closed her eyes and cried out.

"Someone please save me! God, help me!"

The Monroe men had no idea what Anna was experiencing at that very moment. Following a trail that led deeper into the woods, Frank, Brandon, and Luke had to make a decision.

"I say we go back and see if she's gone back to the house," Brandon suggested. "We've seen no evidence she's gone this way."

"Yes," Frank said. "Hopefully, she's there safe and sound, but we need to consider that she might still be out there somewhere. The woods are dense. She's had time to be anywhere by now. And unless she took some food with her, she's bound to be hungry."

"And scared," added Luke. His tone gave away his agitation.

"We need to split up!" Luke exclaimed. "We all know the woods well enough to find our way. Brandon can go back to the house, you can keep on this trail, and I'll back track and check out the river trail toward town."

Frank nodded.

"It's very possible she went that way. Luke's right, let's get going."

The three separated, looking for any clue that might lead them to Anna.

None of them had any idea the scare Anna was facing right then.

Anna held her breath. She wondered what it felt like to die.

The mare slowed as it reached a sharp turn in the path, so Anna sat part way up, hoping to regain control. She reached for one of the dangling reins, and in doing so, she lost her balance.

Anna didn't have time to think about what was going to happen. It just happened.

Her shoulder received the hardest blow, which saved her head from an injury that could have been much worse than it was.

Suddenly, all was quiet.

The horse Anna called Ruby had kicked her hind legs and never looked back, happy to be free of her burden.

The dust hung in the air where Anna laid. She didn't move. Breathing hurt.

Back at the house, Professor Higgins chose to go back to the little house where he could rest. He knew worry was never the answer to any problem, but it was hard not to. He prayed as he walked. His step was steady but labored.

He was just about halfway across the yard when he saw Elisabeth coming from around the barn. She was clearly upset.

"Elisabeth!" he cried out.

She ignored his cry and was practically running at that point.

"Elisabeth!"

David wasn't far behind and slowed when he saw the professor.

"What's wrong, Doctor? What—"

David held up a hand as he passed.

"I can't explain right now, Professor."

The doctor continued his pace.

"But don't worry, Elisabeth is fine. Everything is under control."

The professor stood watching as Elisabeth ran into the house. David had just about caught up with her at that point.

He reached out and stopped the young widow before she took too many steps into the kitchen.

"Elisabeth, please."

She had no choice but to stop and listen. He held her tightly by one arm. His grip wasn't about to let her go.

Both were out of breath, and it took a few moments before David found the words he wanted to say.

He couldn't see her eyes, only the back of her head.

"Let me explain."

She didn't struggle because she knew it wouldn't do any good.

"Will you please give me a chance, Elisabeth?"

She slowly turned his way and looked up at him. He released his grip.

"If you tell me to leave and never come back, I will."

He paused for a reaction.

Elisabeth swallowed but didn't say anything.

"When I saw you standing there at the burial, I saw a woman I knew could make it on her own. I saw a woman who had fought for her life and wouldn't give up. I saw strength and character."

Elisabeth looked to the floor, but the doctor gently lifted her chin so she had to look up at him.

"I saw a woman who loved her husband so much she stayed by his side until he took his last breath, giving him hope to the very end."

Her breathing quickened.

"Why are you doing this to me?" she whispered.

She didn't turn and run, she didn't move at all except to lean just a little bit toward him.

David reached out and enveloped Elisabeth into his arms where he held her until she totally surrendered to his embrace.

He spoke softly into her ear, "I saw a woman that day who had stolen my heart, and there wasn't anything I could do or have done since then to make that feeling go away."

She stayed in his arms.

"So please, I'm asking you to search your heart, and if there is even the slightest chance you could love me back, I'll take that. I'll take that, Elisabeth."

She pulled away, turned, and walked a few steps from him.

"I meant it when I said I'd leave if you want me to. And if that's the case, I need to hear it now."

Elisabeth took a deep breath and squared her shoulders.

"What about the baby? How can you love another man's child?"

He took the steps needed to stand by her side.

"I don't know how, Elisabeth, I just know I can."

She nodded, her eyes full of tears.

"All right, I need some time to think."

David bowed his head and struggled to keep his composure.

"Come with me," he finally said. "Come back with me to Lazy Spring. I will wait as long as it takes for you to love me back. But I'll tell you right now, no one will ever love you as much as I do."

He then took the trembling young woman into his arms and kissed her in a way she could have never doubted that love.

Chapter 53

For God is love.
1 John 4:8

*A*nna was able to roll onto her side, but it was too painful when she tried to sit up. She wondered if she had broken her shoulder because the pain was almost unbearable. The side of her face was sticky from blood trickling down from a cut on the side of her head. She hurt all over, and she felt helpless.

She laid there in the dirt taking small shallow breaths, forcing herself to concentrate on her surroundings. It was a well-worn trail, so she hoped someone would find her soon. She closed her eyes and tried to think of anything other than the pain. Her head began to throb, and she could feel the throbbing pulse throughout her entire body.

She carefully rolled to her back, crying out from the pain. She laid as still as she could. The sun was high above the canopy of trees, and when the wind blew, the branches parted and allowed the sun to find her face. She wondered how long she would have to lay there before someone found her. She was mad, not at the horse or even her situation. She was mad at herself.

She closed her eyes and rehearsed the little song Mrs. McAfee would sing to her.

"Don't be afraid, Anna, don't be afraid."

At about that same time, Luke reached the river trail. He longed for a drink of water. The sun was high in the sky now, and the humidity was on the rise. He looked down the trail as far as he could and just let his thoughts wander.

He tried to think like Anna, like a fifteen-year-old. Everyone treated her so much older, but she was still very young and just learning about the world, he decided. Yes, everyone talked about how mature she was, but he was beginning to think she had a lot of catching up to do.

She didn't grow up doing outdoor chores like many girls her age or work in the kitchen all her life alongside her mother. She didn't know the basic things about cooking, Melissa had told him. She hadn't experienced most of the normal things girls her age had. Megan in some ways knew more than Anna did, he reasoned.

He wiped the sweat from his brow and wished he'd taken time to get his hat from the house before heading out.

Luke's agitation grew. He was almost angry imagining how much neglect Anna probably suffered, living within four walls without a proper childhood, missing out on life just because someone didn't care enough to keep her! Melissa told him all about her talk with Anna concerning her life at the Children's Shelter.

In his frustration, he kicked the sides of his horse and headed down the trail at full gallop. The wind in his thick brown hair felt good. Adrenaline coursed through him.

He knew every twist and turn by heart, and his riding was on the edge of recklessness. The canopy of trees created a calming effect, but it wasn't enough to calm his anxiousness toward Anna and the fact she was nowhere to be found! He was concerned for her but frustrated at her at the same time. If she was brought to Finley Valley to help his parents, she was going to have to prove herself!

He slowed his horse and drew in a deep breath. The air smelled fresh and clean, and the sound of the river was inviting. He knew he was charging ahead with his thoughts and emotions as he often did. And it wasn't time for judgment, he thought, but time to just find the girl.

Maybe Brandon was right, and she was safely back at the house, he thought. He decided he would ride as far as the swimming spot where he could get a drink of water and then he'd head back.

Well, Anna, on the other hand, *was* being very judgmental…
toward herself.

If only I could go back to bed and start over, she thought in desperation. *I have been foolish, as Mrs. McAfee would say, when I made rash decisions.*

"Slow down and think it through," the older woman would tell her. "Haste only causes trouble and more work in the long run!" she'd say.

Trouble—she knew she was in trouble. Even if the Monroe's decided they wanted her to stay, they probably wouldn't now.

She pushed with her good arm and, with much effort and pain, was able to come to a sitting position. She scooted to the side of the trail and looked down toward the river. If only she could make it down the rocky slope, she could get a drink and hopefully wipe the blood from her face and away from her eyes.

She inched her way down the embankment, the rough ground snagging the yellow dress that Melissa had given her. She liked that dress, and now it was ruined! She was too mad to think of crying from the pain in her shoulder.

She began to pray.

"If You get me out of this, God, I will never do anything like this again! I promise."

Then as she sat only a couple of feet from the river's edge, she thought about the inscription in the journal the professor had given her when they left Diamond.

Embrace the adventures God brings into your life and trust Him.

"Trust Him."

You are never alone.

Anna closed her eyes and listened as the river flowed past her.

"I am never alone."

She looked out over the water and watched as leaves and small branches gently flowed with the current.

"I'm ready, God. Take me wherever You want, on any adventure You already have planned for me."

She sat, thinking.

"The professor was right. I *will* understand it all by and by."

"I understand now, God. I give You my heart, my whole heart. Show me what to do now."

"And I'm asking that You give me another chance by making the Monroe's want me as much as I want them!"

Chapter 54

The LORD thy God in the midst of thee is mighty.
Zephaniah 3:17

$\mathcal{M}$elissa was pacing back and forth on Martha and Frank's front porch when she saw Brandon riding up.

He shook his head no to her questioning eyes.

"No sign of her," he said, as he dismounted. "I was hoping to find her here."

"No, we were hoping she'd show up too. Brandon, I'm really worried, and Megan isn't her normal cheerful self. I think this is affecting her more than we realize."

The professor stepped out on the porch, anxiously looking for a good report. But it was clear from Brandon's expression they had been unsuccessful.

"I'm sorry, Professor, but Father and Luke are still out there looking. I came back to see if Anna had come back here."

The professor found a chair and sat.

"Waiting is the hardest part, I think," he said. "I pray nothing has happened to her."

Brandon nodded, not knowing what to say to comfort the old man.

They all stood in silence for a moment.

"So where's Mother?" Brandon asked.

"She's upstairs with Megan, and the boys are running around somewhere, probably the barn."

"Well, if you can round up some food for me, I'll take my horse to the barn so I can get this saddle off her, and I'll check on the boys. Then I'll go up and check on Megan."

Melissa gave him a half smile.

Brandon let the horse's reins slip from his hand, then he walked up the steps where Melissa stood.

He gently pulled her to him, and they embraced.

"Everything is going to be all right."

Melissa looked toward the professor.

"You don't know that for sure," she whispered.

"No, I don't, but we aren't going to give up hope now, are we?"

"No, we aren't."

"You're pretty attached to Anna, aren't you?"

"Yes, yes, I am. We barely had her, now she's gone."

"She's not gone. Even if she wanted to leave for some reason, she can't go far. There's no train until tomorrow."

Both Melissa and Brandon had the same thought at the same time.

"The train station, no one thought to look there."

"I'll take my horse to the barn for some feed and water, and you round up some food for me. I'll go to the station and see what I can find out there."

"Oh, Brandon. I hope she's there."

"I suppose she could be."

The professor was standing, having overheard.

"I'll go too. I can't just sit here feeling like I'm doing nothing."

Melissa gave a slight nod toward her husband.

"Well, I, all right then. I'd enjoy the company," Brandon said.

"Wonderful! I'll change and be right back. I'll just be a few minutes."

"Take your time, Professor. I'll hitch up the buggy."

Brandon threw a look Melissa's way, and she grinned from ear to ear.

"The professor needs something to do, Brandon. He's worried sick."

"It would be faster without him."

"Well, like you said, there's no train until tomorrow."

"Well then, smart girl, how about rounding up that food? I'm half starved."

"Only half?"

Brandon shook his head, and she turned and headed into the house, looking back at the last minute with a grin.

He loved that girl. The first time he saw her, it was love at first sight. He never had eyes for any other girl after that, and he was proud to bring her into the family.

Laughter in the barn brought his attention back where it should be. It was time to see what those boys were up to. And Megan—he needed to see what was going on with her too.

He wondered how things were going with his father and Luke when he heard a horse entering the yard.

He turned expecting his father or Luke, but instead, he watched the small brown mare Anna had taken enter the barn with no rider.

Chapter 55

And to know the love of Christ, which passeth knowledge,
that ye might be filled with all the fulness of God.
Ephesians 3:19

*E*lisabeth was sitting with Megan when Brandon rushed into the upstairs bedroom.

"Elisabeth, I didn't realize you were in here. I was looking for Melissa."

Brandon noticed right away her eyes were red and swollen like she had been crying.

"Is everything all right?" He looked over at Megan where she was sleeping.

Elisabeth nodded.

"Everything's fine with Megan then?" Brandon seemed rushed, irritated.

"Yes, she's fine. I began reading to her, and she fell asleep, so I helped her into bed and—"

Brandon abruptly interrupted her, "I'm sorry, Elisabeth, but have you seen David?"

"Not for a little while. Why? What's wrong?"

"It's very important that I find him right away."

He turned and headed for the door.

She followed close behind.

"What's wrong, Brandon? What is it? Is this about Anna?"

Brandon hesitated at the top of the stairs to answer when he noticed the professor looking up at him from the bottom of the stairs, ready to go to the train station.

"Did you know Anna took a horse when she left?" he asked Elisabeth.

"Yes, I did know that."

"Well, that horse just showed up."

He looked first to Elisabeth and then down at the professor.

"The horse came back all alone and looks like she's been running hard. And I found dried blood on her side."

Elisabeth gasped and didn't wait to hear anything else Brandon had to say. She passed him on the stairs and ran past the professor.

Brandon tore down the stairs after her, ignoring the look of concern on the professor's face.

Elisabeth reached the barn where the brown mare stood, still saddled and feeding from the loose hay on the barn floor that the boys had thrown from the loft.

She ran her hand across the dried blood on the horse's side.

Brandon ran into the barn just as Elisabeth mounted the horse in one fluid motion.

"Elisabeth, what are you doing?"

"I'm going to find Anna. She might be lying out there hurt and afraid. I should have gone sooner."

"No, wait, you can't go!"

Elisabeth pointed the horse toward the barn opening and kicked the horse's sides as soon as she was clear of Brandon.

The professor had just about reached the barn, struggling to catch his breath.

"You shouldn't have let her go like that," he stammered.

Brandon, breathing hard from his run, held his tongue.

"Go after her!" the professor exclaimed.

Brandon looked down toward the ground, thinking the situation through, blocking out the rest of what the professor was saying.

He looked up, ready to answer, when he saw Melissa and David coming from the little house.

"David!"

The professor turned to see.

Brandon ran toward his wife and uncle.

They ran toward him.

"What is going on? What's happened?" were the questions.

"Anna's horse came back alone, and Elisabeth just took off on her to go look for Anna!"

"What!" David exclaimed.

David ran his fingers through his hair then hit his leg with his fist.

He ran for the barn, and with strength he didn't realize he had, he grabbed a saddle and began saddling the last remaining horse.

"I'm going with you!" Brandon shouted as he ran for his horse. "My horse is ready."

The doctor pulled and tugged until he had the saddle on tight and the bridle in place. He mounted the horse, sharply pulling the left rein, which caused the horse to rear his head in protest. He urged the horse toward the barn opening and let out a shout as he slapped the horse's backside.

Brandon followed on the doctor's heels.

Melissa and the professor stood in silence as they rode away, Melissa taking the professor's hand. Her heart felt as if it would beat out of her chest. Her hand hurt from the professor's grip.

"They'll find her, Professor," she said. "I have no doubt one of them will find her."

He nodded and they slowly walked back to the house together.

Chapter 56

We are more than conquerors
through him that loved us.
Romans 8:37

Anna was able to carefully wash the dried blood from her face as well as wash the cut on the side of her head but not without gritting her teeth. She rinsed the one hand she was able to use and then sipped what water she could before it slipped through her fingers.

Her shoulder was throbbing from all her movement, and she wanted to cry, but instead, she held her breath on and off so that wouldn't happen. She had to stay strong. She was fighting the feeling of a very upset stomach.

She prayed God would bring someone soon and then very carefully leaned back until she felt the ground on her back.

All she could do was wait.

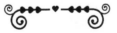

Luke yanked the reins on his horse, almost passing his planned destination.

He carefully guided his horse down the embankment toward the river, and memories flooded his thoughts. How long had it been since he swam there? He saw the rope hanging from the familiar tree branch and smiled. So many good times he had there as a boy with Brandon and the other boys in the area!

He slid down the side of his horse, dropping the reins so his horse could be free to get a drink from the lazy river.

Luke knelt and scooped up handfuls of water until his own thirst was quenched. He threw enough water on his face and hair to cool down before he headed back to the house. If Anna wasn't there, they could regroup and try again.

He bent down to grab the horse's reins when he saw the blood spots in the dirt. Why hadn't he noticed the footprints before and what appeared to be a struggle in the dirt? Was it from Anna or someone else? He started looking around.

That's when he saw Anna's name written in the dirt by the fallen log. She had been there! This was the first clue of where she had gone. Relief flooded through him.

"Anna! Anna!" he called as loudly as he could. "Anna!"

He searched the area around him looking for more clues. He carefully examined the ground, and despite the hoof prints his horse had made and the prints of another horse, it looked like she had proceeded down the river path toward town.

She's bleeding, he thought. He hoped to find her soon.

He rode slowly, calling her name and stopping to listen for any sound.

"Oh, Anna, where are you?" he whispered.

He watched the ground as he rode, but it was hard to follow prints that might have come from her horse.

He pushed his horse to go a little faster and watched both sides of the trail for any clues.

He was just about to push harder when he heard a horse fast approaching behind him.

He turned as Elisabeth reined her horse to a stop.

"Elisabeth! You're the last person I expected."

Her hair was coming loose and she was red in the face.

She wiped the sweat from her hairline and caught her breath. Luke gave her a minute.

"Anna's horse came back to the house without her," she explained.

"And that's not all. There's dried blood. Right here."

That's when Luke noticed the horse was the same.

"Elisabeth, I'll hold the horse while you get a drink. You can get through the trees right there. I'll bring the horse behind you. She needs water, and she clearly needs a rest."

Elisabeth agreed but spoke anxiously of the urgency to find Anna, "She must be hurt."

"I found where she stopped just a little ways back. I also found some blood on the ground, but it didn't look to be an alarming amount. So don't panic."

Elisabeth took a deep breath and looked him in the eye.

"I've never panicked in my life, Luke."

She then thought of the conversation she had with David and decided that wasn't exactly a true statement.

"Well, settle down some then."

"All right, I will."

She pulled her hair up into a loose bun then picked in and out of the trees until she was able to get to the water. She knelt and splashed water on her face. She heard horses fast approaching, and she didn't have to guess who it was.

Elisabeth stood and turned at the doctor's voice.

He was zigzagging through the trees toward her.

"Elisabeth, what were you thinking?" His look was a mix of frustration and relief.

"I was thinking someone needed to find Anna, that's all."

"And in doing so, you decided to throw all caution to the wind and put your life in danger, pushing an exhausted animal to its limit?"

She raised her chin.

"You could have fallen, you could have lost the baby, Elisabeth."

She turned from him.

"I know how to ride, David."

Brandon called from the trail.

David sighed.

"I must go," he said. "You stay here, and we'll go on so we can find Anna."

"You know I won't do that, Doctor."

He sighed again.

"Then ride with me and leave the horse here."

She followed him up the bank and kept up with him despite his long strides.

In one quick motion, he lifted her up on the saddle, then swung himself up behind her, putting one arm around her waist.

Brandon and Luke led the way, and together, they searched all around while keeping a steady pace.

Luke pulled out ahead, and it wasn't long before he saw her.

"There she is!" he cried. "There, down there."

He stopped and ran down the embankment to Anna's side.

She began to sob, and much of what she was trying to say was impossible to understand.

The others were soon by her side, David gently pushing Luke away.

"Let me see her, Luke."

"Anna, we're here. It's over."

She quieted but was still sobbing.

"You need to calm down and talk to me."

Elisabeth held her hand and smiled.

"I'm here, Anna. I'm right here to help."

Anna nodded. It was clear she was in a lot of pain.

"Tell me where it hurts, Anna," David was saying.

"My shoulder. I think I broke it. And my head and stomach hurt."

"Everybody, step back a little, let me check her shoulder."

"This is going to hurt, Anna. But I can't tell what's going on until I check some things."

Elisabeth squeezed her hand.

Anna winched as David examined her shoulder as well as her arms and legs for any cuts or injuries. The cut on the side of her head didn't look serious.

"Can you stand?"

"I think so."

"We're all going to help you up so we can get you home. So on the count of three, we will pick you up. Don't try to help."

Anna nodded.

They sat her up as gently as they could, then Brandon and Luke got on either side of her and picked her up, avoiding the hurt shoulder.

The doctor and Elisabeth steadied her, and together, they all walked her up the bank.

Though wobbly, she was able to stand.

They lifted her up, and with much pain, she was able to straddle Luke's horse. Then Luke pulled himself up and sat behind her.

"I'm going to put my arm around you, Anna. I will steady you the best I can, but it's still going to be a bumpy ride."

She nodded.

"Let's go then."

The group headed home in a single file.

The doctor held Elisabeth tightly as they rode together.

"I don't think it's necessary that I ride the entire way with you if that's what you're thinking, Doctor. I am capable of riding my own horse."

"But then it wouldn't be as much fun. Besides, this way, I know you're safe."

"I was plenty safe before, Doctor."

"Well, *as* your doctor, I say you are never to pull a stunt like that ever again."

"I'm not used to being told what to do."

"I'm starting to see that."

"I can be very opinionated."

"I've noticed that too."

"So what else do you think you know about me?"

"That you're beautiful when you're mad and you are exactly the woman I've been waiting for."

Chapter 57

*God is love; and he that dwelleth in love
dwelleth in God, and God in him.
1 John 4:16*

*A*nna was resting easy on Melissa and Brandon's sunporch.

"So how's my patient?"

David was clean-shaven, nicely dressed, and smelled good.

"Wonderful! It's so good to be back safe and sound."

"Well, let me check that shoulder one more time before I head out."

"I wish you didn't have to leave. Why don't you just be a doctor here?"

"Well, that's a story for another time. Let's just say that sometimes I need my own space."

"I think Luke's a lot like you."

"I think you're right, Anna."

David was careful with his examination.

"There. You might be stiff for a while, but don't let that keep you from using that arm. You're a very lucky girl, Anna. That fall you took could have been much worse. Thankfully, your shoulder was just out of place and not broken. Either way, it can be very painful."

"And the cut on the side of your head looks good. It will heal quickly, and you'll probably only have a small scar. Honestly, the cut on your hand from where you fell on that broken branch might leave the most noticeable scar."

"I'm glad I'll have a scar there."

"Really? Why?"

"It's a good reminder. I'm ready to leave my past behind and go forward. Every time I see that scar on my hand, it will remind me to never think backward, only forward."

"I think you're a very wise young woman, Anna."

Elisabeth came out on the sunporch to tell Anna goodbye as well.

She was dressed in a solid white dress that flowed freely when she walked. Her hair was pulled up on her head, but strands of brown hair fell around her face and accentuated her natural beauty.

"I couldn't help but overhear. I *know* you're a very wise young woman, Anna."

"Thank you. I'm very happy."

"I see that. Everyone sees it."

Elisabeth walked over and kissed Anna on her cheek and spoke so softly the doctor couldn't hear.

"I'm happy we were able to talk in length last night. You will never regret your decision to put God first in your life. I will pray for you."

"Thank you, Elisabeth. I'm just sorry you're leaving so soon, especially after thinking you were going to stay for a couple of months."

"Well, I just have some things I need to get settled, and I can't do it here. I'm not sorry I came, but after getting here, I realized it's not where I need to be right now. I hope you understand."

"I think I do."

The two women hugged and clung to each other for several moments.

"I'm not that far away, come visit soon," Elisabeth was saying.

"I will."

"We better get going, Elisabeth," David said. "Brandon is ready to take us to the train station."

She nodded.

"I'm ready."

Elisabeth and the doctor headed out, and Anna sat looking out the large picture window, thinking. So much had changed in such a short period of time. The Children's Shelter was getting further and further away from her thoughts.

She remembered something Luke told her when she first arrived in Finley Valley.

"Take one day at a time, Anna. Life is too hard to try and think of it all at once."

He was right.

Right then, Luke seemed to appear out of nowhere, and she jumped at the sudden sound of his voice. Her hand flew to her heart.

"I'm sorry, I didn't mean to startle you."

"Oh, that's all right. I just wasn't paying attention."

"Want some company?"

"Yes, I'd love some. Dr. Monroe and Elisabeth just left."

"I know, I just passed them."

"I'm going to miss both of them."

"Everyone will, but he needs to get back to his practice. He didn't plan on being gone this long."

"I guess I'm to blame for that," Anna confessed.

"No, well, actually, yes. You're right."

They both laughed.

"It's good to see you so happy…and safe."

"I was foolish. I caused a lot of trouble."

"Let's just say you've kept us all very busy since your arrival."

Anna blushed.

"I'm here to say goodbye too, Anna. I've offered to go back and help Uncle David out for a while."

"I'm not surprised."

"Really? Why do you say that?"

"I can tell you aren't happy. You're restless."

Luke sat down but then stood right back up.

"I am, Anna. I have no idea what to do with my life."

"Do you remember when I was sick and you told me to just take one day at a time?"

"I do remember. And I also remember you gave us a scare."

"You said that life is too hard to try and think of it all at once."

Luke just studied Anna's face for several moments then nodded.

"That's right."

"Don't think so hard, Luke. Just take one day at a time and see where it leads."

"Look who's all grown up all of a sudden giving advice!"

He sat back down.

"I just wanted to come and tell you goodbye but to also tell you I'm happy Mother and Father invited you to come stay with them."

"If they hadn't asked me to come, I don't know what would have happened to me."

"I think it was meant to happen, Anna, if not for Mother and Father but for Megan. I've watched you care for children, like at Lazy Spring. You have a gift."

Anna was quiet.

"I don't know what your plans are for the future, Anna, and I know you don't either, but I wish you all the luck in the world."

Luke took her hand and kissed it.

"I misjudged you, Anna. When you ran away, I was angry until Mother explained what happened. No one meant to hurt you or give you the impression you weren't wanted."

"I guess I've always felt no one ever wanted me, and that's why I was at the Children's Shelter. Just thinking I might not be wanted again was almost too much to bear!"

"Well, you know differently now."

David came to the doorway.

"We're ready, Luke."

Luke searched Anna's blue eyes.

"I have to go."

"I know."

Luke turned and waved before he disappeared through the doorway. Anna waved too, but he didn't see.

"One day at a time, Luke," she whispered. "One day at a time."

Then she touched her hand where he kissed it.

Chapter 58

But perfect love casteth out fear.
1 John 4:18

𝒫rofessor Higgins thanked Frank then carefully stepped down from the buggy. Frank handed him two neatly wrapped packages then turned the horse toward the barn.

Martha met the professor on the porch.

"I see you've been doing some shopping, Professor. Where have you two been so early this morning?"

"Your husband graciously offered to take me to the train station to see everyone off. I haven't had a chance to talk with Elisabeth much since Anna came home, so I wanted to tell her and Dr. Monroe goodbye since I'll be heading out soon myself. I didn't know when I'd see them again."

"Well, I have some coffee ready. Come on in."

The professor set the packages on the porch and followed Martha inside.

"I didn't realize Luke was leaving too," he added.

Martha pointed to a seat at the kitchen table, and the old man sat down. She poured coffee into a cup and sat it in front of him. Her cup already full, she sat in the seat across from him.

"Luke wasn't the only one who surprised me by leaving," Martha said.

"You mean Elisabeth?"

She nodded as she added a spoonful of sugar to her cup.

"That upsets you?"

"Oh no, not at all. She explained everything to me, and I totally understand. It's Luke that puzzles me."

"How so?"

"I thought he was going to stick around here for a while, and I guess I'm disappointed is all."

"Of course, you are."

Frank came in and hung his hat on the peg just inside the kitchen door and motioned for Martha to stay seated then poured his own coffee. He didn't have to ask what the conversation was about by the look on Martha's face. He took her hand.

The three of them sat in silence sipping their coffee until the professor spoke up.

"Well, I have some good news for Anna."

Martha looked his way.

"While I was at the train station, I inquired about something that came to mind when Anna was missing. And I'm glad I remembered."

"What is it?" Martha asked with keen interest.

"When Anna and I were traveling together, we stopped at Diamond and did some shopping. She was in need of several things, and I was happy to help out. So I had a woman there sew up some dresses and asked her to send them on the train to Finley Valley in care of Annaleigh Thompson."

"The packages you had with you when Frank dropped you off."

"Yes. In all the excitement since the time we left Diamond, I had completely forgotten about the dresses. I guess Anna forgot too. The packages have been sitting at the train station all this time. I can't wait to surprise her."

"That was very kind of you, Professor," Frank said.

Martha nodded, sipping the coffee that was still too bitter for her. She reached for the sugar bowl one more time.

"Yes, Professor, you have done so much for Anna. Thank you for helping her. I'm not sure she could have made it this far without you."

"Oh, she could have made it. I have no doubt. No doubt at all."

There was a pause.

"What is it?" Martha asked. "I can tell you are thinking about something, Professor."

"I was thinking how I'm not sure I could have made it without *her*."

"You helped each other," Frank added with a knowing smile.

The professor agreed.

"But there's something else?" Martha asked, observing the concentration that covered the old man's face.

"Yes, there is. And I'm not sure I'm ready to talk to Anna about it yet."

"Can we help in any way?" Frank asked.

"No, this is something I need to do myself." He scooted his chair back from the table.

"Thank you for the coffee, Martha."

"Don't run off. I was just about to round up something to eat."

"Oh, no, thank you. I'm not that hungry. I'm eager to get over to Brandon's and surprise Anna with her dresses."

"I'll saddle a horse for you."

Frank began to stand.

"No, no, I can saddle a horse. I haven't been doing much around here, and it will feel good to get some exercise. Thanks again for the coffee."

Martha and Frank waved as he left.

"I'm concerned about him, Frank."

"Me too, Martha. Me too."

Chapter 59

Beloved, let us love one another.
1 John 4:7a

*A*nna and Megan were laughing so hard they didn't hear Professor Higgins step into Megan's bedroom.

He stood and watched them for a few minutes before letting them know he was there by clearing his throat.

Anna noticed him first and jumped up from the rug where she and Megan were sitting. Megan waved from the pile of blankets that encircled her.

"Sounds like fun in here."

He and Anna hugged tightly.

"Megan and I are telling stories."

"Well, don't let me interrupt. I can sit right here and listen."

Anna sat back down on the rug across from Megan and urged her to finish her story. But the six-year-old grew shy and shook her head.

"I would love to hear your story, Megan," the professor coaxed.

She continued to shake her head.

"That's all right," Anna said. "We can finish later."

Anna was helping Megan into her chair just as Melissa entered the room.

"I thought I heard a man's voice up here. Hello, Professor."

The professor stood and greeted her.

"I let myself in. I hope you don't mind. I knocked but no one came."

"I'm sorry, I was outside a few minutes." Melissa took a deep breath. "Well, I'm here to take Megan on a walk in this glorious sunshine. Either of you want to join us?"

Before Anna could answer, the professor spoke up.

"That sounds like a great idea, but if you don't mind, I'd like to talk to Anna about something."

"I don't mind at all. Maybe you could join us for lunch?"

"I'd like that."

"Well then, we'll see you two downstairs for lunch in about an hour. Is that enough time for you?"

"Oh, plenty. Here, let me help you take Megan downstairs."

"No, sit where you are. I've been doing this a long time, Professor. We have a routine, don't we, Megan?"

The little girl nodded with a big grin.

The professor noticed Melissa seemed more relaxed lately as well as Megan.

Both Anna and the professor waited until Melissa left to speak.

"So how's my girl today?"

The professor walked over to a small sofa and sat down. He motioned for Anna to join him.

She was wearing a pretty flowered dress with a very fashionable narrow belt. Her brilliant blue eyes brought out all the colors.

"You look very nice today, Anna."

"Oh, thank you. Melissa has been kind to let me borrow some of her dresses. They're a little big but not too much."

"Speaking of dresses, I have a surprise for you."

Anna perked up.

"A surprise?"

"Do you remember shopping for dresses in Wilson's General Store in Diamond?"

"Of course, I do! I love those dresses."

"Mrs. Wilson was going to sew some new dresses for you and send them here."

He waited to see if Anna remembered, and the look on her face gave him his answer.

"I forgot!"

"Well, I did too, but I happened to think about it the other day, so when I went to the train station this morning to tell Dr. Monroe and Elisabeth goodbye, I asked the man at the ticket counter about the possibly of a delivery in your name."

"And they had them?"

"Yes! They have been sitting at the train station all this time. They had no idea who you were."

The professor walked to the doorway and grabbed two packages that were sitting in the hallway.

Anna sat up straight in anticipation. He brought them over and sat them on the sofa between them.

Anna bit her lip and just sat there staring at them.

"Well, go ahead. Open them."

Anna pulled at the brown string that held the package tightly together and was finally able to open the first one.

She lifted up a solid blue dress with a white lace collar so they both could see.

"I asked her to specifically sew up a pretty blue one for you."

"It's beautiful, Professor. Thank you!"

"There's more."

There was a flowered one similar to the one she was wearing and a pink one with white cuffs and a white collar. It had puffy sleeves and a high waist. It seemed much too nice for every day.

"I asked her to do one up real fancy for church and social events. You know, like a picnic or a dance."

Anna fingered the fabric. "I hadn't thought about church or going anywhere like a picnic or a dance."

"Well, I'm sure when you're feeling up to it, Melissa will see that you get to go into town. And soon, you'll be meeting some of the residents of Finley Valley."

"I'll admit I've been wondering about going into town."

"I'll tell you what, why don't you pick one of these nice dresses and I'll see if Brandon will let me borrow their buggy. I'll take you for an early supper, and we can walk around and see the town together."

"Oh, could we, Professor?"

"Of course, we can."

He tapped the unopened package. "Here, open this one."

Anna didn't bother with the string this time; she just tore the brown paper until she could pull out three more dresses.

They were a little heavier weight, but they were just as nice as the others. Anna stood to her feet and ran over to a mirror hanging on the wall. She held a white dress in front of her and stood on her tiptoes to see as much of her reflection as possible. It had little blue flowers all over it.

"This one's my favorite, I think."

"I believe it's my favorite too, Anna. It compliments your blue eyes."

"It reminds me of the little dress I was wearing when Mrs. McAfee found me."

"Then I'm glad Mrs. Wilson thought to sew one just like it."

"I'll wear it tonight."

The professor slowly stood to his feet.

"I better get back to the Monroe's and tell them of our plans, and then I need to clean up a bit. Will you please let Melissa know of our plans and thank her for the lunch invitation and that I'm sorry I can't stay?"

"I will!"

"And don't eat too much for lunch because I'm going to buy you the nicest meal we can find in Finley Valley!"

"Oh, Professor! It's like when we ate at the fancy hotel in Diamond. That seems so long ago now."

He agreed with a simple nod of his head.

"A lot has happened since then, Anna. We can talk all about it tonight."

The professor headed out, and Anna sat on the sofa, surrounded by her new dresses.

Mrs. McAfee would never believe all this, Anna thought. *I can barely believe it myself!*

Chapter 60

For love is of God.
1 John 4:7b

The train rolled into Lazy Spring, and Elisabeth watched from her window. She had missed the little town, and it was good to be back.

Luke and David were sharing a seat directly across the aisle from her, and they started grabbing their bags from underneath the seat in front of them.

"You're looking better now than when we left Burke Mountain, Elisabeth. That nap probably helped," David said.

He reached out a free hand toward her, and she allowed him to pull her to her feet.

"Leave your bags, I'll come back for them."

Elisabeth didn't argue. Between the food at Burke Mountain and the train ride, she was just ready to get off and find a room at the hotel so her stomach would have a chance to settle down.

Luke had already headed out ahead of them and was standing on the station platform talking to someone.

"I'll help you get settled, Elisabeth."

"No, I'm fine. If you can just help me get my bags to the hotel, I'll have someone take them to my room. I think I'll lay down for a while."

They stepped onto the platform where several people had gathered.

The doctor was concerned and pulled Elisabeth to the side. He searched her pale face.

"I'm going with you and stay until your color returns. You don't look well."

"No, David, I'm fine. I just need some rest."

He wasn't convinced.

"Really, I'm fine. I just need some time to rest, and to be honest, I need some time alone. You and Luke should head over to the clinic, don't you think?"

The doctor looked over just as Luke was bringing Elisabeth's bags from the train.

He hesitated.

"David, I'm fine. Really."

The three of them walked to the hotel and entered the lobby. The hotel clerk was glad to see Elisabeth. He nodded toward the men then greeted her.

"Welcome back, Mrs. Landry."

"Hello, Anthony. I'll need a room for at least a few days."

"No problem. I'll put you in the room you were in before."

Elisabeth turned.

"See, gentleman, I'm in good hands."

The clerk stood tall, assuring Luke and David that what she said was the absolute truth.

Uncle and nephew headed toward the clinic while the clerk grabbed Elisabeth's bags and started up the stairs. He turned at Elisabeth's voice.

"Anthony, where can I rent a buggy or a wagon?"

"You mean right now?"

"Yes."

"Well, my buggy is across the street at the blacksmith's shop. If you give me a few minutes, I'll drop your bags in your room then take you anywhere you want to go. I'm done here for the rest of the day."

He looked carefully at the young widow.

"Maybe you should step into the dining room and get a cup of hot tea first. You look tired."

"I am, but no, maybe later."

He nodded and started back up the stairs.

"And Anthony?"

He turned.

"Thank you."

"Of course, Mrs. Landry. I'll be right back."

Meanwhile, Luke and David dropped their bags on the clinic floor with a thud.

"It's good to be back, Luke. I've missed this place."

Luke walked over to the doctor's desk.

"Looks like you have plenty of paperwork sitting here waiting for you."

"I was afraid of that."

"So do you want to tell me what's going on?" Luke asked.

David sat at his desk and leaned back, looking up at Luke.

"What do you mean?"

"You know what I mean."

"No, I'm not sure I follow."

Luke grabbed a chair and turned it so he could sit with his arms up on its back. He looked at his uncle with anticipation.

"You mean Elisabeth?"

"Yes, Elisabeth."

David grinned.

"Is it that obvious?"

"It was obvious long before now. When did *she* figure it out?"

"That's obvious too?"

"Definitely."

David looked through the papers on his desk without really looking then sighed.

"I told myself to wait, to give her some time. But before I knew it, I was telling her I loved her."

Luke sat up straight and tall.

David threw up a hand.

"I know, I know. I see that look. It just…happened."

"What did she say?"

"She hasn't really said anything."

"What did you expect?"

David stood and started pacing the floor, pushing his fingers through his thick hair.

"I don't know. It was too soon, wasn't it?"

Luke relaxed and thought a minute.

"Too soon to declare your love, maybe. Too soon to show her how much you care? No."

David looked strained and unusually flustered.

"I don't think I've ever seen you like this."

"I've never felt this way. I'm not sure how to proceed from here."

"I think you should give her some time. Just see how things go."

Luke thought back to his conversation with Anna.

"Just take things day by day."

David looked Luke in the eye.

"You've changed, Luke."

"Well, you have to admit we have had more excitement in the last couple of months then we usually see in a year, a couple of years!"

"I think we all have changed, Uncle David."

"I think we have, Luke. And if you're going to help out around here again, I think it's time you called me David. You can skip the uncle part."

The doctor wrapped his arm around his nephew's neck and messed his hair.

"But don't let your dad know I said so."

"All right, David. It's a deal."

Chapter 61

Yea, I have loved thee with an everlasting love.
Jeremiah 31:3

*I*t was a beautiful afternoon with a slight breeze and no humidity.

The professor and Anna leaned up against a fence watching two lively horses play.

"Finley Valley is so beautiful, Professor. I especially love the horses."

"Where did you learn so much about horses, Anna?"

"When I was at the shelter, I used to sneak out to the stables and watch Mr. Foley take care of the horses."

"Mr. Foley worked at the Children's Shelter?"

Anna nodded.

"I haven't heard you talk about him before or about loving horses."

Anna shrugged.

"I guess I didn't think about it. I'm sure there are lots of things I don't know about *you*."

The professor laughed.

"You're right, Anna. I guess it would take a lifetime to learn everything about a person, especially me!"

"Did you ever get to ride any of the horses?"

"No, but Mr. Foley used to let me sit on them. He showed me how to brush their coat and mane and how to talk softly to them. Then he used to sit with me and tell me all about things going on outside the shelter, things I could dream about."

"He sounds like a very nice man."

"He was."

"What else did you do?"

"Well, he let me help him saddle the horses because he said it was something I would need to know how to do someday."

"And that's why you knew how to saddle the horse you took when you ran away."

"Saddling was easy, but the riding part wasn't as easy as I thought it would be. It was fun but scary."

"I used to love riding myself. I still do actually."

"Do you think we could go riding together?"

"Perhaps one day. Come on, Anna, let's walk."

"I was going to wait to talk to you while we ate, but I guess now is as good a time as any."

"You're leaving, aren't you?"

"Yes, I guess we both knew this time would come."

"Don't worry about me, Professor. I'm ready for change, and I'm ready for Finley Valley."

The professor wondered if Finley Valley was ready for her.

"Then let's explore, Anna. We have the rest of the day to discover the valley, so let's enjoy our last time together."

"But you'll be back to visit, right?"

"I'll do the best I can to make that happen."

Anna and the professor jumped into Brandon's buggy and headed toward town. The wind felt cool on their faces. Anna's hair flew all around her face, but she didn't mind.

Soon, they reached the bridge that arched over the river that would take them straight into town. The professor stopped the buggy before going over.

"Well, there's the town of Finley Valley, Anna. Looks different from the top of the mountain, doesn't it?"

"I haven't seen it from the top of the mountain."

"Oh, that's right, you haven't. It's a sight to behold, and I'm sure you will have plenty of opportunities to see it from that perspective. Ready to explore?"

"Yes! I'm more than ready."

The professor took Anna's hand and smiled. His white beard was neatly trimmed, but his hair was a little messy from the wind. He wore the same suit he had on when Anna first saw him on the train. He was deep in thought, and Anna noticed.

"What is it, Professor?"

"I was thinking about how much you've grown up, Anna. You're not the same girl I first met on the train."

Anna squeezed his hand.

"That girl was nervous and scared, unsure of herself."

"What do you see now?" she asked eagerly.

"I see a young woman who has faced tragedy and difficulties with grace."

"And a lot of tears!" she added.

"Yes, there have been a few tears for sure! But not as many as when I first met you."

"And I see a young woman with a promising future."

The professor teared up.

"Well, there I go with the tears. I think it's time to head over this bridge, don't you?"

"Yes," Anna said quietly.

Anna snuggled against the old man with her own eyes filling with tears. She wasn't as brave as he thought, but she was determined not to let it show.

Chapter 62

He will save.
Zephaniah 3:17

*A*nthony, the hotel clerk, walked with Elisabeth across the street to the blacksmith's shop.

She waited as he talked with the blacksmith about what repairs were done to his buggy. Her eye caught movement in the corner of the shop, and she strained to see what it could be. As her eyes adjusted, what she saw in the dark corner was a horse with large brown eyes and a golden coat that desperately needed a good brushing. The animal was looking right at her.

She glanced over at the two men before quietly walking over to the horse that greeted her with a wet nose.

"Well, hello there."

She stroked his rough coat.

"You're beautiful."

"He be for sale."

Elisabeth turned to see the blacksmith, a large muscular man, coming her way. Anthony was right behind him.

"He's so beautiful," she said.

"Belonged to old man Adkins."

The big man took off a glove and rubbed the horse's head.

"He passed 'bout a month ago. I sold off his other two horses, but this one here be left."

Elisabeth hesitated only a moment.

"How much?"

"Twenty-five dollar."

She thought carefully but swiftly.

"I'll give you thirty if I can board him here. I'll pay for his feed, and I'll care for him myself. And I'll need a saddle and bridle."

The man raised an eyebrow.

"I gots saddles. I gots bridles. Your choice of any over there. Five dollar."

"I'll give you that extra five dollars for the saddle and bridle if you include that blanket over there. And I want you to throw in a new set of shoes if I don't find them satisfactory."

The man just stood there a moment thinking.

"I see you have plenty of horse shoes hanging there, and I also know you probably do excellent work, so it shouldn't take you long or take away from your regular business," she was saying.

Elisabeth looked toward Anthony. He smiled at her expert bargaining skills and gave her a quick nod of his head.

She flashed a smile at the blacksmith.

"So do we have a deal?"

He held out a calloused hand.

"Deal, little lady. When do you be wantin' him?"

"Right now. I'll take him right now." She shook his hand with renewed energy. "I have something I need to do, so I'll get with you later on those shoes," she explained. "And I can bring your money tomorrow if that's fine with you?"

The man glanced toward Anthony.

"I'm sure she's good for it, Manny. Go ahead."

"All right, I'll saddle him up, and he be yours then. You can settle up with me later. Just bring him back another day if you decides you need them shoes."

Anthony waited until the man walked away then headed toward Elisabeth shaking his head.

"That was quite impressive, Mrs. Landry, but are you sure you're doing the right thing? A horse is a big responsibility, especially one as big as him!"

"Yes, I'm sure. I've missed having a horse of my own. And I know a good horse when I see it. He is worth twice what I'm paying."

"I have no doubt."

"And thank you, Anthony. It was kind of you to offer me a ride."

"No problem. If you need anything else, well, you know where to find me."

"Actually, maybe you *could* help me with something else."

"What is it?"

"I'm going to need my job back in the restaurant."

"I'm sure they'll be glad to have you back, but I'll go over right now and check for you."

"I'd appreciate it."

"Well, then I'll be on my way. I'll see you tomorrow."

"Goodbye, Anthony."

Elisabeth waited for her horse to be saddled then rode down the main street toward the old boarding house where she and all the other train passengers stayed during the illness.

It felt more than relaxing to be in the saddle of her own horse. He was strong and sure. Over time, she determined to have him looking healthy with a brilliant coat and mane. She was excited to have something to occupy her time, to not think of Andrew so much.

She pulled back on the reins and came to a quick stop. She pondered on the weathered building envisioning what it was probably like when it was a successful boarding house. But her thoughts soon drew her toward the weeks of sorrow and sadness she and the other train passengers suffered there.

Why did Andrew have to die? she wondered. Why was she spared? Why hadn't she just gone back home to family? And why didn't God spare both of them instead of leaving her all alone with a baby on the way?

She drew a deep breath.

She and Andrew had only been married a few months. They had just celebrated her eighteenth birthday before the wedding, and they were so happy. He was twenty. He saved all he could in order to afford a piece of land where they could start their new life. It was his dream. Now all that was gone—all at once, no Andrew, no hope for a future with him, no fulfilled dream. All she had left was their unborn child, and she felt badly that Andrew didn't know.

She grew frustrated and fought the terrible feeling of guilt.

She tugged at the front of her dress. She was starting to show, and she wouldn't be able to keep her pregnancy a secret much longer. People would talk about it and ask questions. She tried not to care.

She wasn't prepared for all the feelings coursing through her all of a sudden. David popped into her mind, and she tried to think of something else, anything else. But she couldn't. It felt good to hear words of love again. It felt good to be held. But it made her feel so guilty she tried to make sure she didn't encourage David. People would talk about that too.

Her breathing increased as her thoughts continued.

Elisabeth looked across the field where Andrew was laid to rest under the big oak tree, and she urged the horse that direction. She tied the golden horse to a low hanging branch and walked the few steps to where they buried her husband. The ground was still mostly bare, but grass was starting to form in spots. She bent and pulled the grass away. She tenderly touched the wooden marker with his name, Andrew Foster Landry.

She dropped to her knees.

"Oh, Andrew, what should I do? I thought you'd always be here to help me."

Elisabeth laid down next to his grave and wept. If anyone had been close by, they would have heard her heartbreaking sobs.

Chapter 63

He will rejoice over thee with joy.
Zephaniah 3:17

"I'm heading over to the hotel to check on Elisabeth."

David put the sign in the window that let the townspeople know he wasn't in the clinic.

"I can stay here in case someone else comes in," Luke offered. "If I need you, I'll send for you."

"No, I think we've done enough for today. Honestly, I never expected it to be so busy."

"Word's gotten around that you're back, it seems."

"It would seem so."

"Go get yourself some supper, Luke, and then get some rest. There will be plenty to do tomorrow."

"What about you?"

"I thought I'd see if Elisabeth would have supper with me. We could pick up some food at the hotel and perhaps walk down by the creek."

"Sounds like a good idea, but do you think she'll go?"

"I sure hope so. We don't have all the distractions here like we had at Finley Valley. Maybe I can fix what I've done—a fresh start."

"All right then, I'll catch you later?"

The doctor nodded.

David straightened the papers on his desk then sat in the chair instead of leaving. He ran his hand across the old wooden desk where he spent many hours, including times he fell asleep exhausted. It took a lot of hard work and emotion to be where he was. Even as a child, he always longed to be a doctor, and he was determined to fulfill that longing.

And now here he was, on his own. He hadn't given much thought of getting married or starting a family because he was so wrapped up in his work. He turned away the attention of women through the years. But Elisabeth was different.

He wasn't looking for it, it just happened that day at her husband's funeral. He never meant to express his feelings toward her the way he did. It too just happened.

He was glad to be back where he belonged. The people of Lazy Spring needed him. Maybe his work would help him not think so much of Elisabeth like when he was in Finley Valley where he had so much time on his hands.

David made sure everything was in good order then shut the door of his clinic behind him, leaving the door unlocked as usual. He hoped Elisabeth was feeling better and would give him a chance to start again.

All he could do was hope.

A strong breeze swept through the street kicking up dust. It looked like it could rain any second.

David barely reached the hotel before the first drops fell.

"Good evening, Dr. Monroe."

"Good evening. Do you know if Mrs. Elisabeth Landry is in her room?"

"I'm not sure, but you're welcome to knock on her door. It's room 6."

"Thank you."

David was heading up the stairs when he heard his name.

"Dr. Monroe!"

He turned and saw Anthony, the hotel clerk that was there earlier.

"I overheard you asking for Mrs. Landry. I just left her a little while ago. She was at the blacksmith's shop."

"Oh, thank you. I'll check there."

"What I'm trying to say is she's not there now. She left there and headed out of town toward the old boarding house."

"Walking?"

"No, she was riding a horse she purchased from the smithy."

David didn't wait for any more information; he headed through the steady rain toward the stables.

"Billy! Where are you, Billy?"

"Here, I'm here."

The young stable hand stuck his head out from one of the stalls.

"I need a horse, Billy."

"I don't have any available horses right now. But—"

"But what?"

"You can use *my* horse if you bring her back tonight."

David glanced around.

"Where is she?"

Billy pointed as he made his way toward the doctor.

"There. I can saddle her."

"No, I'll do it."

David saddled the horse and shot out of the stable toward the old boarding house. The rain was coming down in sheets and stung his back.

He knew exactly where Elisabeth would be, and that's where he found her.

"Elisabeth!"

Her horse pulled at his reins from the sudden appearance of the doctor. David jumped from his horse before he came to a complete stop.

"Oh, Elisabeth."

There Elisabeth was, lying on the ground, her rain-soaked clothing clinging to her.

David fell to his knees and pulled her into his arms. He gripped her tightly for a few moments.

"We have to get you inside where it's dry," he shouted over the roar of the heavy downpour.

He pushed her wet hair from her face, and she looked up at him. In one quick motion, he sat her on his horse then pulled himself up behind her.

"My horse."

"I'll get him later."

"But, David—"

"I'll get him later. I promise."

He drove the borrowed horse through the heavy rain then headed straight to the clinic where Luke met them at the door.

"I saw you ride up. What happened?" Luke asked as he stepped aside.

"She's soaked to the bone, Luke. We just need to get her out of these clothes and warmed up."

Luke hurriedly opened the door to one of the rooms used for overnight patients, then David laid her on the bed.

"Elisabeth, I want you out of those wet clothes before you get sick."

She nodded.

David reached down and grabbed his bag he hadn't unpacked from his stay in Finley Valley.

He found a gray flannel shirt and a light weight pair of pants.

"Put these on, and I'll get you some clothes from the hotel when the rain lightens up."

She started to protest.

"I'm in charge this time, Elisabeth, so just do what I say. You have ten minutes before I come back in with some hot coffee."

Elisabeth sat up as soon as he shut the door and began doing what he said.

"I need some coffee, Luke."

"What happened?" Luke asked, as he poured two cups of strong black coffee.

"I'll tell you later. Wait fifteen minutes, then take that hot coffee to her."

"Wait! Where are you going?"

"I'm off to fulfill a promise."

Chapter 64

He will joy over thee with singing.
Zephaniah 3:17

"Doc Stevens, come in!"

The older man greeted Melissa at her door. He looked tired, and his horse did too.

"No, I can't stay. Is Professor Higgins still in Finley Valley by any chance?"

"He's not here right now, but yes, he's still in the area."

"When do you expect him?"

"I don't really know, but he shouldn't be too much longer. He and Anna are spending the day in town. He wanted some time with her before he left."

"So he's leaving Finley Valley soon?"

"Yes, he hopes to leave any day, I believe. He's just wrapping up some loose ends."

The doctor slowly nodded and continued the conversation as if he was distracted.

"So how is the girl?"

Melissa paused while she observed the doctor's furrowed brow as well as his slight frown.

"Doctor, wouldn't you like to come inside? I have coffee."

The doctor paused this time.

"All right. One cup then."

Melissa held the screen door open for him.

"Where's Brandon and the children?"

"Oh, they're over at his parents. They're helping them pick out a puppy."

"A puppy? What do they need with a puppy?"

"It's a surprise for Anna from the professor."

Melissa pointed toward the parlor.

"Have a seat in there, Doc, it's much more comfortable, and I'll bring in the coffee."

"I hate to interrupt your quiet evening, Melissa."

"No, no, it's fine. I enjoy your visits. You know that. I miss helping you with patients, but you know since Megan was born—"

She didn't go on. She knew she didn't have to.

"I know, Melissa."

Melissa and Finley Valley's lone doctor shared a quick moment without saying anything. He knew when Megan was just months old she had difficulties. It was hard to find courage to tell Brandon and Melissa about his suspicions, but that was part of his job as their doctor *and* their friend.

Melissa reached out and squeezed his arm. "I'll get that coffee."

The doctor stepped into the parlor and set his focus on the framed photographs resting casually on the fireplace mantle before choosing a place to sit.

Melissa showed up just minutes later with coffee and biscuits.

"These are leftover from breakfast. Brandon made them actually."

"Are these your parents in this photo, Melissa?"

Melissa sat the tray down and glanced over to where he stood by the fireplace.

"Yes, and that's myself and my brothers in the photo next to them."

"I always supposed you were the oldest in the family," he said with a knowing grin.

"Yes, well, being the oldest and the only girl, I was a little bossy, I'm sure."

He laughed.

"It's a nice photo of Brandon and his family as well."

"Doctor—"

He turned at her voice.

"I'm sure you didn't stop in to talk about the photographs on my fireplace mantle."

The doctor hesitated then took a deep breath.

Melissa searched his face.

"Doc, what is it?"

She held his gaze. "Is it something about Megan?"

He shook his head.

"No, Megan's just fine. Let's have that coffee, and I'm going to share something with you that I'm going to ask you to keep confidential."

Melissa sat on the sofa and handed him his cup of coffee as he sat at the other end.

"The professor came to see me one day. Said he wanted to ask me a few questions concerning Anna."

"Like what kind of questions?"

"He wanted my opinion on whether he should leave her here in Finley Valley or take her with him when he left."

"I guess he was feeling guilty about leaving her, but he doesn't need to worry about that now. Surely, he can see she's loved by our whole family, and she's adjusting very well, I think."

Melissa offered him a biscuit, but he shook his head.

"Melissa, it's not Anna any of us should be concerned about."

There was a pause.

"It's the professor."

Chapter 65

That Christ may dwell in your hearts by faith.
Ephesians 3:17

"Where's the nicest place to eat in town?" the professor asked the handsome couple coming out of one of Finley Valley's many unique shops.

"Well, there's the hotel. They serve up a good meal," the man with the bowler hat said, glancing at his wife for her opinion. She lowered her fine blue and white lace parasol.

The woman had already been observing Anna and decided on a much better idea.

"Go to Emilie's," she said. "She has a place down by the stables."

She was pointing down the street.

Anna looked up at the professor with a big smile, and the woman nodded with satisfaction.

"She serves outdoors, and it's a very nice evening," the woman continued to say.

"Oh Professor, let's do that!"

Professor Higgins thanked them then pulled Anna's arm through his.

"Let's go find Emilie's!"

It wasn't a far walk, and along the way, they peeked in a few windows and talked about the many differences between Diamond and Finley Valley.

People on the street and on the sidewalk discreetly looked their way as Anna and the professor walked arm in arm. They were new to Finley Valley, so everyone was curious.

They stepped off the wooden sidewalk at the very end of the street, and to their right was an outdoor café abuzz with customers.

There were about a dozen tables with red-and-white-striped tablecloths. A colorful mix of fresh flowers graced each table.

They were searching for an open table when they spotted a woman coming their way. She didn't look to be much older than Elisabeth, the professor thought.

She was holding two steaming hot plates of food, and the smell was far more than inviting.

"I have one small table left over there if you want to head that way," she said as she pointed with her head. "I'll come over and get your order as soon as I deliver these."

Anna and the professor circled around all the customers and came to a small table that sat next to the holding pen for the stables. There weren't any horses out, so Anna was disappointed.

"This is very nice, Anna. I'm glad we asked."

"Oh, me too!"

She was looking out beyond the town at the mountains all around when the same woman that greeted them earlier came around.

She wasn't any taller than Anna, but her arms and legs looked strong like she was used to hard work. Her hair, some people would call black, was braided and fell past her waist. Her dark eyes, high cheek bones, and olive skin set off her unique beauty, and Anna couldn't stop staring.

"Hello," the woman said. "It's gotten busy tonight. I think it's because it's an unusually nice evening and the fact I'm serving fried chicken doesn't hurt."

"Fried chicken!" Anna exclaimed. "I love fried chicken."

"It comes with boiled potatoes and peas. There's cornbread and apple or peach pie for dessert. To drink, I have coffee or lemonade. Oh, I have cold water too if you'd prefer."

The professor didn't hesitate and ordered for them.

"Bring us two plates of everything, and I think we'll both have lemonade."

Anna was eagerly nodding her approval.

"We'll let you know about the pie after we eat," the professor said. "And I hope you brew up a good cup of coffee because I'll be needing that with my pie."

"The best coffee in town," the woman answered with confidence. "And I'm Emilie by the way." She shook the professor's hand and smiled toward Anna.

"Are you visiting folks here?" she asked.

"Yes, the Monroe family—"

But then someone called Emilie's name.

"I'm sorry. My little sister usually helps me, but she couldn't make it tonight. I'll be right back with your food."

Anna watched as the woman stepped from table to table, greeting everyone as she went.

The professor watched Anna closely.

"She's pretty, isn't she?" he asked.

"Yes, she is. I've never seen anyone with that color hair. It's beautiful!"

Again, the professor realized Anna had been very sheltered growing up.

"I want to see the world, Professor!" Anna said out of the blue. "I want to meet people and see what the rest of the world looks like."

"Well, maybe you can."

Anna fell back against her chair.

"I'm so happy, Professor Higgins. It just seems like a dream, and I'm afraid I'll wake up and none of it will be true!"

"Oh, it's true, Anna. Believe it."

Emilie returned with their food and told them to wave if they needed anything. She then rushed away to wait on others.

The professor reached across the table and took Anna's hand.

"Let's thank God for our food, Anna, and for all His blessings."

"May I pray this time, Professor?"

"Of course, you may. Go right ahead."

They bowed their heads.

"Dear God," Anna began, "thank you for bringing me here. I was afraid but now I know it was foolish not to trust You like the professor and Mrs. McAfee told me to. I haven't always listened, and I'm sorry. Please be with Elisabeth, Dr. Monroe, and Luke, especially Elisabeth because I know she misses Andrew so much. Please give her a healthy baby."

The professor squeezed her hand as she continued.

"Help Luke find his way, and help Dr. Monroe be a good doctor."

She paused and the professor looked up to find her struggling with tears.

"And, God, thank you for the professor. You brought him into my life just when I needed him. Help me to accept he has to leave, and keep him safe as he leaves to take care of things."

"Thank you for the Monroe family who wanted me to come. And I pray for my parents and any brothers or sisters I may have."

The professor was holding his tears the best he could.

"I understand if they had to give me up for a good reason, and even if it wasn't a good reason, I pray they are safe, and I forgive them."

The professor could barely keep from crying openly at that point.

"We thank you for this food sitting in front of us.

"Amen."

"That was very nice, Anna," he said softly.

"Thank you, Professor."

They were just starting to dig into their meal when a few horses were released into the holding pen.

"Well, Anna, that should make your evening. Look over there. Aren't they beautiful?"

"Yes, they truly are. I would love to have my own horse one day."

It wasn't long before they finished every single bite of their food, and Anna managed to coax one horse to come their way.

It was a perfect evening.

They shared a piece of peach pie, and the professor got his coffee. Anna sipped on her lemonade.

Emilie checked on them often, and most of the other customers had eaten and gone before they decided to leave.

"I suppose we better get home, Anna. We didn't really get to see much of Finley Valley, though."

"Oh, that's all right. I would rather just sit here and spend time with you before you leave. Are you leaving soon?"

The professor sighed.

"Yes, in a couple of days. I told you I'd stay until you were settled, and I think you are."

Anna nodded.

"You don't have to worry about me anymore, Professor."

"Well, keep up that journal. One day, you will be glad you have it."

"Do you keep a journal, Professor?"

"Indeed, I do, for many years now. And I'm glad I have them. Occasionally, I pick one up and read it. It brings back many memories, many things I've forgotten, many things I'd like to forget as well."

It was quiet between them. The night air was feeling cooler.

"I'm sorry I have to leave, Anna. I'm really sorry. And I have to confess that I haven't been completely honest about some things."

"What things?" she asked with a frown.

"Let's head home, and I'll explain the best I can."

Chapter 66

Many waters cannot quench love.
Song of Solomon 8:7

*D*avid stood in the pouring rain looking down at Andrew's grave and where Elizabeth laid not thirty minutes before. The ground was saturated, and his boots saved his feet from the standing water and mud.

He cleared his throat and spoke the words heavy on his heart.

"I love her, Andrew. She's amazing and you were blessed to have her. I wasn't looking for love, it just found me."

The sky opened even more, and as the heavy rains fell, a brilliant flash of lightning lit the night sky allowing the doctor to clearly see the grave marker for just a moment. He was soaked to the bone, but he barely noticed. Raw emotion coursed through him, but he was never given to tears, and this time wasn't any different. He just felt hurt deep within. But it didn't mean he didn't care or didn't experience a silent hurt. It was real, just not on the outside.

"I'm glad I knew you even if it was just a short time so I could understand the type of man Elisabeth would fall in love with and know the father of her baby. I have no idea why things turned out the way they did, but there's nothing any of us can do to change what happened. No one knows that better than myself."

"I did my best to save you, Andrew. You were brave to the end. I will make sure your son or daughter knows that if I'm allowed to be part of their life."

He just stood there. The rain roared all around him.

"I don't know a lot about raising children, but I'm willing to do my best if given the opportunity. I would love him or her as my own."

He took a deep breath, his eyes stinging from the rain dripping from his forehead.

"Well, I guess it's time to face Elisabeth and see where I stand."

The doctor bowed his head in respect.

"Rest in peace, Andrew."

David untied Elizabeth's horse and pulled himself into the saddle, leading the other horse he had borrowed behind him.

He patted the big horse.

"Let's go, boy. A promise is a promise. Let's get you back to your owner so she won't worry."

Both horses were uneasy with the weather, and it was difficult to manage one, let alone two. He just took it slow and easy.

As David rode into town, there wasn't anyone on the street or the sidewalks. Everyone else seemed to have sense to get out of the rain.

He turned toward the stables and hoped Billy was still there.

Billy was waiting, and it looked as if he had been asleep.

"Nasty weather out there, Doctor," Billy said with a yawn. "Thanks for returning my horse. I was beginning to wonder."

"I'm sorry, Billy, it couldn't be helped."

"Oh, that's all right. I decided to just bunk here for the night anyway. I'm not interested in getting soaked on the way home."

"That's a good idea because it's brutal out there. So, Billy, I have a big favor to ask."

"Sure thing, Dr. Monroe."

"Can you board this horse for the night? Rub him down and give him some feed? I can come back for him in the morning."

Billy walked over and ran his hand along the back of Elisabeth's newly purchased horse.

"Nice horse. Sure, I can do that."

"It was a struggle to bring him through all this weather, so he might be a bit skittish."

"Oh, I can handle this big guy. Don't you worry."

David handed Billy some money for his services, and Billy's eyes lit up.

"There's a little extra there. It's late and I can't stay to help you."

"Thank you, Dr. Monroe! I'll take good care of him."

"I'll come back in the morning and get him unless this rain continues."

"Leave him here as long as you need to. There are plenty of empty stalls."

David headed out in the pouring rain. Luke was still up, sitting at his desk when he came through the clinic door.

"Get me something to dry off with, Luke."

"I hope whatever you had to do was worth it," Luke said as he threw his uncle a towel.

"It was. I'll tell you about it later maybe."

David looked over at the closed door.

"She's asleep. I just checked on her."

"Good. She needs to rest. Besides, I would probably have some choice words if she was awake."

"Well, actually, she said when you came in to wake her if she fell asleep."

"She did?"

Luke nodded.

David thought for a moment.

"I'll just let her sleep."

"She was insistent."

The doctor hesitated.

"All right, I'll wake her."

"Well, I'm going to head upstairs and turn in. It's hard to believe we started this day in Finley Valley."

"I know, it seems days ago."

David knocked softly on Elisabeth's door. When he didn't hear anything, he knocked a little harder.

"Come in."

The room was dark, and he could see very little except for what the lamp in the other room allowed.

"Did you get my horse?" Elisabeth asked.

"Yes, he's at the stables. There's a boy there who will brush him down and feed him. I'll go back over there in the morning and get him for you. How do you plan to keep him?"

"The blacksmith is going to let me board him there."

He just stood in the doorway thinking the horse didn't really matter enough to be woken up for.

"I'm sorry, David."

"It's all right. I didn't mind going back for the horse."

"No, that's not what I mean. I'm just sorry—"

He cut her off.

"You don't need to be sorry about anything, Elisabeth. You're a grown woman, you can do what you want. I have no right to be so overprotective. I should be the one saying I'm sorry."

"Can you come in for a minute? I can come out there if you think that's better."

"I'll get the lamp, and I can sit in the chair next to your bed. You'll be more comfortable that way."

"All right."

David returned then waited for Elisabeth to speak first.

"I've been so selfish, David."

"How so?"

"I was worried about my own feelings more than yours. It was wrong of me."

"Elisabeth—"

She was shaking her head.

"No, let me finish. I've been rehearsing over and over what I wanted to say when you got back. And I guess I fell asleep."

He smiled.

"It's been a very long day," he said.

"When we got to the hotel earlier, I was going to rest, but I couldn't relax. I just needed to go out to Andrew's grave. Anthony offered to drive me out there in his buggy, which was at the blacksmith's, and that's where I saw the horse. David, I knew I had to have that horse. He was perfect for me."

"Perfect?"

"I know horses, David. He really is perfect for me. I didn't know it would start raining. I just knew I had to go to Andrew. It couldn't wait."

"You could have gotten sick, Elisabeth, and you still could. And you should've considered the health of your baby."

"I wasn't remembering the baby."

"Obviously not," David said, slightly shaking his head.

She paused.

"David, can we start over?"

"All right."

"I mean *all* the way over from when we were standing in Frank and Martha's kitchen."

"I'm really not sure where you're headed with this, Elisabeth."

"I was scared, David. Never in my wildest dreams did I expect to hear you say you loved me and that you have loved me since Andrew's funeral."

David shifted in the chair.

"I didn't mean to. I was going to wait. I should have waited."

"Maybe you should have."

David's face fell some.

"But you didn't and I've been thinking a lot about what to do and how I should respond."

David couldn't just sit there anymore.

Elisabeth, will you just give it a chance, give *us* a chance? I can wait until you're ready to consider it. And if you don't have any interest at all, I need you to be honest and tell me."

She searched his serious face. The glow of the lamp cast a shadow on his one side.

"It was hard going out to Andrew's grave," she said. "I don't think I've ever felt such strong feelings. It just doesn't seem real he's gone. It wasn't that long ago we talked of dreams and plans."

David's hands were sweaty.

"Elisabeth, what are you trying to say?"

"I'm saying I let him go, David. I was feeling so guilty thinking of love again so soon. But with God's help, I was able to really let him go. I can't live in the past, and I know that now."

She looked David in the eye.

"If you still want me, I'm ready."

David bowed his head and, without looking at her, asked, "Are you sure?"

"I'm sure. You're a wonderful man, David, and I care about you."

"And I care about you more than you know, Elisabeth, and that's why I want you to please follow this doctor's advice and get some rest. You must take care of yourself so you will have a healthy baby."

She laughed. She was shaking her head.

"Always the doctor! Is this what I have to look forward to?"

"Probably," David said with a grin.

The tenseness was lifting.

"I can't believe I'm going to have a baby. I'm even starting to show a little."

"Believe it, Elisabeth. You will be a wonderful mother. I'm sure of it."

David stood to his feet.

"Now get some sleep because starting tomorrow, this doctor is going to do some serious courting."

He bent and gave her a soft, gentle kiss then ran his hand down the side of her face.

Elisabeth smiled sweetly.

"I'd like that, Doctor."

Chapter 67

*See that ye love one another
with a pure heart fervently.
1 Peter 1:22*

$\mathcal{P}$rofessor Higgins pulled the buggy beneath a grove of trees.

"This looks like a nice place, Anna. Would you like to take a walk after that large meal?"

Anna was quiet.

"Are you sleepy?" he asked.

"A little," she admitted.

"Come on then. Let's walk some."

The old man helped Anna from the buggy, and they looked around to see which direction they wanted to go.

"Let's go down toward the river," Anna suggested.

"That's exactly what I was thinking."

They walked toward the sound of the water and discovered a small park hidden beyond the grove of trees.

"Look, Anna, Finley Valley has so many exciting places hidden here and there where you can explore. This looks like a nice place to go when you want to get away by yourself. This isn't far from Brandon and Melissa's house."

He glanced her way.

She wore a gentle smile on her face.

"What are thinking about?"

"I'm thinking about how free I feel."

"Your life is just beginning, Anna. The life you lived at the Children's Shelter is gone, and now you have so much ahead of you to be excited about. You *are* free. Most of your decisions are your own now."

"That's a little scary to think about."

"But that's what makes life fun and challenging, Anna!"

The professor grabbed Anna's hand and walked with her on a narrow path through the woods.

"I love the woods," he said.

"I love the open spaces more, where you can spread your arms and run and run and run."

"Ellen loved the woods too."

"Who's Ellen?"

"Oh, I don't suppose you do know who I'm talking about. Ellen was my wife."

"I overheard your conversation with Mr. Campbell about her and your little girl when we were at the boarding house in Lazy Spring."

"You heard that conversation?"

Professor Higgins stopped and looked at the fifteen-year-old.

Anna nodded.

"That must have been terrible for you, losing both your wife and baby at the same time."

He sighed.

"Want to sit? There's a nice log that should hold both of us."

Anna walked over first and sat, looking up at the professor.

"When I lost my wife and our baby girl, it was like having my arm amputated."

"What is amputated?"

"Cut off. It was like my arm had been cut off. I've just had to learn to live without her. It doesn't mean I've forgotten about her. I will never forget. And I can only imagine what my daughter would be like right now. I'd probably have grandchildren, Anna."

"You would be a wonderful grandfather, Professor Higgins. Mrs. Wilson thought you *were* my grandfather."

"She did?"

"I told her you weren't my grandfather but a really good friend."

He came and sat next to her.

"Tell you what. I'd love to be your grandfather if you would be my granddaughter. Neither of us have real ones. We could be honorary grandfather and granddaughter."

Anna looked puzzled.

He squeezed her hand. "I'm saying it would be an honor to be your grandfather. Will you have me?"

She hugged him with all her might. "Does this mean I can call you Grandpa?"

"Yes, it does, Anna. I would like that very much."

"I'm going to miss you when you leave," Anna said. "But I understand. Just like I had to come here, you have to go back home where you belong."

"Anna, do you remember when I boarded the train the day we met?"

"Of course, I do."

"I was visiting someone there in Logan's Gap. If you remember, I barely made the train."

"And I was disappointed when I saw you coming my way to sit next to me."

"It was the only seat left! I had no choice."

Anna chuckled.

"I'm glad you had to sit with me. I liked you right away."

"I liked you too, Anna. God put us together, I believe that with all my heart."

"Me too."

"Anna, I need to explain something, and I keep putting off telling you."

She watched his eyes.

"I wanted to tell you at the right time, and I think it's time."

She waited.

"The day we met, I was visiting a doctor friend I used to go to school with. I had been feeling run down for a long time, and my day-to-day routine was getting more difficult every day."

"Did he help you?"

"Yes, in one way. He helped me realize I wasn't going to get better. Was he able to help me feel better? Some, by giving me medicine to take."

"The bottles in your bag—I saw you drink from one when you thought I was asleep on the train."

"You're a sharp girl, Anna."

"What's wrong with you?"

"It's my heart. It doesn't want to beat the way it should. I guess you could say it's tired or just plain lazy."

"So the medicine will fix that?"

"No, Anna, it won't. It just helps me along some. What I need to tell you is I won't get better. It will only get worse."

She started breathing a little faster.

"I was taking the train in order to settle some things before my health got so bad that I wasn't able to. But what I didn't expect was to meet you and all the delightful people along the way. I once asked God to allow me to help others, and I thought He was giving me one last chance to do that."

She tried not to cry.

"But you know what I found, Anna? When I thought God was allowing me to help others, He was also allowing others to help me."

Her first tear fell.

"I believe God put us on that train together. You have helped me make this journey, Anna. I couldn't have made it without you."

She hugged him.

"Oh, Professor."

"Now I thought you were going to call me Grandpa."

He carefully pushed her away and wiped the tears from her cheeks.

"Oh, Grandpa, you can't leave. What if something happens to you and I never see you again?"

"It's in God's hands now, Anna. I don't worry about it. I just try to live each day the best I can."

"One day at a time, like Luke said."

"Yes, one day at a time."

Anna smiled through her tears.

"Don't stop trusting God, Anna. Remember, we are never alone no matter what we are going through. And both of us have gone through some hard times."

She nodded.

"Are you going to be all right?" he asked.

She nodded again.

"Well, let's go before they start wondering where we are. Besides, these mosquitoes are trying to eat me alive!"

They walked the short distance back to the small park and lingered there a few more minutes before heading back to the buggy. These were moments they didn't easily let go.

And the buggy ride home was a quiet one. Anna fell asleep on the professor's shoulder, and he hummed one of Anna's songs the whole way back to Melissa and Brandon's.

Chapter 68

For ye yourselves are taught of God to love one another.
1 Thessalonians 4:9

*A*nna lay awake that night.

The professor was leaving on the morning train, and that's all she could think about.

She cuddled her new puppy.

"Oh, Mac, I'm going to miss the professor so much! I can never thank him enough for giving you to me."

The little black puppy had a white tip on his tail and one white paw. He pulled at her blanket and started to growl.

"Shhh. You're going to get me in trouble for having you in the bed!"

She left the puppy in the tall bed she now called her own and opened the balcony door just off her bedroom. The air was cool, but it felt good on her face. The moon still hung high in the midnight sky.

"Let's go outside," she whispered to the puppy.

She tiptoed down the stairs and opened the front door as quietly as she could. She stepped out on the front porch and almost dropped the puppy when someone quietly called her name.

"I'm sorry, Anna, I was trying not to startle you."

It was Frank Monroe sitting in one of the rockers.

Anna set the puppy in the yard then came and sat in the rocker next to him.

"That's a first class puppy, Anna. It was kind of the professor to give you such a fine gift."

"The professor said he would keep me company so I wouldn't miss him so much."

"Well, this place has gone much too long without a dog. He'll add some life to this old place."

"Why did you want me, Mr. Monroe?" Anna suddenly asked, changing the subject.

Frank wasn't expecting the question, but he answered the best way he knew how.

"You mean why did we bring you here?"

"Yes, why me?"

"Well, we saw an advertisement tacked on the bulletin board in the post office explaining that temporary homes were needed for older boys and girls from the Children's Shelter in Logan's Gap. It was a way of giving them a fresh start it said. On the ride home, Martha asked me if I'd consider sending for one of the children. I knew she already had her heart set, so I told her I'd think about it."

"And?"

"The more we talked about it, the more I got used to the idea of helping a child in need."

"So why did you choose a girl?"

"I thought she would be good company for Martha and, honestly, for Melissa."

"You mean Megan?"

"No. Melissa. She has always missed her family. They moved away from Finley Valley not long after she and Brandon married. Her father wasn't in good health, so they moved to a larger town where he could get better medical treatment. Sadly, her father died soon after they moved. Melissa gets lonely, and she struggles with Megan."

"How come? Megan is so much fun."

"I don't know. She just hasn't ever fully accepted that Megan's, well, not like other children. She needs continual care."

"She can't help it."

Frank chuckled.

"No, she can't."

"At least Melissa *has* a little girl. The professor never had the chance to even know his. Melissa should be happy to have a daughter who loves her and make more time for her."

Anna lowered her voice then apologized for her tone.

"Maybe that's why you're here, Anna, to help Melissa see that very thing."

Anna rocked, thinking.

"Well, Anna, I'm going back to bed, and I think you should do the same. The morning will be here sooner than later."

"Mr. Monroe?"

"What is it, Anna?"

"Thank you for bringing me here, for wanting me."

"I can't imagine *not* having you here, Anna. It's like you've always been part of our family."

He said his good nights and left Anna by herself.

Anna sat there, watching the puppy romp in the light of the full moon.

"Part of our family." She was finally part of a family. It felt good to say it out loud, and it felt even better to live it instead of just dreaming about it all the time.

Anna was realizing she had spent far too much time being bitter because no one ever came back for her like they said they would.

Obviously, it wasn't going to happen now. She looked at the scar on her hand.

"I'm not going backward, only forward," she whispered.

She descended the few steps from the porch to the ground where the puppy laid in dirt, sound asleep. She scooped him up and kissed his head.

"I love you, Mac. My family just keeps getting bigger and bigger, it seems!"

Anna tiptoed up the stairs and back into bed with her dog she had named Mac after Mrs. McAfee.

She snuggled under the covers in her very own bed, in her very own room and sighed.

"I've had family all along, Mac, I just wasn't paying attention. God has been watching over me this whole time, just like Mrs. McAfee always told me."

And isn't that what the professor said on the train that very first day when I was scared and upset? she thought.

"Anna, God is looking out for you," he told her. "He watches over all of us."

She lingered on the memory of him sitting there on the train in his three-piece suit. His beard was a little long but neatly trimmed, always trimmed. And peppermint—she remembered he smelled of peppermint!

What else had he said? she thought hard to remember.

"Sometimes, God does things that don't make sense to us."

It was becoming clear to her now.

"I just needed to trust God." Mrs. McAfee had told her that over and over, but when the professor said it, it seemed like the first time she had ever heard it. Somehow, it just didn't sink in before then.

And what did Mrs. McAfee tell her so often: "God has something special planned for you out there, Anna. I just know He does!"

Anna talked to her sleeping puppy.

"It's hard to wait on God's plans for your life, Mac, but I'm finding out His ways are the best ways."

Anna laid there looking out the window at the big full moon, knowing sleep was far away. Her head almost hurt from all the things that were popping into her head, one right after another.

"So much at one time," she whispered. She suddenly jumped from her bed and looked through her things until she found her much neglected journal.

"I've got to write these things down before I forget," she was explaining to Mac who was now awake, watching her every move.

She found her colored pencils and spent the better part of the night writing down her thoughts.

Chapter 69

If we love one another, God dwelleth in us.
1 John 4:12

*L*uke adjusted his cowboy hat.

"So what do you think?" he asked his uncle.

"I think you need to take it back where you bought it. That's what I think."

"It was given to me."

"Well, that explains it then."

"Explains what?"

Right then, Elisabeth came through the clinic door with a large basket.

"Thanks for saving me!" David said as he rose to help her.

Luke just turned away.

"From what?"

She looked from David to Luke and back.

"Luke has a new hat."

Luke turned his head to give her a good look, but Elisabeth was slowly shaking her head.

"Sorry, Luke."

He sighed and rolled his eyes.

"Never mind you two. I'm going to go get some lunch."

"But there's plenty here," Elisabeth started explaining, feeling badly she said anything.

"No, when you're here, I'm invisible anyway."

The doctor and Elisabeth watched Luke head out the door and down the sidewalk.

"What's going on with him?" Elisabeth asked.

"He's just restless as usual, but lately, it's gotten worse."

"You think it has anything to do with you and me?"

"Probably."

Elisabeth lifted the basket to set it on his desk.

"Hey, let me help with that! That looks heavy."

She stepped away and let him help even though she had lugged the basket all the way from the hotel restaurant all by herself. There was no use arguing with her doctor.

"You look very nice today," David said.

He bent and gave her a quick kiss.

"Thank you. I just finished making this dress last night. I was needing more room."

"You sure have a talent for sewing."

"Just one of the many things we had to learn as children. My father wanted to make sure all his girls were ready for the world when they left home."

"So do you think you're ready?"

"For the world?"

"For me."

David pulled Elisabeth into his arms.

"Marry me."

"What?" She tried to push away, but he held her tightly.

"Marry me."

"When?"

"Right now."

"Before lunch?" she teased.

"All right, after lunch then."

"Dr. Monroe, you sure are persistent."

"I am when I know what I want. I wanted to be a doctor, and nothing stopped me until I got there."

He reached for her again, but she stepped just out of arms reach.

"I have to be back to the restaurant soon, David. We should eat."

"Why don't you quit that job? You're on your feet too much."

"And what would I do then? I need to support myself somehow."

"I could support both of us."

Elisabeth began unpacking food from the basket. It was obvious she wasn't going to carry on the conversation any further.

"You can't work at the restaurant when the baby comes."

"I know that."

She stopped and put down the loaf of bread in her hand. "Don't you think I know these things, David? I think about them all the time. The answer to your questions—I don't know. I'm just trusting God will supply what I need when that time comes."

"There's fresh roasted chicken," she said as she changed the subject. "And I brought a piece of that apple pie you like so much."

She felt David's eyes on her, but she didn't look up at him. She finished unloading the basket then walked over to get a chair.

"I'll get that, Elisabeth. You can sit in my chair."

"So what do you think Luke is going to end up doing?" she asked as she reached for a piece of chicken.

"I don't know, but I don't think doctoring is going to work out for him."

"Really? Why not?"

"For one thing, he doesn't have the patience. And he always wants to rush through things."

"Do you think he just wants to do it because he looks up to you?"

"You think he looks up to me?"

"Of course, he does. He would do anything for you."

"Maybe I should talk with him."

"No, let me do it. I think he needs a woman's point of view."

"Oh, really?"

"Stop. I mean it. Someone who isn't family."

"You mean isn't family *yet*."

Elisabeth couldn't help but smile.

"Finish your lunch, Doctor."

"Why are you rushing me?"

"Because I think I see a patient coming your way."

He turned just as a man burst through the door, carrying a little girl in his arms. A distraught woman was following close behind. Blood was coming from the girl's nose.

Elisabeth jumped to her feet as she watched David run to their side. After taking one look at the girl, David had the man lay her on the examining table. Stepping closer, she noticed the girl's face was badly bruised and her arm was hanging awkwardly. There was no question the arm was severely broken.

"What happened?" David calmly asked the man as he carefully felt for other injuries.

"She fell from a tree," the man said anxiously.

He could barely say the words.

The woman suddenly went pale and wobbled as if she was going to faint.

"Elisabeth," David began as he looked her way.

Elisabeth was upset with herself. She should have known to help without David asking!

"Can you get Mrs. Omer a glass of water please? Maybe you could take her into the other room?"

She didn't miss the message in his eyes.

The little girl was in bad shape.

"Of course. Please, Mrs. Omer, come with me."

The woman didn't refuse. She just obeyed.

Elisabeth looked back toward David and the father bending over the unconscious little girl who hadn't moved since they brought her in.

At that moment, she knew. All doubts had flown away. She loved David with all her heart.

Chapter 70

And his love is perfected in us.
1 John 4:12

𝒜 visit from Professor Higgins took Elisabeth by surprise.

"Professor! I didn't expect to see you here."

"I didn't intend to stop in Lazy Spring, but I had something on my mind."

He looked tired and was sweating so much she took him by the arm and led him to a chair at one of the tables in the hotel restaurant.

"Sit right here, and I'll get you something cold to drink."

He nodded.

She motioned to one of the other girls working there.

"Can you run and get Dr. Monroe? This man is ill."

Elisabeth ran for a glass of water then knelt in front of the professor.

"Drink this, Professor."

He just held the glass in his hand, so she helped him raise the glass so he could drink.

"Did you walk from the train station?"

He nodded.

It wasn't an overly warm day, she thought, but it was quite a walk for a man his age.

Just then, David came in with Luke right behind him.

He knelt next to Elisabeth.

Elisabeth could tell he was just as surprised to see the professor as she was.

"He's overheated, David," she explained.

The doctor removed the professor's coat and spoke to the old man with gentle care.

"Relax, Professor. Just rest here and catch your breath."

"Elisabeth, hold his hand and keep him as steady as you can." He asked the other girl working there to get another glass of water.

"Luke—"

"I'm here."

"We need to get him to the clinic. We can try to walk him over, but we might end up having to carry him."

"I'm here. I'm ready."

The professor drank a little water, then Elisabeth watched as Luke and David lifted him and started walking him toward the hotel entrance.

"I'm coming too, David," Elisabeth said.

"No, just stay here."

Elisabeth helplessly watched along with everyone else who had been close enough to know what was going on as they slowly walked the professor down the street to the clinic.

She silently prayed then reluctantly went back to her job.

What do you think is wrong with him?" Luke asked, as they entered the clinic.

The doctor didn't answer. He just nodded toward the examining table.

Together, they helped the professor lay down.

"Take his shirt off, Luke."

David ran to a cabinet nearby and grabbed a small brown bottle. He handed it to Luke.

"Get him to drink some of this. Just take it nice and slow."

David leaned over and listened to the professor's heart.

"What is it?"

"I think his heart is failing."

The professor was unresponsive.

"Professor!" David cried.

There was no response.

Luke held the opened bottle, never able to give the professor one drop.

"Is he...gone?"

"No. But he's barely breathing. Give me the bottle."

David slowly poured the liquid drop by drop into the professor's mouth while Luke watched closely.

"Run and get Elisabeth."

Luke ran as hard as he could and found Elisabeth waiting on customers.

She saw the look on Luke's face and immediately ran back with him to the clinic where he let her go through the door first.

She ran to the professor's side where David stood over him, watching for any improvement.

"Is he going to be all right, David?"

"I don't know. All we can do is watch and wait."

"What's wrong with him?"

"His heart is beating very slowly. His pulse is weak. I wanted you here just in case. He appeared to be failing."

Elisabeth placed her hand on David's shoulder.

The professor was taken to one of the adjoining patient rooms where the men changed him into something more comfortable then the three of them sat and waited.

Luke offered to sit with him while David walked Elisabeth back to the hotel.

"I want to stay, David."

"There's nothing you can do. You need rest."

"So do you."

"Luke and I will take turns. One of us will come for you if his condition worsens."

She didn't argue. She was understanding more and more the ways of the doctor and his medical experience that helped him make wise decisions. He was a gifted doctor. She just prayed that God would help David do whatever was needed to pull the professor through this crisis.

The professor woke during the night and asked for water.

Luke helped him take a few sips, but that's all the professor could manage.

He was trying to say something, but Luke had a hard time understanding him.

"Don't try to talk right now, Professor. Save your strength."

"No," he was saying. His eyes were pleading with Luke's.

"What is it? Do you need something?"

"I have…something…I must tell you. There's something…I need you…to…do."

"Anything, Professor. What is it?"

The professor slowly recited, word by word, the instructions he wanted Luke to follow.

His breathing was labored, and he was beginning to sweat profusely.

"Professor, please don't talk anymore. I understand. I promise I'll take care of it."

Chapter 71

I love them that love me.
Proverbs 8:17

The little girl who fell from the tree never regained consciousness and slipped away quietly during the night.

David did everything he could to help her, but he feared from the very beginning she had little hope of survival. She was never able to leave the clinic and was in one of the patient rooms where her parents never left her side and barely ate.

His heart was heavy as he stood to the side and watched her parents weep over her body. He was glad Elisabeth wasn't there to witness the scene and there was comfort in knowing the girl never showed any signs of discomfort.

He stepped out of the room quietly then walked over to the other room to check on Luke and Professor Higgins.

Luke looked up as he came in.

"The little girl didn't make it," David said.

Luke nodded. "I suspected."

"How's he doing?"

"About the same. Maybe a little more color now than last night."

"Let me see."

The doctor sat on the edge of the bed and pondered on the professor's peaceful face. His breathing was shallow but steady. He did look a little better.

Neither the doctor nor Luke had gotten any sleep during the night.

"I'm glad you're here, Luke. You've been a great help."

Luke didn't say anything but just gave his uncle a look of understanding instead.

The parents' sobs penetrated the wall.

"I think it would be a good idea to go for Elisabeth. Maybe she could be of some comfort to Mrs. Omer. I will sit with the professor until you get back."

Luke stood and stretched his long frame.

"I'll be right back."

The sun was just beginning to rise as Luke crossed the street toward the hotel. The air was cool, and it was just what he needed to clear his head.

The night clerk nodded as Luke came in. He nodded back.

He knocked quietly on Elisabeth's door.

She answered right away. She searched Luke's face.

"It's the little girl. She didn't make it."

"Oh, Luke, the poor little thing. Her parents—"

"David asked me to bring you over. Mrs. Omer is taking it pretty hard."

"Of course. I'll be right down. I'll hurry."

Luke sat in the hotel lobby and began thinking over all the things the professor told him just hours before. He was just nodding off when he felt Elisabeth's hand on his shoulder.

"You need some rest, Luke. You can go up to my room if you want."

"No, David will need both of us. We better get going."

They headed out into the cool air.

Elisabeth sat with Mrs. Omer, and David talked with Mr. Omer about arrangements for their little girl. He glanced over and observed Elisabeth's caring manner with the grieving mother. He was proud of this young widow who exhibited determination and strength and was passing on what little bit she could to Mrs. Omer. Elisabeth had experienced death, and he knew she would be a comfort to the mother. She knew the hurt firsthand.

He hoped he could do the same for the father who could barely speak as they talked of what needed to be done and done very soon.

They buried the little girl in the cemetery by the church that afternoon. The preacher read some comforting scriptures from his worn black Bible, and his wife sang a comforting hymn as many quietly wept over the fresh grave. Most of the town had come to pay their respects.

As soon as the service was over, four of the men started on a new grave. The professor had died shortly after noon.

Elisabeth wept in David's arms.

"I didn't get to tell him goodbye, David. I was so busy with Mrs. Omer."

"And that's exactly where the professor would have wanted you. Mrs. Omer needed you, Elisabeth."

She nodded against his chest.

Luke grabbed a shovel and went to help with the grave. He was stone-faced and barely spoke to either of them.

"He's taking it hard," David said.

"What about Anna?" Elisabeth asked. "She will be heartbroken. She loved him so much."

"We can leave tomorrow for Finley Valley. The train doesn't get here until tomorrow afternoon. It will give us a chance to get some sleep."

"Go get some sleep now, David. I'll wake you when you're needed."

"I'm needed now. I have arrangements to make."

"Of course, I wasn't thinking."

"Maybe Luke can help you."

"No, let him go."

"I'll come with you then."

"You sure?"

"I'm sure."

They stayed until most people had left the cemetery, making sure the Omer's were in good hands before heading back to the clinic.

Elisabeth walked through the clinic door. It was quiet. It was still.

The doctor drew the young widow into his arms.

"I'm very proud of you, Mrs. Landry."

She snuggled against him.

"Life is so fragile, Elisabeth. I want you with me for the rest of my life, and I want it sooner than later."

"I want that too, David."

He hugged her a little bit tighter then laid his head atop hers.

"Two lives have ended, but soon, there will be a new life just beginning," Elisabeth said.

She pulled away and smiled.

"I can't wait, Elisabeth. We can learn all about raising this baby together."

Together, they finalized the professor's arrangements, and soon, the townspeople gathered once more in the cemetery by the church.

David and Luke Monroe and Elisabeth Landry stood by the simple wooden casket as the preacher began. Many others who loved the professor didn't even know he was gone.

Elisabeth barely heard the preacher's comforting words because her mind was on Anna.

Luke stood there in a clean shirt he had borrowed from David. He too had trouble concentrating. He already had his bag packed to leave as soon as the service was over. He would fulfill Professor Higgins' wishes no matter how long it took.

Chapter 72

And those that seek me early shall find me.
Proverbs 8:17

$\mathcal{M}$rs. McAfee was praying. Something seemed terribly wrong. She stepped through her normal morning routine, distracted by a feeling deep within.

She packed her things for another day at the Children's Shelter and headed out into the crisp morning air. The sun would rise soon.

Her step was heavy, and she couldn't concentrate.

The older woman stopped and sat on the bench she passed every morning. Today, she couldn't just pass by, she needed to sit.

She lifted her face to pray as noisy birds in the trees above had just begun their morning tunes.

"Thank you for Your goodness and mercy, dear God. Thank you for hearing our prayers. I need direction right now because something seems amiss. Whatever it is, whoever it is, please help."

She didn't linger because she was needed at the shelter to start breakfast.

She left her burden with her heavenly Father and walked on.

Later that day, David and Elisabeth boarded the afternoon train heading for Finley Valley. Their stop at Burke Mountain was clouded this time. They walked around the trading station, not really looking at anything.

"Let's go get something to eat, David. I'm feeling a little sick to my stomach."

Elisabeth took two more steps, and that's all she remembered. She fell to the ground before David could catch her.

People stopped and watched, some offering assistance.

"I need water for her," David said calmly, as he cradled her head in one of his hands.

Someone swiftly ran.

He bathed Elisabeth's face until she looked into his eyes. She was startled to see so many faces looking at her and tried to sit up.

"Not yet, Elisabeth. Lay there a minute."

"I'm fine, David. I just need some food."

"When is the last time you ate?"

"Last night at supper."

David didn't reprimand this time. He just sat Elisabeth up very carefully then helped her to her feet.

He spotted an unoccupied bench and headed there.

"I'll go get you something to eat. You sit here."

"I'm fine now. I just got a little dizzy."

Her face was flushed, and today, she wore her hair down.

David pondered on her beauty.

"You're so beautiful, Elisabeth, inside and out."

"I'm sure I'm a mess right now." She reached up to push back a strand of hair when the doctor took her hand.

"Come with me."

"Where?"

"Don't ask questions, just come."

They passed through the crowd and all the trading stations until they reached a shaded area.

"Will you be all right if I leave you a minute?"

"Of course, I will."

He reached out and carefully drew her face into his warm hands.

"What is it?" she asked.

"I'm just so happy, Elisabeth. I've never been this happy. Sit over there. I'll be right back."

Elisabeth sat beneath the shade of a large poplar tree. The breeze teased her long brown hair.

The doctor soon returned out of breath.

Under his arm, he held a colorful blanket. And in his hands, he carried a small crate filled with food and drink. On his head was a light tan cowboy hat.

Elisabeth laughed. "That hat looks almost as bad as the one Luke had. It's a little small, don't you think?"

"That's because it's for you."

He placed it on her head.

"Every horsewoman needs a hat."

"Thank you, David. I love it."

"Come on, I want to show you something. Feeling up to it?"

He handed her a braided roll that was still warm from the oven.

She took the bread then followed him down a beaten path through a patch of woods, nibbling as she went.

"I tell you I'm hungry and you bring me into the wilderness?"

He glanced back at her. She looked adorable in her hat and the long flowing white dress that he loved on her.

"Shhh," he said. "Listen."

Elisabeth strained to hear.

"I don't hear anything."

"That's because you're talking too much."

She gave him a look, but he missed it. He pushed on, and she almost had to run to keep up with him.

Then she heard it.

He turned toward her and smiled.

"I hear it. What is it?"

"You'll see," he said with a grin.

They walked a little further, and soon, they stood before a beautiful waterfall cascading from a cliff of jagged rocks.

He watched her face.

"It's one of my favorite spots."

"Anna tried to describe the beauty of the mountains at Burke Mountain," Elisabeth said. "She showed me a picture she drew in her journal. I guess when I was here before I was too busy looking at what was going on instead of what was all around me."

He spread the blanket on the ground and began setting out food.

It was simple—only a couple of pieces of fried chicken and some rolls and a pear and an apple. There was a glass container of grape juice and a pair of tin cups that were dented from lots of use.

She sat down across from him. The air was refreshingly cool from the continuous flow of water as it splashed against the rocks.

They ate and talked about the professor and how it was hard to believe he was gone. They talked about the difficulty of knowing how to tell Anna and the rest of the family.

They also talked about themselves. For the first time, they set aside everything else and just enjoyed each other's company. There wasn't a care in the world right then.

"Walk with me," David said.

He stood and held out his hand.

He led her closer to the waterfall where the reflection of the sun made it sparkle like glass.

Elisabeth lifted her face to the light mist that enveloped them. It was a magical moment.

Then David knelt before her.

She gasped.

In his hand, he held a small, simple ring with a blue stone.

He took her hand and slid it on her finger.

"Elisabeth Marie Landry, will you marry me?"

She openly cried tears of joy!

"Yes, I will!"

He rose slowly then swept her into his arms. She tossed her cowboy hat to the ground.

"You are my life," David whispered. "You are every breath I take. And I want you by my side forever."

"I want that too, David. That day when you were working over the little girl that fell from the tree, I knew then how much I loved you. I love you because you love others so much."

He leaned down and kissed her with purpose.

They walked across the uneven rocks, David concerned with every step she took. The time passed quickly, and soon, they were gathering their things to head back to the train.

On the train, Elisabeth laid her head on David's shoulder and held out her hand to admire her ring again.

"I know it's not real fancy."

"No, I love it, David. It's perfect."

He squeezed her hand.

"I'm glad we have such good news to share with your family during this time. I'm sorry the professor won't be here with us, but we can reflect on his memory together."

They shared a few quiet moments together.

"I wish Luke was here," Elisabeth finally said.

"Me too. But I think it's good he left for a while."

Elisabeth sat up and searched David's face.

"Why?"

"He's restless, he's searching for something to fill a void in his life. I just hope he finds it this time."

Elisabeth looked out her train window, observing the majestic Blue Mountains.

She prayed for Luke to find the peace he needed and for his safety. Luke had no idea at that moment what Mrs. McAfee's and Elisabeth's prayers would mean to him as he pushed his horse harder than he should.

Chapter 73

Love one another; as I have loved you.
John 13:34

*A*nna didn't cry right away. She sat all alone in the little park where she and Professor Higgins lingered after their day away in Finley Valley.

Melissa was worried about her, and was pacing the kitchen floor.

"I don't think it was a good idea to let her ride away on that horse all alone," Melissa was saying.

"Relax, Melissa," Brandon said. "She'll be fine."

"But I don't think—"

"She'll be fine," Brandon repeated. "That horse is older than I am."

Melissa smiled at his logic then nodded her agreement.

"I suppose you're right."

"Of course, I am," he answered with a wink.

"Do you think she should be by herself right now, though?"

"Melissa, Anna needs to grieve her own way. I doubt she's had anyone close to her die before. Let's give her some time."

"I just know when Papa died it hurt so much. I cried for days, remember? I haven't seen Anna cry once."

Brandon reached over and pulled Melissa close. "And Anna is hurting too. She's just handling it differently than you did. It doesn't mean she hurts any less or isn't grieving. In a way, it's a brand new feeling for her and maybe she just doesn't know how to handle it yet."

"I know. I just feel so badly for her."

"Well, she has all of us now, doesn't she? A family to love her and care for her? You know she will be a great help to Mother and that will keep her busy. Plus, she has a basketful of memories to hold on to."

Melissa nodded.

"We will help her through this, and maybe you can help because you know what it's like to lose someone close to you."

Melissa was quiet. Brandon held her tightly for a couple of minutes, then together, they cleaned up from breakfast.

"I'll take the boys to do some chores," Brandon offered. "Want me to take Megan too?"

"Would you?"

"Sure. I'll go round them up. Why don't you go on over to Mother and Father's? Maybe Elisabeth will catch you up on all her news."

"Thank you, honey. I can't believe she and David are going to get married."

"I knew it all along."

Melissa threw a damp towel at her husband.

"You did not!"

"Yes, I did. I saw them hugging one day, and it was too long of a hug not to mean something."

"You never told me that."

"I didn't really think about it until now."

"Oh, you men! Really."

"You go on over and get all the details. I'll just work around here until you get back. And I'll help you with supper since everyone is coming here tonight."

Melissa hugged her husband who looked nothing like the other Monroe men. She loved that about him.

"I'll be back in a few hours then."

"Enjoy your ride over and take your time. It's a beautiful day. The leaves are starting to color."

Anna was noticing the leaves as well. Touches of fall promised cooler days ahead.

She slipped off her shoes and lifted the hem of her simple cotton dress as she stepped into the water at the river's edge. The coarse sand and small pebbles hurt her tender feet.

The water was so clear she could see everything under the water as far as she could see. Small fish began to nibble at her toes, and she giggled. As much as she enjoyed the water, it was just too cold to stay in any longer.

She looked down the path where she and the professor had taken their walk. She chose not to go that way but walked the short distance back to her horse instead.

Stuffing her shoes into the saddlebag, she easily pulled herself into the saddle. Going barefoot felt really good. She drew in a deep breath and looked around as far as she could see.

Her blond hair fell in one long loose braid, tied with one of the ribbons the professor had bought her at the general store in Diamond.

Finley Valley was so serene, so peaceful. The mountains were beautiful and reached right up into the sky through low hanging clouds.

"I'll miss you, Professor Applebee Q. Higgins the Third," she whispered. She held that moment and thought back on all their good times as well as the challenging ones. She had learned so much from him. He and Mrs. McAfee were the ones who always believed in her, always encouraged her. She missed them both.

And now she would take what they taught her and move forward. She looked at the scar on her hand.

Luke popped into her mind, and she wondered where he was and what he was doing. It was no surprise when they said he had taken off somewhere. She just hoped he returned soon. She prayed for him.

She wanted to give in to her urge to cry, but she didn't. The professor asked her not to cry for him but to just pray that he could accomplish the things he felt led to do before he got too sick to do them. Since he passed away only a short time later, she doubted he finished everything he hoped to. And she had no idea that Luke at that very moment was helping with that endeavor.

There would never be another person like the professor, she thought. She was happy God sent him to her. She had him all to herself for many days on the train, and if she had known he was as sick as he was, she would have paid closer attention to what he was saying. But she couldn't change that now.

"They will be memories I will cherish forever in my heart and in my journal," she told the horse, as she trotted away from the park.

She ached inside with each bounce in the saddle, but she held her tears.

"I can do this. I will be strong."

She headed back toward Melissa and Brandon's. There would be a lot to do before everyone came over for supper. It was a planned time to remember the good times with the professor and celebrate the anticipation of the wedding that was sure to take place soon!

Chapter 74

Love worketh no ill to his neighbour.
Romans 13:10

*L*uke rode into the quiet, rustic town called River Branch tired, hungry, and muddy.

He scanned the simply constructed buildings, hoping the office he was looking for was still open. The brilliant orange sun was just beginning to slip below the horizon.

He soon located the office where he wearily dismounted and tied his horse to the railing out front. Every muscle in his body ached. A lantern shone brightly in the office window, and he could make out the hazy outline of someone inside. He seemed to be in time.

He climbed the weathered steps that ran up the side of the building two at a time then knocked on the door. A crude wooden sign nailed to the door read, "James T. West, Attorney." A husky voice shouted for him to "come on in."

Luke opened the door and found an older gentleman sitting behind a large wooden desk. He didn't look Luke's way, he just waved for him to enter.

"Just shut the door behind you," he said calmly, still not looking up. All his attention was on a piece of paper he held.

Luke just stood and waited, looking around the room.

Papers were stacked in careless piles all over the man's desk, and a lit cigar sat on a dish that looked to have probably held his lunch earlier that day. Everything in the room was dusty, and the smell of his cigar made it hard to breath.

The man finally removed his glasses and looked up.

"Now how can I help you, young man?"

"I'm Luke Monroe, and I'm here to pick up something one of your clients left here for safekeeping."

The older man replaced his glasses and looked Luke over head to toe.

"Which client would that be?" the lawyer asked.

He leaned back in his chair and picked up the cigar without taking his eyes off the tall, dirty stranger standing in front of him. He rubbed the gray stubble on his chin.

"I just got into town," Luke started to explain. "I realize how I must look, but I was afraid you might close if I didn't come here first."

"Where are you from?"

"A small place called Finley Valley."

"I know of it. Go on."

"I'm here on behalf of Professor Applebee Higgins."

The man sat his cigar back on the dirty dish and sat forward. He lifted an eyebrow. He was smiling now.

"Well, why didn't you say so? How *is* the good professor?"

Luke hesitated a moment.

"I'm sorry to be the one to tell you, but he just passed away, yesterday, in fact."

The man's expression fell.

"Did you know him well?" Luke asked.

"We were in business together for a time. But that was a long time ago, son. And after Higgins' wife and baby died, well, he left and I never saw him again until recently when he surprised me by stopping in asking for my legal advice."

He just sat there in thought.

"Gone. He'll be missed for sure. What happened?"

"It appears his heart just gave out."

The older man slowly shook his head.

"He seemed in good enough health when he was here. I never would have suspected he would die soon after. He just came and asked if I would help him draw up some papers. Said he wanted to put his affairs in proper order and right some wrongs. Maybe I should have paid closer attention."

The lawyer turned his head toward the window, and Luke patiently waited while the man reminisced.

"You know, he even apologized for running out on me and leaving me to run the business alone. He asked my forgiveness."

The gray-haired man chuckled a little.

"You know, I can't remember anyone ever asking my forgiveness for anything. And in this business, plenty of people do me wrong. He tried to give me money, but I refused. If I had been in his shoes all those years ago, I might have done the same thing. Ellen was a fine woman, and Higgins adored her. To lose both his wife and baby, well, it would make any man crazy."

The older man shook his head and looked up at Luke.

"Anyway, I never figured he'd die so soon afterward."

"It surprised us all, sir."

"So how did *you* know Higgins?"

"Well, he was on a train that stopped in Lazy Spring where I was helping my uncle with his medical practice. A woman on the train had come down with an illness, and the whole train had to be quarantined, and all the passengers were moved to a place where we could treat them. The professor was among them."

"He told me about that. In fact, he had a woman with him that had recovered from that illness."

"That's right. That would be Elisabeth Landry."

The older man looked Luke over carefully then rose from his desk and shuffled over to an old dusty safe.

He turned the dial back and forth until it opened then reached in and grabbed a large, fat envelope.

"This is what you're looking for, I believe. Everything is in order just as he asked. The professor's instructions were very specific."

Luke accepted the envelope, shook the man's hand, and thanked him. He turned to leave.

"Good luck, young fella. Go on over to the hotel and get a warm bath and a hot meal. Tell them Jimmy sent you, and I'll settle up with them later."

"Much obliged." Luke tipped his hat. "That sounds real good right now."

Luke walked the short distance to the livery stable where he made the necessary arrangements to not only have his horse cared for but to be able to leave very early in the morning. The sooner he finished what he promised to do for the professor, the sooner he could get back to Finley Valley with his family.

He stuffed the envelope into his saddlebag, slung the bag over his shoulder, then headed toward the hotel.

The sun was gone now, and the street was dark.

"Stop right there, stranger."

Luke turned and saw a gun pointed at him. He couldn't see the man's face well at all.

"Put your hands up and hand me that bag nice and slow like."

"What's this about?" Luke asked calmly.

"Looking for a couple of men who robbed the bank in Tannersville."

"You have the wrong man."

"You fit the description of one of them. Where's your partner?"

"I'm telling you, you have the wrong man."

"You can explain all you want after we get to the jailhouse."

"What?"

Luke began to protest.

"Now hand me that bag, and don't give me any trouble."

Luke reluctantly handed the man his saddlebag.

"I'm in a hurry to get somewhere."

"Oh, I'm sure you are. Let's go."

Luke walked a few steps ahead of the man, wondering how the timing couldn't be any worse.

Chapter 75

The upright love thee.
Song of Solomon 1:4

*E*lisabeth was showing off her ring to everyone.

The supper Melissa and Anna prepared had already been eaten and cleared away, and dessert was on its way.

"Here we go, everyone!" Brandon exclaimed. "Anna made this herself."

He sat a large peach cobbler in the middle of the table while David started passing out little glass plates.

Anna blushed and accepted all the high praise from everyone while Megan clapped her hands loudly. Her younger brothers, sitting at the other end of the table, just yelled their excitement.

The evening soon ended with the children in bed and lots of hot coffee all around. It was Anna's very first cup of coffee, and Melissa made sure it had plenty of fresh milk as well as a large spoonful of sugar.

Anna sat back and watched the comradery as she sipped her hot beverage. No one treated her like a child, she was welcomed with the adults and all their talk that was thrown around. They were certainly a laughing bunch, and Anna loved watching the evening unfold right in front of her eyes.

Elisabeth caught her eye and winked. Anna felt sure Elisabeth knew exactly what she was experiencing.

The two young women caught up on the porch soon after.

"There you are," Elisabeth said as she pushed open the porch screen door.

Anna was sitting on the steps wishing she had brought her puppy. Elisabeth sat down next to her.

"Oh, it's chilly out here!" Elisabeth exclaimed, rubbing her arms with her warm hands.

"I like it," Anna said. "It was getting hot in there."

"Yeah, it was."

"I like the dress you have on tonight."

Elisabeth straightened out her legs across the steps.

"It's one of the dresses Mrs. Wilson gave me when we were in Diamond. But I won't be able to wear it much longer."

"Are you excited?" Anna asked turning her face toward Elisabeth.

"You mean about the baby?"

"The baby *and* the wedding."

"I am, Anna. I'm so happy right now. Plus, a little nervous to be honest."

"I'm excited too. That means you'll be around a lot if you're part of the Monroe family."

Elisabeth nodded.

"It does."

There was a brief pause.

"So everything all right with you?" Elisabeth asked, doing her best to catch a glimpse of Anna's face in the moonlight.

Anna sighed.

"Is it possible to be happy and sad all at the same time?"

Elisabeth chuckled.

"Well, yes, I've recently had that exact feeling, Anna."

"I really miss the professor." Anna said.

Elisabeth reached for Anna's hand as she spoke softly.

"I know you do, we all do."

They sat quietly looking out at the night sky until Anna broke the silence.

"It feels so good to be here. I hope I get to stay for a really long time."

"Do you think there will be a reason to leave?"

"I don't know. I can't stay forever. I was watching everyone tonight and thinking how good that would feel, but I also know I can't allow myself to get too excited. I'm not family."

Elisabeth was thinking about what Anna had just said. She was right.

"Well, enjoy every moment, Anna. There may be something different later, but I believe God has put you here for a reason. Put your whole heart into what that is."

"But how do I know what that is?"

Elisabeth put her arm around Anna. She had forgotten all about the chilly evening.

"Just wake up every morning asking God what He wants for you that day. Do you have a Bible?"

Anna shook her head. "I've never even seen one close up. Mrs. McAfee used to tell me things from the Bible, though."

"You can borrow mine. I will show you some verses to read. It will help you understand who God is and what He wants us to do."

"I'd like that."

"I'll get it out tonight, and we can read a little before we go to bed."

Just then, Elisabeth heard David calling her name.

"Well, sounds like we may be leaving now."

"You go ahead. I want to sit here a few more minutes."

Elisabeth gave her a quick hug and headed inside.

Anna looked up at the moon. There was a dull haze all around it, and the stars didn't seem to shine as brightly as usual, she thought.

She wondered where Luke was. She wished he could have been there with everyone else while they shared memories of the professor. She was a little miffed he would decide to leave at this time.

Then she heard someone calling her name, but she was reluctant to move from her comfortable spot.

She took one more real good look at that moon, and as she got up to go inside, she thanked God for helping her, and then she asked God to help Luke.

Chapter 76

Luke had no idea how many prayers had been said on his behalf. It would have been nice to have known at that moment.

The sheriff turned the key in the cell lock and told Luke to plan on sleeping there for the night.

Luke was hungry.

"I was on my way to the hotel," he explained. "Think I could get a bite to eat somehow? I've been on the trail a long time."

The sheriff hesitated a moment but then told his deputy to head over to the hotel and bring back enough food for all three of them.

Luke thanked the sheriff even though it was difficult. He sat on a narrow cot, trying to figure out how he could get out of the situation.

The sheriff opened Luke's bag and pulled out the fat envelope.

"This yours?" he asked, ignoring Luke's protests.

"Yes, in fact, I just got that from the town lawyer, James something."

"Jimmy?"

"Yes, he said his name was Jimmy!"

"I can check that out."

He opened the envelope and showed it to Luke.

"And all this money is yours?"

Luke couldn't believe his eyes.

"Looks like a lot of money to just be carelessly carrying around."

"You have to believe me that I didn't know that money was in there. You can see the envelope was sealed. Send your man out to find Jimmy."

"I might just do that myself. Right now, you rest easy."

The sheriff slid his hat on his head and checked his sidearm. He paused and looked at Luke.

"You better be telling me the truth, boy. I'm not in the mood to be wasting my time."

"Just find the lawyer."

The sheriff left without another word.

Luke was alone and frustrated. He lay back on the cot and woke up when the deputy brought in the food.

"Where you coming from?" the deputy asked, as he bit into a cold chicken leg.

"Lazy Spring."

"That so? So you came through Tannersville?"

"No, I didn't. I didn't even come close to there."

"You're awful dirty, like you've been riding hard."

Luke held his tongue for a moment then calmly answered.

"I'm trying to get some things done in a short amount of time, and I wanted to get here before the lawyer's office closed. I already explained that to the sheriff."

"Riding alone?"

Luke swallowed hard.

"Yes, all alone. Do you mind if I finish my supper?"

"No, go right ahead. Take your time, you aren't going anywhere."

Luke ate the small amount of food given to him and lay back down. He hoped the sheriff was talking with the lawyer right then so he could just get his horse and leave the little town that needed a good painting and more than one or two repairs.

The sheriff finally came back, and Luke jumped up, grabbing an iron bar with each hand.

"Jimmy wasn't in his office. You'll have to wait 'til morning when he gets back in."

"Surely, you know where he lives. Can't you go there and talk to him?"

"Look, fella, it's getting late. All of us will get a good night's sleep, then we'll talk about all this in the morning when things settle down."

Luke had no choice but to sit back down. This was one crummy little town he would be glad to ride away from and never return.

He lay down with his face against the wall, but sleep eluded him as he listened to the deputy's annoying snores.

Chapter 77

*In every thing give thanks: for this is the
will of God in Christ Jesus concerning you.
1 Thessalonians 5:18*

"Good morning, Jimmy."

"Sheriff, what brings you here so early this morning?"

The lawyer was on the floor rifling through a stack of papers.

"I have a man in my jail cell who says he knows you. Tall, lanky fella."

The lawyer laughed as he started digging in a different pile.

"Well, I know plenty of shady characters that would fit that description. Does he have a name?"

"Monroe."

"Monroe. Let me think."

He slowly rose to his feet then sat in his chair with a huff.

"Says he stopped in here to see you yesterday."

"Yes, yes. I was forgetting that name. Seemed like a nice young man to me. What did he do?"

"The bank in Tannersville was robbed yesterday afternoon, and he fits the description of one of the men. I found an envelope full of money in his saddlebag."

Suddenly, the lawyer grabbed his hat and cigar.

"I'll walk over with you so we can get this business straightened out."

"You saying you'll defend him if necessary?"

"No, I'm saying he's not your man."

"How do you know that? He could have robbed that bank and still got here last night. He said he rode hard to get here."

"I know bank robbers, and he's not one. And he would've had to ride a lightning bolt to get here from Tannersville by the time he stopped in to see me. It wasn't even dark yet."

The lawyer lumbered down the steps toward the street, and the sheriff had no choice but to follow.

The air was crisp, and the town seemed to be waking up slowly.

Luke jumped to his feet as soon as he saw the lawyer come through the door. His clothes were caked with dried mud, and his face was still streaked with dirt from the trail.

"Am I ever glad to see you!"

"I'm sure."

"Explain to the sheriff that I'm not their man, that you gave me that envelope full of money."

"I've done that. But just tell us where you were yesterday afternoon before riding into our town."

"I was on the trail. I never came close to Tannersville. I came straight here from Lazy Spring."

"That's quite some distance, but I believe you. Now you'll have to convince the sheriff."

All eyes were on the sheriff. He looked toward his deputy who was waiting to see what he would do.

"Sorry, son, but I can't let you go until I investigate this further."

Luke threw his hands into the air.

"This is ridiculous!"

The lawyer asked to talk to Luke alone.

The sheriff motioned to his deputy.

"Come on, we can get some breakfast and come back."

Luke started to say something as soon as the door shut, but the older man held up a hand.

"There's no use arguing right now. The sheriff is just doing his job."

"I can't believe this. Of all things to happen right now."

"If need be, I'll represent you. But hopefully, it won't come to that."

Luke ran his fingers through his dirty hair.

"Can you get my saddlebag so I can at least see what's in the envelope? That might help me understand more of what the professor was expecting of me."

"You know I can't do that, son."

Luke shook his head and sighed loudly.

"I give up."

Chapter 78

Watch and pray.
Matthew 26:41

A telegram was delivered to the Monroe home very early one morning.

Frank Monroe read it first.

"Who's it from, Frank?" Martha asked, as she brushed through her thick graying hair.

Frank looked toward this wife with concern written on his face.

"It's from a man named West. Says he's a lawyer."

"What's he want?"

Martha turned on the cloth covered stool that faced her dressing table. A handsome oval mirror hung directly above.

Frank walked to the closest bedroom window and looked out toward Finley Valley's rugged mountains, which seemed very far away at that moment.

"He wants us to know that Luke is in jail."

Martha dropped her brush, her hand flew to her mouth.

"In jail? Luke? Oh, Frank, what else does it say?"

"He's asking us to verify that Luke is our son."

"Of course, he's our son!"

Frank abruptly turned from the window.

"Well, they don't know that, Martha."

Martha jumped to her feet.

"I know, I know. I'll go with you to the telegraph office so we can send a quick reply."

"No, I'll go. It will be much faster if I go on horseback. You stay here, and I'll be back as soon as I can."

Martha walked with Frank to the barn and waved as he left the yard. She then went and sat in one of the rockers on the porch. Her heart was pounding; her head was too.

She turned as the screen door opened.

Anna stepped out, and Martha held out a hand toward her.

"Did you hear?"

"Yes."

"Oh, Anna, I can't imagine Luke doing anything bad enough to be in jail!"

Anna set her puppy down and watched him as he mastered the steps a little better this time.

"At least we know he's fine and where he is."

She wasn't about to show Martha how worried she was.

"You're right, Anna. No sense worrying about it until we have more information."

Anna nodded and kept her thoughts to herself.

Together, they tried to be patient as they awaited Frank's return.

Luke, on the other hand, wasn't being patient at all. He convinced the sheriff to let the deputy escort him to the hotel where he could get a bath and change clothes. The sheriff kept the large envelope in his top desk drawer.

One day passed on the heels of another, and Luke felt like an animal trapped in a cage. At least the lawyer came by every day and brought a decent lunch. Then one day, he explained that there would be a hearing soon to determine where and how they should proceed. The sheriff wasn't going to budge, and the lawyer explained that having someone in jail he *thought* could have robbed the bank made the sheriff look better than no leads at all.

"Don't worry, Luke. A hearing is not a trial. I've done plenty of these."

Luke knew he couldn't do anything but trust this man who told him stories of the days when he and Professor Higgins were in business together. There wasn't anything else he could do—nothing.

Luke lost a little weight, and the stubble on his face looked more and more like a beard. No one was willing to give him a razor or afford him the luxury of a trip to the barbershop. Frankly, he was miserable, and there wasn't much the lawyer could do to cheer him up.

The night before the hearing, Luke sat on his cot, hugging his legs. He rested his head on his knees. He wished he was home. At least he was given permission to wire his parents and David so they would know what was going on. He instructed them not to come unless he told them to. The lawyer said it might complicate things. He knew his mother would worry and Anna too for that matter. There wasn't anything he could do but wait it out.

He stood on his cot so he could look out the barred window above him. Wooden slates had been nailed across the bars to help keep out the cold, but he could peek through one little spot and see the moon and the stars.

He began to pray from deep within his heart. He spoke out loud but quietly.

"God, I haven't paid much attention to You over the years, but I need You now. Anna says to trust You, but I didn't want to admit that I wasn't sure I even knew how. I'm not sure You even care to listen. But if You *do* care to listen, I'm ready to make some changes. So will You please help me?"

Anna was still awake the same night, looking at the same moon. She just happened to be praying for Luke.

"Luke needs you, Father. I don't know what You are doing in his life, but help him learn what he needs to from this. Dr. Monroe and Elisabeth's wedding is soon, and we want him here. Please bring him home."

Anna snuggled up against Mac. He was sound asleep and snoring like dogs sometimes do.

"I can't believe how much you've grown, Mac."

The puppy stretched and looked up as if he understood.

"Go back to sleep, puppy. At least you can sleep without worries."

Anna slid out of bed and opened her balcony door. She shivered in the cold, night air. The moon was bright in the clear night sky, and the stars seemed to sparkle more brightly than other nights.

Suddenly, she began to weep. It just came out of nowhere.

"I'm sorry, Professor, I just can't hold it in anymore. I miss you so much, and it's hard to believe you aren't going to one day step off the train and surprise me. Now Luke is in trouble, and I'm not sure when he will ever come back home."

She cried until she couldn't cry anymore then slipped back into bed where she fell into a fitful sleep.

Luke finally slept as well and just as fitfully.

Chapter 79

The secret of the LORD
is with them that fear him.
Psalm 25:14

"*I*'m almost done."

Elisabeth stood as still as she could while Martha marked the hem of her wedding dress. Her wedding day was swiftly approaching.

"There, all done!"

Martha helped Elisabeth step down from the stool.

"It's prettier than I ever imagined," Elisabeth said. "How did you get it done so quickly?"

"Well, I admit I was up late several nights, but I couldn't have done it without Anna. She has jumped in and done anything I ask, and you know me, I'm not afraid to ask!"

Elisabeth just smiled.

"How *are* things going with Anna?"

"Better than I ever expected. I had my reservations bringing her here, but now I don't know what I'd do without her!"

"I'm glad it's working out well. She's such a sweet girl. I liked her immediately when we first met in Lazy Spring. She was a great help there too, helping with the children and even helping David at times when he was so exhausted from treating patients. Everyone at the boarding house loved her caring ways. I've always thought it was amazing how well she turned out despite her upbringing."

Elisabeth hesitated only a moment before changing the subject.

"Any word from Luke?"

Martha shook her head and sat on a long sofa.

"It's still hard to believe he's in jail."

Martha looked across the room but wasn't focused on any one thing.

"What's wrong?" Elisabeth asked, as she sat down next to her future sister-in-law.

"Don't say anything to anyone just yet, but Frank is going to leave early in the morning. He says he can't sit back and not do anything. He's determined he can convince the sheriff that Luke is innocent."

"But the lawyer said to wait. That it might hurt the situation."

"I know, but he's a Monroe, and more than that, he's a father."

"Maybe Brandon should go with him. That's a long ride."

"That's what I said, but no, he wants to go alone."

"If David was here, he'd go."

"I know, dear. We just have to let him do it his way. We can't stop him, Elisabeth. And frankly, I wouldn't want to."

Elisabeth squeezed Martha's hand.

"Well, enough of that!" Martha exclaimed. "We have a wedding to plan! I'm glad you're here so we can plan the wedding together. I was hoping you'd come here to get married."

"David and I talked about it, and we both agreed we'd rather get married here instead of all of you having to travel to us. But it wasn't easy for David to let me come ahead and leave him in Lazy Spring."

Martha began helping Elisabeth out of her dress.

"It will be good for him to be without you a little while before the wedding."

"I know you're right, but I miss him terribly."

"As the way it should be, dear. Let's go grab a cup of tea before Melissa and the children show up. It will be the quietest moments we have all day, I imagine."

"Where's Anna?" Elisabeth asked.

"I'm not sure. Lately, she's been out riding more and more. She seems preoccupied."

"By what, do you think?"

"Well, certainly, she misses the professor."

"But it's something else, you think?"

"Honestly, I think she's pining for Luke."

Elisabeth stopped what she was doing and turned.

"You really think so?"

"I do. Ever notice how she lights up when he's around?"

Elisabeth thought a moment.

"Now that I think about it, maybe you're right. But she's young. What girl wouldn't notice Luke? He's as handsome as they come! She's never been around men like she has now. And she's growing up. Certainly, she's going to have feelings for boys like other girls her age."

"But Luke's not a boy, Elisabeth."

"And Anna isn't far from womanhood," Elisabeth added.

Martha pondered on that.

"I just hope she doesn't get hurt," Martha said.

"Me too, but that's also part of growing up sometimes. It's another situation she can learn from. She's a big girl. She'll survive."

"I know you're right. I worry too much about such things," Martha said with a sigh.

Elisabeth laid her wedding dress out on Anna's bed, smoothing out all the wrinkles.

"This is a beautiful dress, Martha."

"You could have done as well, Elisabeth."

"I'd be too nervous to stitch a straight line! And besides, it wouldn't be as special."

"Well, as you know, I don't have a daughter, so this has been a treat for me. Thank you for giving me this opportunity."

"I wouldn't have it any other way, Martha. I'm so happy knowing I'll soon be part of the family."

"I know you must be missing your own family."

Elisabeth nodded.

"I do."

"But what is it? You don't seem so sure."

"Oh, I love my family. I love them dearly, but now that I've come west, I don't have any desire to go back home. When Andrew died, I thought I should go back, but something kept me here."

"David maybe?"

"Maybe. Or God's leading. I can't imagine leaving now because of David. I do love him, Martha. With all my heart, I love him."

"And he loves you, dear. No one would ever doubt your love for each other."

Elisabeth blushed.

"If you don't mind my asking, does your family know about David? And the wedding?"

Elisabeth sighed.

"I wrote my parents a letter about Andrew's death and my decision to stay here, and it was days before I found the courage to mail it. But sending a telegram just seemed too impersonal."

"Did they write back?"

"Yes, they did."

"And?"

"They were heartbroken, of course, and while father understood my decision to stay here, mother wasn't as pleased. She worries."

Martha was nodding, smiling.

"She's a mother. We do that. Wait until you have your little one, you will understand then. But I know that must be hard, knowing she worries."

"It is but I know I have made the right decision and they are supporting me."

"And the baby?"

"I told them. They are very excited, and Mother insists on coming when he or she arrives."

"That will be nice since I'm assuming they won't be here for the wedding."

"I wired them about the wedding, but I'm sure it's the last thing they expected."

"You haven't heard back?"

"No, everything happened so fast, and I'm not in Lazy Spring to get a message if they did reply."

"Well, I think it's a wise choice, and they will too. If not now, later when they meet David. They will love him."

"I know you're right."

The two women hugged tightly. Then Elisabeth changed into a simple, blue cotton dress and pinned her hair up out of the way.

"I'm ready for that tea, I think," Elisabeth said.

"Oh yes! I completely forgot! Let's hurry."

But before they hit the bottom step, they heard Melissa's buggy pulling into the yard.

Elisabeth turned and laughed toward Martha who was a couple of steps behind her.

"Well, there goes our quiet," Martha said, shaking her head. "I'm just glad we were able to have what time we did this morning. I doubt we'll have another moment like it the rest of the day!"

"I'm sure you're right about that!"

Chapter 80

Let us therefore come boldly unto the throne
of grace, that we may obtain mercy,
and find grace to help in time of need.
Hebrews 4:16

"The hearing has been postponed."

"What! Why? What's the hold up this time? I think the sheriff is purposely trying to detain me."

"Keep your voice down, Luke. You aren't helping matters at all."

"If I ever get out of here—"

Luke looked over at the sheriff leaning back in his chair with his feet on his desk. His face was buried in a newspaper.

Jimmy West was a shrewd lawyer, but the sheriff had him stumped this time. He was being unreasonably stubborn, he thought. And he couldn't figure out why.

"I'm not sure what the answer is right now, Luke, but they can't hold you forever without some type of legal proceeding. It's the law."

"From what I see, I don't think they follow the law around here."

"I'm going to make some inquiries, and I'll be back as soon as I know anything that will help you."

"I might rot by then."

The lawyer stood as close to the bars as he could and looked up into Luke's blue gray eyes, lowering his voice to a gruff whisper.

"I like to think I'm a patient man, Luke, but I'm tempted to walk away from all this mess unless you show me you have a fight somewhere deep inside of you."

The men held their gaze a few moments, then the lawyer grabbed his hat and cigar and left through the door without another word to anyone.

Luke didn't move, he just stood there thinking. The sheriff and the deputy looked his way then laughed among themselves.

"I need a miracle, God," Luke whispered. "And I need one right now."

The day was long and lonely. The sun was going down, and the jail cell was cold. Luke lay on his cot with his face against the wall. Both the sheriff and the deputy had gone to get their supper.

Luke didn't bother to turn over when he heard the door.

"Son?"

Luke turned.

His father stood before him looking very dirty and very tired.

Luke had a hard time saying even one word. He flew to the bars that held him captive, and father and son tightly gripped each other.

"I should have come sooner," Frank said. "I'm sorry, son."

He tried not to stare at Luke's unkempt hair and the long stubble on his face. His heart sank over the dark circles under his eyes. Anger rose within him, and anyone who knew Frank Monroe well rarely saw him reach that point.

This was one of those times.

Neither of them had a chance to say anything before the door opened again.

"Turn around nice and slow, Mister," a voice said.

Frank turned and faced the sheriff and the gun he held in his hand.

"So, you the partner we've been looking for? You aren't exactly what I was expecting."

"As you see, Sheriff, I'm not carrying a gun."

Frank held his arms away from his sides.

The sheriff never lowered his gun.

"I'm Luke's father, Frank Monroe."

Even the sheriff could see the resemblance.

"You're wasting your time coming here. He's not going anywhere until he can prove his innocence. And how do I know you're who you say you are?"

"I suppose you're just going to have to trust me."

Frank stood his ground.

The sheriff took a few moments to look over the tall, dirty man in front of him then lowered his gun about the same time the deputy came through the door with Luke's supper.

"What's going on?" the deputy asked.

"This man says he's Monroe's father."

"You believe him?"

"I think I do."

"Well, that's the first bit of sense I've heard come from your mouth," Luke spouted.

Frank didn't stop his son from speaking his mind, his eyes never left the sheriff's, and the sheriff finally looked away.

"Give him his supper!" the sheriff barked.

The deputy just stood there with a questioning look.

"I said, give him his supper!"

Frank stood aside as the deputy passed the food through the bars. Frank then walked over to the sheriff where he sat at his desk.

"I'm going to the hotel to clean up," Frank told the man.

He paused, leaning in toward the sheriff.

"Then I'm coming back with enough water and soap to help my son wash off all the grime and filth from this place."

The sheriff held the father's gaze but didn't argue with the man who stood in front of him with fire in his eyes.

Chapter 81

*Thou therefore, my son, be strong in
the grace that is in Christ Jesus.
2 Timothy 2:1*

$\mathcal{T}$he wedding date would have to be moved forward.

David had gone with his older brother, Frank, to help free Luke.

Frank walked over to the hotel where David was waiting for him.

David stood to his feet when his brother came through the hotel doors while the desk clerk watched the two men with a nervous eye.

"How did that go?" David asked. "Did you see Luke?"

Frank shook his head in frustration.

"He's there all right. The poor boy looks half starved and needs a bath and a haircut. It was all I could do to hold my composure."

"What do we do now?"

"First thing we need to do is get some food in us and get a room or we won't be any good to anyone."

Frank approached the desk clerk.

"We don't want any trouble," the clerk said.

Frank noticed his hands were slightly trembling.

"All we want is a room and a bath. We're not here to cause any trouble."

Frank laid money on the counter.

"Think you can arrange that?"

The clerk looked at the generous amount of money then pulled a key from a hook.

"I'll send a boy up with a tub and some hot water directly."

Frank laid a few more coins on the counter.

"I'm going to need more hot water hauled to the sheriff's office when we're done. I trust you can do that as well?"

The man nodded.

"Yes, sir."

The Monroe men wearily climbed the stairs to their room.

"Thanks for getting the horses settled," Frank said. "I'm beat. That hot water will feel good."

"Thanks for asking me to come with you. This isn't something you should do alone, Frank."

Frank chuckled.

"I have a confession. It wasn't exactly my idea to ask you to come with me."

David turned the key.

"Who did then? Martha?"

"No, it was Elisabeth's idea. And I found out she's a hard one to say no to."

David stepped into the room and threw his bag on the bed closest to him.

"Yep, that's Elisabeth. And it's that spunk I fell in love with."

"Well, for a girl to postpone her wedding day to help someone else says a lot about her."

David landed on the bed next to his bag.

"And here I was this entire trip wondering how I was going to explain having to postpone our wedding."

He looked up at the ceiling and recited an imaginary telegram.

"Dear Elisabeth, I regret to inform you, but I can't make our wedding after all. With all my deepest affections, your husband to be."

Frank laughed just as a knock sounded at the door.

"That was fast. I wasn't expecting the boy to bring that water so soon."

He opened the door to a short, stocky man gripping a cigar.

"James T. West," the man said. "May I have a moment of your time?"

"Of course, Mr. West, come on in."

David sat up and surveyed the country lawyer.

"Call me Jimmy, everyone else does."

The men took turns shaking hands.

The lawyer spotted the only chair in the room and pointed with a stubby finger.

"Do you mind?"

"No, please sit. Do you have information that might help us free my son?"

"I wish I could say yes to that question, Mr. Monroe, but no. I just left Luke, and he said you were here, so I just wanted to come over and introduce myself."

"Well, I'm Frank Monroe, and this is my brother David. I'm well aware you advised us not to come, but I couldn't stand by and not help my son, Mr. West."

The lawyer nodded with his unlit cigar held firmly between his teeth. He dug into his pocket and pulled out a folded piece of paper and held it out toward Frank.

Frank walked over and took it.

"What's this?"

"Read it. It's something I was going to show Luke, but I think it's better you see it first."

Frank unfolded the paper and read it over.

"I'm not sure I understand. Who is this from?"

The lawyer appeared to ignore his question and instead turned the conversation a new direction.

"When Higgins," the lawyer began to say, "when Professor Higgins and I—"

"Wait, you're saying you knew the professor?" Frank asked.

"I did. Luke told me of his passing when he came to see me. I was deeply saddened to hear the news."

"I'm sorry, I'm confused as to where all this is leading."

Frank looked toward his brother. David shrugged.

"Well, hear me out. Luke came to me wanting some paperwork that Higgins left with me for safekeeping. Apparently, before Higgins passed, he asked Luke to finish up some of his affairs."

"So that's why Luke left in such a hurry after the funeral," David said. "It would have been nice if he had told someone where he was going. I'm going to wring his neck."

"I don't know about any of that, but as a friend of the professor, I was thinking of trying to help Luke out with his promise to the professor when I came across that bit of information in your hand."

"All right, we're listening."

"I think we can pull together and honor the professor's wishes at the same time we work to free Luke."

Frank looked over the paper again and handed it back to the lawyer.

The lawyer stuffed it in his pocket and stood to his feet.

"I have some ideas, and now that you're here, maybe you can help me."

Chapter 82

Beareth all things, believeth all things,
hopeth all things, endureth all things.
1 Corinthians 13:7

The Monroe women sat out on Melissa and Brandon's sunporch. Anna and Elisabeth were a pleasant addition to what was usually only two.

"It was nice of Brandon to take the children for a while," Martha said.

"Well, you raised him well," Melissa said to her mother-in-law. "He's always eager to help."

"He was like that as a child. Always there to help. Now on the other hand, Luke was never around because he was always off somewhere getting into something."

They all laughed at her description of her sons. They knew she was doing her best to be cheerful despite the fact that Luke was in jail and Frank and David were gone to try and help him.

Melissa stood and starting clearing the table, telling everyone just to sit.

"Does anyone want anything else? There's more cake."

Elisabeth looked around the table at the others.

"I'll take another piece. I'm eating for two you know."

"If you aren't careful, that wedding dress isn't going to fit," Martha teased.

The room grew quiet for a moment.

"I can't believe how big I'm getting so quickly," Elisabeth said good-naturedly. "Hardly anything I have fits anymore."

"I'll split a piece with you," Anna chimed in. "Chocolate is my favorite."

"I'll bring the cake out, and we can all have a sliver. How's that sound?" Melissa asked. "I think we're all ready for more."

Everyone wholeheartedly agreed to that brilliant idea.

"Anna, would you mind helping me?" Melissa asked.

Anna followed Melissa out to the kitchen that was rather small for their family.

"Are you feeling all right, Anna? You're awfully quiet."

"I'm just tired, I think. Elisabeth and I have been staying up late talking and reading. It's been so much fun having her here."

"What ya reading?" Melissa asked, as she looked around for the knife she used earlier.

"Her Bible. I'm learning so much, and I can't believe I never knew about those things."

Melissa handed Anna some clean plates.

"What things?"

"Like all the stories. I never knew that the rainbow was a promise from God after He flooded the whole world. It was a promise He would never flood the entire world like that again. I'll never look at another rainbow the same way now. Oh, and the man that was swallowed by the big fish. I've never heard of such a thing!"

Melissa thought right then how much she cared for the fifteen-year-old.

"That was Jonah. I used to hear those stories when I was a child at church."

"Why don't you go to church now?" Anna asked.

Melissa put the cake back on the table.

"You know, Anna, I guess we never really think about it. We have gone here and there for picnics and special meetings but not on a regular basis. I guess we're just too busy to be honest."

"Megan and the boys would like it. Maybe I could take them in the buggy with me if you and Brandon can't go."

"Hold on there. I don't think that's a good idea. You and all the children? I'm sorry, Anna, that just wouldn't be a good idea."

"Then maybe you and Brandon could come too."

Anna searched Melissa's face with anticipation. She held her breath.

Melissa picked the cake back up.

"I'll ask Brandon. How about that?"

Anna smiled her answer, then the two headed back to the sun-porch where all the talk was about the upcoming wedding.

Chapter 83

Charity suffereth long, and is kind.
1 Corinthians 13:4

*M*rs. McAfee started a fire in the cookstove. The warmth soon found every corner in the kitchen, and the older woman hummed a lively tune.

She was mixing a large batch of pancakes when she noticed an envelope sticking out from between a couple of crocks on the cluttered work table.

She pulled it out and looked it over.

It was addressed to Mrs. Eleanor McAfee c/o of Logan's Gap Children's Shelter, and it was dated almost two weeks earlier.

She wiped her hands down her apron and forgot about the pancake batter. She held the envelope close to the lamp she had lit earlier.

The return address said it was from Professor AQ Higgins.

How had she missed it sitting there?

She hurriedly pulled a chair next to the stove where it was nice and warm. But for some reason, she had a hard time wanting to open it just yet.

It must be about Anna, she thought. *Why else would this professor be writing me again?* She dreaded its contents. *Was she sick? Had there been an accident?*

She remembered the feeling she had walking to work that one morning, a feeling to pray fervently for someone. Her breathing increased, and her palms grew sweaty.

She finally opened it with trembling hands.

It was a lengthy letter, and she had just started reading it when her helper came to assist her with serving the children.

So she had no choice but to slip it into her apron pocket and get back to the pancakes. The letter was like a hot coal burning in her pocket. She could hardly stay focused on what she was doing, but she managed.

She couldn't wait to get the children served then slip away where she could read it with no interruptions.

And back in River Branch, Luke was still waiting for a positive outcome to his situation.

He was clean-shaven, and David was almost finished cutting his hair. The deputy stood over them like he was afraid they would all of a sudden try to make a getaway. His hand never left the gun in his holster.

"You're breathing down my neck, deputy," David said, as he looked the deputy's way. "Relax. We aren't getting all cleaned up so we can go rob your bank."

Frank cringed and tried to make eye contact with his younger brother, but David wasn't looking his way.

"Your time is almost up," the deputy said forcefully. "It's time to close everything up for the night."

David stood to his feet and brushed the hair from Luke's shoulders.

"We'll be back as soon as we can, Luke."

"Who's going to clean up all that hair on the floor and dump that dirty water?" the deputy asked as he walked out of the crowded cell, pointing to the floor around Luke's feet.

"I'll send someone back over from the hotel to take care of it," Frank explained.

"You—"

The deputy pointed toward David.

"You go get someone now. The sheriff would be upset if he knew you were still here."

"You're in charge now, aren't you, deputy?" Luke taunted as he walked toward the open cell door.

The deputy pulled his gun. "You get back in that cell!" he exclaimed. He pointed his gun toward Luke then waved his gun toward David then Frank.

Frank raised his hands a little.

"Relax there, young man. We're leaving. Don't get excited."

David held his tongue and left Luke in the jail cell, pulling the door behind him until it clicked shut.

"Better not push our luck, or we'll be sharing that cell with you," he whispered toward Luke. "We'll talk in the morning."

The brothers left the deputy *and* the mess from Luke's bath and haircut. When they reached the hotel, they looked back and saw the deputy pulling the tub of water out of the sheriff's office and into the street. They both had a good laugh.

"Let's get some sleep," Frank said. "I don't think we'll get much from here on out."

"You're right about that," David replied.

Eleanor McAfee was too wound up to think of sleeping. She had slipped away right after lunch and read the professor's letter, and that's all she had on her mind the rest of the day. Now that she was home, she planned on fixing a hot cup of tea and reading the letter again so she could slowly absorb everything the professor was saying. But first, she knelt by her chair and thanked God for His care and provision. But most of all, she asked for wisdom to make the right decisions.

Chapter 84

I can do all things through Christ which strengtheneth me.
Philippians 4:13

$\mathcal{F}$rank and David settled in for the night. Their beds were lumpy and scratchy, but they didn't care. They were weary from travel and from dealing with the situation that kept Luke behind bars.

The lawyer knocked on their hotel room door before the sun came up. And he knocked a second time before Frank had a chance to answer.

"Good morning, gentlemen."

Jimmy West walked straight to the only chair and sat down. He took his time lighting his cigar while David sat up in bed rubbing his eyes. Frank sat on the end of his bed facing the lawyer.

"I hope you slept well, gentleman. I have horses waiting at the livery all saddled and ready."

"Do we get to eat first?" David asked, as his feet hit the cold wood floor.

"Food is ready and waiting in the hotel dining room."

The stocky man stood.

"Get dressed and I'll wait for you there."

And with that, he closed the door behind him with a bang.

David and Frank just looked at each other. And Frank spoke before David had a chance to get a word out of his mouth.

"Just do as the man says, David."

"I guess we don't have a choice, do we?"

"No, we don't, so let's get dressed and head downstairs."

The three men ate and worked out a detailed plan. The lawyer was just finishing up and pushed away from the table.

"I'll head up to Tannersville, and you know what you need to do, right, Mr. Monroe?"

"You can call me David, and yes, I think I have it."

The lawyer looked toward Frank.

"Tell Luke we're on it and not to worry. You keep your eyes and ears out for anything that might help us here."

Frank headed to the livery with them and waved goodbye as they rode off in different directions.

This wasn't going to be easy, Frank thought. But they each had a job to do, and hopefully, their efforts would pay off and pay off sooner than later.

Frank walked over to the sheriff's office and was glad Luke was there alone. The hair from Luke's haircut had been neatly swept away.

"Son?"

Luke rolled over.

"Good morning. I brought you some food."

Luke sat up and stretched.

"I'm surprised I slept so well," Luke said. "I think it's because you're here and I feel like something is finally getting done. And the blanket you brought didn't hurt any."

"I'm glad we came. I'm just sorry we didn't come sooner. Let's just hope all goes as planned."

Frank handed the food through the bars.

"This is a lot of food," Luke said.

"I was thinking we better fatten you up some because we don't want your mother seeing you like you are now."

"How *is* Mother?"

"She's worried, but that's to be expected. Everyone is concerned."

"And Anna?"

"She hasn't said much, but I know she's worried about you too."

"I was thinking more about how she reacted when she was told about the professor."

Frank nodded.

"She took it better than any of us ever imagined. She's been very strong."

"That's good. I'm sorry I wasn't there when the family found out, but the professor was so insistent that I carry out his plans immediately."

"Why didn't you tell David or even Elisabeth why you were leaving? It would have made things a lot simpler."

"I don't know," Luke was saying, shaking his head a bit. "I guess I just wasn't thinking."

Luke's father smiled, knowing the nature of his younger son.

"Well, all that is behind us. Now we need to concentrate on getting you out of here. Mr. West and David have left already, and I'm going to see what I can do to persuade the sheriff to improve your conditions until we hear back from Mr. West."

Chapter 85

Mercy and truth are met together.
Psalm 85:10

Elisabeth savored her last bite of cake and pushed her empty plate away. She had even wiped her plate clean of all lingering crumbs.

"Good thing we've postponed the wedding," she said. "I'm going to need time to work off some of this weight. I've done nothing but eat since I've been here!"

Everyone laughed as she pushed back in her chair and groaned.

Melissa told everyone to just leave their plates and suggested they all retreat to the parlor where it was more comfortable. Martha and Elisabeth followed Melissa toward the parlor, but Anna headed upstairs to check on Megan who was taking her afternoon nap.

"Anyone interested in coffee?" Melissa asked.

"I think that's a great idea," Martha suggested. "Otherwise, we may all need a nap."

"Coffee it is then. I'll be right back."

"Melissa sure has made this house cozy and inviting," Elisabeth said, as her eyes searched out every corner of Melissa's parlor. "I hope I can do as well."

"I remember when Brandon and Melissa wanted to buy this old house," Martha said. It was run down and needed a lot of work. I honestly thought it was a poor idea, but Melissa has rolled up her sleeves, and she and Brandon have achieved the impossible."

Elisabeth scanned the room. It wasn't a large room, but Melissa had been wise to place the long sofa against the wall so there would be plenty of floor space. A braided rug took up much of the wooden floor, and many a cool night the boys laid on the rug in front of the warm fireplace while Brandon read a book to the family. Melissa and Megan often preferred the oversized rocking chairs that sat between the tall windows that let in plenty of light during the day and allowed the moon to peek in during the night. A simple but very functioning table sat in front of the sofa.

Martha had skillfully sewn all the curtains in the house as a wedding gift while Frank worked many long nights in the barn carving the handsome wood mantle that hung above the fireplace. Melissa proudly displayed family photos and precious keepsakes there.

It was the place where family and friends shared many good times together. And it was a perfect retreat for Melissa and Brandon after the children were tucked in bed.

Martha and Elisabeth relished the calmness of the moment, each with their own thoughts for a few minutes until Martha broke the silence.

"Have you and David settled on where you will live after the wedding?" Martha asked.

"I was wondering the same thing," Melissa said, as she returned with a tray of filled coffee cups.

"Well, with the wedding on hold for the moment, I was tossing around a new idea. I just hope David will agree."

Elisabeth took the cup of coffee Melissa handed to her.

"Agree to what?" Melissa asked.

Elisabeth stood to her feet and walked over to one of the windows, carefully taking a sip of her steaming coffee.

Melissa and Martha glanced toward each other, each taking a cup of hot coffee from the tray.

Elisabeth finally turned and explained.

"Andrew always dreamed of moving west when he was old enough to be on his own. It was all he talked about. So when we talked of marriage, he made sure I could support him on that dream."

"And did you?" Melissa asked.

"Not at first. I was very close to my family, and I wasn't sure I could leave them. I wasn't very supportive in the beginning to be perfectly honest."

"What changed your mind?"

Elisabeth chose one of the rocking chairs and sat down.

"Andrew's excitement, his passion, and the way his eyes lit up when he talked of our future and the opportunities that only the west could offer. He wanted his children to grow up loving what he loved and to love and serve God with all their hearts. I wasn't about to take that dream away from him."

Melissa and Martha got comfortable on each end of the sofa and let Elisabeth talk. Anna quietly slipped in and sat in the other rocking chair, nodding to Melissa that all was fine with Megan.

"Andrew worked very hard and saved all the money he could to make his dream happen. When he felt he had enough, he asked me to marry him, and we made quick plans. We had grown up together, and everyone expected us to marry."

All eyes and ears were attentive to Elisabeth's story.

"Of course, it wasn't possible to fulfill that dream since Andrew died."

All heads turned when Anna suddenly spoke up.

"What happened to the money?"

"I have it. I wasn't going to spend it on myself since it was Andrew's money he worked so hard for in order to fulfill a specific purpose. So I have prayed that God would show me what to do with it. I even thought of giving it away, but I didn't know to whom or for what."

"And you've got an idea now?" Martha asked.

"I do. Since David went with Frank, I've had time to think about a lot of things. I'm actually glad we had to delay."

Elisabeth gave Martha an understanding smile. They both had to wait on someone they loved to return.

"I want to buy the old boarding house in Lazy Spring so David can have a place to set up a real hospital and medical clinic in order to serve the people better. The place he's renting now is small and ill-equipped. And if he had a place of his own, he could do whatever he wanted to with it."

"Where would you live?" Anna asked.

"I thought we could fix up a couple of rooms for ourselves, a bedroom and a sitting area, a comfortable room like this one, only smaller. Then over time, maybe we could build a house of our own nearby."

"I think it's a great idea," Melissa said. "Brandon and I could help. We all could!"

Elisabeth was getting excited about the idea now that she had some positive feedback.

"I agree. It would be a very worthwhile project," Martha chimed in. "It would be a very unselfish way to spend the money."

Everyone was talking at once, all except Anna.

"What do you think?" Elisabeth asked Anna.

"I think it's a good idea, but wouldn't you feel strange?"

"I think I understand what you mean, Anna, but I've really thought a lot about it, and I know I could get past my feelings. And if done properly, it could be a way to honor Andrew and the rest who died of the illness. Would it bring back some less than desirable memories? Yes, it would. But in time, a better medical facility that could help or even save others would help all of us get past the hurt and bad memories, don't you think?"

Anna sat thinking.

"It would be a way of taking something bad and turning it into something good," Elisabeth added.

Anna nodded.

"I guess so," was Anna's reply.

"Well, it's just a thought anyway. I have no idea what David will think."

"In the meantime, we'll just have to pray that David and Frank will be home soon, bringing Luke with them so we can all be back together again."

"And with that said, we need to finalize some wedding plans," Martha added, setting her empty cup back on the tray.

They all agreed and once again talked of dresses, flowers, and food.

Chapter 86

Righteousness and peace have kissed each other.
Psalm 85:10

*E*leanor McAfee was dressed in her finest Sunday outfit. She had an appointment in the nearby town of Weaver's Corner, and she wanted to look her absolute best.

She stepped carefully from the carriage with the assistance of the driver, and when she offered a coin for the ride, the driver politely refused.

"You keep it, ma'am," the driver said. "I was coming this way anyway."

"I appreciate your kindness," she said.

The man just tipped his hat and wished her a good day.

Mrs. McAfee was nervous yet excited. She opened her bag to make sure she hadn't forgotten to bring the professor's letter with her. But it was there, exactly where she had placed it.

She wasn't paying attention to the sound of carriages and horses all around her. Even the cries of the children playing in the street didn't grab her attention. Her full attention was on the building in front of her.

She looked up at the four-story brick building that loomed before her with its magnificent arched windows and fancy scalloped trim that ran along the top of the building and the covered sidewalk. There were no buildings in Logan's Gap that compared. Everything was so neat and tidy, she thought, from the sparkling window panes to the polished brass door knobs on the painted entry doors. Two large wreathes made from a mixture of beautiful white flowers hung on each of the two dark mahogany doors.

She took a deep breath and climbed the wide steps that led to the neatly swept wooden sidewalk. Most people appeared to be patient as they wove around her while she collected her thoughts.

She couldn't recall the last time she took a day away to do something of a personal nature. She wondered how they were managing in the kitchen without her, but she knew the staff at the Children's Shelter was efficient. She felt she didn't need to worry because they had managed just fine when she was sick and had to miss work the day Anna left for Finley Valley. She felt good knowing they could manage without her because that way she didn't have to feel so guilty for taking a couple of days off.

She felt out of place as a few passersby glanced her way. But she straightened her hat and took another deep breath as she entered through the heavy doors.

The foyer was quietly abuzz. People stood in small groups here and there, speaking in hushed tones. Those who passed by her seemed busy and made their way around everyone without a word. The oak floor was polished until it shone, reflecting blurry images of everyone in the foyer.

No one seemed to notice her except the man at the marble topped counter. She couldn't take her eyes off the winding staircase that curved up and out of sight until she heard his voice.

"May I help you with something, ma'am?"

She walked over and stood before the smiling man dressed in a dark suit and collarless white shirt.

"Oh, well, I'm here to see Mr. Connor."

She squeezed the handle of her bag.

"Today?"

The man hesitated a moment.

"Is he expecting you?"

She fished into her bag and produced Professor Higgins' letter. The man patiently waited until she opened it and found the spot she was looking for. She pointed.

She watched the man as he read. His eyebrows rose a little.

"Mr. Connor is very busy this morning," he explained, "but I'm sure he'll want to see you considering the unexpected circumstances and the nature of your letter."

She had no idea what he was referring to, but she didn't let the look on her face reveal her confusion. She just politely smiled.

He turned and looked up at the large round clock behind him then waved toward a boy who looked to be no more than twelve or thirteen years old. He was also dressed very nicely, his hair parted and combed over to one side.

The boy responded quickly.

"Will you escort Mrs. McAfee to Mr. Connor's office please?"

The boy smiled and held out his arm to assist her.

"This is my son, Benjamin. He will show you the way."

She wasn't used to such attention. She straightened the front of her dress and stood as tall as she could. She grabbed ahold of the boy's extended arm.

Together, they climbed the elegant staircase to the second floor. The carpet on the floor matched the red carpet on the stairs. Everything looked expensive, from the gold-framed pictures on the walls to the rich furnishings in the long hall. She walked slowly as she admired everything in their path.

The boy smiled and politely walked at her pace.

"Is this your first time here, ma'am?"

"Oh yes!" she exclaimed. "I'm not from here."

"Oh, where are you from?"

"Logan's Gap."

"Oh, that's not too far from here. Did you arrive today?"

"No, I came in yesterday so I would have time to rest before coming here."

"That was probably a wise decision. You look lovely today by the way."

Mrs. McAfee blushed. She couldn't remember anyone other than her husband saying anything like that, and her husband had been gone over fifteen years.

"Thank you, son. You are very kind to say so."

"Well, here we are. Do you want me to go in with you?"

As the older woman stood before the closed door, her hand tightened around the boy's arm. The name Charles R. Connor was displayed on a brass nameplate.

"Would you mind? I'm a little nervous."

"I don't mind at all."

He opened the door and let her go first. She stepped into a small office furnished with a couple of padded chairs and a matching royal blue sofa. A handsome oak desk stood against one wall facing the center of the room. There was no one there, but voices could be heard coming from behind the closed door of an adjoining office.

She looked over at Benjamin with a questioning look.

"Sit wherever you like. I'll let them know you're here."

She chose the chair closest to a large picture window where she could observe the busy street below.

The boy leaned down and took her gloved hand.

"Will you be all right now, or should I stay? I could get you some cool water if you like."

"No, I'm fine. You've been very helpful. Thank you."

"You are very welcome."

She nodded. Her palms were sweaty beneath her white dress gloves, and her heart was pounding so hard she was certain they could hear it in the next room.

She and the boy looked over when a nicely dressed woman came into the room from the inner office. She was surprised to see Mrs. McAfee but was very cordial. She looked toward Benjamin.

"This is—"

He paused as he glanced toward the older woman, biting his lip.

"I'm Mrs. McAfee." She stood to her feet.

"Yes, this is Mrs. McAfee. She is here to see Mr. Connor."

"Well, he's with someone at the moment, but I'm sure he'll be glad to see you as soon as he can. I will let him know you are here."

Mrs. McAfee couldn't help but notice the woman had been crying. She sat back down.

Benjamin excused himself, and Mrs. McAfee sat looking out of the window. The woman slipped back into the inner office, and everything was quiet and peaceful. The bright sunlight warmed her face, and she struggled to keep her eyes open.

She woke by someone gently shaking her shoulder.

"Mr. Connor will see you now, Mrs. McAfee."

She gathered her gloves and her bag then followed the woman into a large office, which had bookshelves that lined one entire wall. A tall, smartly groomed man stood as she entered. His hair was graying at his temples, and he had a neatly trimmed salt and pepper mustache. His smile was genuine.

He walked around his desk and greeted her, gently leading her to a comfortable chair facing his desk. He returned to his desk chair and sat down.

"I apologize for the delay, Mrs. McAfee. We received some very sad news yesterday, and I'm afraid, well, I'm afraid we are a bit preoccupied right now."

He was very professional in all his actions, but his face revealed a reflection of sadness.

"I'm so sorry," she said. "Should I come back another day?"

"Oh no, no. How is it I can help you?"

She opened her bag and carefully pulled the professor's letter from its envelope then laid the letter on the man's desk so it was facing him.

He pulled the letter toward him as he listened.

"I received this letter from Professor Higgins asking me to come see you, bringing the letter with me. I'm humbled that he would do this for me, someone he has never met."

The man smiled a sad smile toward her.

"What is it?" she asked.

Mr. Connor sat forward and sighed, not even glancing at the letter.

"Mrs. McAfee, I'm sorry to be the one to tell you this, but we just received word yesterday that Professor Higgins recently passed away. We're all deeply saddened by the news."

The blood drained from her face.

"I, I didn't know."

"I understand. We're all in shock."

She thought back to the way everyone was dressed when she arrived. The quiet murmur from everyone in the foyer, the wreaths on the doors, the woman who had been crying—it all made sense now.

"I'm sorry to take up your time," she said. She held out her hand for the letter. "I won't take up anymore of your time."

"Do you mind if I read it, Mrs. McAfee? Perhaps together, we can work on what the professor has to say. It doesn't surprise me that even after his death, he is still very much alive in many ways."

Just then, there was a slight knock on the door, and the woman Mrs. McAfee met earlier stepped in.

"What is it, Mary Alice?"

"I'm sorry to bother you, but Dr. Monroe is here again and says he just wants to see you a minute before he leaves town."

Chapter 87

Greater love hath no man than this,
that a man lay down his life for his friends.
John 15:13

*J*ames T. West woke with the sun and dressed and shaved away his thick, gray stubble. He rode hard to reach Tannersville just to find out the judge wasn't due back from trying a case until the next day. He had no choice but to find a room at the hotel and wait.

Tannersville was clean and neat, and the lawyer remembered the days when River Branch was just as well cared for.

The food at the comfortable hotel was filling and surprisingly good. He asked the waitress to express his compliments to the cook. He sipped his coffee and glanced up at the interesting looking clock above the door. The sheriff's office should be open, he thought. He left his payment on the table and headed that way.

Tannersville's wide main street with its large variety of stores and establishments gave way to several residents already busy with their day. The lawyer scanned the well-constructed buildings and admired the carefully planned details that gave Tannersville its own unique look. As he crossed the street, he couldn't help pondering on the brightly painted red and white striped barber pole. River Branch didn't even have a barber anymore, he thought.

The green and white pinstriped awning above the confectioner's shop had been added since the last time he was there and frankly, it added just that right sparkle of appeal to the specialty shop that tempted the most cautious eaters into its doors. The tried and true tailor's shop had the most interesting sign, he thought. Its fancy design gave the impression that more than just plain tailoring was done there and maybe it was, he further thought. Maybe it was. If he had more time he would have gone in and asked, but he didn't. He was headed to the sheriff's office and he was almost there. There was no time to waste lingering on a town that had advanced far beyond what River Branch ever was or ever could be again. He just focused on the sheriff's office that had come into view. It's lively shade of bluish green with its lime green border around the door would catch anyone's attention as they rode into town. And he imagined that was its intended purpose.

The sheriff was coming out of his office just as he walked up.

"Can I help you, Mister?"

"I sure hope so. My name is James T. West. I'm a lawyer in River Branch, and I'd like to talk to you if you have a few minutes."

"I'm needed at the school this morning, but you are welcome to walk over with me."

The two men walked the dirt street toward the school. The tall sheriff with the tall hat made the lawyer look shorter than he really was. The tin star pinned to the sheriff's denim shirt was polished to a perfect shine.

"I'm looking for Judge Peters. Has he arrived back in town yet?"

"I haven't seen him. What do you need with him?"

"I represent a man that's currently in jail," the lawyer explained, "who's been arrested for the bank robbery you had here recently. I've heard the judge is the best in the territory for fairness, and I'm looking for a lot of fairness. Frankly, our sheriff has dragged his feet on this so long I'm losing my patience."

The sheriff stopped midstep and looked down on the stocky man.

"But we have already arrested and tried the men involved with that robbery. I knew of your man being held, but I wired your sheriff soon after the trial. The men are locked up in my jail this very minute awaiting their fate."

The lawyer took the time to relight his cigar and take a few puffs before saying anything.

327

"Well then, my suspicions were right. I knew something stank about all this."

He pulled out a folded piece of paper and showed it to the sheriff.

"Is this the wire you sent?"

The tall man examined the paper.

"Yes, the very one. How do you happen to have this?"

"Let's just say I may have accidently noticed it in one of the sheriff's desk drawers and took it for safekeeping. I plan on showing this to Judge Peters. I have a very irritable yet innocent young man waiting for justice to be served."

"No need waiting for the judge. Meet me at my office in a couple of hours, and I'll ride back to River Branch with you and redeliver this wire to your good sheriff in person."

The lawyer tossed his cigar to the ground and crushed it with his dusty boot.

"Now we're getting somewhere. Two hours it is. I will be ready."

Chapter 88

For God so loved the world, that he gave his only begotten Son, that whosoever believeth in him should not perish, but have everlasting life.
John 3:16

*A*nna's puppy was growing.

The little black-and-white puppy ran back and forth through the hay, and Anna was having a hard time keeping up with him.

Martha heard Anna's laughter and walked out to the barn to see what was going on. She stopped at the barn's door and just watched a few moments before letting Anna know she was there.

"Sounds like fun in here," she finally said.

Anna and her puppy looked her way. Anna was out of breath, and hay stuck out here and there all through her messy blond hair. She grabbed the puppy while he was distracted, and he wiggled to get free, but Anna easily won the struggle.

"I forgot how much fun having a dog could be," Martha said. "We haven't had a dog since Luke was a boy."

"I never had a dog growing up," Anna said, as she stroked the puppy's head. "I'm so happy the professor thought to give him to me."

"Yes, the professor, he was a very generous man."

Anna nodded her agreement as she released the puppy into the yard.

"Care for some lemonade?"

"That sounds really good right now."

"I'll go get some, then I'll meet you on the porch. That way, we can keep an eye on Mac."

"I can help you," Anna offered.

"No, you have done a lot this morning already. It's time I waited on you for a change."

Anna watched the older woman head into the house. She walked with a slower step since Frank left to go help Luke. Not knowing what was going on was the hardest part, Anna decided.

Martha found Anna sitting in one of the rockers on the porch that wound around much of the house. She handed her a glass then sat in the other rocker. Neither said anything for a couple of minutes.

"Anna, I was thinking."

Anna turned to listen carefully.

"Are you happy here?"

"Of course, I am. I've never been happier."

"When will you be sixteen?"

"I guess I haven't thought much about my birthday, but it's not until Thanksgiving time. Mrs. McAfee picked the date for me. Going by how old she thought I was when I was dropped off at the shelter, she figured it should be near that time."

Anna laughed a little.

"What are thinking, Anna? Why the laugh?"

"Mrs. McAfee tried to make something good out of everything, even giving me a birthdate around the time we're supposed to be thankful."

"I think that's a nice way to be, don't you?"

"Yes, I do, but you'd have to know Mrs. McAfee to fully appreciate her. She was loud and a little clumsy, and her red hair always looked like she forgot to comb it all out before she headed out the door to come to work."

Martha shared in the laugther, envisioning the woman Anna thought so much of.

Anna paused a moment then kept on going.

"She loved to sing and make up stories. She loved to eat too. I think that's why she cooked so well. She would sing and cook and sing and cook all day long, not caring so much about the spills around her. She just enjoyed having fun and making others laugh."

"You miss her, don't you?"

"I do miss her, but I don't miss the shelter."

"Were they unkind to you?"

"Not really. There were so many children, they didn't have time to spend quality time with any of us. The only way they knew how to control all of us was to yell most times. And when it came to our chores, they sent us to bed without supper if we didn't do them as well as they thought we should. I used to go to bed angry all the time. Others cried themselves to sleep."

"And now? Do you think about the shelter and all that went on there?"

"I do think about it. Probably too much. When Professor Higgins was around, he always made me feel important. You know, like I was special. When I'd start talking about negative things about my time at the shelter, he would change the subject, and we'd end up laughing. He was always reminding me to think of what I could be thankful for when I wanted to complain about something."

"You had two very important people in your life, Anna. And you certainly have a good attitude after having such a tough childhood."

Anna stopped her rocking and took a long drink.

"I wish I knew more about God then and what Jesus did for all of us. If I had, I would have told the other children so they would have hope. We didn't know we could pray and ask God to help us. We didn't know He was watching over us even though we didn't know to pray."

"Anna, before you came, I didn't think much about religion. You have shown me by your actions that I need to think about some of the things I hear you talk about."

"It's not religion, Mrs. Monroe. That's what the professor told me to be careful about. He said it's a relationship—a relationship with Jesus Christ, accepting His death on the cross for our sins and then being sorry for all those sins by asking Him to forgive us while we let Him guide us to do what He wants, not what we want."

"Well, I need to do more thinking on that, but whatever has changed you into becoming the fine young woman you are deserves some more thinking."

Martha stopped her rocking as well.

"You know, Anna, when we talked about bringing you here, it was for selfish motives, *my* selfish motives. I just wanted someone who could help me with the work around here and be here when Megan and the boys were too much to handle. Sure, I wanted to help an orphan find a home, but more than that, I wanted others to think that I was being a good person by bringing you here. So my main reason for bringing you here was very selfish."

"Well, the professor once told me that sometimes people will do things for less than perfect reasons but God often turns the situation into a good one."

"Well, I owe you an apology. Will you forgive me?"

"Are you telling me all this because you're thinking of sending me away now that I'm almost sixteen?"

"Oh no, Anna. Just the opposite. Frank's not here, but I think I speak for both of us that we'd like you to consider staying here."

"You mean all the time?"

"Yes, I mean all the time."

"Like adopting me?"

"No. I don't think that's necessary. You're not a child anymore, Anna. I just mean that you're welcome to stay until you decide to leave on your own."

"I don't think I'd ever want to leave."

"Well, one day, Anna, you will meet a nice young man who wants to marry you. You'll be happy to think about leaving then."

Anna blushed.

"I guess you're right."

It was quiet between them a few moments while they rocked and sipped their drinks.

Anna turned toward Martha when she started the conversation back up.

"I'm going to make some changes around here, Anna. I'm working you so hard I haven't given you time to pursue your dreams and aspirations. From now on, we will do more of the work together. Then you can think about doing some of the things you possibly missed by growing up in the shelter."

"I really don't mind all I'm doing. I did more at the shelter."

"No, Anna, when I make up my mind, that's final."

Anna just smiled because she found out early on that that was true.

"What do you say we head into town and eat at Emilie's Outdoor Café for an early supper? Just maybe we will be able to see some of the horses at the stables next door."

"You mean it?"

"I mean it. I'll get Mac and put him in the barn and hitch up the buggy. You go wash up and change."

"Do you think Mac will be all right running loose in the barn instead of being pent up?"

"Yes, I think it's time to let Mac do some exploring on his own as well, don't you?"

"Yes. I think that's a great idea!"

"Let's just hope he doesn't terrorize all the livestock while we're gone."

Anna fairly flew from the rocker but stopped at the door before going in.

Martha studied her face.

"Thank you for believing in me, Mrs. Monroe. You have no idea what it means to me that you'd want me here."

"I'm just happy to see you've started believing in yourself, Anna."

Chapter 89

Rejoice in the Lord alway:
and again I say, Rejoice.
Philippians 4:4

$\mathcal{F}$rank Monroe had the privilege of turning the key to Luke's jail cell to set him free. And James T. West, the town lawyer, had the privilege of closing the cell door after putting a new prisoner in Luke's place.

The sheriff of River Branch pled guilty to plotting to bribe the Monroe family for a large amount of money in exchange for Luke's freedom, falsely suggesting that the suspects for the robbery were never found and out of an exchange of "kindness" he could be persuaded to let Luke go. The terms of his conditions were written in a note and was found hidden at his prosperous cattle ranch. The deputy, on the other hand, chose to leave town even after he was cleared from being any part of the scheme.

River Branch was now without a sheriff or any law enforcement. The lawyer suggested offering the job to Frank Monroe.

But Frank quickly gave his answer.

"I appreciate such confidence in me, Mr. West, but all I care about is getting home to my family."

He slapped Luke on his back.

"We have some catching up to do, don't we, son?"

Frank then reached out and shook the lawyer's hand.

"We owe you a debt of gratitude," he said, as he squeezed the man's hefty hand.

"My lawyer instinct told me something was amiss," the lawyer said. "I just had to follow my gut feeling and a little evidence to find the truth. I never like to see an innocent man suffer while the criminal runs free."

"And that's why I'm prepared to pay you well for your services," Frank said.

He began to pull something from his vest pocket.

"No, sir, none of that," Mr. West said waving a hand. "Let's just say we were all blessed to know the professor, and if this was part of what it took to honor his wishes, well, I'm not going to argue with how it got done."

Frank nodded.

"Well, Luke and I are heading over to the hotel for a meal and a hot bath. Then we'll keep an eye out for David's return. Would you like to join us?"

"No, but thank you anyway. Tell them Jimmy sent you, and I'll settle up with them later. I owe Luke a meal, I believe."

Neither of them had any idea he owned the hotel.

Luke accepted the lawyer's firm handshake.

"Thank you for believing in me, Mr. West."

"It's Jimmy, remember, kid? You just need to start believing in yourself, and you'll go somewhere in life."

"You're right. I've had a lot of time to do some thinking about that very thing."

"Go home and make some plans for your future. And if you're ever back this way, look me up. Who knows, maybe the sheriff's job will still be open."

Luke laughed.

"I'll do that."

"And let me know when the doctor gets back. I'd like to know what he was able to accomplish."

"If he had half the success you had in solving this case, I'd say our plans have gone well," Frank said.

"Well, I'll bid everyone good day. I have work waiting for me back at my office."

River Branch's only lawyer and hotel owner made his way across the street and up the long flight of stairs to his small, unassuming office. He paused at the nameplate on the door: James T. West, Attorney. He ran his hand across the rough piece of wood. He remembered the day he nailed it there and nodded his head.

It took a lot of effort and hard work to get that title, he thought, and even more to win the trust of his ever-growing clients. He had become a successful lawyer, but you would never know it from his meager lifestyle and his choice of clothing.

He turned the knob and stood in the doorway, looking around as if he had never seen the inside of his office before. There were the careless piles of papers on the floor, his desk a mess of scattered paperwork and dirty plates and cups. The sunshine streaming through the only window spoke of the thick layer of dust that clung to everything.

He took a deep breath as he stepped inside, the smell of lingering cigar smoke assaulting his senses.

He made his way into the room, stepping around the piles until he reached his desk chair. He slowly lowered his thick body into the leather seat that perfectly fit his form. He leaned back and released an audible sigh.

"Where did the time go?" he said out loud, squeezing the arms of his chair.

His mind drifted back to the days when he and the professor, along with the professor's wife Ellen, tossed around ideas of starting a business. With the professor's education and the lawyer's legal mind added to Ellen's enthusiasm, they opened the Homestead and Farm Store. It was agreed to be founded on honesty and integrity and fairness. Through their joined excitement, they brought in merchandise from every corner of the territory. Their store was unique, and the townspeople found merchandise and friendship through their doors.

Ellen displayed each item with extreme care. The professor kept track of incoming and outgoing inventory by devising a system of accuracy and speed. The lawyer, on the other hand, handled all the legal aspects while assisting the professor and his ideas. It ran efficiently with the added smoothness of three friends working in harmony.

But it all came to an abrupt stop the day Ellen died along with her newborn daughter. It seemed everyone in River Branch suffered, especially the professor, of course.

No one faulted the professor for leaving after the funeral. But on the other hand, everyone expected him to return, most of all, the lawyer, his friend.

James West sat forward and leaned heavily on his desk. He groaned. Memories and emotions coursed through him, and he pounded his fists until his hands hurt. Dishes hit the floor, and dust filled the air. Papers flew and added to the piles already there.

Everything in his life changed in one moment because of the actions of someone else. The professor had left him with the store and all its responsibilities. The townspeople mourned in different ways: first, losing dear friends; second, losing the comradery they came to love when the store was vibrant and alive. When he was forced to sell the store, it was never the same, and its new owner soon shut its doors, a general store moving in down the street trying to copy something they never could.

He sat back once again and looked up, wondering why he had never noticed the cracked ceiling before. He tried to ignore the cobwebs in the corners by lowering his head and shutting his eyes.

That long year having to recover from selling the store and beginning a law career was forever etched in his mind. It was possibly the most difficult thing he ever had to go through. But he knew the professor's change of fate was more difficult than his own. He did his best to not fault the man. But honestly, it was hard.

Time had passed, and wounds healed very slowly.

The lawyer scanned his office and all its contents. He had become successful and admitted most of his success was based on the principles he learned from the professor and Ellen: honesty, integrity, fairness, and hard work!

He fished a new cigar out of his pocket but didn't light it. Instead, he stuck it back into his pocket and began clearing his desk of its clutter. Minutes turned into hours, and at midnight, his oil lamp was still ablaze.

His shoulders hurt, and he was hungry from missing the supper meal. But when he looked around the now clean office, all that was forgotten. The open window had brought in a steady breeze that helped pull away the staleness of years of half-smoked cigars.

He blew out the oil lamp and headed home, rehearsing the events of the past weeks. The sheriff was behind bars, the deputy gone, and the Monroe family reunited. And most fulfilling of all, Luke was free.

But was *he* free?

Yes, after today, he believed he finally was. Most of the bitterness he harbored toward Professor Higgins melted away that day he showed up at his office humbly asking for help and forgiveness. He listened as the professor told of his struggling story after leaving River Branch. At first, he found pleasure in knowing the professor's struggles were more challenging than his own through all the years. But as the story progressed, he realized the professor had found something much more valuable that he never possessed. And he pondered on who really succeeded and who didn't.

It troubled him enough that he couldn't stop thinking about all the professor shared with him. But it was late, and he needed sleep after all the long days leading up to Luke's freedom. He needed to go home.

He walked the dark street of River Branch toward his small cottage just on the edge of town. And along the way, he stopped in front of the building that was once owned by him and the professor. It sat dark and empty after one business or another moved from there. It needed paint and a lot of repairs.

The lawyer rubbed the gray stubble on his chin. He wasn't a young man anymore, but he couldn't dismiss the longing to see the building come alive once again. It was a thought he would have to sleep on.

"Rest in peace, Professor," he said, as he stood before the building. "May your memory continue and your deeds produce fruit throughout the ages."

James Theodore West tipped his hat then slowly walked home, his cigar in his pocket.

Chapter 90

But be ye glad and rejoice for ever.
Isaiah 65:18

"I'm sorry, Mrs. McAfee, I'm sure this will only take a few minutes."

The older woman looked over at the ruggedly handsome man who had stepped into Mr. Connor's office.

"I'm sorry to intrude," the man said, nodding toward her.

She nodded back.

"Dr. Monroe, I'm glad you stopped back in to say goodbye," Mr. Connor said.

"I wish our meeting could have been under better circumstances," David replied.

"Yes, it was hard to receive such news. Professor Higgins was beloved by all who work here."

Mrs. McAfee turned her head away from the men, realizing her reason for coming was now for naught. She released a sigh she didn't realize was loud enough for anyone to hear.

The men turned toward her sigh.

"Oh, I'm sorry," Mr. Connor said. "Dr. Monroe, I'd like you to meet Mrs. Eleanor McAfee."

David stepped over and shook her hand, trying to place where he had heard the name before.

"She also knew the professor," Mr. Connor explained.

"Not actually 'knew,'" she said. "We just corresponded. Well, he wrote to me. I never actually wrote him."

She felt awkward, and she stumbled over her words.

"Well, I can tell I've intruded, and I'm sorry," David said.

He looked back toward Mr. Connor who had just sat back down behind his desk.

"I was just wondering if you had a chance to look over the contents of the envelope I brought," David said. "I admit I'm more than curious of what's inside."

"No, actually, I haven't. As soon as word got out about the professor's death, I've been busy seeing one person after another."

Eleanor McAfee reached across the desk to take the professor's letter, hoping to politely excuse herself and go back to her hotel room.

Mr. Connor stopped her by laying a hand on the letter.

"Please, Mrs. McAfee, don't leave."

She stood and straighten her shoulders. "I'm sorry to have taken up any of your time. I can see you have business to discuss, and *my* business isn't relevant anymore."

"But, Mrs. McAfee—"

"I really need to get back to the Children's Shelter. They will be needing me in the kitchen."

The Children's Shelter! Of course, thought David.

"Excuse me, Mr. Connor, but I need a word with Mrs. McAfee if you don't mind."

The man behind the desk couldn't hide his confusion.

The older woman just wanted to leave before she cried.

"Mrs. McAfee, I know Anna—Annaleigh Thompson."

Her hands flew to her burning cheeks.

"You know my Anna?"

"Yes, I couldn't remember where I had heard your name before, but when you said you were from a Children's Shelter and you needed to get back to the kitchen, I realized that you were probably the woman Anna speaks of so often."

"She speaks of me?"

She began to cry.

"Dr. Monroe, pull up a chair and join us," Mr. Connor was saying. "Please, Mrs. McAfee, have a seat. We'd like you to stay. I think we all have something in common, it seems."

She nodded then she let the doctor assist her as she sat back down.

Mr. Connor called for his secretary, and she promptly responded, not surprised by more crying that day. Everyone who came and went through Mr. Connor's office had cried about losing the professor.

"Will you please get Mrs. McAfee some water?"

"Of course, I'll be right back."

Soon, the boy who had escorted Mrs. McAfee earlier showed up at the office door. He brought the water but also cups of strong coffee.

"Benjamin, thank you," Mr. Connor said.

The boy smiled at the older woman, his eyes reflected his concern.

The room was quiet until Mrs. McAfee spoke again.

"My tears are not from sadness but joy. I never met Professor Higgins, but I can tell he was loved by many and his correspondence to me during a hard time in my life expressed the type of man he most certainly was. But just to hear about Anna, anything about her, brings joy to my heart. God is very good to me to use this situation to let me hear about Anna."

They let her cry a moment, then Benjamin quietly slipped away.

"You see, the professor wrote to me." She pointed to the letter. "He said Anna told him all about me and my long days as cook at the shelter. Well, in short, he offered me a job."

Mr. Connor held his expression, but he couldn't think of any job that would be suitable for her in the company.

"He told me to come see you, Mr. Connor, and that he would explain everything to you. I realize now he never had that chance."

"No, he didn't."

"I realize he must have been a valuable employee and for him to ask your help in finding me a more suitable job is more than kind."

Mr. Connor smiled at this precious woman.

"Mrs. McAfee, I want to show you what I showed Dr. Monroe earlier this morning. Come with me."

They left the coffee and water, and she followed Mr. Connor out of the office, David right behind them.

They walked the long corridor and up the winding staircase to the top floor. She was out of breath as she reached the top step, but David took her by the arm as they followed Mr. Connor to the end of the hall. They waited as he turned a key to open a very small office.

The office was unoccupied and didn't look like any of the other offices. It was plain. It was simple. It was ordinary.

"Here, Mrs. McAfee, is Professor Higgins' office. He wasn't an employee, you see, he owned this company."

David just smiled at her shocked expression.

"I was just as surprised," David explained. "He never told any of us who he was or what he really did."

Mr. Connor continued.

"He originally built this company for the wealth it would afford him, and he achieved that goal. He was rich and had accumulated many possessions, including real estate holdings in this town and many other locations, even in your town of Logan's Gap. But he wasn't a happy man in the beginning. He was hard and ran his company...well, sternly."

"Life had been cruel to him, and he was searching for happiness in all the wrong places."

Mrs. McAfee had pictured him a different way, and David listened closely since Mr. Connor hadn't told him this story when he brought him there earlier in the day.

But then Mr. Connor explained further.

"One day, Professor Higgins returned from a long trip. He was quiet and stayed in his large, plush office located on the main level, not wanting to be disturbed. But then one day, he sent for me.

"The professor had changed. He explained how he ran into a man who had been beaten and left for dead on the side of the road. At first, he said he was frustrated, thinking he needed to be on his way to meet someone about pressing business affairs. But the man's desperate cries touched him in a way he hadn't felt in many years. He knew he couldn't leave him, so he turned back to help and took him to the nearest town where he was cared for and eventually recovered. The professor paid all his expenses and gave him money to help him on his way.

"It was the first act of true kindness he had done in many, many years."

Mrs. McAfee listened carefully as she stood looking around the simply decorated office, a small framed photograph of a woman sat on the desk.

"The man returned his favor by offering him a gift much greater than anything the professor did for him."

The older woman knew what that was. She had received the same gift as a child. So before Mr. Connor could finish, she finished for him.

"He found Christ, forgiveness, and true happiness."

"Yes, he did. And in time, because of his testimony, I did too and many of our employees."

David grew uncomfortable, but no one noticed.

"Before you is the office of a humble man. And within these walls is a company dedicated to serving others and the community."

"What does this company do?" Mrs. McAfee asked.

"We manufacture, publish, and distribute printed material, mostly books. Professor Higgins holds the patent for the Higgins Printing Press. He started his life immersed in education, so he turned what he loved to do into a business, and it flourished. Now up until his death, he used his influence to distribute wholesome books and literature literally everywhere, including schools. And by owning a large portion of the rail service that brought you here to Weaver's Corner, he was able to do just that.

"So now, Mrs. McAfee, you know a small portion of the story behind the man in your letter."

Chapter 91

Rejoice with them that do rejoice.
Romans 12:15

Elisabeth and Anna took a walk. The days were much cooler, and most of the leaves had fallen from the trees.

David was coming home!

"Won't be long now," Anna said. "You will soon be married."

"I know! I want to pinch myself. With David gone, I realize more than ever I would never want to live without him."

Anna was quiet as they walked.

"What are you thinking about, Anna?"

"Oh, I was thinking about how old I feel."

"How *old* you feel? A comment like that makes *me* feel old."

Anna chuckled.

"I'll soon be sixteen."

"And I'll be nineteen. I would call that far from old, though."

"I wasn't thinking 'old' like in years, but I was just thinking about how much things have changed for me in such a short period of time and about what has taken place. You know, difficult things. At the shelter, it was the same routine day in and day out. Pretty plain and ordinary."

Elisabeth stopped and reached out and stopped Anna from walking as well. She took both of Anna's hands in hers.

"For me too, Anna. My life has changed so quickly I almost forget how things used to be. My father once told me to not let my past control my future. Difficult times or not, Anna, we have to keeping looking forward."

Their eyes held. They had developed a special bond.

"I like what your father said. I'm going to remember that and write it in my journal—don't let your past control your future."

"It has helped me many times these past months. Sometimes, I would just say it over and over in my mind. Otherwise, I wanted to cry all the time."

They continued their walk. The leaves crunched beneath their feet.

"When did you know you loved Andrew?"

Elisabeth wasn't prepared for the question that came out of nowhere.

"Well, we grew up together, and we were always close. We enjoyed the same things, so I guess we just expected to marry one day. Why?"

"I was just wondering."

Elisabeth didn't miss an opportunity to speak freely.

"It's nice to have Luke home, isn't it? He's changed, I think."

Anna blushed.

"It sort of seems everyone is changing," Anna said. "Luke said the Monroe family has been 'shook up.'"

"That's a funny way of saying it, but in a way, he's right. I'm sure everything was routine until we came along!"

They both had a good laugh. Their friendship was growing.

"Did Luke have anything else to say?"

"He says he wants to travel."

"That's exciting! And why am I not surprised?"

They laughed some more.

"He said he's always wanted to explore places he's never been before, but he felt held back because he thought no one would understand."

"Isn't that what you said you always wanted to do? Explore new places?"

Anna nodded.

"Well, I'm content settling here," Elisabeth said, "in Lazy Spring. I haven't been there that long, but it feels like home now. I miss being there. Do you think Finley Valley will become your home?"

"I don't know. I don't know what's beyond Finley Valley. I never even knew much about Logan's Gap where the Children's Shelter is located. Only what Mr. Foley told me really."

"And who's Mr. Foley?"

"He worked with the horses at the Children's Shelter. He let me help him with the horses, and he told me stories about Logan's Gap and the places he had been."

"Maybe that's why you have a desire to explore."

"Maybe. Probably."

"No matter what you choose to do, Anna, I will always cherish our friendship."

"I guess I'm not as old as I think, really. Just wishing about how things might be. Just getting in a hurry probably."

"Wishes can be desires, Anna. God plants thoughts and desires in our hearts so we can accomplish what He wants us to do for Him. We just have to be careful not to act on our own desires that are just selfish."

Anna thought on what Elisabeth was saying.

"Thanks for helping me understand more about God and the Bible. I will miss our talks when you marry David and he takes you back to Lazy Spring."

"I'm not that far away, Anna. Come visit. I could use some help when the baby comes, I'm sure. You have such a natural way with children."

"I do love helping with children," Anna said, as she realized it more and more as the months passed. "And I want to travel to discover new things."

Anna sighed.

"How in the world am I ever going to know what I'm supposed to do! I'm finding out I like a lot of things."

"Trust God to show you," Elisabeth explained. "But you have to just take one day at a time. You can't rush things."

"That's what Luke says."

Elisabeth looked shocked.

"I mean the part about taking one day at a time, not the rushing part."

"I wondered! I was thinking if Luke was slowing down and not rushing into things, he was the one getting old!"

They laughed and laughed as they talked about Luke and all the stories the family told about him and his impulsive growing up years until their sides hurt.

They slowed as they walked.

"I think it's time to check on lunch, what do you think?" Elisabeth asked, rubbing her stomach. "I'm so hungry."

"Me too. I think it's this mountain air."

So the two young women turned around and quickly retraced their steps, singing songs and laughing about some very girlish things.

Chapter 92

Let us draw near with a true heart in full assurance of faith.
Hebrews 10:22

*D*r. David Monroe escorted Mrs. McAfee home to Logan's Gap so she could settle her affairs.

"I appreciate you coming with me," she said.

"It's my pleasure. I never thought I'd be standing in the foyer of the very same Children's Shelter where Anna grew up."

He glanced around and understood better what Anna had described. It was a very plain and ordinary place.

"I admit, I'm a bit nervous," she went on to say.

"Don't be. I'm here to support you."

After a brief meeting with the Children's Shelter's administrator, Mrs. Eleanor McAfee felt at peace with her decision. After many years, she was no longer the head cook at the shelter. She would miss the children, but she knew the timing was right. She had no regrets. She silently thanked Professor Higgins for making it possible.

She was allowed to walk the halls, telling each of the children goodbye. Some of the staff members gave her small gifts.

At long last, she headed toward the kitchen she knew so well, and as they climbed the uneven porch steps that led to the kitchen's back door, she pointed out to David the exact spot where she found Anna.

All goodbyes had been said, and the older woman was determined not to look back, only forward, something she always encouraged Anna to do as well.

David helped her pack a couple of bags, and soon, they were on the westbound train heading for Finley Valley.

"Thank you for giving me this opportunity to visit Anna."

"Remember, it was Mr. Connor's idea. It was his generous money gift on behalf of the company and Professor Higgins that is making this possible."

"I can't believe this is all true."

"Well, believe it. Now you can experience the exact same train ride that Anna took. And I'll warn you, it's a long trip to Finley Valley."

The trip did take a long time, but Mrs. McAfee learned a lot about the Monroe family and their large part in Anna's life. She heard for the first time about the illness that plagued the train passengers who were taken to Lazy Spring and that David was the doctor who treated them. She wasn't surprised the professor was right in the middle of things, helping others. And it was no surprise that Anna was so helpful with the children.

"She loves children," she told David. But he already knew that firsthand.

She enjoyed hearing all about Elisabeth and was saddened when she heard the story of her husband's death. She couldn't imagine the pain and heartache the young woman suffered. She lovingly listened when David declared his love for Elisabeth and thought she had never heard a sweeter love story.

She sat wide-eyed when he explained what happened to Luke and how he was thrown into jail. She would never know that her prayers helped him through. She sat quietly as he told her of Anna's illness and how Luke and Melissa nursed her back to health.

She couldn't wait to meet Martha as well as David's older brother Frank or Brandon and Melissa and the children. She wanted to meet Megan most of all.

She had most of the Monroe family names memorized, including who belonged to whom before they reached Burke Mountain Station.

"This is our last leg of the trip, Mrs. McAfee," David explained. "I think you'll enjoy this place. It's a favorite for many people because traders come from all around to sell their wares."

The older woman was no longer timid and shy around the doctor. She sang and hummed a bit too loud on the train at times, and when they reached Burke Mountain Station, she practically pulled David from table to table. There were so many tempting things to buy, and she bought plenty.

"I can't go visiting people I don't know unless I bring a gift or two," the older woman explained.

David didn't argue with her. He was just ready to get to Finley Valley where Elisabeth was waiting for him.

Another hour passed, and he convinced Mrs. McAfee to slow down.

"I think we should slow down some and get a bite to eat," he said. "There's a favorite spot I'd like to take you. It's called Barney's Place."

David was glad she agreed it was time to find something to eat. And both of them were finally able to catch their breath.

On the last part of their trip to Finley Valley, David could barely keep his eyes open. She, on the other hand, stared out the window at the beautiful Blue Mountains. They were the tallest, most rugged mountains she had ever seen.

This was a trip she knew she would never forget. And the thought of seeing Anna again made all the miles worth it.

Chapter 93

And let us consider one another
to provoke unto love and to good works.
Hebrews 10:24

*W*ord came that Mr. Connor had arrived at the Finley Valley train station. Brandon was asked to pick him up and bring him to Frank and Martha's house. The man from Weaver's Corner was in awe at the beauty of Finley Valley as they crested the small mountain.

Brandon stopped the buggy. It was a clear cold day, and they could view the entire valley and the town below that was divided by its river that brought life to the valley. The rugged mountain range stood tall on all sides as if it was protecting those who lived there.

"I had heard of Finley Valley, but I never knew it was so beautiful. No wonder you and your family settled here."

"I have no desire to be anywhere else," Brandon explained. "I like to stay close to home, and I wouldn't care if I never had to travel outside of Finley Valley again."

"I enjoy being close to home with my family as well," Mr. Connor said, "but I'm glad I was given the privilege to see this mountain hideaway. What's beyond the mountains?"

"Nothing. We are literally on the edge of nowhere."

Mr. Connor nodded.

"Beautiful, Brandon, beautiful!"

Brandon urged the horse on, and soon, they pulled up in front of Frank and Martha's comfortable home. Frank greeted Mr. Connor as Brandon reined the horses to a stop.

"Welcome, Mr. Connor!"

"Thank you. It's a pleasure to meet you. David has told me a lot about his family."

The men shook hands.

"I hope it was all good."

"Yes, it was all very good."

"Well, I hope you're hungry. My wife is in the kitchen preparing some food for us right now."

"I admit I'm very hungry, and to be very honest, I'm tired as well."

"I'm sure. We'll have a bite to eat, and then you can choose when you want to retire. You can meet all the family tomorrow. If all has gone as scheduled, David and Mrs. McAfee should only be a day or two behind you."

"Excellent. I don't want to impose on your time any longer than necessary."

"We don't mind the company to be honest. We don't get many travelers up our way."

"That's a shame. It's such a beautiful place."

Martha met Mr. Connor in the dining room where she was setting out her best dishes. Anna was there by her side, doing her best to calm Martha's nerves. Martha wanted everything looking just right for their important guest.

"Mr. Connor, this is my wife Martha, and this is Anna."

He shook Martha's hand, and since Anna was across the room, he just nodded.

Anna just smiled.

"It is nice to meet you both so I can put faces to the names David told me about. Anna, I have heard many wonderful things about you. Dr. Monroe tells me you're adjusting very well here. Is that right?"

She felt uncomfortable, and Martha noticed it right away.

"Mr. Connor is here to bring us news concerning the professor," Martha tried to explain.

Anna frowned.

"Here, Anna," she said in an attempt to change the subject. "Let's get the food on the table and we can talk while we eat."

Frank showed Mr. Connor where he could wash up, and soon, the four of them were at the table enjoying the meal that Martha and Anna prepared.

"Professor Higgins was a very good friend of mine, Anna," Mr. Connor was saying. "He and I worked together in Weaver's Corner, not far from where you grew up in Logan's Gap."

Anna sat up straight and politely listened.

"I'm here at the professor's request."

Anna was frustrated, and no one at the table missed the look on her face.

"He wrote a paper, sort of a letter, with detailed instructions about how he wanted things done after his death."

As much as he tried, Mr. Connor found he was unable to say exactly what he meant. He knew Anna was young, and well, he just decided to stop trying to say anymore about why he was there.

Martha looked first at Frank and then toward Anna, fearing this might be upsetting for her. But Anna in the end seemed more interested than upset.

She finished her last bite and sat her fork on her empty plate.

Frank spoke up.

"We are very interested in hearing what he had to say, Mr. Connor. It must be very important for you to come all this way."

The man nodded.

Frank suggested they take their dessert into the parlor where they could be more comfortable, and Martha ran to put the coffee pot on the hottest part of the stove, reprimanding herself for not thinking of it sooner.

Anna excused herself and said she was tired and wanted to head to bed a little early.

She first headed out to the barn to see Mac and was surprised when she found Luke sitting in the hay playing with the black-and-white puppy.

Luke heard the barn door.

"How was supper?" he asked.

"Fine. I didn't know you were here," she said. "You could have eaten with us."

Anna sat on the barn floor and reached for the feisty overgrown puppy.

"I ate at Brandon's. They offered to let me stay with them tonight, but I wanted to come back here. Much more peaceful."

He smiled and Anna knew exactly what he meant. Sometimes, she tired of Melissa and Brandon's rambunctious children too.

They sat without either saying much.

Mac soon climbed out of Anna's lap and flopped down in the hay where he could stretch out.

"I've been thinking, Anna."

"Oh? What about?"

"About when I was locked in that jail cell."

"Was it scary?"

"Some, but don't tell anyone I said so."

She smiled.

"I had time to think about a lot of things."

He waited for her to respond, but she seemed unusually quiet.

"Are you feeling all right, Anna?"

"Yes."

"Are you sure?"

Anna stood up and walked over to stroke the horse she usually rode.

Luke hesitated but then followed her, standing on the other side of the horse where she couldn't help but look at him.

"I'm not leaving here until you talk to me, Anna."

He liked her stubborn little way of subtly asking for attention, and he was determined he had her figured out more than she knew.

"You were talking first," she said. "I want to hear what you were going to say."

"My stuff can wait. I can tell you're bothered."

Anna kept stroking the horse until Luke took her hand and led her to a nearby bench.

"You're going to rub off all his hair stroking him like that."

That brought a smile to Anna's face. She was surprised when Luke didn't let go of her hand.

"I'm just tired of talking about the professor," she said. "I want to just let him go, but everybody seems to want to talk about him all the time."

Luke nodded.

"I'm sure it will all settle soon. Mr. Connor is here at the professor's request even though he isn't with us anymore."

"That's what he said."

Anna hesitated.

"Luke, were you with the professor when he died?"

"Yes, Anna, I was."

"Did he suffer?"

"Anna—"

Luke was still holding her hand.

"Well, did he?"

"No, Anna, he did not. He slipped away very quietly and very peacefully."

"I wished I could have been there to tell him goodbye and tell him how much I loved him."

"He knew how much you loved him."

Luke lifted her chin with his other hand.

"Look at me, Anna. He loved you more than the air he breathed."

"I know."

"He asked me to help him finish up some of his affairs. I'm glad I was there to hear what he had to say. In a way, it was nice to feel like I was doing something good for him when he did so much good for all of us."

Suddenly, the barn door opened a little wider.

Luke pulled his hand away from Anna's but not before his mother saw.

"Hello, Luke. I didn't know you were here. We were worried about Anna. Is everything all right?"

"Yes, Mother, we were just talking."

"All right, son. I can walk you back to the house now if you're ready, Anna."

Anna thanked Luke with her eyes then walked over to pick up her puppy.

"No, leave him, Anna. I think I'll sleep in the barn tonight, and I'd like some company."

"Are you sure?" his mother asked. "It's going to be a cold night, son."

"Yes, Mother, I'm sure. I just want to be alone. Besides, there are plenty of blankets."

She wanted to ask more questions, but Luke had turned away.

"Good night then, son."

Then Anna headed out with Martha.

"And, Anna—"

She turned at Luke's voice.

"I'd like to finish our conversation real soon."

"I'd like that too," she said softly.

The two women walked in silence toward the house. And Martha wisely left Anna with her thoughts.

Chapter 94

And now abideth faith, hope, charity, these three;
but the greatest of these is charity.
1 Corinthians 13:13

*A*nna and Elisabeth were washing the supper dishes, Martha and Frank had gone for a walk, and Luke had taken Mr. Connor over to Brandon's for a return match of checkers.

Anna was laughing so hard at Elisabeth's antics she decided to sit down before she dropped the wet plate in her hand.

"You can't quit on me now, Anna!" Elisabeth exclaimed, attempting to throw soapsuds toward her with no success.

"Then stop making me laugh!" Anna shouted back, as she threw a towel that landed in the tub of soapy water, Elisabeth successfully dodging her throw.

"Now you've done it!"

Elisabeth grabbed the wet towel, but instead of throwing it back, she just stood there, water dripping on the floor as well as soaking the front of her dress and her stocking feet.

Anna suddenly lost her smile, her eyes following Elisabeth's gaze.

There David was, standing in the doorway. His hair was messy, and he definitely needed a shave.

But all Elisabeth saw was David, not his rumpled clothing or his messy appearance, just David and his cheeky grin.

Anna's heart warmed as Elisabeth ran past her, dropping the wet towel before she ran.

David opened his arms, eagerly waiting for her to reach him. He scooped up his bride-to-be in one fluid motion.

Anna quickly turned away and just listened to their sweet expressions of love as she picked up the wet towel from the floor. She took a deep breath and sighed. She was so happy for Elisabeth.

Then as she reached up for a clean towel hanging on a hook beside her, she heard another voice.

She froze.

Someone was singing, and there was no mistaking that voice.

Anna hesitated for fear her mind was playing tricks on her. She wanted to turn around, but her body wouldn't let her. Her heart pounded a little faster. She dropped her head and listened.

Eleanor McAfee slipped past David and Elisabeth who eagerly waited to witness the reunion between Anna and the woman who was more of a mother figure than a friend.

The older woman quietly called Anna's name.

Anna turned and unashamedly cried tears of joy.

"Oh, Mrs. McAfee! I thought I'd never see you again!"

"Nor I, sweet child."

One tight embrace turned into another tight embrace.

"Look at you, Anna! You have grown so much! Your hair has gotten so long."

Anna pushed her wayward hair away from her face and straightened her dress. She didn't know how to respond. She just kept smiling.

"Come, come, let's sit down," Mrs. McAfee said. "Where is there a good place to sit?"

Anna looked over and saw that David and Elisabeth had slipped away without them noticing. She never thought anymore of the supper dishes soaking in the tub of soapy water but turned all her attention on Mrs. McAfee instead.

"I can fix you a cup of tea," Anna offered. "What about something to eat? Would you rather have a cup of coffee?"

"Anna, Anna, my dear. Listen to you, so grown up! And so polite and hospitable."

Anna blushed at her compliments.

The older woman took Anna's hand.

"So where is there a place to sit, my dear? My new shoes are hurting my feet."

"Oh, of course, the parlor! Let's go into the parlor."

"You lead the way, and I'll follow."

They reached the sofa, and Mrs. McAfee sat down with a long drawn out sigh.

"This feels so much better than those hard seats on the train."

"Mrs. McAfee, how have you come to be here?"

"Your friend, Dr. Monroe, rode on the train with me all the way from Logan's Gap."

"What was he doing in Logan's Gap?"

"I'm tired and it's a long story, Anna. I just want to hear about you. Are you happy here?"

Anna knew asking any more questions was a waste of time.

"I'm so very happy here, Mrs. McAfee!"

The older woman sat back and finally relaxed.

"God is good, Anna. He answers my prayers."

"Thank you for praying for me because I knew you were. I had no doubt."

"Yes, every day, all day. I was so worried. Professor Higgins was good to write me about you. It sounded like you were in good hands."

"About me? He wrote about me?"

"Yes, he sent me a telegram when you were so sick, and then he remembered to send me another one when you were well. Not long ago, he wrote me a long letter. I have it with me so you can read it."

"I don't know what I would have done without Professor Higgins. He rode on the train with me the entire way to Finley Valley when he wasn't even coming here himself."

"Finley Valley, Anna! It is so beautiful! The mountains are so big!"

Anna laughed at the woman and her facial expressions. She missed their times in the kitchen at the shelter. Mrs. McAfee brought life to a gloomy day.

"I do love it here, Mrs. McAfee. The Monroe's are good people, and they have treated me kindly. Mrs. Monroe has asked me to stay as long as I want."

"That's wonderful news, Anna! God answers prayers! I heard all about the Monroe's."

"You did?"

"Yes, David told me all about his family. I know all their names by heart."

Anna sat wide-eyed.

"You do? That's wonderful! I can't wait until you meet them."

"I look forward to it. Tomorrow maybe."

"Yes, tomorrow. How long can you stay?"

"I don't know. I guess it depends on the Monroe's. I no longer have a job at the Children's Shelter because I quit. I have plenty of time for a nice visit if they are willing."

"Wait, what? You quit? Why did you quit? Did something happen?"

But Martha and Frank walked in at the moment, and Anna didn't get any answers. Mrs. McAfee just politely smiled their way.

"You are welcome to stay as long as you like," Martha said, rubbing her cold hands together.

"Oh, Mrs. Monroe, this is Mrs. McAfee," Anna said.

Martha told Mrs. McAfee to stay seated and came over and gave her a quick hug. Frank shook her hand.

"We've been looking forward to this, Mrs. McAfee," Frank said.

"You knew?" Anna asked.

"We did know," Martha replied. "It was so hard not to tell you, Anna. I almost slipped once."

"This is so unbelievable," Anna said. "This is such a surprise! I still can't believe it. Someone needs to pinch me!"

Martha turned toward Mrs. McAfee.

"Anna and I have readied the little house for your visit. I believe you will be comfortable there."

Anna's mouth flew open.

"I wondered why it was so important to clean the little house!"

Martha smiled real big.

"Well, now you know. We thought it would be nicer than one of the rooms upstairs. It will give you more privacy, Mrs. McAfee."

THE EDGE OF NOWHERE

"That's very thoughtful. Now I know why Anna loves it here so much. You are very kind."

Frank stood.

"I can tell you're very tired. I'll take you on over right now so you can settle in from your long journey. I'm sure Anna will want to visit some more, and you can do that more comfortably over there. There's everything you need. It's fully furnished, just like this house, only smaller."

"I'll just take her," Anna said. "We will be fine."

"All right then, I'll leave you women to what you need to do. I have some things to do in the barn."

Anna reached out to help the older woman to her feet.

"Oh, and, Anna—"

"Yes, Mr. Monroe?"

"Mr. Connor has asked that we all meet sometime tomorrow. He is eager to get back home. I suggested we meet at Melissa and Brandon's for an early supper. I thought the sunporch would be the best place to meet since it's large enough for all of us. That way, none of us have to be in a hurry tomorrow morning."

"Thank you, Mr. Monroe. I have so many questions for Mrs. McAfee, we may stay up all night!"

"I have an idea," Martha said, as she stood. "Let me walk Mrs. McAfee over and get her settled, and you can go get some of your things so you can stay over in the little house with her tonight."

"I'd like that," Anna said, as she squeezed Mrs. McAfee's hand. "I'll run right up and get my things. I'll see you soon, Mrs. McAfee!"

Anna ran up the stairs, humming as she went. Just when she once again thought her life couldn't get any better, it did. She continued to be amazed. She couldn't wait to hear about all the children at the Children's Shelter. Even news about the selfish Rebecca Dunlop would be welcomed!

Chapter 95

As the Father hath loved me, so have
I loved you: continue ye in my love.
John 15:9

Martha woke to the smell of bacon and coffee. She turned over, and Frank's side of the bed was empty.

She grabbed her bed coat and walked down the hall then peeked in Anna's room where Elisabeth was staying. They were gone too. David's door was open, so she guessed he was probably downstairs as well.

She stood at the top of the stairs and listened. Quiet laughter and lively voices drifted up toward her. The wooden steps were cold beneath her feet as she descended the stairs. She pulled her bed coat around her a little better then looked toward the dining room, but it was dark. To her surprise, everyone was in the kitchen.

"Mother!" Luke exclaimed, as she appeared in the doorway. "Come join us."

Frank pulled out the chair next to him.

"Come, Martha, sit down. Mrs. McAfee is making breakfast for everyone."

Martha didn't move.

Mrs. McAfee was busy at the hot cookstove while everyone else crowded around the small kitchen table.

David and Elisabeth sat hand in hand, smiling her way. Luke was messing around with something at his feet, and Anna was laughing at what Luke was doing. Frank winked at her, casually sipping his coffee and motioning for her to come sit down.

The table was filled with cups of steaming coffee, hot biscuits, bacon piled high, and large pancakes piled even higher. Everyone was eagerly filling their plates.

"We can't possibly eat all this food," David said, as he stuffed a piece of biscuit in his mouth. "Martha, you have to help us!"

His voice sounded desperate, and they all laughed.

Everyone had messy hair and wore the clothes they slept in. Mrs. McAfee had found an apron, but it barely fit around her. She was dressed in a simple cotton dress like you'd wear at home after a long day. Her hair looked to be the messiest of all.

Martha just stood there, staring.

Frank finally got up and walked over to his wife.

"Wake up, sweetheart," he whispered, as he pecked her on the cheek. "Come join us."

Martha wiped a few strands of graying hair away from her face. Her one long braid fell down her back, and Anna realized she had never seen Martha with her hair down before.

Martha quietly took her seat between Frank and Luke.

"I'm so embarrassed," she said. "I can't believe I slept so long. Frank, you should have woken me."

"Look outside," Luke said. "It's not that late."

He was right. The sun was just beginning to rise.

Martha turned when she heard Mrs. McAfee's voice.

"I'm sorry. It's my fault."

"And mine," added Anna.

"I'm so used to getting up very early to feed the children at the shelter, I just couldn't sleep anymore. So Anna and I came over here to make some hot tea. Before I knew it, this young man showed up, and I was fixing food."

Luke raised his hand, and they all laughed again, this time with no restraint since Martha was up and awake.

"Elisabeth dragged me down here," David added, pointing at her.

Elisabeth hit him on the arm.

"I did not! Don't tell them that!"

David gave her a look.

"All right, maybe I accidently knocked on your door when I passed your room," Elisabeth admitted. "But you found the kitchen on your own."

"I'm guilty too," Frank said. "I smelled coffee, and you know I can't resist a good cup of coffee."

He raised his cup toward Mrs. McAfee, and she smiled, waving her hand toward him like she was shooing something away.

Martha looked at the woman at her stove.

"But there's food in the little house. Didn't you show her, Anna?"

"I did show her, but she wanted to come over here where we could all be together when everyone woke up."

"And I saw them crossing the yard," Luke said. "So Mac and I followed them."

"You were in the barn again? What were you doing up so early?"

"That dog kept me awake. Have you ever tried to sleep with Mac?"

Just then, Mac stuck his head out from under the table, and Luke looked at his mother sheepishly.

Martha's eyes grew wide.

"Well, we had to introduce Mac to his name sake, Mother. But I'll take him outside."

Luke jumped up and opened the door.

"Imagine, a dog named after me! The things that go on behind your back!" Mrs. McAfee exclaimed.

They all laughed again, only harder.

Elisabeth and Anna seemed to be laughing the loudest. David looked very tired but laughed along with the rest as he occasionally tried to suppress his yawns. Frank, who was usually the quieter one, squeezed Martha's hand as he joined right in. And Luke—she noticed Luke looked happier than he had in a very long time.

Mrs. McAfee began to sing, and Anna joined right in, knowing every word to the silly song. Soon, everyone was singing, and the sun had come up while no one was looking.

Martha watched the scene unfolding in front of her. She finally relaxed against Frank's shoulder and just closed her eyes and listened. Frank put his arm around her and pulled her close. It was a comforting sound to hear everyone so happy. It was music to her ears and peace to her soul.

Soon, most of the food was eaten, and they talked Mrs. McAfee into sitting at the table with them. They had squeezed in one more dining room chair, and they all sat elbow to elbow in the warm kitchen.

Everyone began asking Anna and Mrs. McAfee about their days together at the Children's Shelter. They were amazed how much more they learned about Anna and how much she could blush in one morning. It didn't take them long to understand the deep love Anna had for this woman who rescued her that day from the kitchen's cold back porch.

Anna and Elisabeth convinced Martha and Mrs. McAfee they could do the cleanup and insisted they just sit and get to know each other. Luke and David were volunteered by the girls to dry the dishes, and it wasn't long before Frank suggested to Martha and Mrs. McAfee that they take their coffee to the parlor where they wouldn't have to talk above all the noise at the sink.

In both the kitchen and the parlor, everyone was discussing what they thought Mr. Connor might have to say later that day.

Chapter 96

Know therefore that the LORD thy God, he is God.
Deuteronomy 7:9

The day was a relaxing one, but it was time to head over to Brandon and Melissa's soon.

Anna looked out the parlor window and frowned.

"Looks like rain," she said. "Maybe we should head over soon."

Frank stepped up beside her.

"Anna's right. Those are some angry-looking clouds. I'll hitch up the horses, and we can head on over if everyone is ready."

"I'll go tell David and Elisabeth," Martha said.

Soon, everyone was piled into the large wagon, David driving the horses with Elisabeth by his side.

"Are you warm enough?" he asked her.

"Yes, I'm fine."

Not convinced, he pulled her blanket up around her neck then kissed her sweetly.

"Maybe that will warm you up."

Her eyes brightened, and she just smiled.

"What about everyone else back there? Everyone ready?" David shouted before he pulled away.

Everyone pulled their blankets tightly around them, and with a resounding yes from the bed of the wagon, David pulled away from the yard. They could hear Mac franticly barking in the barn.

Luke noticed Anna's concerned look as she glanced toward the barn.

"He'll be fine," Luke said. "There are plenty of animals in there to keep him warm. He'll settle down before we make the first turn."

"I hope so."

Luke kept watching Anna, but when she noticed, she shyly looked toward his parents then looked away.

Frank couldn't help but notice and glanced toward Martha. They both smiled, and he squeezed her hand.

Mrs. McAfee insisted on sitting near the back so she could see the scenery on the way over, and she quietly hummed as the wagon bounced its way along. She cradled a warm pie against her while the rest of the pies rode safely in a wooden crate. She was happy to contribute to the supper everyone was looking forward to. And she was even happier to be with Anna and her newfound friends.

Melissa and Brandon welcomed everyone as they noisily climbed the porch steps. The boys ran circles around everyone, and Megan waited very impatiently just inside the screen door.

"Hurry, it's so cold out here tonight," Melissa said. "We hoped you'd come early. I almost sent Brandon over to get you! Megan has been crazy with excitement."

"Looks like rain so we decided to head on over," Frank said.

"I know," Brandon said, "we were worried you'd get caught in a downpour."

Luke brought in the crate of pies, and Frank carried the side dishes Martha had prepared. David took the pie from Mrs. McAfee, and everyone headed down the hall toward the large sunroom.

Anna lingered in the foyer along with Mrs. McAfee, letting the others go on ahead of them.

"I want you to meet a very good friend of mine, Mrs. McAfee," Anna said.

Megan beamed and did her best to straighten in her chair.

"My, my, what a beautiful girl you are!" Mrs. McAfee exclaimed. "Anna has told me so much about you!"

"I'm six years old," the little girl said, holding up six fingers.

"You are so grown up," the older woman said, appearing to be shocked beyond belief.

"Mommy let me help her."

"Well, that's great, Megan," Anna said. "I'm sure she is very proud of you!"

Anna pushed Megan's wheelchair, and the three of them headed into the sunroom where everyone was already seated. Mr. Connor was there, and the men were discussing his uncanny checkers skills to which it was decided they would have to pull the board out later that evening.

Melissa and Brandon were busy finishing up the touches on the table, talking with everyone as they went.

Brandon pulled his wife aside while no one was looking.

"The table looks great, Melissa. You've outdone yourself tonight."

"Megan helped me."

Brandon raised an eyebrow.

"I took Anna's advice and let her set the table. It took a long time, but as you can see, she did an astounding job."

Brandon squeezed her hand.

"I'm proud of you, Melissa. I'm a blessed man."

"We are all blessed, Brandon. Just look around."

Once again, the Monroe family was all together, and the room was filled with laughter along with the usual shouting from the boys. Mr. Connor and Mrs. McAfee might as well have been family the way everyone included them.

Martha and Frank insisted on bringing in the rest of the food from the kitchen to give Brandon and Melissa some time to sit and enjoy the rest of the family.

And Frank soon raised his voice to get everyone's attention.

"I know everyone is eager to eat this fine meal, and I want to thank everyone who had a part in its preparation. We also want to welcome our guests, Mr. Charles Connor from Weaver's Corner and Mrs. Eleanor McAfee from Logan's Gap. They have both traveled a long way to be here."

Elisabeth squeezed David's hand, knowing he endured that long, tiring trip as well.

Frank paused.

"The last time we gathered like this, we had one more person present who is not with us today."

Some of them were nodding, the room grew very quiet.

"We miss Professor Higgins' contagious laugh and his very detailed stories."

They all quietly laughed.

"And before we eat, I want to commend Luke on his bravery and willingness to execute the professor's final wishes, never expecting the difficulties he would endure."

Luke's face burned hot, and Anna, sitting across from him, smiled.

"Let us give thanks as we always do."

Frank prayed and the meal commenced. Everyone agreed to save the pies until later.

Before long, the table was cleared with everyone's help, and the women washed the dishes while the men retreated to the parlor where they talked about the upcoming cold weather and the snow that would soon come to the high mountains.

The children enjoyed a small piece of pie and a glass of warm milk and were soon ushered upstairs to bed. The three young children sat wide-eyed as Mrs. McAfee told them stories she had heard as a child, the very same stories she told Anna when she was growing up.

Melissa and Brandon stood quietly just beyond Megan's bedroom door, watching and listening.

"She's an amazing person, Brandon. None of Anna's descriptions of her come close to who she really is. I'm so glad she came for Anna's sake."

Anna came upstairs and settled Megan into bed while Mrs. McAfee sang a gentle, relaxing lullaby. The boys ran off and put themselves to bed with a lot of prompting from their father.

Melissa stuck her head into Megan's room.

"Pie is served on the sunporch, ladies. And Mr. Connor is just about ready to begin."

Megan sleepily said good night, and soon, the adults were sitting around the table enjoying pie and coffee, eagerly awaiting what the rest of the evening might hold.

Chapter 97

The faithful God, which keepeth
covenant and mercy with them that love him.
Deuteronomy 7:9

$\mathcal{M}$r. Connor stood, clearing his throat, and everyone looked his way.

"I am pleased to be with you tonight," he said. "My entire stay has been a very pleasant one and one I will never forget. Thank you to everyone for making that possible, and many thanks to Brandon and Melissa for their hospitality and allowing me to share their home."

Everyone was nodding with their full attention on the man who won every checker game he played since he arrived in Finley Valley.

He cleared his throat again.

"So with that said, I believe it's prudent we get started. This might take a while, so everyone should relax and get comfortable."

Everyone quietly stared with anticipation, but no one was relaxed or comfortable.

"Professor Higgins was someone whom we all loved," he began saying. "He made an impact on more people than we will ever know. Only heaven knows. And tonight, we want to talk about his influence on everyone here."

The tall, well-groomed man sat a handsome leather case on the table and opened it. He pulled out a large, fat envelope.

"This envelope, I understand, has passed through several hands. I'm just happy it finally made its way into the *right* hands so I can share its contents with you tonight."

Luke drew a deep breath. Other than the large amount of money he assumed was still in there, he had no idea what else the envelope he once held in his hand might contain.

Mr. Connor went on to say, "And we thank David for picking up the task of delivering it safety to me when Luke was unnecessarily detained."

The room was so quiet, other than the sound of Mr. Connor's voice, nothing could be heard except the steady rain hitting against the windows.

"In short, I want to thank everyone who has played a part in Professor Higgins' life. And that is all of you. And what I have to share with you right now will be a testament of his never-ending generosity."

He then pulled from the envelope a large amount of money and sat it on the table. Beside the money, he laid out a document looking to be several pages long, smoothing it out as flat as he could.

"If you don't mind, I will sit down as I read a handwritten document that was written in the professor's own hand that he wished to be included along with his original will. There is no legal wording since it is written in layman's terms, but it is a bound and legal document authorized by James T. West, Attorney, River Branch."

Frank glanced toward Luke and then David. He wondered how the lawyer was doing.

"And as far as I can see, everyone but one person is present who is included in this will."

Mr. Connor sat and looked around the table and smiled.

"Please, everyone needs to relax."

So everyone tried to, but it wasn't easy.

"All right then, I will address Mrs. Eleanor McAfee first."

The older woman sat, amazed she was included.

"This money is yours."

She gasped.

"The job Professor Higgins spoke of in the letter he sent you is a simple one. Even though he didn't explain what your job description would be, this document does. It reads."

"'I leave this money from the sale of a portion of my railway holdings to Mrs. Eleanor McAfee who unselfishly poured her life and energy into Annaleigh Thompson to help her through life. No amount of money would ever come close to compensating her for her devotion and care. Her job is to use this money wisely as she uses it not only for her own needs but for anything else she deems worthwhile. I also leave enough railway stock in her name to last her for the rest of her life. Annaleigh Thompson is to be the sole beneficiary of any funds that may remain after her death.'"

Anna took a deep breath and didn't look toward anyone.

Mrs. McAfee was stunned. God had provided in a way she never dreamed. She squeezed Anna's hand until it hurt.

Anna's heart was beating rapidly from the magnitude of the evening, and it had just begun.

Mr. Connor waited until everyone quieted, then he spoke again.

"Next, Mr. and Mrs. Frank Monroe."

The senior Monroes looked toward each other, then listened intently.

"'To Frank and Martha Monroe, I have included a deed for fifty acres of land located on the upper northeast edge of Finley Valley. The exact location is recorded and filed with the clerk at Finley Bank.'"

Mr. Connor handed it to Brandon and let him pass it to his father.

"I don't know what to say," Frank began. "I don't know how the professor could have acquired that land. As far as I know, it's protected property owned by Finley Valley and not for sale. How do you think the professor was able to purchase it?"

"Well, Mr. Monroe, Professor Higgins knew many people in high places. Perhaps we will never know the answer to your question and the other questions that will surely come."

"Thank you doesn't sound adequate enough, but thank you."

"There's actually more concerning that property. I'll continue."

"Brandon and Melissa Monroe."

The couple gave him their full attention.

"The adjoining fifty acres have been deeded to you."

Brandon couldn't believe it. He didn't deserve such a gift. Melissa just sat there speechless along with everyone else at the table. It was almost as if they were all having the same dream and no one wanted to wake up.

"Now there are some conditions you need to understand," Mr. Connor warned.

Frank and Brandon and their wives paid close attention.

"The land is never to be sold but forever left in the Monroe family. A portion of the combined land has been designated for the construction of a school. It's all explained here. The professor believed in education, and he has left his entire collection of rare books to Brandon to establish a learning library within the school.

"Well, read for yourself. Here is his explanation in full."

Mr. Connor handed a set of papers to Brandon.

There was a low murmur around the table. No one ever expected such generosity.

Melissa stood and all eyes were on her. She took a deep breath.

"I don't know about the rest of you, but I could use another cup of coffee. I'll go put the pot on the stove and be back in a few minutes."

David quickly spoke up.

"Melissa, let Elisabeth and myself do it. That way, you, Brandon, Frank, and Martha can talk about all this. And I wouldn't mind stretching my legs." He took Elisabeth's hand, and they headed to the kitchen.

Everyone else sat and talked among themselves.

Elisabeth pushed the coffeepot to the back of the stove, and David stepped out on the kitchen porch.

"Are you all right?" Elisabeth asked, as she walked up behind him.

"There's a lot to think about. I just needed some air."

David put his arm around Elisabeth, and they watched the cold, steady rain.

Neither of them spoke of what was happening on the sunporch.

"I'm ready to go home," David said.

"Me too, David."

"I'm watching everyone in there, and don't get me wrong, I love being here with family, but—"

He shook his head.

"But what?"

He drew Elisabeth close.

"I've been gone too long. I have patients that need me. Like Mr. Bowers, he will need more medicine for his stiff joints soon."

Elisabeth squeezed his hand.

"And May Potter, she's most likely had her baby by now. I wanted to share that special event with her and her husband since they had almost given up on ever having a child."

The rain was more of a drizzle now.

"David, you are a wonderful doctor, and Lazy Spring is honored to have you. You will be back there soon. Until then, you have Sam filling in. Just a little longer and we can have the wedding and head home."

"Elisabeth, when we're here in Finley Valley, it isn't reality. I have no responsibilities here. Are you sure you're ready to be a doctor's wife?"

"You forget I've been in Lazy Spring to see how hard you work, your passion for the people."

"But you haven't been married to it, Elisabeth. Like the nights I'm woken when a patient comes to the clinic or when I have to leave and not be back for a day or two."

"No, but I've been eating lunch with you when we've been interrupted. I've had to walk home alone when you had to leave on an emergency call."

She paused.

"And I've been there to pray for you and your patients."

David squeezed her shoulder.

"And you've never once complained."

Elisabeth chuckled.

"I can't promise I'll never complain, but I want to be there by your side helping. When the little girl died after falling from that tree, I was glad to be there for the grieving mother. And I think God will open more opportunities like that in the future. We will be a team, David, a good team."

"I don't deserve you, Elisabeth."

The air was cold and damp, and Elisabeth was shivering.

"We better go in, Elisabeth. I don't want you getting a chill."

"Everyone will be wanting their coffee too," she added.

"One more thing, Elisabeth."

She looked up into his face.

"I can't give you riches like the professor has been handing out. Sometimes, things can get pretty tight. All the townspeople don't pay in cash. Sometimes, it might be in chickens and eggs or meat and vegetables."

"I don't mind that, David. You know I don't. I'm happy for your family and all the professor is doing for them. He has changed their lives. But I don't need change. I just need you."

Elisabeth started to head toward the kitchen again.

"One more thing."

Elisabeth smiled and studied his face.

"I've been thinking. I've been thinking a lot."

"About what?"

"Remember I was telling you about being in Weaver's Corner and Mrs. McAfee and I found out the professor owned his own company and was a wealthy man?"

"Yes."

"His testimony was—"

He couldn't find the words.

"Was what, David?"

"I don't know. I can't explain it."

Elisabeth heard someone in the kitchen and turned her attention that direction.

"We can go in, Elisabeth, we've been gone too long."

"No, finish, I want to hear."

"All I'm saying is after hearing the professor's life story and riding with Mrs. McAfee on the train and hearing about her life and Anna's, well, I'm missing something in my life."

Elisabeth reached up and hugged David around his neck.

"You've tears in your eyes, David. What is really going on?"

"I've been doing a lot of thinking, Elisabeth. I want to be a husband you can respect."

"David, look at me. I do respect you."

David looked long and hard into Elisabeth's brown eyes.

"I'm not a man of strong faith, Elisabeth, and I don't want to disappoint you. I've always relied on myself. I never thought that much about God until I met you and Andrew. Then to be around the professor and to hear how his life changed and then to listen to Mrs. McAfee's solid and unwavering faith in everything she says and does, it does something to you."

Elisabeth wiped a tear from his face.

"Something deep within me won't let me sleep at night, Elisabeth."

Elisabeth ignored the noises in the kitchen while David continued.

"Your faith in God was so strong right up until the very end of Andrew's life. I'm not sure I can compare to that *or* him."

"I'm not looking to compare, David. You and Andrew aren't the same man. I would never compare you to him."

"Can you be patient with me? I asked God to help me be a good husband, and I prayed for Him to show me what I need to do. I'm sorry, I'm really bad at this, Elisabeth. I can sew up wounds, I can deliver babies, I can sit up all night listening to someone moan from pain, not being able to do anything but hold their hand. But I'm not very good with words."

"David, you are great with words. I think I understand why you're struggling. We will work on it together."

They stood hand and hand. Rain dripped steadily from the porch roof, and the night air seemed to be growing colder with each passing minute.

"I can't wait until our wedding day," David said. "I'm ready to begin a life with you, one that has some structure and routine."

"I'm ready too, David. But I think we better get back to the others, don't you? Besides, I'm freezing."

"I'm sorry, Elisabeth. Let's go."

David quickly led Elisabeth back to the kitchen where the coffeepot was gone and the noise and laughter on the sunporch drifted down the hall toward them.

Chapter 98

And keep his commandments to a thousand generations.
Deuteronomy 7:9

$\mathcal{T}$he wind whistled through the bare trees, and the windows on the sunporch shook.

"Sounds frightful outside," Mrs. McAfee said, as she glanced out the window next to her.

Anna looked toward Luke with concern, and he knew exactly what she was thinking.

"Mac will be fine," he whispered. "He's safe in the barn, remember?"

"I know," she whispered back, "but he'll be frightened."

"He'll be fine."

The look on Anna's face told him she didn't quite believe him.

Mr. Connor stood to his feet just as David and Elisabeth came back into the room.

"Good," Mr. Connor said. "Since we're all back together, I'll continue with the reading."

Brandon pushed a piece of pie toward the engaged couple along with two forks. Melissa poured their coffee.

Every eye was soon focused on Mr. Connor while they tried to ignore the ugly weather.

The tall, nicely dressed man turned a page and looked it over. He smiled.

"Well, the next person in line that the professor mentions is Megan."

Brandon reached over and took Melissa's hand, and she squeezed his in return as they waited to hear what the professor could possibly give a six-year-old.

"'A trust fund in the name of Megan Taylor Monroe has been set up to help her with any medical needs she may have in order to advance her physical well-being. I have included the name and location of a doctor that has helped other children with similar needs.'"

Melissa tried to hold her tears, Frank just let his tears run down his face, and Brandon lowered his head and bit his lip.

Mr. Connor hesitated but only a moment as he readied to move to the next name. The wind continued to blow, but no one except Mrs. McAfee noticed.

"'To Mrs. Elisabeth Landry.'"

Elisabeth sat very still, and David squeezed her hand that he was already holding.

"'I agonized over this decision, but one day, I knew what to do to help this strong-willed woman who encouraged me during one of my hardest moments in life. I owe her a debt of gratitude.'"

Elisabeth took a breath as she vividly remembered that moment at the professor's old homestead.

"So to you, Elisabeth," Mr. Connor said. "The professor has given you a building."

"A building?" she asked. "Where? What on earth would I do with a building?"

"Well, uh, it's a building located in Lazy Spring."

"You mean the old boarding house?"

She held her breath, dreaming it was true.

"Apparently not, Elisabeth," Mr. Connor said. "It says the building on Main Street facing the general store. Here's the paper giving you the precise information."

David and Elisabeth looked it over. He knew the building well that had sat empty as long as he could remember.

Elisabeth wasn't sure she understood it all, but a building *was* a building.

"David, maybe you could set up your practice there." She pushed aside her idea of converting the boarding house.

Mr. Connor interrupted.

"I'm sure the professor would want you to do whatever you wanted to with the building, but he says more."

Everyone was listening.

"'A banknote for her to start her own café has been left at the Lazy Spring bank.'"

"A café!" Anna exclaimed, after sitting quietly during the reading. "Elisabeth, that's what we were talking about on that last walk we took!"

Elisabeth cried out!

"Oh, David, I never dreamed—" but then she stopped. "But the need for a larger clinic is so much greater. My dream can come later if things work out."

"I never knew you dreamed of owning a café, Elisabeth," David said.

"Oh, I never imagined I would ever have the opportunity, so I didn't really think much about it."

"Did you mention it to Professor Higgins?" Brandon asked.

"No, I didn't."

Everyone at the table started talking among themselves, so Mr. Connor sat back down.

"I'm sorry, Mr. Connor, I didn't mean to interrupt," Elisabeth said. "It's just that I'm so overwhelmed—overwhelmed like everyone else here. I honestly can't believe this is happening. Can the professor possibly afford all this?"

Mr. Connor chuckled.

"I assure you he can." He crossed his arms and sat back comfortably. "Looks like he was a very busy man while he was here." He glanced at his pocket watch just as the clock in the hall began to chime.

Time had flown by.

"Well, I believe we need to move on or we might just be here all night."

Mr. Connor looked toward David.

"David, I believe you're next in line."

All eyes were now on David—the tall, rugged thirty-year-old man who knew exactly what he wanted to accomplish early in life and along with a lot of hard work and perseverance felt like he had finally fulfilled his goal of becoming a successful doctor. And now to have Elisabeth in his life, he couldn't possibly imagine what the professor had for him that could be any better than what he already had. But somehow, the professor seemed to know what everyone needed more than they did. And so far, the professor had far exceeded everyone's expectations.

David raised his eyebrows toward all the faces looking his way and gave a crooked smile. He wasn't the only one wanting to know what the professor had chosen to give him.

Elisabeth had to nudge him to get him to pay attention to Mr. Connor who was holding out a key toward him.

"What's this?" David asked, as he stood up to reach over and get the key.

"I'll let the professor tell you.

"'I leave for Dr. David Monroe a key to the chest in my office, which contains all my journals that I have written in almost daily since the day my wife and baby girl passed away. I believe you will find many life answers that might help you as you marry and start a family.'"

David didn't say anything at first. It wasn't at all what he was expecting, but he didn't know what he had expected. The professor had once again given a gift with meaning and purpose to just the right person.

He missed the next few words and had to ask Mr. Connor to repeat them.

"'Along with my journals, I leave you the controlling interest in my company, giving you 51% ownership.'"

David was trying to process what he had just heard. The whole room was quiet. Even the wind had died down to nothing more than a whisper.

David finally found his voice and was shaking his head.

"I'm not sure I want it."

The room seemed quieter at that moment.

"I'm, I'm a doctor, not a business man."

David looked to Elisabeth for support, but she was just as dumbfounded.

"Do I have to take it?" he asked sincerely.

He then grew somewhat agitated.

"He leaves Elisabeth a building for a café in Lazy Spring, and he leaves me his company?"

"Well, not *all* his company," Mr. Connor added.

"All his company or just part, I can't run a company in Weaver's Corner and leave Elisabeth in Lazy Spring. Did he forget we're going to marry? And did he forget I'm a doctor?"

David paused.

Maybe the professor was confused at the end, he thought.

Elisabeth gently tugged at his sleeve, so he took a deep breath and sighed.

"I'm sorry, everyone. I know I sound utterly selfish and disrespectful. I haven't had much sleep, and frankly, I just need to get home where I'm needed."

He then sat down, and no one said anything.

Mr. Connor looked around the room.

Anna was sitting quietly, looking down toward her lap, and Mrs. McAfee looked as if she needed some rest. The entire Monroe family looked to be in shock. The initial excitement had died down, and reality was setting in. The professor was unbelievably generous, but with his generosity would come change. And even good change wasn't always easy.

Melissa quietly asked if anyone wanted something to drink, but no one took her up on her offer.

Mr. Connor set aside the document in front of him and cleared his throat.

"Melissa," he said, "I believe I'm interested in that drink. Maybe something other than coffee?"

"Absolutely," she replied and started to get up.

"And is there anymore of Mrs. McAfee's delicious pie?"

"We have about a pie and a half just sitting in the kitchen. I'll bring some fresh plates."

"Bring the leftover biscuits too," Luke added.

Melissa nodded.

"I'll help you," Brandon offered, as he pushed back his chair.

"Well, Brandon," Mr. Connor said, "I was hoping for one last game of checkers before I leave tomorrow."

That's when Frank spoke up.

"And I think I could use some coffee after all. Martha, would you like to help me—"

But before he could finish, Mrs. McAfee interrupted him.

"Mr. Monroe, I've been sitting too long and could use something to do, so I'll help Melissa, and maybe the rest of you can head to the parlor."

Melissa was nodding her way when Luke's voice suddenly rose above all the others.

"Look everyone!"

He pointed toward the window.

"It's snowing!"

Chapter 99

*For whatsoever things were written aforetime
were written for our learning, that we through
patience and comfort of the scriptures might have hope.
Romans 15:4*

The fire popped and crackled as Brandon threw a couple of more logs on the glowing embers. The parlor was cozy and warm, and everyone retreated there so the checker game could commence.

Any tension from the evening was beginning to mellow, just as the businessman from Weaver's Corner had hoped.

Light snow was falling, dusting everything in its path. Anna was staring out one of the tall, narrow windows when Luke walked up behind her.

"It's pretty, isn't it?"

She turned slightly at his voice, still watching the snow.

"Yes, I don't think I've ever seen anything as pretty."

They watched from the window a little longer.

"This is incredible, isn't it?" Luke asked.

"You mean the snow?"

"Well, the snow and the reading of the professor's will. Life sure can change in a moment."

Anna nodded.

"Have you thought about what he might have given you?" she asked.

"I'd be less than honest if I said I haven't. He was certainly generous by making you the beneficiary for Mrs. McAfee."

"It's just the professor's way of taking care of me. I'm beginning to think I could never be surprised by anything anymore!"

"Not anything?"

"Well, you know what I mean."

Luke pondered on what she said, but just then cheers erupted from across the room. Brandon jumped to his feet in victory. He had finally beaten Charles R. Connor, the checker champion.

"Well, that's icing on the cake for Brandon," Luke laughed.

Mr. Connor stood to his feet as well then shook Brandon's hand.

"It's been a pleasure, Brandon. Great game."

He looked around at the Monroe family and the friends before him.

"I'll be leaving all of you tomorrow. Professor Higgins was blessed to know all of you," he said, "and I'm glad to have played a small part in all this."

He looked over toward Anna still standing at the window.

"Little did the professor know when he boarded that train and sat down next to a frightened young woman where God would lead," Mr. Connor was saying. "He boarded that train with some fairly definite plans, but then God appears to have changed them. God certainly answered his prayers through Anna and through all of you. And along the way, God supplied the needs of others."

He looked down at Mrs. McAfee who was sitting comfortably on the sofa near him.

Anna tucked her head from the sudden attention then looked out into the darkness instead of looking at anyone, including Luke.

Soon, everyone sat quietly after enjoying a bite of pie along with biscuits and leftover ham pieces. The fire continued to pop and crackle. The wind whistled, and the snow began to swirl.

Luke leaned toward Anna.

At first, he hesitated but then said what was on his mind anyway.

"I have another surprise," he whispered. "Come with me."

"We can't leave now, Luke. Mr. Connor is getting ready to finish reading the professor's will. He looks like he's about ready to head back to the sunporch anytime."

"It will only take five minutes."

Luke's eyes were pleading.

Anna looked around. No one was paying any attention to them.

"All right, five minutes."

Luke took her hand and led her to the front porch then out to Brandon's barn. It was bitterly cold, and the wind whipped through their clothing as they crossed the yard. Heavy, wet snow flakes were hitting them in the face.

"Luke, it's freezing out here!" Anna yelled as she took off running, following Luke's lead.

"Just a few steps more and we're there!" Luke yelled back.

Anna ran into the barn just as Luke opened the door.

He pulled one of Brandon's old coats from a peg and wrapped it around her shoulders. He lit the lantern that always hung in the exact same place, and light slowly illuminated the area around them.

Anna looked frozen, and she felt frozen in the cold barn.

"You're crazy, Luke."

"I know."

Luke stood there, a huge grin on his face.

Anna watched his face, and his eyes seemed to dance in the light.

"But you're happy," she added.

"I am, Anna. Happier than I've been in a very long time. Probably in my whole life."

"Me too," she said softly.

Luke forgot about the cold a moment and looked into her brilliant blue eyes. Her long blond hair was a mess from the wind.

She didn't turn away.

Luke cleared his throat.

"Listen. David might kill me, but I'm going to show you something. Close your eyes."

"What is it?"

"Just close them."

Anna obeyed by putting her hands in front of her eyes.

"No peeking."

"I'm not!"

Luke lifted the lid of a wooden box and pulled out a smaller box. He took Anna's hands and placed the smaller box there.

Anna opened her eyes.

"Go ahead, open it."

Anna just stood there, not responding.

"What's wrong? Open it."

"This is only the second gift I've ever received. Well, the third if you count Mac."

"Well, relax, it's not really a gift."

Anna was confused.

"At least not a gift from me. David brought this back from Logan's Gap. Says it belongs to you."

Anna turned the box around in her hands. It was hand-carved on all sides, including the top. The initial B was beautifully carved on the top amid the handsome swirls created by someone's skilled hand.

"It's beautiful, Luke, but it's not mine."

"Well, open it so we can see what's inside anyway."

"You don't know?"

"No, Anna, I don't. Open it for goodness sake."

Anna lifted the lid and stood spellbound as she listened.

"It's a music box!" Luke exclaimed, as he tried to get a better look.

Anna forgot the cold. She had lost her smile.

"I know that song," she said softly, as she handed it back to Luke.

"I thought you'd be happy."

Anna's eyes were filling with tears.

"Look, it has your name carved just inside the lid."

Anna wiped her eyes with her cold fingers and looked.

"Annaleigh Rose."

Then Luke almost dropped the box when a voice came out of nowhere. His and Anna's attention flew to the open barn door.

"David!"

"What's going on, Luke?"

David noticed the box in his hand and walked over and took it from him.

"I'm sorry, David. I just got caught up in the moment of all the excitement and, well, the snow, and I thought I'd just bring Anna out here to see this."

David handed the box back to Anna.

"I was going to save this for the right moment, but Luke is right, maybe this is a good time to show this to you. It is definitely a night of unexpected surprises."

"Luke says it's mine."

"It is. Someone gave it to me when I was at the Children's Shelter in Logan's Gap and asked me to give it to you when I felt the timing was right."

"Who?"

"Tom, the man who works in the horse stables."

Anna looked to the floor.

"The tune is a song he would hum when we worked on the horses together. And one day when I asked about it, he taught me the words. After that, we sang it often."

Luke stood quietly, his breath evident in the frigid air. He looked toward David then Anna.

"The professor figured it out, Anna."

Anna waited to hear.

"Tom is short for Thompson."

Anna was holding back a sob, searching David's face.

"It was *his* name on the note that was left with me when Mrs. McAfee found me?"

David was nodding.

"Does Mrs. McAfee know?"

"No, she doesn't."

Anna turned away from both Monroe men. She had mixed feelings.

David spoke louder.

"His name is Thompson Foley, and he's the man who left you on the porch that day. He watched to make sure Mrs. McAfee found you, knowing she came to work exactly the same time every morning."

Anna didn't respond.

"He knew you'd be safe at the shelter, Anna. And since he worked in the stables, he could keep an eye on you. When he found out Mrs. McAfee had quit and that we were coming here where you are, he thought it was his last chance to have any contact with you."

Anna clinched her fists.

"He made this music box shortly after you were born and wanted you to have it."

Anna whirled around, the glow from the lantern casting a dim light around her.

"But why!" she exclaimed. "Why would he do that and not ever tell me! I lived all my life at the shelter, and *he* was the one who left me there?"

Anna was trembling. Luke just listened, but his heart was racing.

"My middle name is Rose," she finally said in a soft voice. "I've never known my middle name until now."

One of the horses snorted and stamped its foot.

"Look on the bottom of the box, Anna."

Anna turned it over, and there in small, carefully carved letters was her name, her full name with a date: Annaleigh Rose Bentley, November 21, 1864.

"My birthdate?"

"Probably, that's what I was thinking."

"Mrs. McAfee was right then. The date she chose to celebrate my birthday was so close to my real birthdate."

Anna shook but not from the cold. Luke wanted to put his arm around her but didn't.

"I'm sorry, Anna," Luke said. "I didn't know. I thought it was just something you left behind at the shelter, and I wanted to surprise you with it."

Anna swallowed hard.

"My last name is Bentley?"

"Yes, it is," David answered.

"Does Mr. Foley know where my parents are? And why they didn't come back for me?"

"Anna, let's go in the house where it's warm."

Anna shook her head.

"No, I'd rather hear it now and out here, away from everyone."

David took a deep breath.

"He's your grandfather, Anna. Thompson Foley is your mother's father."

Chapter 100

Make a joyful noise unto the LORD, all ye lands.
Psalm 100:1

*E*lisabeth met David at the door.

"I've been worried, is everything all right?" she asked.

Anna walked straight past her and ran up the stairs. Luke just nodded her way and headed back to the sunporch where everyone had regathered.

Elisabeth looked up at David.

"I'll explain later," he said.

Elisabeth started to say something, but David put his finger to her lips.

"Trust me on this one, Elisabeth. Everything will be better in time."

"All right."

Elisabeth looked up at the empty stairs then reluctantly followed David to the sunporch.

"I think we can conclude quickly if everyone is ready," Mr. Connor was saying.

He looked around and realized Anna wasn't there.

"Could someone go find Anna?" he asked.

Martha caught Elisabeth's eye, and the expression on Elisabeth's face told her that something wasn't right. Luke was just sitting in his chair, staring at nothing.

Mrs. McAfee was carefully watching the expressions on everyone's faces and was beginning to worry about Anna's absence.

"Anna's not feeling well right now," David started to explain. But he no sooner had spoken when Anna entered the room.

She walked over and sat next to Mrs. McAfee, then smiled toward Luke and his furrowed brow.

"I'm fine, Luke," she whispered.

She held out her hand that had the scar.

"Remember? I'm not looking backward anymore, only forward."

Luke smiled and nodded. He was so proud of her.

Her gesture didn't escape David and Elisabeth's notice. They smiled at each other, feeling certain they knew what Anna had whispered to Luke.

"I believe we're all ready to conclude, Mr. Connor," David said confidently. "And I think I speak for everyone else that all of us are grateful for the professor's generosity."

He smiled at Elisabeth and continued.

"And we accept whatever the professor has given us, even though we may not be able to understand his reasoning now, I believe we will in time."

Elisabeth squeezed his hand.

"So, Mr. Connor, please continue. We are ready to hear what that last page says."

"Very good," Mr. Connor said. "Let's finish up!"

The snow had stopped and so had the wind that couldn't seem to make up its mind. All was calm.

As Mr. Connor finished, everyone gave him their full attention.

Luke was given the responsibility to care for the professor's old homestead with instructions that the cabin was to be completely burned so no trace of it remained. The old fence around Ellen and his baby girl's grave was to be replaced, and someone was to be hired to maintain the property at all times. Money was available to make sure all that could happen. The professor, in his wisdom, decided the project would be good for Luke as he contemplated his future.

"Hard work and responsibility has a way of defining a man," the professor wrote.

Luke didn't question what seemed to be an odd request. He would do as the professor asked.

He listened as Mr. Connor continued.

"'At the completion of three years, the interest of the company given to Dr. David Monroe will transfer to Luke Monroe. With the stipulation that David can extend it another three years if he feels Luke is not up to the responsibility. Neither man is required to live in Weaver's Corner to fulfill their responsibilities. The only requirement is to be present at the annual meeting of board members.'"

Everything was beginning to make sense.

"'Luke's immediate responsibility with the company will be as 'purchasing agent,' which will require travel to many parts of the surrounding territories and states. He is given free access to all rail lines, and no one will ever question his presence. My two horses are his as well.'"

"'Both Dr. David Monroe and Luke Monroe will receive monthly wages toward their basic living expenses for as long as the company exists.'"

"And that concludes all the Monroe's but one," Mr. Connor said.

Everyone was thinking the same thing: what Monroe was left?

"The professor has employed Mrs. Agnes Wilson from the Wilson's General Store in Diamond to sew a variety of children's clothing for baby Monroe when she is notified of its gender."

Elisabeth gasped.

"David, how sweet of him to include our baby."

"Yes, Elisabeth, our baby."

There was a lull for a few moments, but then everyone suddenly began the cleanup, and the usual Monroe laughter began.

Mr. Connor quickly held up a hand and whistled, getting everyone's attention.

"I'm sorry, but we have one more person on this page."

Everyone stood as statues until one after another sat back down.

"Anna, the professor hasn't forgotten you."

"But he has left me so much already."

"Well, he has more to say concerning you."

Anna looked toward Mrs. McAfee, and the older woman gave her a nod, the same reassuring nod she had given Anna many times throughout the years.

"'To my sweet dear Annaleigh, to you I give the greatest treasure of all.'"

"'Alongside my journals in the chest in my office, I have two Bibles. One is for you, and the other is for the man you marry one day. Follow God's guidelines within their pages, and you will have true success.'"

"'And upon the day you marry, you will be given my entire homestead located in River Branch along with the remaining 49% of controlling interest in my company.'"

The murmur around the table began one more time.

"Wait, wait, there is one last thing, Anna."

Everyone felt fairly exhausted from all they had heard throughout the evening but listened as the last few lines of the will were finally read.

"And, Anna, the professor has purchased a building in Lazy Spring for you as well—an old house right outside of town."

"The boarding house." Elisabeth whispered toward David.

"The professor has left funds for it to be renovated into a children's home under the supervision of anyone Anna chooses."

Elisabeth knew that was the best use for the boarding house. Her idea of converting it into a medical clinic was dismissed with no regret. And she and David would soon agree that the money Andrew had saved for his dream of moving west to start a new life would be set aside and used for the baby's future education.

Anna sat trembling. That day she stepped on the train headed for Finley Valley had changed her life forever.

Chapter 101

I will sing of mercy and judgment:
unto thee, O LORD, will I sing.
Psalm 101:1

Goodbyes were said to Mr. Connor as David rounded up everyone going back to Martha and Frank's house.

Everyone was tired, and the ride would be a cold one. Brandon gave them extra blankets as they climbed into the back of Frank's wagon. David grabbed one to put around Elisabeth since they would be up front driving the team.

Once everyone was settled, Anna grew quiet, and Luke slipped his hand into hers, causing her to turn her face his way.

It was too dark to see his smile, but she held onto his hand tightly.

"So you're sixteen tomorrow," he whispered.

"It seems so. A new birthday will feel strange."

"But it's the correct one."

She nodded in the dark.

"And now you know your full name."

She nodded again.

Mrs. McAfee, who was sitting across from them, had fallen asleep almost the moment they pulled away from Brandon's yard. Frank and Martha were in the corner of the wagon toward the front, huddled under a thick blanket. If they were talking, Anna and Luke couldn't hear them.

Anna kept her voice low.

"All my life, I've wondered about my past, and plenty of times, I was bitter when the other children at the shelter teased me."

"Teased you? About what?"

"I would tell them I wasn't going to be stuck there like them because someone was coming back to get me."

"And because no one ever did, they gave you a hard time."

"Yes, they did. I shouldn't have been so hateful."

"You, hateful? That's hard to believe."

"Believe it. But all that seems so long ago now. Thanks to Professor Higgins, I'm not the same person I used to be."

"Well, if they could see you now, they would know you are a rich woman."

"I don't feel rich the way you mean. I'd rather have Professor Higgins back than have any of his riches."

"Me too, Anna, but life goes on, remember? You can't change what has happened, you just have to take one day at a time with how things are at the moment."

Luke squeezed her hand.

"You know, I'm not sure I want to know all the details of my past," she said.

"David said he'd sit with you tomorrow and tell you the rest of what Mr. Foley told him."

"I know. I wasn't really surprised when Dr. Monroe told me my parents aren't alive. Somehow, I think I always knew they weren't."

"I'm sorry, Anna. I wish I could make things right."

Anna grew quiet for a moment, and Luke wondered if she was crying.

"Well, at least it explains why no one came back for me. It's nice to know."

"I know, Anna, and when you know more details, hopefully, it will answer some of those questions you've had all these years."

Mrs. McAfee groaned a little, and they waited to see if she was going to wake up. But she continued sleeping through all the ruts in the road.

"I need to tell Mrs. McAfee. She will want to know."

"Will you feel comfortable having her hear what David has to say when he talks to you tomorrow?"

"Yes, certainly. She's like my mother even though she's older. She's been the only mother I've ever had, Luke. I thought I'd lost her forever when I boarded that train, but here she is, sitting right across from me. I still can't believe my good fortune."

"Sounds like God has taken care of you."

Luke felt Anna turn his way.

"What is it, Anna? What did I say?"

"That's what the professor said the day I met him. I was telling him about myself, and he said it sounded like someone was looking out for me.

"When I asked who, he said God watches over all of us."

The wonderful memories of their train ride were flooding over her.

"God knew when you were left on that kitchen porch, there was someone at the Children's Shelter who would love you as a mother. You didn't know as a baby that your parents would die from a terrible illness, but God knew. He placed Mrs. McAfee in your life to plant the seeds you would need for the next part of your life journey—your journey to find God."

Anna was nodding as she thought through what Luke was saying.

"And the professor was there to take over where Mrs. McAfee left off," Anna said softly.

"Exactly."

"And now I'm here with your family who has taken me in. I'm learning so much about things I never had a chance to learn at the Children's Shelter."

"And each day of your life will continue to teach you something. You just have to trust God to guide you. He will bring more people into your life. You wait and see if I'm not right."

"Like Elisabeth teaching me things from her Bible."

"Yes, like Elisabeth."

"And you, Luke."

"And me, Anna."

They were silent a few moments. They would be back at the house soon.

"I'm glad we've had this time to talk, Luke. You've changed. I've never heard you talk like you have tonight."

"I've been watching and listening, Anna. You know the night when you and I were in the barn with Mac and Mother came out to take you back to the house?"

"Yes."

"I wanted to tell you then. After being in jail, wondering if I was ever going to be free, I cried out for God's help, and I know He heard me. You're not the only one changing, Anna. We are all working out our own journeys. We just have to decide if we want to continue down our own selfish path or follow the path God has designed for us."

Anna was quiet.

"Luke, I don't understand why Mr. Foley just left me in the care of the shelter and didn't try to raise me on his own once my parents died, but I think I'm beginning to understand the grace of God that Elisabeth talked about when she lost Andrew."

"Well, I'm sure he was doing what he thought was best or he wouldn't have left you. Perhaps he thought the shelter could provide for you in ways he couldn't. At least he was there to watch over you the best he could."

"I suppose. He was very kind to me, and I learned a lot from him. It just seems strange to think he's my grandfather."

"One day, you'll be able to thank him for making sure you were taken care of, and then you can ask him all those questions rolling around inside your head right now."

Luke squeezed her hand.

Anna laughed softly.

"I look forward to that day."

"Well, for right now, I'm thinking of how we can celebrate your birthday tomorrow."

"Don't you dare, Luke Monroe! And keep your voice down."

"No, ma'am, I've been waiting for you to turn sixteen for a long time, Anna."

She asked Luke why, but she was certain she already knew the answer. She just wanted to hear him say it.

"So I can ask Mrs. McAfee's permission to court her daughter proper like."

Chapter 102

But thou, O LORD, shalt endure for ever.
Psalm 102:12

*D*avid ever so gently lifted Elisabeth's chin then tenderly kissed his bride.

Her veil fell freely down her back, softly covering her long brown hair. Tiny bits of dried baby's breath were carefully arranged about her head, and her wedding gown sparkled from the tiny pearls lovingly sewn in place just the night before by Anna and Martha. Care had been taken to give Elisabeth's growing waistline plenty of room.

Anna stood by her side. Elisabeth wouldn't have wanted anyone else to stand with her. They had grown so close over the months. They were the outsiders now lovingly welcomed into the Monroe family.

Melissa had carefully arranged Anna's soft blond hair loosely atop her head, allowing small wisps to sweetly encircle her youthful face. Her royal blue dress complimented her bright blue eyes.

Anna sighed and smiled toward Luke, standing with David, who was more like a brother to David than a nephew. He looked handsome in his dark pants and collarless white shirt, his thick brown hair was neat, but left free enough to reflect his spirited ways.

Everyone seemed to hold their breath as David finished his kiss and then tenderly placed a cool hand on Elisabeth's flushed cheek.

"I love you, Mrs. Monroe," David whispered to his bride.

"I love you too," she said through her tears.

Then shouts of joy rang throughout the church as bride and groom turned to face the congregation.

The preacher spread his arms wide.

"Dr. and Mrs. David Monroe, my friends!"

All of Finley Valley appeared to be there, as word spread quickly of their wedding plans. Doc Stevens stood proudly as David nodded toward him when he spotted him among the others.

As the couple began their walk down the aisle, Anna slipped to the side and knelt to look on Megan's beaming face.

"Ready to go?" Anna quickly asked the six-year-old.

Megan smoothed her new dress, then Anna wheeled her down the aisle behind the happy couple. The little girl clung tightly to the basket she used to drop flower petals when Brandon and Melissa sang leading up to the magnificent entrance of the bride. Frank had offered to walk Elisabeth down the aisle, and she happily accepted.

Luke guided Brady and Ramon behind their sister then took his place behind them. Melissa and Brandon were already at the back of the church to see that every detail of the wedding was still going smoothly.

Martha and Frank stood quietly at the front of the church and watched as family and friends congratulated David and Elisabeth as they walked hand in hand.

Despite the cold weather, most everyone followed the bride and groom out the doors to their awaiting buggy that was decorated with evergreens and pinecones and red bows. Cries of well-wishers filled the air as David slapped the reins, urging the horse to move forward. Elisabeth tossed her bouquet just as they pulled away, and many a single girl, no matter what age, scrambled to be the first to catch it.

The buggy left tracks in the new fallen snow, and soon, the couple disappeared from sight. Mrs. Brown's oldest daughter hugged Elisabeth's bouquet, and she and the rest of the townspeople quickly headed their own directions, and all was quiet.

The remaining greens and pinecones in the church were left for the upcoming Sunday service, and the floor was swept clean. Brandon brought the wagon around, and everyone loaded up and headed to Frank and Martha's where fresh cinnamon rolls made that morning by Mrs. McAfee were waiting alongside the pot of coffee to be heated to just the right temperature.

Frank and Martha's house was cozy and warm after Frank built a fire while everyone else had gone to change their clothes.

Martha stood at their bedroom window, still wearing the clothes she wore to the wedding when Frank came to see what was taking her so long.

"You're going to miss out on the cinnamon rolls if you don't hurry," Frank said, as he came through the doorway. He was surprised she hadn't changed. He stepped alongside his bride of many years.

"What are you looking at?" he asked.

"Our little house. The one you worked so hard to build so we could marry."

She leaned toward him, and he put his arm around her.

"Remember those days, Frank?"

"Of course, I do. I worked night and day to make that house just livable enough to convince your parents it was fit to live in so we could marry."

Martha laughed.

"We worked for days to plug up the holes where the raccoons kept coming in."

"And the birds, don't forget the birds, Martha."

"Those were good times, Frank."

"We were so young."

"Yes, but in love. No one ever doubted our love for each other."

"Where has all the time gone, Martha?"

"I don't know, Frank. But every moment has been wonderful, not always easy, but wonderful."

They stood together, gazing out at the snow that had fallen the night before.

"Elisabeth's dress was lovely, Martha. You did an amazing job."

"She looked radiant," Martha said. "She'll be good for David."

They both agreed that was true.

"You know, Anna looked so grown up today in her new dress. And the way Melissa fixed her hair, well, she's not at all like the girl who first came to Finley Valley," Martha said.

Frank nodded.

"She's so confident now and much more relaxed. And just think, if you hadn't answered that advertisement about taking in an older orphan, who knows where she'd be now?"

"And none of us would have met Professor Higgins," she added.

"That's right."

"*And* who knew Mrs. McAfee would accept your offer to come stay with us and live in the little house? Everyone in Finley Valley will envy you, Martha. Not everyone has their own personal cook."

"Oh, Frank."

They laughed here and there as they talked about everything from raising two very different sons to helping with their overactive grandchildren. Then they backtracked and filled in things they forgot the first time.

"Our lives have radically changed, Martha."

She snuggled hard against him.

"Who would ever believe an elderly, educated gentleman and a backward, young orphan girl could do so much to change one family?"

"Probably no one, Martha. Only God, in His perfect timing and eternal purposes."

That if thou shalt confess with thy mouth the Lord Jesus, and shalt believe in thine heart that God hath raised him from the dead, thou shalt be saved.
Romans 10:9

About the Author

*L*aura Bratcher Goins creates believable Christian fiction. Daughter of a southern Baptist pastor, she grew up in Kentucky's bluegrass region with a love for southern hospitality, quiet country living, and barbeque. She currently lives an empty-nester life in southeastern Pennsylvania with her husband, Bobby, and their two Cavalier Spaniels.

Her faith in God draws her to write about believable, fictional characters who encounter everyday joys and struggles. Her desire is to help her readers find encouragement, hope, and real-life solutions throughout each story.

You can reach her by emailing lbgstories@gmail.com

CPSIA information can be obtained
at www.ICGtesting.com
Printed in the USA
BVHW081000030720
582582BV00001B/6

9 781645 699767